Smiling at Heaven

Karen J. Hasley

Karen J. Hasley [signature]

A special thank you to Ann, whose eagle-eyed proof reading uncovers what I missed. You [and your red pen] are invaluable!

This is a work of fiction. The characters described herein are imaginary and are not intended to refer to living persons.

ISBN-13: 978-1494208608
ISBN-10: 1494208601

It is not death
Without hereafter
To one in dearth
Of life and its laughter,

Nor the sweet murder
Dealt slow and even
Unto the martyr
Smiling at heaven:

It is the smile
Faint as a (waning) myth,
Faint and exceeding small
On a boy's murdered mouth.

The Young Soldier by Wilfred Owen, b. 3/18/1893
d. 11/4/1918, one week before the Armistice

Prologue

$\mathcal{M}$y father died in my arms, and despite the accumulated memories of many years, the words still hold the power to steal my breath as I write them on the page. At the time I was too young and sheltered to suspect how quickly and irrevocably the people we love can vanish. One day here and without warning or premonition gone the next, but that's how it was with my father, and his passing changed me forever. Whether for better or worse I'll never know, but the circumstances of his death changed me all the same.

On the last day of his life Father and I crossed the street and opened the store together exactly as we did every morning except Sunday, and he was his usual hearty self, teasing about something or other, a good-humored, friendly man always ready with a joke or riddle. He didn't display a hint of what was to come, but just before noon he complained that he didn't feel well. When Father went home mid-afternoon to lie down, I knew something was very wrong—I had never known him to be ill a day in his life—and by evening the sound of his labored, uneven breathing echoed through the big house. The doctor exited the sick room with a sober shake of his head and a look on his face that brought unbidden tears to my eyes. I knew we would lose my father. He fought for breath all night, my grandmother and I on each side of his bed, until finally with a last desperate flail of his arms and the throated gurgle of a drowning man he died.

Jeffrey Hansen was an energetic child from his first kick in the womb, my grandmother once told me, and he grew into a vigorous man, forty-three years old in 1918 and no apparent reason he would not live another forty-three years. I'd read about the mysterious, deadly illness sweeping through the major cities of America and, in fact, through the world. I even read about a similar mysterious illness that ravaged Haskell County in the spring of '18, arriving without warning and departing the same, but the summer months passed without any additional doomsday prophecies, and Haskell County was a full county away from our Blessing. Blessing, Kansas, was so far removed from any major city that we never imagined the same Spanish Influenza mercilessly decimating the populations of Cleveland and Chicago would ever find its way to our little town. But it came, nevertheless, overrode our innocence, slid into Blessing without warning, wreaked chaos and horror for eight weeks, and just as silently moved on.

When the bells of the Lutheran church sounded on the afternoon of the eleventh day of November, 1918, I at first thought they announced another influenza death. By then the county had banned all gatherings including funerals for fear of spreading the disease, and we were reduced to receiving immediate announcements of any importance via the steeple chimes. I soon found out that instead of grief those particular bells tolled joy. At exactly eleven o'clock that morning, Germany had surrendered and an armistice was declared, the Great War over and peace and Lloyd home at last, please God. Since my brother's enlistment nineteen months earlier I had often told myself that we might put a Hansen in the grave before the war ended, but I never once imagined it would be Father. We buried Blessing's last influenza victim that same November day, thanked God for peace and pleaded for good health all in the same prayers, mixed our mourning with joy in an unnatural way that kept me off balance for days afterward. I didn't quite know how or what I should feel.

Father's death was one piece of so many horrible things that year: young Joey Buchanan's death in France, my brother's transformational injuries at the Front, brutal murder closer to home, the unexpected malice of people I thought I knew, obsession and assault, fear and helplessness. Yet it would be a mistake to forget that something good emerged from that time, too, something more lasting than an armistice that would be shattered within two decades.

I recently came across a retrospective picture of Belgian farmlands in 1919, pockmarked by the shells and guns of battle with only the jagged skeletons of black, barren tree stumps to show that the place had once held life and vigor. A nightmare vision of an earthly Hades. But next to that picture the photographer had juxtaposed the same landscape twenty years later, hills lush with a carpet of thick grass covering the scars the Great War had inflicted on the terrain. New branches sprouted from the same trees that had looked so bleak and irretrievably dead years before. I stared at the two photographs in the book a long time, felt like weeping but smiled instead. The picture reminded me of so much that was dreadful and so much that was hopeful, a paradox of time I would not change even if I could.

Because of what I discovered during that terrible October and because of who discovered me.

Chapter 1

Wednesday, October 1, 1919

$\mathcal{A}$ year after my father's death I had grown accustomed to bearing sole responsibility for the success of Monroe's Emporium, the family store I inherited with Father's passing. To my knowledge no one wondered at my inheritance and that had nothing to do with my older brother being at the Front. Lloyd was a bright young man of many talents but no one, especially Lloyd, expected that he would have received the store. His talents and interests lay in directions other than business and commercial enterprise. I was the one that knew the internal workings of the store inside out and had been its bookkeeper since I was sixteen. Even before then I'd followed my father around the departments, watched him evaluate displays as he encouraged his employees, listened to him hail customers with a cheerful, heartfelt greeting that never failed to inquire after their good health and the well-being of their children. My father had a gift for remembering customers' names and birthdays and anniversaries. More than once I'd overheard comments to the effect that people preferred to shop at Monroe's because of the personal touch my father offered every visitor. When the full realization of my inheritance finally managed to sink in through the numb shock of Father's death, I struggled for weeks with uncertainty and something close to fear. I knew I was more than competent to keep the books, balance the accounts, set the prices, hire the staff, place the orders, and design the window displays for a small, Midwestern department store. What I doubted, and doubted acutely, was my ability to present the same cheerful and sincere welcome customers had come to expect from Jeff Hansen. Truth be told, I never was able to match him in that regard and always felt somewhat the failure because of it. Fortunately, people continued to shop with us, but I'm certain their doing so had nothing to do with the force of my personality. I was a girl that kept her own counsel and grew into the same kind of woman, though it would be a mistake to confuse quiet with shy. I was never shy.

On October 1, 1919, Father had been dead for just a year and my brother, Lloyd, had been home from the Front for seven months. My life was not exactly settled, not with the changes in Lloyd caused by the War, not with an ailing grandmother and the responsibility for a store and the subsequent impact its success or lack of would have on my family and the families of my employees. How could a girl of twenty feel settled with so much resting on her shoulders? But I was at least able to maintain a certain equilibrium, and I didn't want to be completely settled, anyway. Not just yet. I was only twenty and I'd seen nothing of the world beyond the confines of Blessing, Kansas. Suffragettes had changed the possibilities for women, thousands of Ford Model-Ts were coming off something called an assembly line, Fanny Brice made people laugh, Mary Pickford made people sigh, and Douglas Fairbanks was the handsomest man I'd ever seen.

For all my responsibilities during the war years, I still managed to see *His Majesty, the American* three times at Blessing's only movie house. No young woman of the time could ever get enough of Douglas Fairbanks. I'd lost both parents and in a way lost a brother, too, but I wasn't miserable. I grieved, of course, but because I was busy all the time I didn't have the luxury of ongoing unhappiness. I was young and hopeful of the future, besides. Clearly, dashing Douglas Fairbanks, having recently divorced one wife to invest in a newer model, was not pining away for love of a twenty-year old Kansas store keeper, but that didn't mean I must forego marriage all together and forever. In between the burdens of family and daily business tasks, I nurtured my own dreams and thought I had a good chance of finding my own hero. I was only twenty, after all, and still believed in happy endings. Until the morning of Wednesday, October 1, that is. The morning that changed both my routine and my life into something completely unexpected.

I braved the residue of early morning fog, our local river's reaction to a humid summerlike day replaced by a cool fall night, to drive our new Oldsmobile Economy truck to the railroad depot, picked up a waiting order of crates and boxes, and brought them back to the unloading platform at the rear of the store where our little warehouse backed up against a broad alley. Whoever had planned out the store's design years ago had done it thoughtfully and wisely, allowing easy access and room for growth. I loved that Oldsmobile truck and looked for any excuse to get behind the wheel. It was a dream to operate and while we didn't really need such a large truck, the store's budget accommodated and I rationalized its purchase because even then I loved to drive.

Kinsey Carr waved when he saw me back the truck up to the platform and hopped down beside the truck to yell over the motor's noise, "I could've picked this up for you, Thea," knowing even as he spoke that his hope for a chance behind the wheel always took a back seat to my availability.

"You wish!" I yelled back as I shifted the gear and took the big step down to the ground. "But you can put her in the garage after you unload her, if you want."

"Really?" To Kinsey's way of thinking such an opportunity did not come often enough. The boy looked pale and tired that morning and the influenza had not been gone for so long that I did not feel a pang of worry when I first saw him. But the idea of driving the truck restored his natural color and I squelched my concern. Kinsey's mother had died early in the epidemic, and if he hadn't contacted the illness at such close quarters he was almost certainly immune to it by now.

"Really. But don't rush with the boxes. There's a crate of fine Lenox china that's come all the way from New Jersey, and if you break any of it I'll figure out a way to take it out of your hide."

"You wish!" he retorted and we both laughed. Kinsey was fourteen to my twenty so we could take that tone with each other.

I went in through the side door, walked through the warehouse and into the back of the store proper. Monroe's Emporium was two stories, home goods and all sundries on the first floor, clothing and personal items on the second. Not so large or so busy that either floor needed more than two employees at any one time but busy enough to keep those two employees occupied for the day. Kinsey's sister Cecelia oversaw the second floor and Raymond Cuthbert, methodical and older than my father, supervised the ground level. Raymond was my father's opposite and never my father's friend, but he was devoted to the store and more regular than the seasons. Sometimes I thought Monroe's could run itself without me, but I doubted it could manage without Raymond.

Once in my office, I tossed my hat onto the credenza and sat down, first to examine and then to record and file the shipping invoices for the items I'd just picked up. The Lenox china was a special order for Cynthia Marks, a wedding present from her parents and hugely expensive, though when I'd quoted the price to George and Priscilla they hadn't batted an eye. Cynthia was their only daughter and their youngest, besides. Nothing was too good—or too expensive—for her. "If it's good enough for the White House, it's what we want for our Cynthia," George had said without a modicum of self-consciousness, and I placed the order with a straight face. If Mr. Marks believed that Washington, D.C. and Blessing, Kansas, needed to share china patterns, who was I to argue?

Busy with recording the costs, I nearly missed the first tentative knock on my door. I hardly ever closed my office door, only to concentrate when I worked on the books, and Raymond, whose knock I had come to recognize over many years, rapped again with more force. He could have simply stepped in after making his presence known, since it's not as if I changed clothes or took a bath in the office, but as many times as I invited the man to do so, he refused to take what he called a "liberty" with me. He kept a distance, I believed, to make me more aware of my youth and his seniority, but I didn't allow Raymond Cuthbert to make me uncomfortable. Monroe's was my father's store and now, whether Raymond approved or not, it was mine. Both floors and every inch of it.

"Yes," I called. Raymond pushed the door halfway open.

"Someone to see you," his voice unnaturally strained so that I felt a little stir of alarm.

I put both palms against the desktop to rise, asking as I did so, "Is everything—" and stopped abruptly when Sheriff McGill, the head of Blessing's police constabulary, stepped past Raymond into the office. At the sight of the officer, my alarm grew.

"Mort," I said, standing upright and looking straight at the sheriff, "is something wrong?" I don't know exactly why I had that thought, his sober face, maybe, or the worry and fear I carried with me ever since Lloyd had come home from the war. I saw something in McGill's face that made my heart start to beat unnaturally fast.

"I'd like to talk to Lloyd," he said without answering my question. "Do you know where he is?"

"Home, as far as I know. I left him there this morning still asleep. He didn't say anything about having plans today." Mort McGill shook his head.

"No, he's not there. The house is empty. I took the liberty of looking in."

"Did you?" I said. I knew something was very wrong if Mort McGill stepped into my home without invitation or permission.

He nodded. The knuckles on the hand that held firmly to the brim of his hat showed white with strain. Something very, very wrong.

"Rudy Stanislaw was killed this morning, Thea."

"Rudy?" I repeated, horrified and for a moment at a loss for more words. Finally, I was able to speak. "My God, I'm so sorry. Was it an accident? He's always so careful with his tools."

"No, not an accident, Thea. Someone, I don't know who yet, shot him. It looks like somebody interrupted him this morning while he was working in the garage. The way that shot took him, killing him was the only intention. So, no, it wasn't an accident." Behind him Raymond Cuthbert, still listening from the doorway, made a little sound at the news, clearly shocked. I was shocked, too, but being so did not interfere with my ability to think quietly and furiously about what McGill's presence in my office asking for Lloyd might mean.

"I'm so very sorry," I said evenly. "It will be a blow for his father and for Lloyd, too. You know they've been best friends since they were in Sunday School together."

"I'd like to talk to Lloyd, Thea," McGill said again.

"Why Lloyd, exactly? How can he help you?"

"I won't know that until I find him, but—" for all his easy tone, McGill's eyes were dark and sharp "—a couple people saw your brother leave the garage this morning so maybe Lloyd saw or heard something that could help identify Rudy's killer." And just maybe Lloyd's the killer himself, McGill was thinking. I could read it on his face.

"Lloyd would never hurt Rudy. They fought together. They came home together. They're best friends." But that was before, I thought, even as I mentally backed away from the disloyal notion. Before the war changed Lloyd, made him start at sudden noises, gave him a temper he'd never had before, woke him with violent dreams, changed him from my bright, daydreaming brother into a brooding and occasionally belligerent stranger. Almost no one was spared Lloyd's temper, not even I or Rudy. Regardless of how I presented the friendship to McGill, I'd personally seen Lloyd strike out at Rudy. Only Cecelia had the ability to calm my brother.

"Maybe a stranger broke in and surprised Rudy," I suggested. "Some vagrant off the train passing through town and thinking he'd find something valuable in the garage."

"There wasn't any struggle, Thea. Do you think Rudy Stanislaw would let a stranger break in and point a gun at him without defending himself? Rudy?" He paused. "Does Lloyd have access to a revolver, Thea?"

"I don't know. I suppose so. I remember my father had a pistol in the house, but I don't know what happened to it. I haven't thought about it in years."

"Then Lloyd could have come across it and you wouldn't have known."

What the sheriff said was true enough, and I could only repeat, "Lloyd would never hurt Rudy, Mort."

"That may be so but I need to talk to him."

"I don't know where he is," I replied. "He was asleep when I left this morning, and I haven't seen him since."

"Maybe your grandmother would know."

"I doubt it, but by all means stop down at the hotel and ask her. Just remember she hasn't been well lately."

"I'm headed there now." I could tell from the sheriff's implacable tone that he wasn't asking my permission to question my grandmother.

"You do what you have to, Mort, to find out who committed such a terrible act, but don't for a minute think Lloyd had anything to do with it. He loved Rudy like a brother. He'd never hurt him." After he left, I sat down behind my desk like a balloon that lost all its air.

"Can I do anything?" Raymond asked, sincere concern in his voice. He'd stood in the doorway immobile during the entire conversation.

"Would you ask Cece to come and see me, please? I'd like to talk to her." Raymond nodded and disappeared, shutting the office door behind him. I sat behind my desk without moving, but my thoughts banged around inside my head like balls bouncing off the sides of a billiards table. Bouncing and colliding and bouncing and colliding again. Where was Lloyd and what had he been doing all morning? I would not be able to rest until I had answers to both questions.

Cecelia Carr gave a quick rap on the door and came in before I had a chance to say a word. "Raymond said you wanted to see me." With the familiarity of many years, she sat down without being asked and continued, "What's wrong, Thea?" Cecelia Carr might be young, but she was also perceptive beyond her years. "Is it Lloyd?"

"I don't think so." Ashamed of my doubts I said more firmly, "I'm sure not, but I need to speak to him and I don't know where he is. Have you seen him today at all? Maybe when I was away at the depot?"

"No, I haven't seen him once today." Her smile faded. "Which is odd, really? He almost always stops by first thing to say hello." Cece stared at me for a long moment. "Something's wrong, isn't it? I can tell."

"Rudy Stanislaw was killed today."

Cecelia gasped, her eyes filled with sudden tears, and one hand went briefly to her lips. "Oh, no! What happened?"

"I don't have details," I replied evasively, "but I wouldn't want Lloyd to find out by accident."

"No, of course, not." She rummaged around in a smock pocket for a handkerchief. "Poor Rudy, Thea, and poor Dolf. How awful to make it through the war and come home only to die a few months later in the safety of your own hometown. I'm so sorry. I don't know what to say."

"I know." After another brief silence, both our thoughts racing on different tracks, I said, "If you see Lloyd, Cece, please don't say anything about Rudy. Just tell him I need to talk to him about something important. I know you're his friend, but let me do the telling, okay?"

Cecelia stood. "Of course." She took a quick swipe at her tears with the fingertips of both hands. "Poor Rudy," she said again at the door before she left.

I was too restless to stay at the store for very long and left well before closing, not something I did very often; Raymond volunteered to close up for the day when he returned to ask me if there was anything else he could do.

"You'd better go talk to your grandmother," Raymond advised. "No doubt McGill's already been there and she'll be worried. If Lloyd shows up here, I'll send him down to the hotel, tell him you're looking for him."

"Thank you, Raymond." I was surprised and touched by his concern. "Grandmother's legs have been bothering her, and I don't want her trying to walk from one end of Blessing to the other in search of either Lloyd or me."

Along with the store, the Hansen House was one of the oldest establishments in Blessing. I loved the refined antebellum look of the place with its grand front porch and stately white pillars. The rooms were spacious, the lobby plush and comfortable, and the restaurant on the first floor famous for its fried chicken. My father's parents had started it on a shoestring forty years earlier, and now it was renowned in Kansas, as much for its amenities as its history.

I expected to find Sheriff McGill there, but he had come and gone quickly, my grandmother not being a woman to suffer fools or prolong the unnecessary or unwelcome. I found her in her spacious second-floor apartment and knew from the look on her face that she was disturbed. Grandma Liza, as Lloyd and I had called her all our lives, was an opinionated, forceful woman, who never shied away from sharing her views on everything from politics to fashion. I had learned that I was most convincing when I refused to engage in battle with her; she viewed silence as a strength because it was so foreign to her nature.

"I thought you'd be by, Thea," she said without additional greeting. "Have you located that brother of yours?"

"No. You haven't seen Lloyd either?"

Grandmother sat in a rocking chair, one swollen leg propped on a hassock. She emphasized her "No" with a sharp rap on the floor with the wooden cane she held in one hand. "He doesn't come see me very often in the best of times."

"Lloyd doesn't sleep well and his days are all mixed up. I hear him up at night and then he sleeps the day away. He doesn't mean to be—" My grandmother cut my words off with a snort.

"I know that, Thea. My legs don't work, but my eyes and ears still work fine. Lloyd hasn't been himself since he came home. That damned war! Wilson was going to keep us out of it and what does he do as soon as my back is turned but send our boys across an ocean to a place they had no business being." She observed my expression and softened. "I haven't seen Lloyd, but I know that boy and he'd never hurt Rudy. They were like brothers. McGill's got a bee up his butt about somebody seeing Lloyd over at the garage at the time of the killing, but I told him that didn't prove anything. Like as not there were a lot of folks at the garage one time or another this morning. Just because Lloyd is still recovering from his time at the Front doesn't make him a murderer."

I smiled at that. For all her forthright talk, our Grandma Liza was loyal to her family and especially to her grandchildren. She couldn't have been bribed to compliment us to our faces, but let anyone criticize or belittle any of us and she was our staunchest defender. She gave me a long look.

"Ring the bell for Lizzy, Thea, and then sit down a while. You look worried."

Lizzy, Grandmother's help, showed up at the door with a pot of hot tea. The two women had been together since my Grandpa Steven died in '98 and after twenty years hardly needed to use words with each other at all.

I sipped the tea, careful not to slurp even by accident because my grandmother absolutely detested poor table manners.

"I am worried," I admitted. I couldn't tell my grandmother everything that was happening, but I could still say things to her that I wouldn't divulge to anyone else. "But only because Lloyd's disappeared. Cecelia hasn't seen him at all, which is odd because she's one of the few people he seeks out. She can make him laugh when no one else can. And the sheriff said Lloyd's not at home, either. And if he was seen at the garage, where would he go afterwards? I'm confused and worried, but—" my tone firmed "—like you I know my brother would never hurt Rudy, not really. They had a couple of loud arguments but that's just men being men." We talked a little longer as I finished my tea. Then, feeling better for both the refreshment and the conversation, I stood and said, "I'd better get home and see if Lloyd's showed up there."

At the door Grandmother said, "Let me know what happens, Thea. I'm old and crippled but I'm family, and family sticks together. Everything'll be all right. Hard times come and go but family lasts." I smiled at the words, one of her favorite phrases and one I'd heard ever since I was a little girl.

Once outside I headed toward the opposite end of Blessing, taking my time to peer down side alleys and stop by any establishments Lloyd might frequent, but my brother was nowhere to be found. The hotel and the store had once been Blessing's two largest commercial enterprises, but through the years the town's main street had expanded, had added businesses and side streets and traffic, including motor cars. My grandmother had a scornful opinion about what she considered to be a "fad" over motor cars, but while I didn't bother to argue with her about their usefulness or future potential, I had no doubt the automobile was here to stay. I was glad of it, too, although it seemed to me that simply owning a motor car did not make a person qualified to sit behind its steering wheel. The way some of the drivers chugged, careened, and jerked their ways down the middle of Blessing could make crossing the street a challenge, especially at dusk.

By twilight I'd exhausted every possible place Lloyd might be and finally reached our house, comforted by the lights blazing from several windows. Lloyd must be home, I thought with a surge of relief, but that was before I saw the two police officers at the side of the house peering around the corner toward the back yard, both men still and watchful. I began to run, yanking up my slim skirt as I did so, rushed past the two officers despite their muted, surprised cries to me, and halted abruptly at the sight of Mort McGill, hands in his pockets, conversing calmly with my brother. Lloyd stood on the porch, one hand on the screen door handle and McGill stood midway on the back walk facing the porch.

"I only want to talk with you, Lloyd," McGill said easily. Lloyd shifted from one foot to another as he listened to the sheriff. Both men turned their heads to me as I rounded the corner, my panting clearly audible in the evening air.

I had to take a moment to catch my breath before I said, "I'm glad you're home, Lloyd. I didn't know where you were."

My brother shifted his weight again and said in a voice almost too low for me to hear, "Rudy's dead, Thea."

I heard misery in his voice and a grief beyond bearing, heard it with joy and knew for a certainty that Lloyd had not had any part in Rudy Stanislaw's death. There was too much pain in his voice, too much loss. I hoped Mort McGill heard what I heard but doubted that was the case. McGill didn't know or love Lloyd as I did.

"Yes," I said, taking a few steps past the sheriff so that I stood at the foot of the porch steps. "I know, Lloyd. It's a terrible thing. Where were you just now?"

Lloyd considered my casual question. "At the cemetery."

I didn't expect that and had to ask, "Why there?"

"I don't know. I wanted to see Father's grave. I missed him all of a sudden and just wanted to see his grave."

With unhurried steps Mort McGill came to stand next to me. "I'd like to talk to you, Lloyd." My brother's eyes shifted from my face to McGill's and back again to me.

"Please, Lloyd," I said. "Let's go inside and sit down. The sheriff has a job to do and those of us who loved Rudy need to help him." A brief, breathless moment passed and Lloyd nodded.

"All right. All right, Thea." His voice had a dazed tone to it, the same tone I heard immediately after he awoke from one of his terrible dreams, as if he did not know where he was, did not know what was real or imagined or even if he were alive or dead.

Mort made a negligible wave toward the side of the house where his two officers still waited before he followed Lloyd and me into the kitchen. I turned on the gas under the tea kettle, trying to act as if life were normal and it was any evening I came home, put on hot water, reached for something from the icebox, took down the carving board, and brought bread from the breadbox.

"Sit down, Lloyd." Mort's tone was that of a man in charge and I think my brother recognized it from his years in the military because he sat as ordered and rested his folded hands on the tabletop. "What's that on your shirt cuffs?"

Even with my back turned to them I heard the sudden change in McGill's voice, whirled still clasping the loaf, and stared at Lloyd's hands where they lay on the table. The unfastened cuffs of his shirt showing beyond the sleeve of his jacket were stained red. It was all I could do to keep from dropping the bread, and I know McGill heard my quick intake of breath. Lloyd heard it, too, and looked down with bewilderment at his sleeves.

"I don't know," his words halting. He looked at the stain on both cuffs with bewilderment. "I don't know." He turned his head toward me, eyes beseeching. "Thea?"

"It looks like blood, Lloyd" I said with a calm I didn't feel. "Did you cut yourself?"

"No. I don't think I did. I don't remember any cut." He pushed both sleeves up above his wrists and began to search his arms for injury. There was something not right with Lloyd, I realized. He had not lost that dazed tone to his voice. Did he think he was in a dream? I sat down beside him, laid my hands on his to stop their unnatural activity, and pretended to examine his lower arms.

"No," I agreed, clasping his hands in both of mine tightly. "You're right as rain, love. I'm glad you're not hurt." I smiled directly into his eyes and felt him relax a little.

"Then where—?"

I shook my head at his unfinished question. "I don't know."

The sheriff broke his silence to ask, "Were you over at the garage today, Lloyd?" I watched my brother consider the question with unusual intent.

"I can't remember, Mort. I don't think so but maybe I was."

"I ask because a couple of folks thought they saw you go in the garage and then a couple of other folks saw you hightail it out of there some time later. Do you remember that?"

Without a word Lloyd shook his head. "I'd remember if I was there." Again Lloyd turned to face me. "I'd remember, wouldn't I, Thea?"

"I think you would, Lloyd, though anybody can be forgiven for a lapse of memory now and then."

You'd remember if you killed your best friend, I thought firmly. I know you'd remember that. I was even more convinced, despite witnesses and unexplained blood, that my brother had had no part in the morning's murder.

"Did you hurt Rudy, Lloyd?" Mort asked pleasantly. It was the right tone to take, light but not too light, the tone of a father questioning a son's mischief or an officer interrogating one of his troops for some slight infraction.

"Hurt Rudy?" Lloyd repeated, incredulity in his voice. "Hurt my buddy? No! No, I didn't! I'd never hurt Rudy. We fought together. We came home together. I'd never hurt Rudy, Mort!"

There, I thought, hearing the outraged grief in his voice, that settles it, but I knew it didn't, not really. Mort could no more ignore the blood on Lloyd's sleeves than I could ignore a rat in the cupboard.

The sheriff stood up and thrust both hands back into his pockets, the picture of nonchalance.

"Well, you come with me, anyway, will you, Lloyd? I'd like to talk with you some more and Thea's had a long day. We don't need to involve your sister in our discussion."

"Come with you where?" Lloyd asked. To me it sounded as if he were slowly returning from a distant place, his tone sharper, his words less plaintive.

"Over to the jail, Lloyd. It's private there and we can talk without bothering anyone."

My brother gave McGill a long quiet look, stared down at the blood on his sleeves for an even longer time, inhaled deeply, and gave a slow, shuddering sigh. Through it all the sheriff and I did not take our gaze from Lloyd. What I saw was a young man coming to grips with the death of a good friend and finally understanding the reason for the sheriff's presence in our kitchen. What McGill saw I didn't know but was certain it was something else entirely. Lloyd stood up.

"You think I killed Rudy," he stated. He turned to look down at me. "I didn't hurt Rudy, Thea. I'd never hurt Rudy."

"I know." I spoke firmly, rose, and reached across to straighten my brother's coat lapels. "You go on with Mort. Everything will be all right."

McGill said to me, "I wouldn't expect Lloyd home tonight, Thea." And not for any night in the near future, he would have added if he wasn't worried about setting Lloyd off and spoiling the peaceful way the evening had progressed. "It might not hurt to let Ian Buchanan know what's happened and tell him to come see Lloyd first thing in the morning." Mort McGill, a good man and longtime friend of our family, added, "I'm sorry about this, Thea."

My brother heard the name Ian Buchanan and said, "No."

McGill and I both stared at Lloyd, startled by the firm syllable. McGill stiffened somewhat at the word, perhaps expecting some kind of resistance from my brother, but Lloyd wasn't reacting to the sheriff's direction to accompany him to the jail.

"Not Ian Buchanan. I don't need or want his help. Wire Captain Davis, Thea. I heard he went back to being a lawyer and I bet he's a good one. He's a damned good man all around. One of the best. He never left any of us behind and he said he never would, even after we came home. I believe him, Thea. He'll help me. He knows Rudy and me. He knows I wouldn't hurt Rudy and he'll help me." Lloyd had mentioned Captain Davis on several occasions, but I didn't know he was a lawyer and I certainly didn't know where he lived. Come to think of it, I didn't even know the captain's first name. I guessed that would all change soon enough.

"Where do I find him?" I asked.

Lloyd shook his head as if clearing it of excess information and finally answered, "Wyoming. Laramie, Wyoming. That's where he's from. We used to razz him about being a cowboy, ask him why he didn't wear a cowboy hat. He never acted better than the rest of us. A good officer and a better man."

"What's his first name?" Even with the seriousness of the situation my brother grinned at the question. The thought of

Captain Davis coming to his aid seemed to restore Lloyd to some semblance of normal behavior.

"Augustus, must have been. We called him Gunny Gus. He never asked us to pick up a weapon unless he already had his in his hands. He's the man to help me."

"Help us," I corrected. "I'll get Jimmy to open the cable office and wire Davis tonight. We can have it delivered to the Laramie court house. If he's a lawyer they'll probably know him there."

With that reassurance Lloyd turned back to the sheriff and held out his hands, wrists together, but McGill shook his head.

"No need for that, Lloyd," he told him quietly and together the two men walked out the back door and into the darkness.

I didn't bother to follow them. Instead, I went in search of my heavier coat because an October evening in Kansas turns cool as soon as the sun goes down and the cable office was several blocks away. If my brother had wanted the man in the moon I'd have found a way to get him, so walking only a few blocks to wake up Jimmy Long and have him open the office to send a cable on Lloyd's behalf was child's play by comparison. I knew the situation was as far from child's play as it could be, but something in the hope I'd heard in Lloyd's voice at the mention of Davis had heartened my spirits as well. If Lloyd wanted Captain Gus Davis, he would have him.

Chapter 2

Thursday, October 2 – Monday, October 6, 1919

*T*he pragmatic side of my nature did not expect Lloyd home that night, but that did not keep me from stoking the fire in the pot-bellied stove for extra warmth and curling up in the rocking chair next to it in case my brother walked through the back door and needed sustenance.

At first light, I considered my list of tasks as I dressed for the day. First stop, of course, was the jail. Danny Merritt, one of Blessing's five police officers, stood when I entered.

"He's fine, Thea," Danny announced before I had a chance to say a word. Danny's younger sister and I had been friends all through school, although with her departure to college that friendship had been interrupted.

"Lloyd has bad dreams sometimes," I said. "From the war." Danny nodded. I held out the covered plate I held. "I brought him breakfast. Can I take it back to him?"

"I don't know any reason why not." Danny opened the drawer of the desk and took out a ring of keys. "I don't suppose you brought anything for me." I knew he was trying for a light touch and it was funny in its way since Danny was a big, meaty man with a renowned appetite for anything set before him.

"That would be Estelle's responsibility," I said, trying to smile so he'd know I understood his kind intent, "not mine." His wife was a tiny thing with the appetite of a bird, and they were Blessing's own Jack Spratt family.

Lloyd sat on the bunk in his cell with his knees pulled up to his chest. He didn't look a day past fifteen and I felt a sudden tenderness for him. He'd gone off to war dreamy-eyed and cheerful and come back a haunted stranger. I longed for the return of the boy I'd waved good-bye to three years ago but realized he was gone forever. This thin man with shadows under his eyes had returned in his place, and he was my brother now.

Lloyd's face brightened at the sight of me. "Did you send for the captain, Thea?"

"I did," I said with a cheerfulness I didn't feel.

"Good. It'll be all right, then." We were wordless as he started his breakfast, but he looked up after a few bites. "You know, Thea, I don't hold this against the sheriff. I know it looks bad, the blood on my cuffs and all, but Captain Davis will sort it all out. He'll know I'd never hurt Rudy, not with what we went through together, and he'll figure it out. The captain always knew what to do. I didn't dream last night, and I think it's knowing the captain's on his way that made the difference." He gave me the open smile I remembered from years ago. "It'll be all right, Thea, I know it, and I'm okay here. I just wish I knew who hurt Rudy. He was a good friend. He didn't deserve what happened to him. It doesn't seem right, does it, that he made it through the Huns only to have someone in his own hometown kill him?"

"No," I agreed. "It doesn't seem right and it doesn't make sense. I can't see anybody doing something so horrible. Maybe it was a stranger passing through, a tramp or a thief trying to steal something from Rudy."

"Maybe."

Lloyd finished his breakfast and handed me the empty plate, which I placed inside my small satchel until I was next home. Since I had a number of errands, I imagined that wouldn't occur until evening.

"You'll bring the captain to see me straight off when he gets here, won't you?"

"Yes, but give him some time, Lloyd. He'll just receive the wire this morning, and since he's a lawyer he might have other cases he needs to wind up." I hoped that wasn't so because I was as anxious as Lloyd to have the mythic Davis show up, but I didn't want my brother to be disappointed if the man didn't appear in front of him by suppertime.

"He promised he'd stand by us, and he'll be here sooner than you think. You'll see."

As I walked from the jail to the store I pondered Captain Augustus Davis and wondered what kind of man could inspire that kind of confidence in other men. What if Davis's departing words were all façade? What if captain's stripes had blinded my brother to the man's true character? What if, looking around for anything to hold on to, Lloyd had latched on to an officer and imbued him with the traits and characteristics he needed him to have so that my brother could believe in his own survival? I thought I might be even more eager than Lloyd to have Gus Davis appear in Blessing.

I arrived at the store earlier than usual and still found Raymond and Cece waiting for me.

"The sheriff arrested Lloyd for Rudy's murder," I told them immediately; Cece gave a small gasp, "but I know he didn't do it and we're waiting for a lawyer from Wyoming to help prove Lloyd's innocence." At their unspoken question I continued, "He's a man Lloyd served with in the war and Lloyd trusts him. I sent him a wire last night so if a stranger shows up looking for me, let me know right away."

"But, Thea, since Lloyd didn't kill Rudy, who did?" Leave it to Cece's open nature to ask the obvious question I hadn't allowed myself to dwell on.

"Let's not think about who's guilty," Raymond advised, "only about getting the innocent out of jail." To me he said, "Take all the time away you need, Thea. Cecelia and I can handle the store."

"I know you can," I replied with gratitude, "and I will be gone this morning. I need to let Grandma Liza know what's happened before she hears about it through the grapevine. But I'll be back this afternoon." I hesitated a moment, searching for the right words. "And thank you both. You're good friends to Lloyd and me. I appreciate that." Cece smiled, but Raymond flushed with emotion I hadn't expected. After a moment, as his Adam's apple continued to bob from the effort of holding back his feelings, Raymond turned away to unlock the front doors. Despite the fact that we had an elevator, Cece headed for the stairs to the second floor. Perhaps, like me, she needed exercise to release her anxiety.

By store opening I knew that everyone in Blessing had heard that Lloyd Hansen had been arrested for the murder of Rudy Stanislaw. The next edition of the local newspaper, The Banner, wasn't due out until Monday, and by then the paper's headline announcement of the crime would arrive to no one's surprise. Blessing's grapevine would put any print edition of news to shame. Because I was so young at the time I had an expectation that at least a few people, people I considered particularly good friends, would appear to offer encouragement and support. When I said as much to Grandmother later in the morning, she gave a snort of disparagement.

"Lord, Thea, what world do you live in? There's nothing like a good scandal to turn friends into strangers." She sat with her swollen leg propped up and a blanket over her lap but still very much the old-world dowager. "How did Lloyd handle the arrest?"

"He was calm. He doesn't remember what he did yesterday morning."

"So he says." I glared at her, wordless and surprised. "There's no use you giving me one of those looks, Thea. I'm just saying out loud what Mort McGill and probably the whole town are thinking. You'd better get used to it." I knew she was right but the knowledge made me angry.

"Most people in Blessing have known Lloyd his whole life. They know the kind of boy he is."

"The kind of boy he was. Lloyd came back a man with little resemblance to the whistling boy he was when he left. You know that better than anybody."

"What we are inside at our core doesn't change, no matter what." I snapped the words from pique but realized I believed them.

"Have you had time to talk to Ian Buchanan yet? Tell him we don't care about the cost if he gets our boy free and home."

"Lloyd doesn't want Mr. Buchanan. He asked me to get him another lawyer, someone he knew from the army, and I wired the captain last night to ask him to come. I expect I'll hear back from him today."

Grandmother eyed me with suspicion. "We need the best man for Lloyd's defense, Thea. This isn't something that'll go away if we pretend it doesn't exist."

"Lloyd thinks Captain Davis is the best man for the job. He trusts him. Just knowing he might come calmed Lloyd down. He actually smiled. The old Lloyd smile, the one I haven't seen in a long time. We're going to give Captain Davis a chance, Grandma. I just wish he were closer."

"Where's he coming from?"

"Wyoming."

The name sharpened my grandmother's gaze. "Wyoming is it? What's the man's name again?"

"Captain Augustus Davis. Well, he's a private citizen now so I don't suppose he uses the captain part any more."

"Augustus Davis." Grandmother rolled the name over her tongue like she was tasting it and a slow smile pulled at the corners of her mouth. "You bring that man to see me when he arrives, Thea. I want to meet him. And tell him he's to lodge here as our guest however long he ends up staying. There's some justice to that after all these years." I looked at her with curiosity, sure there was something behind her enigmatic words and half-smile that she ought to share with me, but she wouldn't say any more on the topic.

My last stop of the morning was a difficult one, but I thought for Lloyd's sake I needed to visit the Stanislaw garage and express my sympathy to Dolf Stanislaw at the death of his son. I knew he might not want to talk to me but didn't think he would direct any anger he felt about Lloyd at me personally. I had to be my brother's face now, speak his words, act on his behalf. I believed in Lloyd's innocence, and I was not going to sneak from alley to alley like a criminal trying to escape capture.

The Stanislaws had always lived over the garage in a small apartment, at one time much too small for the parents and five children but now, sadly, probably feeling much too large for one man, wife dead, and children grown and moved away. Rudy's enlistment had been a blow to his father and when the boy returned from the fighting without injury to mind or body, Dolf had handed out cigars the same as a new father would have. He was not a man given to smiling, but the day Rudy came home from the fighting and stepped off the train onto the Blessing platform I thought Dolf's cheeks would split from the smile. Now after all that joy and all that hope, I was knocking at a house of mourning.

Dolf Stanislaw opened the door and at first glance his appearance shocked me, dark stubble on his face, unkempt hair, and clothes with the noticeable air of having been worn too long and probably slept in. He said nothing, only looked at me with eyes red from lack of sleep. Here was grief in its rawest form, I thought, and felt a pang of pure compassion for the man.

"What do you want? Come to gloat?" My compassion vanished quickly at the rough words and the rank smell of alcohol Dolf exhaled with the words.

"No," I replied, calmer in my tone than I felt inside. "I wanted to say how sorry I was about Rudy." He started to speak and I put out one hand, palm forward to keep him quiet. "And I wanted to say that Lloyd didn't do this terrible thing. He'd never hurt Rudy. He loved him, we both loved him, like a brother."

"Shit, Thea, do you think you standing there all prissy and fine could make me believe that? Your brother came back messed up in his head. You know it; the whole town knows it. You saw him hit my boy. You saw how many times Rudy had to calm him down, and yesterday your goddamned crazy brother picked another fight with my boy, only this time he brought a gun with him. Must've planned to kill Rudy the moment he walked into the garage because he never gave him a fighting chance. And now you want me to believe your brother had nothing to do with it, that he loved him like a goddamned brother? There ain't nobody else would have hurt Rudy and you know it. You can both go to hell." He closed the door carefully with the exaggerated gesture of a drunk.

I stood there long enough to catch my breath, pulled my coat closer around my chest, carefully descended the outside steps, and headed back to the store. No one had ever spoken to me so crudely or with such contempt, and in all my life I'd never had hatred directed at me. While I knew part of what I heard was grief and another part alcohol, I also realized that Dolf Stanislaw truly believed my brother had killed his son. Grief and alcohol aside, I recognized that most of the man's emotion was hatred in its most elemental form. The knowledge made my hands shake so noticeably that I kept them in my pockets all the way back to Monroe's.

Ian Buchanan waited for me in the store office. When I entered the room, slipping off my coat as I did so, he rose.

"Thea, is what I heard about Lloyd true? I don't want to believe it, but if it's true, I hope you know you can rely on me to help you."

I hung my coat on the hook behind the door and turned to the man with a sincere smile. Ian Buchanan was handsome, gray-headed, and dignified. His son Joe had been the third of the youthful triumvirate of army enlistees from Blessing, Kansas, and the one that didn't come home.

"Hello, Mr. Buchanan. Please sit down." I went to my chair behind the desk and did the same. "I don't know what you heard exactly, but if it was that my brother was arrested for the murder of Rudy Stanislaw, then it is certainly true."

"I heard about Rudy, poor boy. I think everybody I talked to felt the same about it. A damnable shame that he should come home safe from the war and be killed in the peaceful security of his own hometown, his own place of business. A damnable shame." Memory of his son's death in France colored his voice and gave the words an unspoken implication.

"Lloyd didn't kill Rudy, Mr. Buchanan. It doesn't look good for my brother right now, but I am absolutely sure that someone else did this terrible thing."

More than twenty-five years of practicing law had taught Ian Buchanan to put on the proper face, but even with that history I saw the skepticism and the pity in his eyes before he composed his expression into one of benevolent concern.

"You're a good sister, Thea."

"I may or may not be a good sister, Mr. Buchanan, that evaluation could change based on the day we discuss it, but I know my brother and I know how he felt about Rudy. You remember as well as I that Lloyd and Rudy and your Joe were closer than peas in a pod all their childhood and there wasn't a mean bone in those boys. Even in his worst times, Lloyd would never have hurt Rudy."

Ian Buchanan did not take his gaze from me and smiled slightly as I concluded.

"That's true enough, Thea." He paused. "Well, I'll go talk to Lloyd, find out what the arrest warrant says and if McGill's already petitioned for a court date. You know Kansas abolished the death penalty over twelve years ago now so that's one worry off your mind."

I did not welcome that final comment, as if Buchanan already had his mind made up about Lloyd no matter what I said, and I responded in a sharper tone than was warranted by the man's kindness.

"That won't be necessary. I value your kindness and your willingness to help, but Lloyd has asked for legal assistance from a man he met in the army. His commanding officer, in fact, a Captain Davis. I wired Davis last night and although I haven't heard back from him yet, Lloyd is confident in the man's willingness to help and in his competence besides."

Buchanan's impassive expression changed to one of surprise at the news. "Do you know this Davis fellow, Thea?"

"Lloyd's talked about him now and then, always with respect and admiration, but no, I don't know him, not really."

"Then I think you and your brother are making a serious mistake. Lloyd needs someone that knows him, someone that knew Rudy, too."

"Captain Davis does know them both, Mr. Buchanan, knows what they're like in the heat of battle, and has had the opportunity to observe them under difficult circumstances."

"You know what I mean."

"I do, and I appreciate your willingness to help, but I'm going to wait to hear if Captain Davis is willing to take on Lloyd's case. It's what Lloyd wants."

I could tell Ian Buchanan felt inclined to argue the matter further, he was a lawyer after all, but he wisely refrained from doing so. He stood and put on his hat before speaking again.

"You remind me of your grandmother at the most unexpected times, Thea," he commented with a smile. "Do what you feel you must but know I'm ready to help any time and any way I can. If Davis takes you up on your request, don't hesitate to send him to me if he needs advice or information."

"Thank you, I will. That's good to know." I was touched by the offer. "How is Mrs. Buchanan?"

Always at the mention of his wife a faint shadow passed over the man's face. I wondered if I was the only person to notice how his lips compressed, however briefly, whenever Delta Buchanan's name was brought into the conversation.

"She's fine, Thea. Just fine. Thank you for asking. Delta and I just saw Rudy a day or two ago. He was good about stopping by for a word now and then. She'll be heartbroken to hear he's gone." Buchanan always had a ready answer to an inquiry about his wife and the response was always superficial. We both knew that Delta Buchanan had never recovered from the knock on the door and the telegram bearing the news of her son's death. War did not damage only soldiers on the battlefield. It had long-reaching power to wound on the home front, too.

Jimmy Long personally delivered the response from Captain Davis I'd been awaiting, a kind gesture from Jimmy done, I was sure, because all his young life he'd idolized my brother and felt sad because of what had occurred. In a small town like Blessing you grow up in other people's pockets. I slid open the flap of the envelope, unfolded the notepaper and read: *Sorry to hear of Stanislaw death. Brother's arrest seems all wrong. Will arrive Monday.* Short and sweet. Tears pricked my eyes at the words *seems all wrong.* Did he really mean it? Did this man who'd led my brother into combat and fought beside him truly trust in his innocence? I needed a fellow believer as much as Lloyd needed a good attorney. That my grandmother loved Lloyd I could hear in her tone, but I could also hear that she had doubts about his innocence. She would never verbalize such treasonous thoughts, but I could tell she wouldn't be surprised if Lloyd confessed to killing Rudy Stanislaw in a fit of unbridled rage. Augustus Davis might share those same doubts but how I hoped not! How I wanted him to mean *seems all wrong* with his whole heart, believing it with the same certainty I felt. Because even then and later, too, as the situation grew even darker, I knew that Lloyd was not the killer people thought him to be. Someone else in my little town of Blessing was, however, and the realization held its own fear and disbelief. If not Lloyd, then who?

The flow of customers through the store the next two days was so slow as to be non-existent. People had heard about Lloyd and were working out what to do if they should come face to face with me. Offer sympathy? No, Lloyd wasn't the one that was dead. Offer encouragement? Not if Lloyd ended up being guilty; were that the case, justice should be swift and forceful. Nod and not make eye contact? That seemed to be the general consensus of the few customers we had. I was tempted to close early on Saturday, so empty was the store, but my spine stiffened at the idea because I would not act like we had done something wrong and needed to rush home to hide. So I rambled around Monroe's Emporium, ignored Cecelia's flushed cheeks and glistening eyes, and at the usual time turned the key in the lock and the sign on the door. The week had taken a turn I could never have imagined in my wildest dreams. I supposed Dolf Stanislaw felt the same and felt a sharp pity for him despite his coarse rudeness to me. Grief, I knew, affected everyone differently.

Look at Delta Buchanan, a petite, Georgia beauty with a flair for fashion and a sharp tongue that could both amuse and wound at the same time. But that was before the wire arrived announcing her Joey's death in France. I wondered if she saw the terrible words written on that piece of paper whenever she closed her eyes and that was why she hadn't been able to sleep for weeks afterward, why—so I'd heard from more than one person—she demanded the table be set for three people long after the devastating news had irretrievably reduced her family to two. Poor woman. Poor Dolf. Poor Rudy. We seemed to be a town of *poor* people right at the moment, thanks to the effects of war and the deadly influenza. Whatever normal was, and at the time I couldn't quite recall what normal looked or felt like, was what I longed for.

Grandmother took over providing Lloyd's meals from the hotel's kitchen, but I visited my brother twice a day over the weekend. I was pleased that he hadn't slipped back into the black suspicion, so unlike his usual self, that could take over his mood since the war but wished he could recall more of his movements Wednesday morning. No matter how I probed, however, he said he couldn't and I believed him. My brother had been a transparent lad, clear-eyed and mischievous but always tender-hearted, a boy who wrote poetry and loved music. He had never lied well. I, knowing him all my life, did not believe he was lying now.

Sunday brought worship service at the Lutheran church, which had dropped the word *German* from its name at the start of the war along with its German language early service. We ended the service on a somber note praying for President Wilson, who'd been taken seriously ill over the weekend, a chastening reminder to me that Lloyd wasn't the only person in the world in need of divine support. Once home, I spent the afternoon trying to compose a letter to my Uncle Carl and Aunt Louisa. I valued their advice, but unfortunately they were in Topeka visiting their recently married and relocated twin daughters, Beverly and Barbara. In one wedding service the sisters had conveniently married brothers and then moved to Topeka where the husbands/brothers worked and lived. Privately I considered such tandem togetherness slightly obsessive, but then I was not very gregarious and certainly not a twin so I kept my thoughts to myself.

Aunt Louisa was my father's only sister and she and her husband ran the hotel for Grandmother, who had made it clear early on that they would one day inherit the business. My father didn't mind the arrangement because he'd already received the store as an unexpected bequest from its previous owner, old Frank Monroe, Mr. Monroe's only stipulation being that Father not change the name of the establishment. So *Monroe's Emporium* still showed in an ornate scrawl on the building's façade although it was owned by Hansens and probably always would be.

Eventually, distracted by musings of my family both past and present, I gave up on the letter, visited Lloyd for a few games of checkers instead, and went to bed early.

Monday morning I awoke surprisingly cheerful and realized it was because Captain Augustus Davis had said he would arrive in Blessing today. Whether by train or motor car or carriage or horseback I had no idea—maybe one of those airplanes I read about in the papers would drop him from the sky—but I had begun to imbue the man's arrival with the same glorious anticipation I attributed to The Second Coming. Trumpet fanfare and a break in the clouds would not have surprised me at all.

Which was why my first meeting with Gus Davis seemed almost a letdown. Right after a quick lunch, Kinsey and I crouched next to the Olds truck in the alley examining one of the tires for a leak.

"I don't see anything," Kinsey said.

"I felt it, though," I replied. "There's a pull to the driver's side when I steer so check it, will you, please? I bet I picked up something at the depot this morning."

I stood and gave Kinsey a friendly thump on his shoulder as he peered at the offending tire, turned, and discovered a man standing a few yards away eyeing our little tableau. Impressed by the Olds, perhaps, because it was a vehicle worth every penny of the fourteen hundred dollars it had cost to get it to Blessing, Kansas. Not, however, impressed with the sight of me, wearing my oldest work smock over my skirt and shirtwaist and a bandanna holding back my hair.

"May I help you?" I asked, my voice curt because I was startled and because it never dawned on me that my first meeting with the nearly-mythical Augustus Davis would be anything other than dignified.

"Miss Hansen?" A pleasant baritone with only the slightest drawl, not southern but western maybe. By then Kinsey stood beside me and we both stared hard at the stranger.

I took in the duffel at his feet and in a moment realized who it must be that stood there. I had a quick debate with myself whether I should whip off the offending bandanna so I looked a little more the mature store owner and a little less the kitchen maid. Then I thought, why bother, the damage is done and stepped quickly forward.

"You're Captain Davis," I pronounced as I put out a hand, quickly jerked it back, and wiped tire grime from my palm onto my smock before extending my hand once more in greeting.

"I am," he agreed gravely. "Well, to be accurate, it's not captain any more." He gave me a firm handshake, apparently oblivious to grease.

"Esquire in its place now," I commented and liked that he didn't need even a blink of a moment to understand me. That boded well.

"Esquire would be more accurate."

For a moment we stood, each taking the measure of the other. I liked the look of the captain, a tall, lean man with light brown hair and hazel eyes in a weather-browned face. I could understand from just his stance and appearance that men like my brother would follow him without question and remember him with respect. There was something indefinable in his expression that reminded me of Lloyd, despite the fact that my brother's eyes were the blue of a Kansas sky in summer and Davis's held a hint of autumn-leaf brown. It wasn't a season that the two men shared but a kind of shadow, something dark and almost bruise-like resting in the depths of their eyes. A vestige from the war, no doubt. It was one of the very few times I wondered if we might have made a mistake enlisting the legal services of Augustus Davis. Could a wounded man help a wounded man? Too late now, of course, because the captain stood in front of me, had dropped his Wyoming life at my request, and responded to a plea from a woman he didn't know. For the time being, at least, he would have to do.

He nodded toward the truck. "Nice. How does it handle?"

"Like a dream. I never thought a truck would have such a smooth ride. Electric starter, four cylinder valve-in-head motor, and Goodyear tires front and back. It's a lot of fun." After a brief moment that could have been awkward but only felt comfortable, a shared but unspoken admiration for things mechanical, I invited him into the side door of the warehouse. "You can go around and come in the front door if you like," I spoke over my shoulder, "but if you don't mind a dusty short cut, we can get to the office more quickly this way."

He didn't bother with a response but followed close on my heels and grasped the edge of the door with his free hand to hold it open for me in the way a gentleman who'd been taught good manners would do. Something else in his favor.

Once in the office, I kept my back to Davis long enough to pull off the bandanna and run fingers through my hair to untangle and smooth it. After a quick, calming breath I turned to face him. He'd hung his overcoat on the coat tree behind the door and stood waiting for my attention.

"Thank you for coming," I told him. "I should have said that first thing. This is good of you."

His unsmiling nod of response made short shrift of my words. Not a man for unnecessary amenities, then. I liked that, too. Really, except for that dark caution—not the word I wanted but the closest I could find at the moment—lurking in his eyes he seemed as admirable as my brother thought. I nodded toward the empty office chair and seated myself behind the desk, an arrangement with incongruous overtones because it gave me an authority that seemed wrong. A twenty-year old girl who'd never been outside Kansas state lines and a man of several years' seniority who'd crossed an ocean to spend months if not years on the European continent, who'd led soldiers into battle and had surely left some behind buried on foreign soil. In normal times the differences between us would have given him the authority and placed him behind the desk. But, of course, the current situation was anything but normal.

"I was sorry to hear about Rudy Stanislaw," Davis told me. His sober tone supported the sentiment.

"Did you know Rudy well?"

"I wouldn't say well, but I knew him. One of the Blessing boys." The name made me smile, which he caught and smiled slightly in return, but his smile did not brighten anything on his face. I realized suddenly that it was not caution or illness I saw in him but sadness at Rudy's death, a personal and heartfelt sadness.

"Then you must have known Joey Buchanan, too."

"Yes," with no further embellishment. "Tell me what you know about Stanislaw's murder and why your brother is suspect."

He dropped the word *murder* into the room and whatever warmth I'd felt was replaced with a sudden chill. To hear it on the lips of a stranger, even one who'd come to help, had the effect of a chunk of ice dropped down one's shirt. I willed myself not to shiver and leaned forward, both elbows on the desktop and hands folded.

I prefaced my story with, "I don't know very much," and proceeded to tell him everything I could think of and everything I'd heard, even if it was a rumor.

"Blood on his shirt cuffs and no alibi for the time in question. Not good, but there are ways to explain both circumstances. Who were the witnesses that saw Lloyd at the garage that morning?"

"I don't know."

Davis took a small paper notebook and pen out of his inside coat pocket and scratched a few words before he looked back at me.

"Is there anything else I should know?" He saw my hesitation and the look on his face softened. "Your brother was the best of the Blessing boys, Miss Hansen. There's not a mean bone in his body, which was why I always had the highest admiration for him. He'd go over the top with everyone else, shouting what soldiers shout at the time to keep their nerve up and I never saw him waver, but I knew he'd have been happier to meet a German, shake his hand, and sit down with him to discuss poetry."

Davis's kind words brought me to unexpected tears and I blinked quickly to keep them off my cheeks. This was not the time or place to turn weepy.

"Fiddle tears."

"What?" I stared at him, puzzled by a phrase that seemed to have no relevance to the discussion at hand.

Shaking his head, he said, "Sorry. For a moment—" A pause to consider whether he should finish the thought, then, "My mother always calls them fiddle tears, those times when you tear up without warning and almost without reason. I didn't mean to distress you."

"I was distressed long before you got here, Captain."

"Gus."

"Gus, then. I'm Thea, by the way."

"I know. Your brother talked about you a lot." I hadn't expected to hear that but refused to indulge in Davis's fiddle tears twice in the same afternoon.

"Well, your description of Lloyd was right on target. He was always such a cheerful boy and a great brother. He loved music and books and he had a completely unrealistic picture of what going to war would be like. I think he envisioned snappy songs and uniforms with bright buttons. He was such a little boy in his own way and if my father or I had guessed his intention to enlist, we'd have locked him in his room until the notion passed. Father always said I was more soldier material than Lloyd."

"Your father—?"

"Died last fall in the influenza outbreak. He never got to see Lloyd come home and the last time Lloyd saw Papa was in '16 when we waved goodbye on the train platform."

"I'm sorry."

"Yes, well, so am I, but I can't make the past any different than it is. I can only work on the future and bringing my brother home again."

"Then you'd better tell me what it is about Lloyd that you don't want to tell me. I'll be his attorney, Thea, and I'll be on his side, but I need to know everything, good and bad. Is there anything else I should know?" repeating his earlier question with deliberation. A perceptive man, he had noticed how I'd mentally backed away from the query the first time.

"When Lloyd came home, he was different. The cheerful boy who couldn't hurt anything, whose heart was never in hunting and who brought injured birds home for me to tend, who never threw a punch that I know of came home with a temper. He wasn't the Lloyd that left. He was suspicious of everybody, even me. The first month back he shouted at me if I dared to even knock on his bedroom door. He'd yell, asking who I was and what did I want. He never started anything for the pleasure of it and this may sound odd but he wasn't mean exactly, only he seemed to think people were out to get him. He jumped at everything, every loud noise and every shout whether it had to do with him or not. So what you should know is that one time Lloyd was walking with Rudy, and a Ford way down the street backfired. At the sound, Lloyd shouted something and turned and hit Rudy with his fist. Hard. It knocked Rudy down. I know it's normal enough to jump when you're startled, but it's not normal to punch your best friend just because a motor car backfired. It was so public, too, right in the middle of town and a lot of people saw the incident. They'll remember it."

Davis watched me carefully through the telling, his hazel eyes alert and intent.

"Have there been other incidents like that with other people or did they happen only with Stanislaw?"

"He turned on me once and I thought he'd swing at me. I came into the kitchen when he didn't hear me and had his back to the door. I didn't expect to see him, either, and surprise made me drop the pan I carried. It made an awful clatter and Lloyd whirled around in a crouch, his teeth bared and his fists clenched. For just a moment I was frightened of him." I'd never told anyone that story and was ashamed to confess that I had feared my own brother. "After that I always made it a point to somehow announce my arrival whenever I entered the house or even a room where Lloyd might be."

"He didn't strike you?"

"Oh, no," I replied quickly and noticed Davis's face relax at the answer. "My brother would never hurt me, not really, any more than he'd hurt Rudy. Lloyd must have seen the fear on my face that time because he was so sorry he almost wept. He kept saying how sorry he felt, and I know he was. It wasn't like it was me he had turned on. It was a reaction he couldn't help, that's all. Something about the war, right?"

"Yes, something about the war." I could see that Davis was thinking through what I'd told him. He wrote in his notebook again before stuffing it back into his pocket and rising.

"I think it's time for me to see your brother."

"All right. You can leave your bag here. I'll ask Kinsey to carry it down the street to the Hansen House."

"Related?"

"I'm related to a lot of people in Blessing," I replied with a smile, "one way or another, but the Hansen House is really family. My father's parents started it over forty years ago and my aunt and uncle run it today. There are rooms waiting for you. My grandmother said to tell you you weren't to stay anywhere else and you weren't to try to pay for anything, not for meals or for your rooms."

"I don't expect that."

"I'm afraid that what you expect isn't very important to Grandma Liza. All that's important is that she gets her way, which she has been known to arrange by completely reprehensible means. So take what she offers, say *thank you, ma'am*, and bow to the inevitable." I paused and added without humor, "She loves Lloyd, too, Gus, like I do, but I'm not convinced she's sure of his innocence."

"You're sure, though, aren't you?" No humor there, either.

"I am," I answered with a nod of my head. "I am completely sure. But it troubles me to think that since that's the case, little Blessing, Kansas, has a cold-blooded murderer wandering its streets." I shook off the chill of the words. "I'll take you to the jail. Lloyd will be so happy to see you. He's been waiting for you like a child waits for Santa Claus." I had a sudden picture of Lloyd as a very little boy on Christmas Eve, nose pressed against the window watching for Santa's sleigh, eyes sparkling with anticipation. If I wasn't careful, I'd have a third attack of fiddle tears and that was completely unacceptable.

Gus Davis, perhaps sensing the depth of emotion that rested just beneath my skin, grabbed his overcoat and quickly opened the office door.

"Lead on," he said lightly.

No murmurs of sympathy, no too-hearty affirmations of Lloyd's innocence, no encouragement with a false bottom. Nothing but *lead on*. I heard sympathy there and encouragement, too, but Gus Davis knew he didn't have to validate the feelings with an abundance of words. I liked the man a great deal at that particular moment.

Chapter 3

Monday, October 6, 1919

$\mathcal{M}$ort McGill didn't bother to hide his scrutiny of Gus Davis and took the attorney in from head to toe with leisurely inspection. Then he nodded toward the hallway that led back to the cells.

"Lloyd's this way."

My brother lay on his bunk, apparently dozing, one arm thrown across his eyes and one leg dangling off the edge of the cot. He'd always slept in an abandoned sprawl and seeing him like that reminded me of the boy he'd been, the boy he left behind in France.

"Company, Lloyd," declared McGill as he unlocked the cell door with a jangle of keys against metal and my brother sat up with a start, eyes wide and staring. He had the look on his face of a bewildered, frightened animal.

Before I could say or do anything, Davis stepped into the cell saying, "At ease, Private" with comfortable authority. Lloyd stared at the tall man in front of him and I saw how my brother relaxed almost immediately, saw the stiff tension of his shoulders and neck ease. He stood, smiling somewhat sheepishly.

"Yes, sir. I'm glad to see you, sir." Davis took my brother's outstretched hand in a firm grip.

"I imagine you are, Hansen. Looks like you've gotten yourself into a tight situation."

"It seems so, though I'm damned if I know how I got here, sir."

"Language, Private. Your sister's present."

Lloyd, who'd returned from the war with a vocabulary far expanded from the one he'd left with, often awoke from his dreams using words I'd never heard before. I might not know their exact meaning but I had no doubt that if my father had been alive, he'd have sent me out of the room at such profanity and coarse language. But my father wasn't alive, and Lloyd in the depths of fury or terror didn't care a bit about my sensitivities, so a simple *damned* seemed as innocent as a nursery rhyme, both to Lloyd and to me.

My brother's face, however, colored slightly and he looked over at me to say, "Sorry, Thea."

"That's all right. It won't corrupt me." Lloyd looked pale but composed and I was pleased to see how his eyes had brightened at Gus Davis's presence. A good sign.

Davis motioned with one hand toward the bunk. "Sit down, Lloyd. Between the two of us maybe we can figure out how you managed to get yourself behind bars." He smiled when he spoke to rob the words of any implied accusation. Lloyd sat down at one end of the bed and Davis at the other, turning in a way that faced Lloyd and gave him all his attention. With the man's back to us, it was clear that McGill and I were excluded from their conversation. Neither the sheriff nor I moved, however, until Gus Davis spoke over his shoulder in a tone not to be disputed.

"My client and I need to have a private conversation." That was for McGill's benefit because Davis's tone softened when he added, "It's best if Lloyd and I talk alone, Thea. It's nothing personal."

"Of course. The two of you need to talk." I felt flustered and somewhat resentful despite my calm response, suddenly the one on the outside looking in and not liking being excluded even as I knew lawyers talked privately with their clients all the time. "I'll go back to the store. Lloyd, if you think of anything you need, let Mr. Davis know and he can pass the word along to me." My brother looked at me long enough to nod, but his attention returned to Davis almost immediately. The attorney, his back turned to McGill and me, had already taken out his small notebook and pen and flipped it open. He had questions to ask, and I was as unnecessary and unwelcome as a third thumb.

Back in the jail office, Mort McGill said, "Seems like a competent enough fella. Hope he can do Lloyd some good."

"He already has. I haven't seen my brother so relaxed since he got home."

"Relaxed isn't going to mean much in front of a jury."

"Well, it means something now," my tone sharp. "Maybe Lloyd will be able to remember what he was doing at the garage and what happened there."

"You know what happened there, Thea," but the sheriff spoke with a gentle tone and I didn't let his inference anger or even annoy me.

"No, I don't, and neither do you, for all the answers you think you have. You may have people who saw Lloyd come and go from the garage, but I know for a fact you don't have a soul that saw my brother shoot Rudy Stanislaw because Lloyd didn't do it. Somebody else did, and finding that somebody else is what you should be doing instead of accusing my brother of a terrible crime he wouldn't do in a hundred years."

I am not ordinarily a woman that indulges in displays of emotion, but I did that afternoon. I glared at McGill, yanked open the door, flounced through it, and shut it behind me with a noticeable bang. Though I think, if truth be told, I was reacting more to being excluded from the conversation taking place in Lloyd's cell than I was to anything Mort McGill said. Since Lloyd's return from the Front, I'd been his most loyal supporter and in an instant I'd been replaced by a man Lloyd hadn't seen in months. On the walk to the store I gave myself a stern talking to so that by the time I walked through the front doors whatever hurt feelings I'd felt had disappeared. I knew they were childish and unseemly and was truly relieved to share the burden of Lloyd's future with Augustus Davis, but I had to confess that I was still curious about what the two men said to each other that afternoon.

I spent time in the warehouse, then roamed about on the store's second floor where I stopped to ask myself if the women's fashions we carried on the rack were right for Blessing. Too progressive? Too old-school? True, females had possessed the vote in Kansas almost a full three months now, but that didn't mean the women of western Kansas had fully embraced rising hemlines and the startling casual lines of Paul Poiret's draped dresses. I might privately believe that the sight of a woman's ankle was unlikely to drive the men of Blessing, Kansas, mad with lust, but I had to sell what my customers would buy. Perhaps I needed longer skirts on the rack regardless of fashion trends.

When I asked Cecelia's opinion, she gave a faint smile, the first I'd seen since Lloyd's arrest.

"Priscilla Marks wants the very latest from Paris—" Cece changed her tone to gently mimic Mrs. Marks's distinctive, rather snobbish voice "—but Frieda Hoffman practically averts her eyes with horror every time she sees one of the new style of dresses that are meant to be worn without a corset. She'd have the bustle back in a second." Cece gave an exaggerated shiver. "Honestly, Thea, I'd throw myself in the river if that contraption ever returned." I was in complete agreement with the sentiment and we both laughed.

"I think the end of the war changed a lot of things, Cece, things you wouldn't have expected like women's hemlines and the need for corsets." My comment sobered the conversation.

"I heard Lloyd's lawyer got here from Wyoming," Cece said. "Do you think he can help Lloyd?"

I considered Gus Davis's lean, sober face and his depth of intelligence impossible to miss.

"He already has, in a way. Lloyd thinks so highly of the man that the moment Mr. Davis stepped into his line of sight, it seemed a hundred years dropped from Lloyd's face. He laughed, too, the way he used to laugh. Before the war."

"Before the war," Cece repeated. "Gosh, that seems a lifetime away, doesn't it?"

I thought of the many new headstones in the cemetery, all showing the date 1918, Cece's mother and my father among them, and remembered how handsome Joe Buchanan surprised me with a kiss on the train platform before he left for the army never to return.

"Yes," I agreed. "Several lifetimes."

"But it will work out for Lloyd, won't it, Thea? I mean, he didn't do this awful thing, and you can't be convicted for something you didn't do."

I felt a wave of affection for this girl with her fresh face and trusting soul. Only two years separated us in age but sometimes it felt like twenty. Cece had emerged from the loss of her mother with her hopeful innocence still intact, but I couldn't say the same about myself.

Of course, innocent people can get convicted for crimes they didn't do, I thought. The statue of Justice wears a blindfold so how can she ever be sure she's got the right person? The law is made up of people and people make mistakes. Instead of saying any of my unbecoming thoughts, however, I gave Cece a quick hug.

"You're right. Lloyd didn't hurt Rudy and everything will work out. Lloyd's captain is smart, and he knows Lloyd and likes him."

Gus Davis, the man in question, stood behind the counter engaged in a serious discussion with Raymond when I stepped off the elevator later. At the creak of the elevator gate both men turned toward me, Raymond concluding his comment just as I got within earshot. By their sudden silence, I knew they'd been discussing Lloyd or me or both of us but supposed that was only the first of many similar conversations that must take place if Lloyd were to have a creditable defense. The Hansens were no doubt being discussed all over Blessing, and there was no reason Monroe's Emporium should be any different.

"You must be hungry, Captain," I commented, saw his expression and grinned a little. "I know it's not captain any more, but you might as well learn to expect an occasional slip of the tongue. You've been Captain Davis and only Captain Davis for months and it will take a while for me to adjust to you as an ordinary civilian. I sometimes thought your christened first name was Captain."

He had an easy laugh that took the form of a warm chuckle. "I was named after my grandfather, but Augustus was such a mouthful when I was a boy that I would almost have preferred Captain."

"Augustus Davis?"

"No, my mother's father. Augustus Caldecott."

The name sounded familiar, one I had previously seen or heard somewhere and should recognize, but by then we were out on the sidewalk briskly walking toward the hotel and I had to concentrate on keeping up with Davis's long strides. I'm a brisk, steady walker myself, but he had a good six inches on me in height and I hadn't slept well the last few nights so I felt somewhat tired besides. Not that I would give him the satisfaction of asking him to slow his pace on my account. He was quiet for the walk, thinking hard about something and not until we reached the bottom of the hotel porch steps did he stop abruptly, suddenly aware that he'd ignored and outpaced me for the last few minutes.

"I'm sorry. I was—"

I waved off the explanation, having found my second wind, and climbed the steps ahead of him.

"Never mind. You were thinking deep thoughts and I wasn't going to interrupt them, not with my brother's freedom and future in the balance. You don't have to entertain me." Without waiting for a response, I pulled open the door to the hotel lobby and headed for the stairs to the second floor and my grandmother's apartment. The Hansen House had the latest in elevators throughout, and the one that opened directly across from my grandmother's apartment was especially roomy to accommodate her wheeled chair, but I wasn't going to give the captain the impression that he'd tired me out.

"No, I can see that," he murmured behind me, taking the steps two at a time until he caught up with me.

At Grandmother's door, I asked, "Did I mention that my Grandma Liza is known for her sharp tongue and strong opinions?"

"Not exactly."

"Well, she is, so don't let her intimidate you. She'll try."

In answer to my rap on the door, my grandmother's strong voice called us in—the word *invited* would have been too mild for her tone of voice. She wasted no glance on me; her gaze went straight to Gus Davis's face and stayed there, examining him the way I imagined a scientist would analyze a specimen under a microscope.

"Grandma, this is Augustus Davis."

"I can see that." She continued to look at him with an unblinking and rather disconcerting stare that she finally dropped to the cane in her hand. "I can't stand, young man. My legs are having a bad day, I'm afraid."

A bad year, I amended silently, but didn't speak.

"That's just fine, Mrs. Hansen."

"Is this your first trip to Blessing?"

Davis seemed surprised by the question, but his answer was calm and respectful. "Yes, ma'am."

"But you'd no doubt heard about Blessing, Kansas, before."

This time her words surprised me, and I found myself looking between the two of them, aware that they shared knowledge from which I was excluded, a circumstance becoming something of a habit with Gus Davis and my family members.

"Yes, ma'am, I had."

Grandma Liza nodded, satisfied with the answer. "Your mother's well, I hope."

"Yes, she is, thank you for asking. She said to greet you on her behalf." I wanted very much to ask some questions of my own but thought I would wait for another place and time to satisfy my curiosity.

"Is she still married to that man?"

"She and my father just celebrated thirty-nine years of marriage."

"They spent their wedding night in this room, young man, this very room. Back then it was the finest room in the hotel. My Steven and I held a little reception in the hotel lobby the day they were married, and then we offered them this room for the night. They left the next morning, the two of them and that boy, that slow boy—what was his name?"

"Billy."

"Yes, that's right. Billy. I recall now. He had a flair for the fiddle. Well, I haven't seen hide nor hair of any of them since. Are there others besides you?"

"I have an older brother and two older sisters."

"Sounds like they did all right, then. I never expected that man to do right by her, but she had her heart set on him and your mother could be a force. Lou Caldecott liked to have her own way."

That would be two of you, then, I thought, and wondered how two such women had gotten along in the little town that Blessing must have been forty years earlier, even smaller than it was today.

"He was a violent man your father, and I never could tell what she saw in him." I sensed Davis stiffen a little at that. My grandmother noticed it, too, and in her way tried to soften the words. For all her years, however, she had not mastered the art of appeasement.

"Everything looks different when you look at it through the eyes of love, I suppose, but he was a violent man, Mr. Davis. Make no mistake. I saw it with my own eyes. He even convinced my Steven to carry a gun for a while, as if my husband ever knew one end of a firearm from the other. He was an innkeeper, for God's sake." She knocked her cane against the floor quietly in memory of whatever frustrating emotion she'd felt at the time. "Well, times were different back then." Her reflective tone changed. "And now you're here to help my grandson. Have you talked to Lloyd yet?"

"Yes."

"He spent most of the afternoon with him," I interjected, thinking I'd been kept out of the conversation long enough.

"And what do you think?" I might as well not have spoken because she asked the question directly to Gus Davis.

"I think he's innocent of the charge." At Davis's matter-of-fact response I had to keep myself from hugging the man. He sounded so certain! His words took my grandmother aback for a moment.

"Can you prove it?"

"Not yet."

"Then you'd better stop wasting your time talking to me and get on with it. I take it Thea told you you'll sleep here and eat here."

"She did, but I don't need to take advantage of you."

"A funny kind of taking advantage since I made the offer before we ever laid eyes on each other. You bring my grandson home, Mr. Davis, and you and your entire family can stay here free of charge the rest of your natural lives." Her voice and even her face softened with the words. "You've no doubt been told this before but you favor your mother."

"Thank you. I'll take that as a compliment."

"It was meant as a compliment," she retorted, the quiet moment past. "Lou Caldecott had her faults, but she was a fine looking woman and smart as a whip. Too bad about that sister of hers. Now go have something to eat. Thea can help you find your way to your room and to the dining room. I recommend the chicken. We're famous for it. Thea, I told Lizzy to be sure we put him in the room on the opposite wing of this floor. It's all by itself on that side of the hotel and has that big desk in it that a lawyer can no doubt find use for."

Once out in the hallway, I remarked, "Well, I warned you. She's never given much thought to people's feelings, and I'll apologize for her if she said anything that got under your skin. Grandma Liza's blunt, I know, but she's transparent as window glass, and there's never any malice behind her words. She speaks her mind."

"She'd make a good witness on the stand. Nothing sentimental in her opinions, just the facts."

"The facts as she sees them," I amended slightly, and he laughed.

"You're right there." I led him through the second floor hallway to his room and pushed open the door to show his bag already there.

"Here you are," I said, feeling awkward for no reason I could name. "The dining room is downstairs off the lobby. You can't miss it. Just follow your nose. Will I see you—?"

"Thea," Davis said quickly, almost as if he were uncomfortable in the asking, "I wondered if you'd join me for dinner. If you don't already have plans. Seems funny to ask you, since I'm not paying for it, but I'd like the company, and I'd like to ask you a few questions."

It's not like he's asking me to join him because he's enamored of my presence, I thought, but I'd appreciate the company and had no desire to eat at my kitchen table, a solitary diner in a big, dark house. I'd never liked that house from the day my father purchased it from a distant cousin of the previous owner. As the widow Fairchild's closest surviving relative, the man had inherited all her possessions, including the house, but he was eager to return to Wichita and sold off most of his inheritance as fast as he could. My father, who'd long admired the big house with its distinctive crescent of wine-colored glass over the front door, could hardly believe his good fortune.

"Of course," I told Davis. "You must have a lot of questions. I'll wait for you downstairs if you want to unpack first."

"Ten minutes is all I'll need," and he was as good as his word.

After we sat down at the most private table in the dining room and gave Mavis our order, I said, "I'm sorry I didn't place the name Caldecott when you first said it. I was too preoccupied, I guess."

"You have a lot on your mind."

"Still, the name has a history with my store that I should have recognized straight away. Your mother's family owned Monroe's at one time, didn't they?"

"My grandfather Caldecott started the place from scratch, and my mother inherited it from him. She sold it when she married my father and moved to Wyoming."

I nodded, digging the story out of my memory. "There's always been a little mystery about that, or I should probably say myth."

The tale I'd been regaled with as a child had to do with desperadoes and danger and a brave uprising in the streets against villainous tyranny. Thrilling to hear but hardly in keeping with a quiet little town on the Kansas prairie. It would not be the first commonplace happening to take on storybook greatness through years of telling. Davis didn't respond, simply smiled and raised both brows in an expression that could have meant a lot of things, could have meant *You're right about that* or *That's how life is* or even *Maybe it's not the myth you think.*

I couldn't read him and continued, "I've seen the name Caldecott in the Lutheran cemetery. I can show you where if you'd like."

At that he did speak. "I would like. Thank you. My mother's parents and sister are all buried there. I'd like to see the markers."

Our meal came and we ate in silence. The appetite I thought I possessed had disappeared and I picked at my food until my companion put down his fork and looked across the table at me.

"Thea, I'm convinced that your brother did not kill Rudy Stanislaw, and I'll prove it."

The words came in the midst of my efforts to trim chicken from the bone, and I stopped, placed knife and fork on the table top, and let my hands rest there palms down. The confidence and kindness in his voice raised a quick spring of hope in my heart.

"Are you convinced? Really and truly convinced? You don't have to say things to placate me, Gus. Please don't do that. I don't want to be patronized."

He reached one large hand across the table and placed it over one of mine. "I am convinced. Really and truly. And I promise never to patronize you. You're too genuine and too bright for that. You'd see through me right away."

I was very aware of his warm grasp, noticed that his hazel eyes were flecked with gold, felt a strong pull of attraction toward him and then saw on his face that he had become conscious of me in the same intent way. A little color came into his cheeks and he pulled back his hand abruptly. More a lawyer than a man, I thought with disappointment.

"I'm sorry if that seemed presumptuous."

"That seemed kind," I said, "kind and hopeful. It's 1919, Gus. Touching a woman's hand in public won't raise a stir, even in the parochial confines of Blessing, Kansas." I smiled to show I was teasing. "If you ever are presumptuous, I'll be the first to let you know." With his normal color returned, he picked up his fork once more.

"Well, good. I'll count on it."

After Mavis whisked away our dishes, Gus loosened his tie and leaned forward on his elbows. "I know it's getting late, but could you take some time yet to answer a couple of questions?"

"Of course, I could. I have all the time in the world. Raymond is completely capable of handling the store in my absence—and secretly thrilled to be in charge, although he'd never admit that or even show it. I told him that right now Lloyd was my priority and if I had to do it, I'd close the store until this ordeal was over. Raymond was as horrified at the idea as I expected, and we've worked out a temporary measure for him to take over whenever necessary."

"The store means a lot to you."

"My father left it to me and it's all I have of him. I've never been outside the borders of Kansas and I probably never will now, what with the store and Lloyd needing me, but Monroe's is a world of its own and I like knowing what's out there."

"You like that Olds truck, too, if I read you right."

"I love mechanical things more than Lloyd ever did. He loved music and poetry and I was the one fascinated by the combustion engine. I had the head for business, too. None of that is very ladylike but I never really cared."

"You're ladylike enough for me," and went on hastily, "One of my sisters is a doctor, and I remember her saying the same thing. She found what she loved and she stuck with it."

"Right now it's my brother I love," I reminded him gently, "and for all your hopeful words, I know he's in a lot of trouble."

All business again, Davis said, "I'm going to work under two assumptions going forward, Thea. One is that someone intentionally killed Rudy Stanislaw. By that I mean, it wasn't an accident and it wasn't done by a stranger that wandered into the garage and killed Rudy for no reason other than random craziness. The other assumption is that the person that killed Rudy wasn't Lloyd Hansen. Since it wasn't Lloyd, finding out more about him won't do much good, which leaves us with Rudy Stanislaw. I believe that the more I know about Rudy, the better defense I can provide your brother because maybe I can uncover other suspects with better motives than being startled by an automobile's backfire."

His words were the first sensible thing I'd heard in days, and I found myself nodding along as he spoke.

"Tell me what you know about Rudy Stanislaw. What kind of a man was he? Who were his friends? How did he spend his time? Who knew him best?"

"You knew him," I pointed out.

"I did, and it's true that war shows what a man is made of, but I haven't seen anything of him in over a year. The last few weeks before the armistice I was working on a special assignment for General Pershing, and by then—" He hesitated before asking, "You knew that by the summer of '18 Lloyd was in the hospital, didn't you?"

The unexpected information made me stare at him. "No. We never heard a word from anyone for weeks. Then Papa died and I had my hands full, but I never heard anything about Lloyd being in the hospital until the Armistice. I wrote him about Papa but I never heard back. I thought that probably meant Lloyd never got the letter because it was so close to the end of the war, but that would explain—" I didn't finish the sentence and Davis didn't prompt. After a thoughtful moment I met his gaze. "Rudy and Lloyd came home together, and now I think that was because Rudy waited until Lloyd was released from the hospital so he could accompany him. They were practically the last ones home compared to other soldiers from neighboring towns, and if I thought about it at all, I guess I thought it was just the way their numbers came up when they were rostered out. All the Stanislaws and all my family were waiting at the train station when our two boys finally came home."

I recalled clear as day how relieved I'd felt when my brother stepped off that train and how I'd rushed forward to throw my arms around him in a hug. And I recalled how stunned and speechless I'd been when Lloyd asked, "Where's Father? Don't tell me he couldn't pull himself away from the store for my homecoming," his dark-circled eyes searching the crowd for the familiar figure of a father he'd never see again. The memory of that moment still held the ability to shock me. Gus Davis watched me wordlessly as I gathered my thoughts.

"Lloyd didn't receive my letter and he didn't know Papa was dead. For a time I was angry at the army for allowing my letter to slip through the cracks, but if Lloyd was in the hospital, if he was confused or not himself, then maybe the doctors didn't think he was strong enough to hear the news. Or maybe when the letter arrived no one forwarded it to the hospital. Maybe no one knew where he was. Or maybe the letter never got there at all. Oh, there could be a lot of reasons, I see now. But someone should have let me know about Lloyd."

"Yes, someone should have, but at the end of the war we were shipping thousands of soldiers home, and it sounds like Lloyd got lost in the confusion. I'm sorry."

"It's not your fault and it's all past now, anyway." I brought the conversation back to Rudy. "What I was going to say was that Rudy Stanislaw was blunt, honest, loyal, and a good friend to my brother, but he wasn't very tactful. He didn't bother to hide his scorn for pretense and hypocrisy, and he always said exactly what he felt whether you liked it or not." I pictured Rudy in my mind, short and broad chested like his father, swarthy complected with dark eyes and heavy dark brows.

"What family did he have?"

"He had his father. Dolf was looking forward to running the garage with Rudy because his other son, Leo, didn't appear to have any interest in automobiles or the garage or working with his father at all. Leo was always on the wild side but Rudy seemed content to work in Blessing, live with his father, have a beer with his friends once in a while, live a normal life. Rudy wasn't a deep thinker, not like Lloyd, who was always pondering the mysteries of the universe even when he was a boy. Rudy saw life in black and white, everything either right or wrong, good or bad. He was one of the least complicated people I knew. It's funny to think of them being such good friends for all they were so different. Then if you threw Joey Buchanan into the mix, well, then it really got interesting."

"How so?" Davis had fished out his notebook and pen and made notes as I talked.

"Joe was the handsomest boy in Blessing, and he was charming, besides. Every girl I knew had a crush on Joe Buchanan at one time or another, but Joe was also full of mischief. He had a feel for people, for their weak spots, really, and he knew how to rile people, how to get them to say things they didn't mean just for argument's sake. Joey liked mischief and he wasn't above playing jokes on his two best friends." It wasn't hard to picture the three boys as they'd been before the war. "But they still called themselves The Three Musketeers and they stuck together closer than glue. It was Lloyd that wanted to enlist and the other two followed him. And now it's only Lloyd that's alive." I looked across the table at Davis. "You knew Joey Buchanan, didn't you? So you knew what he was like."

"Yes, I knew Buchanan."

A nuance in the man's voice, a tone that seemed purposefully devoid of emotion, made me think sharply, there's something he's not telling me, something serious, but I couldn't bring myself to inquire further. I wasn't even sure I wanted to know.

"Besides his father, you said Rudy had an older brother?" I didn't miss the quick subject change.

"Yes, Leo. He lives—well, honestly, I don't know where or how he lives. He's different from Rudy. Always was. He likes to flash his money and brag about how good he's got it. I imagine he'll be here tomorrow for the funeral."

The thought depressed me. A few years ago when I was still little more than a child Leo Stanislaw had shown an interest in me and refused to believe that I was serious in my rejection of him. My father had had to get involved to convince Leo to keep his distance, and I'd always been a little afraid of Leo ever since. I loved Rudy as an extension of my brother but that affection never extended to Leo. I didn't like Leo one bit, and I didn't want to think about how he'd take the news that Lloyd was implicated in his younger brother's death.

With a sigh, I continued, "There are three sisters in between Leo and Rudy, all of them married. Darla lives in St. Louis so I don't know if she'll make it for the funeral, but the other two live with their families in Liberal so I imagine they'll take the train up. They're probably already here." It was the thought of facing the family, of having them think the worst of Lloyd, that made me sound suddenly weary and sad. I heard it in my own voice and knew Gus Davis heard it, too, because he tucked his notebook away and pushed back from the table.

"That's enough for tonight. Come on, I'll walk you home."

"You don't have to do that. I've walked home on my own from this hotel more times in my life than I could count."

"No doubt, but humor me. I can use the exercise." It was no sacrifice to humor the man. I liked being with someone who believed in Lloyd's innocence as wholeheartedly as I did. Truth be told, I liked everything I'd seen of Gus Davis so far and enjoyed his company, and I didn't bother to protest further.

Chapter 4

Tuesday, October 7, 1919

When I made my morning stop at the jail the next day, I found Gus Davis there ahead of me despite the early hour. He and Lloyd were deep in conversation and only stopped their talk when McGill opened the cell door. Davis was casual, his suit coat thrown at the foot of the cot and shirt sleeves rolled up. Clearly he and Lloyd had been engaged in serious talk: strategy, I guessed, or maybe just Davis's gentle but persistent and thorough probing for information. He rose when he saw me and my brother did the same, but more slowly. I thought Lloyd looked tired and guessed he'd had a bad night. Apparently not even Gus Davis's magic spell could withstand a hard bunk and bad dreams.

I spoke a good morning to both and said to my brother, "You look tired. Do you need anything?"

"Besides a breath of fresh air and a prairie walk? No." I knew he didn't like to be constrained. "Well, on second thought, Thea, next time you come could you bring that book of Longfellow poetry I left on the table next to my bed? And a pad of paper and a pen? The captain wants me to write down whatever I remember, thinks that writing it down might help me remember even more."

"That makes good sense. I'll bring what you need this afternoon after the funeral."

The words startled Lloyd, puzzled him almost, until he figured it out. To him, Rudy's death had been more theory than fact and the word *funeral* gave substance to the terrible thing that had happened.

"That's today?" Lloyd asked.

"Yes."

"You going?"

"Yes." I paused. "I've got to get to the store. I'll see you later. I promise." As I spoke Davis rose, rolled down his sleeves, and quickly slipped into his coat.

"I'm leaving, too," he said, although he'd looked pretty intent on his conversation with Lloyd just a few minutes earlier. Outside on the sidewalk, he asked, "Are you sure attending the funeral is wise?"

"No, I'm not at all sure, but if I don't go, tongues will wag and say I couldn't face the Stanislaw family because I felt guilty about the terrible thing my brother did to Rudy. I know this town and these people, Gus, and I won't let them think that. Besides, I knew Rudy all my life. He was always underfoot in our kitchen, always getting into mischief with Lloyd. I cared about him and I'll miss him. If for no other reason than that, I should go."

"Then may I attend with you?"

I stopped abruptly. "Why would you want to do that? You don't have some crazy notion about watching out for me, do you?" He resumed walking and I picked up speed to catch up and hear his answer.

"Now that would be crazy. I was Rudy's commanding officer for over a year, Thea, so I think that might be enough reason to attend the man's funeral."

"Not if the family knows you're defending Lloyd."

"I'll take my chances. And I would very much like to get a look at brother Leo and anyone else in Blessing who'll be at the funeral. Someone killed Rudy, Thea."

"Well, the culprit won't have the word *guilty* tattooed on his forehead," I retorted, "but if you think seeing the people at Rudy's funeral will help Lloyd, then by all means come along with me." I added more quietly, "But how awful to use the occasion for anything other than mourning that young man's death."

By then we had reached the front of the store and Davis had opened the door for me.

"Rudy Stanislaw is dead and all the mourning in the world won't bring him back. Our goal, yours and mine, has to be to protect the living. That doesn't mean I don't sincerely regret Rudy's passing or feel for his family's loss, but somebody stole that young man's life and finding out who that someone is does more than free Lloyd from suspicion. It offers justice to Rudy, too. I don't want to see any more young men die. Every one of them was a life cut short before its time. A waste of good men." I knew he had passed from talking about the here and now, about Lloyd Hansen and Rudy Stanislaw in Blessing, Kansas.

"You talk about young men like you're Methuselah, Gus. You're not that much older than the men you led."

I stepped into the store and heard his quiet rejoinder, "I feel like Methuselah most of the time. Like I've lived a hundred years and seen the worst the world has to offer."

I didn't know what to say to that because I hadn't seen anything of the world, let alone led men into battle and watched them fall around me. I supposed such an experience could age a man; it had certainly changed Lloyd, yet Rudy had come back apparently unaffected by his experience. I didn't understand any of that and instead of responding to Davis's words, I said only, "The funeral's at two o'clock this afternoon at the Catholic church. If you want to stop by here about one thirty we can walk to the funeral with time to spare."

"All right. I'm going to visit the garage and then spend time organizing my notes and writing out some questions I want answers to. Tomorrow I plan to take the train to the county seat and see if they've assigned a date and place and prosecutor for the trial."

"You can take the truck."

"I couldn't do that." He looked alarmed at the prospect.

"Why? Don't you know how to drive?"

"Of course, I know how to drive," his tone indignant. "I traveled the byways of France in vehicles that wouldn't be allowed on roads here in the United States. But I can't take your truck."

"Yes, you can. That way you can get there and back on your own schedule without waiting for the train. It's a pretty straight shot northwest to Scott City, but I can sketch you a map before you go if that would help." I saw Raymond bearing down on us.

"Don't stand on pride and principle right now. You're the one who said we should focus on protecting the living, which means my brother Lloyd, so the quicker you get to Scott City and back the better."

I knew instinctively that Davis was a man that wouldn't want to borrow anything from anyone at any time and especially something big and expensive like a vehicle that cost much more than a year's salary. But he knew I was right and I was pleased that he didn't argue the point any further. Instead, he greeted Raymond, nodded at me, stepped outside, replaced his hat, and strode purposefully away.

Dreading the thought of the funeral made me watch the clock on the wall too closely to be able to get any office work done, and finally I pushed back from my desk and headed out into the store. We had more customers than yesterday but the numbers were still down. I supposed that until this awful situation was concluded I should expect a general loss of customers and business. A few people greeted me but more avoided eye contact and shifted to another part of the floor as I approached. I was reminded of the days during the heart of the influenza outbreak when people avoided each other and a quickly-passed local ordinance forbade more than six people in the store at a time. People had stayed out of each other's way then, too. Influenza and murder had more in common than I thought.

I was relieved to see Gus Davis step through the Emporium's doors. Despite my earlier words, I was thankful and happy to have him as a companion. The idea of stepping into that church and facing the Stanislaw family had my stomach in knots. I knew I was right to attend but that didn't mean I wanted to go.

I nodded at Davis, returned to the office to don hat and gloves, and joined him by the front door.

"All right?" he asked. Have you changed your mind? he meant.

"I'm all right, but I dread this. Why did this awful thing have to happen?" I knew as soon as I said the words that I sounded childish but I couldn't help it. I wanted so much to go back in time, back to when Rudy was alive, back even further, to a time when Lloyd was happy and Father was in charge and I didn't feel like I carried a yoke across my shoulders.

"I don't know why anything happens," Davis admitted. "My mother would say there's a good reason behind everything, that good always follows bad and you just need to hold on and not give up. But I don't know if I believe that any more."

I appreciated that he didn't feel a need to use platitudes and polite phrases with me, that he felt comfortable being honest in front of me. After all we'd been through in the last five years, surrounded by sudden death from pestilence and war, I understood exactly what he meant and how he felt. But there was the memory of my father's enduring good nature and the unexpected kindnesses I'd seen from people I never suspected of any tender feeling to balance Davis's shared uncertainty.

"I think we should take your mother's words to heart," I told him. "I like the hopefulness of it."

We walked side by side without further conversation until we had the Catholic church in view. The sight made me stop a moment to smooth my skirt, tug unnecessarily on my gloves, and take a deep breath. I let it out in a sigh.

"Are you ready now?" Davis asked.

"Yes," I answered in a calm voice that belied the butterfly wings fluttering wildly in the pit of my stomach, "or as ready as I'll ever be, anyway."

My entering the church was nothing like I'd feared. The people already sitting in the pews did not turn in one concerted motion to stare at me and hiss their disapproval of my presence. Several people noticed, of course, and I saw nudges and surreptitious glances, heard a few whispers I was certain were comments about my arrival, but Gus Davis and I nodded at Father Keenan as he stood inside the front door and slid into the back pew at the rear of the sanctuary without any fuss. The Stanislaws were already seated in the front pews and the closed casket lay at the end of the aisle before the large ornate altar with its statues and candles. By the end of the service I had relaxed, was able to use the sonorous Latin liturgical words as a backdrop for my own silent prayers. When the pallbearers carried the coffin down the center aisle followed by the grieving family and people began to exit the church row by row, I told myself that the funeral hadn't been as bad as I'd anticipated. I was grateful it was over but attending had been the right thing to do, and I thought I would survive the experience, after all.

Ian Buchanan and his wife paused as they passed the rear pew where Gus and I sat. Whether from pride in his wife or simply because she was so petite, the lawyer always seemed to add a few inches to his otherwise average stature when he stood beside the petite, raven-haired Delta, a woman with a glamour foreign to the simple folks of Blessing, Kansas. I'd been fascinated with Delta Buchanan all my life, still was in a way. It was she that spoke first, placing a gloved hand on my shoulder.

"Oh, Thea, this is awful news, just awful! My Joey gone and now Rudy gone and Lloyd in jail. I don't know what's happened to this world!" Whenever she spoke, I heard Georgia peaches and cotton fields in her soft consonants and drawled vowels. That day she appeared calmer than I'd seen her in a while but knew that her equanimity was uncertain at the best of times, which this certainly wasn't.

"Hello, Mrs. Buchanan," I said. "Yes, it is awful, but I'm sure everything will turn out all right." I wasn't sure of anything of the sort, but Delta Buchanan had a helplessness about her that made a person long to offer solace. Gus Davis had stood when Delta Buchanan began speaking and I introduced him. "Mr. and Mrs. Buchanan, this is Mr. Davis. Gus, Mr. and Mrs. Buchanan are old friends of the family. Gus is acting for Lloyd as his attorney to help get this misunderstanding settled."

"Thea said you'd be coming," Ian stated and put out a hand, which Gus shook. The older man made no mention of the war, although he certainly must have known that Captain Gus Davis had a connection with his son. Gus followed Buchanan's reticence and only nodded.

"If there's anything we can do, Thea," Delta said, "you let us know. Of course, we don't believe for a minute that Lloyd had anything to do with this dreadful thing. No one in his right mind would believe that. I told Ian it must have been an accident. Unless—" She paused and added in a quieter voice, "Well, Ian and I both noticed that Rudy wasn't himself lately, so high strung and difficult and quick to argue about the most inconsequential matters. Sometimes he said the most awful things! Not like the old Rudy, at all. I wondered if the war ended up being too much for him, after all. There's no hint that he might have taken his own life in a moment of despair," her statement really a question.

"No, nothing like that." I thought the comment poorly timed and almost macabre but answered calmly enough.

Mrs. Buchanan shook her head in distress. "I suppose that's good—oh, I don't know what's good any more, to tell the truth. What a world we live in! So much death! So much loss! I don't see how we can bear any more."

Her voice rose on the last words, and Ian gave her a quick, sideways glance and took her hand in his as he said, "Come along, my dear. You'll tire yourself out. Thea knows she can come to us if she needs anything." To Gus he added, "I'm an attorney myself, Davis, so don't hesitate to look me up if there's any assistance or information you need."

Mrs. Buchanan leaned down to give me a cool, dry kiss on the cheek. "I hate to see you distressed, Thea. You've always been like a daughter to me. You know I always had hopes about you and Joe—" But at that, her husband drew her away with an insistent tug, and she didn't finish the thought. Delta Buchanan may indeed have had "hopes" about her son and me, but she'd only given voice to them after his death and whenever she did so, I felt a discomfort I feared I was sometimes unable to hide. Joe Buchanan had flirted with every girl in Blessing but settled on none, and if he had happened to settle on me I'd have sent him packing without hesitation. He'd never held appeal for me.

Davis sat back down and with desultory conversation about only the most superficial topics we waited until everyone had exited the church, waited a little longer still, and then exited ourselves. The only conversation I'd had was with the Buchanans and that had been an encouraging interaction. I felt a wave of relief that the ordeal was nearly over and nothing unpleasant had occurred.

But when I stepped outside I lost my feeling of satisfaction because I ran into the solid chest of Leo Stanislaw. If anything he was heftier than I recalled, a big, rough, broad, swarthy man, who now stood so close to me I could feel the buttons of his suit coat pressing against me.

He put his face very close to mine, smelling of alcohol and an underlying perfume-like fragrance, something he might have splashed on to try to hide the smell of spirits.

"Who the hell do you think you are, coming here like you owned the place, like it wasn't your family that put my brother in the grave?" I couldn't retreat with Gus Davis immediately behind me so I tried to step to the side to get away from him.

"Leo, I'm so very sorry—"

"I bet you are. I just bet you are. Always thinking you're so much better than me and now here you are with a crazy murderer for a brother. Somebody should show you—" He grabbed my upper arm in a grip tight enough to make me wince and would have pulled me back against him except by then Gus Davis had stepped beside me and put the palm of one hand to Leo's shoulder. He gave him a hard push backwards and Leo, startled by an interference he hadn't anticipated, let go of me and stumbled back a step.

"That's enough." If I hadn't known it was Gus Davis speaking I wouldn't have recognized him from his voice just then. Here was the captain that commanded men and tolerated no opposition, stern and just a shade short of ferocious. I certainly wouldn't have crossed him when he spoke with that tone.

Leo Stanislaw was shrewd enough to hear what I heard in the voice and contented himself with asking, "Who the hell are you?" Behind him Father Keenan, suddenly aware of trouble on his sanctuary's doorstep, was hurrying back up the walk from the gathering of mourners that waited by the horse-drawn hearse.

"This is Captain Davis." I introduced him with a shaky voice and felt slightly absurd making polite introductions after the latent violence I'd just felt from Stanislaw. "He was Rudy's commanding officer in France."

Leo examined Davis with a sneer. "And now you're defending the crazy bastard that killed him." He'd have said more, something rude and angry and insulting, I was sure, except by then Father Keenan was with us and had laid a hand on Leo's shoulder.

"Your father and your sisters are waiting for you, Leo." Leo turned to see that the group by the hearse had all turned to look back at him. He gave his shoulders a visible shake.

"I'm not done here," he said in a low voice, "not by a long shot. You Hansens always acted like you couldn't be bothered with the likes of us."

"Only you," I said evenly. "Rudy was a better man than you could ever hope to be, Leo, and he was always welcome in our home. We loved him."

The priest said Leo's name a second time and tried to draw him away from Gus and me.

"Well, you sure got a hell of a way of showing it." Leo shook off Father Keenan's hand and made a show of adjusting coat lapels and tie. "Just remember what I said. I'm not done here." By then Davis had somehow managed to insert his shoulder between Leo and me.

"You're making your family wait, Stanislaw." The same tone of voice as before with a touch of steel underlying all the words. Leo gave me a last threatening look and turned away.

"I'm sorry. Grief can turn people into strangers," Father Keenan said before he went to join the Stanislaws for the trip to the cemetery.

No, I thought, something deep and dark and angry motivated Leo Stanislaw, but it didn't have any kinship with grief.

"Thea?" I was relieved to hear that Gus Davis's voice had returned to normal. "I'm sorry that happened."

"You said you wanted to get a look at Leo. I hope that was close enough for you."

"He's nothing like his brother."

"Not in any way that matters. I've always been frightened of him."

"I never would have guessed that," his tone both admiring and sincere. Gus Davis really was a kind man, I thought, and held out my hands so he could see that they still trembled.

"Because I had my hands in my pockets," I said, trying to smile. "See?"

In a completely natural and almost brotherly way he took one of my gloved hands and tucked it under his arm.

"Let's go home, Thea. I think you've had enough drama for today." We walked together as far as the jail. "I want to spend some time with Lloyd," Gus said. "Are you going back to the store?"

"Yes." I disengaged my hand from his side. "I think I'll close up tonight. I feel the need to do something safe and familiar and Raymond deserves an early afternoon. Tell Lloyd I'll see him later."

"When you're done at the store, would you come back to the jail? We could walk to the hotel together and maybe you'd join me for dinner again."

I thought that two nights running might be noticed and remarked on by people that didn't have better things to do with their time, and I found that I didn't care one bit. I liked how safe I felt in Gus Davis's presence. A world that over the past few years had often seemed frightening and baffling and inchoate had with Rudy's murder become even more so, and we were partners, after all, joined together in the common belief that my brother, for all his nightmares and emotional outbursts, was innocent of killing his best friend. Dinner with Gus Davis would not turn back time or bring the dead back to life, but it might be able to shift the world back onto its axis for a little while, and I was not about to refuse the opportunity.

Later that evening, our meal done and the dishes whisked off the table by Mavis, I passed a rough map of the route to Scott City to Davis as he savored his postprandial cup of coffee. Besides chicken, the Hansen House is known for its coffee, and I understood why he wore a slightly beatific expression as he held the cup in his two hands. After a moment he caught my look and grinned.

"It sounds petty and superficial, but in France one of the things I missed the most was really good coffee. When I first went over I trained with the Brits and tried to make do with their tea rations. Later, when I was assigned to my own company, we had coffee, but sometimes we didn't have a fire to heat water, and I still believe the dried coffee in our rations wasn't the real thing. It had a vegetable taste to it. When I got home and my mother asked what she could fix as a favorite homecoming meal, I said coffee and nothing but coffee. This," he concluded, holding out the cup, "is the best I've had since I've been home."

"I'll share that with the cook," I responded, smiling, as he took the paper with the directions to Scott City. "Tomorrow morning I'll meet you in the alley behind the store to get you the truck. We're almost due south of Scott City so if you go north out of Blessing and stay on the main north road, you'll be in Scott City in under two hours. Keep the truck as long as you need it."

We had talked about Lloyd and Davis had asked a number of questions about several of the people at the funeral. By the end of the meal I felt tired and sad and I suppose those feelings showed on my face.

"I know you feel bad about Rudy and I know that exchange with Leo Stanislaw was unpleasant for you."

Davis's voice was gentle; his manner nothing like the fierce, implacable man I'd heard earlier in the afternoon. I found it intriguing that two such distinctive natures, which he could seemingly turn on and off at will, inhabited the man and wondered if even more sides of Gus Davis would appear depending on the situation. I had to force myself back to the conversation at hand.

"I can't make any promises, Thea, but I have a strong feeling there's a lot more to this situation than meets the eye, and I believe we'll get to the bottom of it eventually."

"In time for Lloyd, though?" I responded. "I can tell being incarcerated is beginning to take a toll on him, and I don't know what to do about it. In his nightmares he's always buried or trapped and trying to crawl out of a deep, dark place. He can't tolerate being confined and he hates the dark. He never had those fears as a boy."

"In the war," I noticed how my companion's hands tightened on his coffee cup with the words, "the shells would hit and dig out deep craters in the ground. Sometimes the force of the blast would throw men into the holes and if the dirt was loose it would come back on top of them. It would bury them. Sometimes we got them out in time but often—" He didn't finish the sentence, didn't have to. In my mind a quick unbidden picture played out like a motion picture reel, men buried alive under the dirt and their comrades digging furiously with their hands as the shells continued to crash around them.

"I shouldn't have told you that," he said.

"Why not? Why should you think you have to spare me, spare anyone? If we don't understand what happened, how can we help?"

"If you weren't there, Thea, I don't think you can understand, so why distress people with the details?"

I wanted to argue with him, tell him that maybe civilians and statesmen wouldn't speak so cavalierly about war if they knew those very details, but I didn't. I thought that part of the reason Gus Davis didn't choose to speak about the war was because it was he, more than his listeners, that was not ready to put words to the memories. I'd noticed shadows in his eyes, too.

Instead I asked, "Did that happen to Lloyd, the shells and the being buried?"

Gus nodded. "But he was lucky, believe it or not. Lloyd was only shoulder deep and we got him out right away. Rudy Stanislaw stayed right there with him, talking to him all the time and digging just like the rest of us. There were men deeper than Lloyd, though, men we never could have reached, men we had to leave." There was a subdued grief in his voice that made me want to comfort him, to reach across and place my hand on his this time, but I was more guarded than he'd been the previous night and remained still.

"Something changed in Lloyd that day. I didn't notice it right away but after a while, well, there's a stare men get, a look in their eyes that says something's not right."

"And Lloyd got that look?"

"Yes. I had him shipped out to the closest American hospital for observation and they kept him until the war ended. It was only a few months. Stanislaw could have come home earlier than he did, but at the end he asked me to send him to the hospital and he waited there until the doctors thought Lloyd could travel without incident. I know you may not believe this, but there's a big improvement in your brother since I last saw him. I was pleased with what I saw. He looks a lot better."

I was quiet for so long that Davis said with quiet contrition, "I'm sorry. This is hardly proper dinner conversation."

At that I spoke. "If it's not proper to talk about a dearly loved brother, then I don't know what is. I'm not fragile, Gus, not any more if I ever was. I held my father as he died an awful death, and I've listened to my brother shout his terror into a dark room many a night. I'm not the girl I was three years ago. Sometimes I can't even remember what that girl was like. I'm different now, though I can't say if it's better or worse. Just different."

He smiled at me, the warmth of the smile turning the gold in his eyes warmer than you'd think eyes could be. "Lloyd's lucky to have you."

"Wouldn't your sisters do the same for you?"

He nodded. "Either or both of them."

"Well, there you are then. There's nothing special about me." He pushed his chair back from the table and I couldn't see his face.

"More special than you know," is what I thought I heard him say, but I might have been mistaken about that, might have just been a wishful young woman looking for approval.

Chapter 5

Wednesday, October 8 – Thursday, October 9, 1919

*G*us Davis drove off in the Olds truck doing his best to hide the pleasure he felt at being behind the wheel of such a fine vehicle. I know he felt that showing enjoyment would hardly be right, considering the terrible circumstances necessitating the excursion he was about to make, but I recognized the way his face brightened when the engine fired up. No doubt my face showed the same gratification every time I took the Olds out, and I couldn't hold his momentary lack of gravity against him. At that moment I caught a glimpse of what Davis must have looked like as a boy and found the picture unexpectedly endearing.

Kinsey and I stood at the end of the alley and watched the Olds head north, past the sugar factory and on to Scott City. Kinsey sighed.

"Well, I hope we don't lose it."

"The Olds or the lawyer?" I asked, trying for levity.

"Both, though I think we could replace the lawyer easier than the truck."

We smiled at each other, and for a moment it could have been a week ago, Rudy Stanislaw still alive and Lloyd asleep in his room in the big house across the street from Monroe's. Then Kinsey patted his shirt pocket.

"I almost forgot." He pulled a folded envelope out of the pocket and handed it to me. "This was sticking out from under the door when I got here this morning." The sealed white envelope had my name printed on the front in black, square letters.

"The alley door to the warehouse?"

"Yup. Seemed odd to me, like somebody's got a secret."

Somebody does have a secret, I thought, a dreadful secret, but I feigned a nonchalance I didn't feel and put the envelope, to be opened later in privacy, in my skirt pocket.

"Thank you," I said and stepped into the warehouse, walked into the store proper, toured the glass display cases with their treasures of cigars and belt buckles and handguns and a host of other sundries, discussed inventory levels with Raymond, and finally moseyed to the office where I closed the door and immediately flung myself into the desk chair. That envelope had been burning a hole in my pocket since Kinsey had handed it to me, and I couldn't wait another moment to read it, even when I feared what the contents might be. Something rude and unkind is what I expected because it had been slid under a door anonymously, something about Lloyd's being in jail and being accused of murder. But the note held nothing malicious, only a few plain, printed words that purported to be helpful: *Maybe knowing what gets shipped out of Dolf's Garage every Wednesday night would help. A friend*

I had no idea if there really were surreptitious deliveries being made to and from the garage, but it was the location of Rudy's murder and not coincidentally the note had appeared on a Wednesday. With the seed planted, I knew I'd have to find out whether the words held any truth or would send me on a wild goose chase, a very late and somewhat tiresome wild goose chase. Still, I wasn't sleeping much so I might as well use my night hours in a more useful fashion than staring at the ceiling wondering if my brother would spend the rest of his life in prison. Why this "friend" couldn't simply have given me the information face to face instead of dropping the hint in a secretive, slightly dramatic manner I couldn't begin to guess, any more than I could guess the author of the note. Nevertheless, I was thankful to have something on which to focus, something I could do that involved activities other than visiting Lloyd or having dinner with Gus Davis. The first was important and the second enjoyable, but I wanted to be doing something that held the possibility of more visible and valuable results. Spying on Dolf's fit the bill perfectly.

Davis brought the truck home well after supper but fortunately before it was fully dark; the prairie roads that seemed perfectly navigable in daylight turning into bumpy sandpaper once the light disappeared. I didn't worry about Gus Davis but felt a little protective about the Olds, the fact that it was on a necessary mission for Lloyd's well-being notwithstanding. I'd just closed the store and was home warming up leftovers on the stove for my supper when someone rapped sharply on the back door. Gus Davis stood on the porch, and I pushed open the screen door to invite him inside.

"I left the truck in the shed like you asked," he told me, "but I thought you'd feel better knowing for sure that your baby was home safe and sound." Other than a coating of dust on his clothing he looked none the worse for wear, and I assumed it was the same for the Oldsmobile.

His words made me smile but at the moment I was more interested in the information he brought back from Scott City.

"Sit down and I'll pour you a cup of coffee," I suggested, "and in exchange you can tell me what you found out at the courthouse." He shrugged out of his coat and draped it over the back of a chair but did not sit immediately. Instead, he gazed around the kitchen without bothering to hide his interest.

At my questioning look he explained, "About sixty-five years ago or so my mother was born in this house. She didn't talk about it a lot, but when she did I could tell from her voice that that time was special to her. She told us about how her father ordered the colored glass over the front door as a present for my grandmother and about—well, other things a person would remember from her childhood. She lived here with her sister until my Aunt Lily married some banker fellow, and then Mother moved across the street to rooms over the store. It seems funny in a way to have stepped into a house I've heard stories about all my life."

"My father bought the house from the Fairchild estate a few years ago when the banker's widow died," I said, "but she wasn't your aunt, was she?" I couldn't quite get the people and the timing straight in my head.

"No. My Aunt Lily died young. She was married to a Fairchild, though. Maybe she was the banker's first wife. I should have asked my mother more questions about what happened, I suppose, but I never took the time. Too busy being a kid myself." He gave an apologetic shrug and small smile.

"Mr. and Mrs. Fairchild are buried in the same cemetery as my parents and your grandparents. You said your aunt was buried there, too. I'll take you there the first chance I get. Now sit down and tell me the news from Scott City." He sat obediently and abandoned his musings about the past for news of the future.

"The trial's scheduled in twelve days, a week from this coming Monday. The judge is Samuel Plumquist and the prosecutor a fellow named Ben Marquart. Do you know either of them?" I shook my head.

"I met them both and they seem like decent enough men. Marquart's pretty sharp. I thought we might have run across each other sometime in the past, but since he's Kansas educated and I'm from the state university of Wyoming all we had in common was prosecuting criminals." I stared at him.

"You're a prosecutor?"

He had the good sense to look a bit sheepish. "Sorry. I thought you knew that."

"How would I? I didn't know your first name before Thursday night, and all Lloyd said was that you were a lawyer." I eyed him. "Are you able to switch sides like that and do Lloyd justice?" The term seemed doubly appropriate.

"I believe that Lloyd is innocent, Thea, and that makes all the difference in the world." I observed him without comment until he added, "Unless you'd feel better asking someone else to take over your brother's defense. I hope that's not the case, but I'd understand if it was."

"It's not up to me," I said finally. "It's Lloyd's decision."

"But if it was up to you?" he persisted.

"My grandmother always says don't change horses in the middle of a stream, so I suppose I wouldn't make a change." Not the most ringing of endorsements but he seemed to be content with it.

After a small silence, I offered, "I have leftover meat loaf and scalloped potatoes if you'd care to join me for supper. Grandmother sent it over from the hotel so I can't take credit for it, but even second hand it's better than I could do on my own."

"I'd hate to intrude."

"Suit yourself, but I have more than enough for two." The words overcame his token resistance and after washing his hands at the kitchen sink, he loosened his tie and sat down at the table. He looked tired and hungry and I felt a small pang of guilt that we'd called him away from his work and his home and family using an appeal of military loyalty that he could hardly refuse.

I filled plates from the stove and set them on the table, then sat down myself and remarked as I picked up my fork, "I don't recall that we've talked about your fees, Gus, but I hope you know we won't quibble about anything. It was good of you to come. I know it's probably not what you expected to be doing with your time."

"We can talk about that later. I have to make a trip to Cheyenne early next week to handle some business, but coming to Blessing isn't that much of an interruption. I'm too new to my job to be indispensable, and I have an understanding boss." I thought he was being kind but decided to accept his explanation at face value.

"The judge surprised me by saying he was agreeable to holding the trial in Blessing's town hall. I thought they'd transfer Lloyd to the jail at Scott City, but Plumquist seemed to be looking forward to a stay at the Hansen House."

"Must be the chicken." At Davis's laugh, I added, "I told you it was famous," and laughed a little, too. It felt good to have ordinary company across the table, not an empty chair or what was sometimes worse, a young man unable or unwilling to make cordial conversation. Lloyd was often on edge and jumpy, caught up in his own thoughts and not interested in amiable dialogue.

I remained conscious of the anonymous note still resting in my pocket, and intended to mention it to Davis. He was my brother's lawyer, after all, and deserved to know about any developments, but every time I thought I'd say something about it our conversation veered off to another topic. And by the end of the meal, just as I decided it was now or never, I opened my mouth to speak and surprised myself by yawning instead. Gus struggled for a moment about whether to comment or ignore the yawn and gave way to the obvious.

"You're tired and I'm keeping you up," he said, pushing back from the table. "This was kind of you, Thea, and I've enjoyed the company, but I have some work to do tonight yet so I need to get going."

The note can wait until later, I told myself, and felt relieved. I'd wanted to have a more active part in helping my brother and now I could do a little spying and perhaps have something of real worth to share: an alternate suspect or at least suspicious behavior that would offer an interpretation of Rudy's death that did not include my brother. Of course, I needed to tell Gus Davis about the note and I would, but what difference would it make whether I did so tonight or tomorrow? None that I could see.

"Gus," I asked as we stepped out into the crisp night, "have you thought about how the blood got on Lloyd's shirt cuffs?"

"My guess is that he was at the garage Wednesday morning, but when he got there Rudy was already dead. I can make a persuasive case that when he saw the body of his friend, Lloyd did what any decent person would do. He touched the body, maybe lifted it or turned it, to see if there was a chance to save Rudy's life. I believe that's what happened."

"But why wouldn't Lloyd remember doing such a thing?"

"Shell shock is a funny thing, Thea. It's not like an illness you can see and you can't always explain it. I imagine seeing his friend dead on the ground would have been an awful shock to your brother. You told me he seemed a little dazed Wednesday night, and that would make sense if Lloyd had been deeply disturbed by the sight of Rudy's body. I've heard that a sudden shock like that can cause a man to lose ground for a while. Do you understand?" I shook my head.

"Honestly? No, I don't understand." I felt ignorant and confused by that ignorance, a modern young woman discovering how much of life she really knew nothing about. "I want to and I'm trying to, but I just don't, and I don't think most other people will either. What if Lloyd goes to prison, Gus? I'm afraid he'll lose even more ground, the way you put it, and what will happen to him then?" I knew Davis didn't have an answer, but at the moment I just needed to speak my worry.

He didn't reply for a long moment and his response when it came surprised me—surprised him, too, I think. He reached out one hand and ran the back of his fingers down my cheek, a feather light touch that held cool comfort and something else that was neither cool nor comforting. I didn't take my gaze from his face.

"I won't tell you not to worry, Thea, because that would be useless, but I wish there was a way I could lift that burden from you. You need to trust me."

I did not back away from him—he was not the kind of man a woman would ever want or need to back away from—and it was he that pulled back his hand, thrust it into a pocket, and took a quick step that was almost a stumble toward the porch railing.

"I do trust you," I told him in an even tone. After a pause we concluded the evening with mutual good nights in voices that were back to normal. He went down the porch steps and disappeared around the corner of the house.

I stood there on the porch a few moments longer, stared at the night sky, and considered what I'd just told Gus Davis. I'd met the man less than a week ago, barely knew his whole name, possessed the sketchiest of family details, and had only just found out what he did for a living. But still. But still…

There was something integral to Augustus Davis that made him as solid and trustworthy as the Rock of Gibraltar, something fundamental to his nature. I understood why men like my brother had followed Davis into battle with confidence and unquestioning allegiance, and it was the same for me, I realized, mine a different kind of battle but a battle, nevertheless. If I were honest with myself, however, and if for a moment I ignored the serious situation in which Lloyd and I found ourselves, I'd have to admit that there were certainly other, more enjoyable ways to spend time with Gus Davis than fighting battles. I shook the thought away and went inside, washed up our few dishes, and hurried upstairs to change my clothes. There might be a place for Gus Davis in the future, that remained to be seen once my brother's prospects were settled, but the present night belonged solely to Dolf's Garage. Not as romantic a thought but in its own way just as exciting.

Before the turn of the century, Dolf's Garage was Blessing's livery stable, situated at the edge of town and owned and run by a man named Caleb, who died well before I was born. When Caleb passed away with no living relatives to be found, the livery reverted to the town, and the town maintained the place by hiring a man to run it on Blessing's behalf. That arrangement might have continued indefinitely except for Henry Ford's Model-T, which, despite those who predicted the automobile to be a passing fad, changed the need for a town stable to the need for a town garage. Dolf Stanislaw, a young man recently arrived from somewhere in Poland, came to Blessing at the invitation of an aunt and uncle who farmed in the area, but from the beginning, so my grandmother related, it was apparent Dolf wasn't cut out for farming. Instead, he had a gift for fixing things, for fixing almost anything, in fact, especially anything with a motor, and somewhere along the way the city fathers put it all together and asked Dolf to run the stable as a garage on Blessing's behalf. By the time I was born Dolf had saved his money, purchased the garage from the town, married, and started a family. Not everyone liked Dolf Stanislaw but no one would have argued the fact that the man was a hard worker with a mechanical bent that he passed on to his youngest child, Rudy.

The garage still sat on Main Street as the last building at one end of town with a narrow path separating it from its only neighbor, the undertaker's. The other side of the building, the side with the steps that led to the upstairs living quarters, was exposed to the prairie. A broad double door at the rear of the garage opened onto a wide back alley that ran parallel to Main Street. Vehicles accessed the garage and the undertaker through that back alley, which opened onto the side street Lincoln Avenue to the south and onto the prairie via a rutted dirt road on the other.

Dressed in a heavy dark jacket and an old pair of my brother's trousers and with my hair stuffed under a soft black cap, I slipped through the back streets of Blessing like a moon shadow. Part of me found it an adventure. Blessing at night acquired a mystique it did not possess in daylight and became so unexpectedly altered that I could almost convince myself I had stepped into a foreign city of inscrutable, exotic mystery and adventure.

Another part of me, the wiser and more responsible part, kept asking, what in the world are you doing, Thea? This is business for the authorities and for the law! But there I was, pressed against a wall of the undertaker's establishment with my gaze fastened on the garage that sat just across the footpath.

Every door looked tightly shut, exactly as one would expect at this time of night, and the garage, the undertaker's, and the drug store, its blank rear wall directly across the back alley from Dolf's, were all silent as a tomb. Perhaps not the wisest simile to think of just then but there was no activity to be heard or seen anywhere. Like Blessing itself, the alley seemed shut down and sleeping. I slid my back down the wall and rested on my heels, determined to wait through the darkest part of the night, until dawn began to lighten the sky if necessary, to be sure I didn't miss any Wednesday night action at the garage. I might end up being the victim of an unkind and ill-timed practical joke, but if that were the case all I'd lose was a night's sleep.

Eventually I slipped into a sitting position, knees pulled up against my chest and my arms wrapped around my legs for both warmth and compactness. I slept sporadically, my cheek against my leg, and didn't feel the slightest surprise when I heard the first rustle of movement. In my heart I had believed the note writer all along.

A wagon, pulled by two horses, their hooves wrapped in cloth, came slowly down the alley from the direction of Lincoln Avenue and stopped at the back doors of the garage. The driver pulled up and hopped down to take the reins of the team, then a second figure jumped lightly from the back of the wagon. I crept closer to get as good a look as I could, but clouds obscured the nearly full moon and the men were too distant for me to recognize any of their features. The back doors of the garage creaked as they were pushed open from within. In the still night air the creak sounded like a train whistle, and a man gave a muffled oath at the noise, the only human sound I heard during the entire transaction. As the driver held the horses still, two men began to load the wagon with boxes from the garage. I was too far away and there wasn't enough light to see exactly what was being loaded but I heard the muted clink of bottles as several crates filled the back of the wagon. Then, silently and so quickly I almost missed it, the garage doors closed—no creak this time— and the wagon, its cargo, driver, and passenger continued down the alley and disappeared onto the worn prairie track that led north over a ridge and away from Blessing.

I found that I'd been doing my best not to breathe and let out a long exhale as I considered what I'd seen. Two men on the wagon but there'd been a third man to push open the garage doors and help load. Dolf? Impossible to tell because I couldn't distinguish the features of any of the men.

The activity had been so methodical, quick and silent, the men such phantoms, that I could almost have convinced myself it had been nothing but a dream. I knew differently, of course. Not a dream but a silent, surreptitious shifting of merchandise had just taken place. What and who and why I had no idea, but whatever I'd seen might have a role in gaining my brother's freedom, and I considered it a night well spent.

Gus Davis, on the other hand, did not agree with my evaluation.

"You did what?" he asked, his usual attractive and moderate voice taking on a tone that was neither attractive nor moderate.

I had decided not to wait to share my observation and so had met him in the lobby of the hotel and joined him for coffee over breakfast. He was dressed casually, expecting to spend the morning with Lloyd and the afternoon working on defense strategy in his room, and my relating of the night's alley adventure clearly took him aback. I thought he would be pleased at the knowledge of something furtive taking place at Dolf's Garage but he looked anything but pleased. Astonished (not in a good way,) alarmed, even angry, but definitely not pleased.

"You needn't act like I did something dangerous or risky," I replied, somewhat annoyed by his reaction. "I crouched in the shadows and observed. Simply observed. Don't you find it at least curious? I mean, something illegal is going on at Dolf's Garage." I lowered my voice. "Really, Gus, somebody is doing something they shouldn't and aren't you at least curious about what it is?"

"Thea, there is a murderer in your little town of Blessing. Someone killed Rudy Stanislaw and since we both believe that person isn't your brother, the murderer is still walking around big as day and bright as morning. It might have been one of those men in the alley."

I felt myself growing more irritated with each word. "Well, maybe it was and maybe it wasn't, but nobody saw me so what difference does it make?"

'You didn't know no one would see you."

"Of course, I knew. Do you think I planned to burst into a rowdy version of 'Tell That to the Marines' as I danced a jig down the middle of the alley?"

He did not find my comments amusing. "You put yourself in danger."

"I did not." I glared over my coffee cup at him. "And even if I did, you are not my master. If I choose to put myself in danger—which I didn't—to help my brother, I will, and you should just get used to it." My words and tone had a bossy edge to them that could have been considered rude, but I didn't feel contrite and wouldn't back down.

I watched Davis get control of his temper in an elaborate sequence of gestures: an audible deep breath, a glance away from me (since apparently the sight of me across the table at that moment tempted him to ungentlemanly conduct,) a reach for his fork, and an exaggerated bite of hotcakes, all done without speaking a word.

Finally, temper in check, he said, "Thank you for this information. Yes, it may prove valuable but that remains to be seen. Do you have the anonymous note with you?"

"No. It's in a desk drawer at the store."

"I'd like to see it. May I?"

His questions, asked in the tone one would use with a slow but excitable child, aggravated me even more with their implicit rebuke than his earlier remarks had.

"Of course, you can see it," I snapped.

"Thank you." Silence. "Thea, I'm sorry if I seem less than appreciative about the information you just shared. But—" We made eye contact across the table. "—in Lloyd's absence, I feel somewhat responsible for you, and I don't want you to forget that there is a person walking around Blessing who killed Rudy Stanislaw."

Trying to match his same even tone, I answered, "I understand your reaction was kindly intended, but you are not my brother and you are not responsible for me. I am of age and in full possession of my mental faculties." I glared at him waiting for a comment and when none came continued, "As such, I am responsible for myself. I don't need a keeper. I realize a mysterious someone killed Rudy and you may rest assured that I have no intention of allowing that person to repeat the offense, not against me or anyone else. You aren't the only person capable of rational thought and reasonable action."

Gus did not look especially cowed or impressed by my lucid response, but he took the time for another bite of hotcakes and another sip of coffee before he said, "Agreed. However, as your brother's legal representation, I wonder if it would offend you too much to at least share with me all information pertinent to your brother's defense upon receipt of said information. If you had met an untimely demise in that alley last night, I would not have known about the note and that would hardly benefit Lloyd's defense."

He had a point, I thought, and as much as it pained me to admit it, he was probably right in expecting to have any and all information about the murder dropped into his lap before anyone took any action about it.

"All right." I heard an unattractive grudging tone creep into my words and repeated the words more lightly.

"Promise?"

I shouldn't have to promise, I thought, he should trust me exactly as he asked me to trust him the night before but, of course, I had kept information about the note to myself so he might have a small but justifiable reason for requesting a promise.

"Yes, I promise."

"Thank you." He took another deliberate sip of coffee. "Now let's go over one more time what you heard and saw in the alley last night."

I spent the rest of the morning at the store, keeping busy with account books and inventory calculations. My concentration kept slipping, however, to the horse-drawn wagon in the alley, the muffled hooves, the furtive loading of a mysterious cargo, the clink of glass. What in the world was going on? If only there was a way to get into the garage on my own and poke around, but even I, motivated as I was by a desire to aid Lloyd, couldn't quite picture myself sneaking into the garage after midnight and prowling its contents. Recalling my last meeting with Dolf and the loathing I'd heard in his voice and seen in his eyes made me catch my breath at the thought of coming face-to-face with the man as I rummaged around his property uninvited and unwelcome. Of course, if I had a collaborator, someone who would watch outside while I was inside, it might be possible. There was no way to enter the garage directly from the upstairs residence where Dolf slept, and he would have to descend the stairs in order to catch an intruder. But surely the man would make enough sound on the wooden steps to be heard by an accomplice, who would have more than enough time to give me a warning so we both could skedaddle before Dolf entered the garage. By the time I'd thought the plan all the way through, I had forgotten about the account book and was tapping my pencil on the desk, deep in criminal contemplation.

It took two small coughs to get my attention. The first didn't register with any emphasis, so deeply was I contemplating the illegal act of breaking and entering, and only the second, more pronounced cough caused me to look up and see Cece in the open doorway.

"Thea, there's someone I think you ought to talk to," Cece said. She stepped fully into the office and closed the door behind her.

"All right," I replied with caution. "Who would that be exactly?"

"Rachel Holiday."

I stared at Cece, taken by surprise at the name. "Why?" was all I could think to say at the time.

Cece shifted from one foot to the other, a posture that indicated a level of discomfort with what she was about to share.

"I've thought and thought about it," she finally said, "and I know it's wrong to betray a confidence, but then there's Rudy dead and Lloyd in jail and it doesn't seem right not to say anything, either."

I tried to listen patiently and wait for her to get to the point. Clearly, Cecelia was having difficulty with the ethics of what she was about to say, and I thought if I made it any more difficult for her, she'd backslide into silence. By now I'd figured out that she might have information to help Lloyd and for that I would cultivate the patience of Job. I said nothing and simply waited.

"And she's here right now, here in the store. The timing is perfect. I can occupy her mother easily enough—you know how Mrs. Holiday loves to talk about the latest fashions—and you could make up some reason to speak to Rachel privately here in the office. Doesn't she have a dress on order or something? I think that would work."

"Cecelia, why would I want to talk to Rachel Holiday, privately or otherwise?"

"Because," Cece answered, misery creeping into her voice, "Rachel was keeping time with Rudy. A lot of time. They were sweethearts."

"Rachel Holiday and Rudy Stanislaw?" I couldn't keep the incredulity out of my tone.

Cece nodded. "Yes. Lloyd and I surprised them once down by the river. They were sort of preoccupied and didn't hear us. Lloyd and I were out walking one night earlier in the summer, June I think it was, and there they were. Rachel was beside herself and made us promise not to tell. She was so afraid her father would find out. You know how he is."

"Rachel and Rudy," I murmured, only half listening. I was having a difficult time picturing the match: stocky, swarthy, dark-browed Rudy and fair, ethereal Rachel Holiday, the closest thing to a fairy queen Blessing had, hair the color of very bright sunlight and so slender she looked breakable. I'd never have guessed it in a million years. And yes, indeed, I knew exactly how Charles Holiday was, the owner of several sugar factories statewide and a man that wanted what he wanted when he wanted it. As a girl I had heard him use a tone with my father that no one had ever used before or since when something Mr. Holiday had ordered didn't materialize on the promised due date. At the time my father's easy temperament and natural diplomacy had refused to respond in kind and the Holidays continued to purchase from Monroe's, but even as a girl I recognized that when Mr. Holiday said he would take his business elsewhere if such an occurrence happened again he meant exactly what he said. We would have missed the man's business then and still would today. The Holidays were the wealthiest family in Blessing.

I came back to the present as Cece concluded, "I'll be right back with Rachel."

"Wait!" I called after her but she'd taken my retrospection as agreement, and I heard the brisk click of her shoes fade as she disappeared down the hallway to send Rachel Holiday back to the office.

When Rachel finally appeared in the open doorway of the office I was startled by her appearance. True, she was not a girl one would ever have described as robust, much too slender and fair for that, but she still usually managed to give the impression of good health, aided by a natural rosy flush on her cheeks and eyes of rich violet that sparkled despite their dark color. That morning, however, Rachel Holiday looked ill with an ashen complexion and smudged circles under her eyes.

"Cecelia said you had word on that cape Mother ordered from Montgomery Ward and since Mother was occupied—" Rachel started to finish the sentence but gave a small gasp and put a hand over her mouth instead. "I don't feel very—" Another sentence unfinished but there was no mistaking what was going to come next. I jumped up, grabbed the waste paper receptacle next to my desk and made it to Rachel without a moment to spare. After it was clear she had nothing else to contribute, I set the container out in the hallway and propelled the girl into the office before I closed the door behind her.

"Sit down," I told her but kept my voice gentle.

Rachel dabbed at her lips with a handkerchief for a moment, then met my gaze with a miserable expression. "I must have eaten something at breakfast that didn't agree with me."

"I've been told it feels like that." Neither of us said anything for a while.

"Or a touch of stomach influenza, perhaps. I've heard there's—"

I said her name quietly to interrupt the flow of words I could see trembling on her lips. "Rachel, it's all right. I understand exactly why you're unwell." I couldn't have said how I knew with such certainty, but I was absolutely sure that Rachel Holiday was pregnant.

"You do?" the words breathless and faint, fearful and relieved all at the same time.

"I'm so very sorry about Rudy," I told her and watched with alarm as her beautiful eyes filled with tears. A small sob escaped her and I rose, went to the chair where she sat, bent down and put both arms around her. Her shoulders shook but she made no sound and I wondered with a pang of pity how many times she'd wept exactly that way to hide her grief and her secret.

After a moment, she pushed away from me and wiped at her eyes with the crumpled handkerchief she still clutched.

"I'm sorry to have been such a bother, Thea. About that cape—"

"Rachel, have you said anything to your parents about your current unwellness?" I couldn't think of another word and thought she was not yet prepared for me to say pregnancy out loud. Her eyes widened with alarm.

"No. No, Thea," she repeated even more firmly, "and you must promise not to say a word."

"Sooner or later it will not be hideable."

Her mouth thinned into something unattractive. "There are ways to take care of the condition." It was the twentieth century, after all, and I was as modern as the next girl, but I still heard the words with alarm and a small jolt of shock.

"True, but I wonder how long any inquiry you make will remain confidential in Blessing? Sneeze on one end of town, hear *God bless you* on the other. You know that's what they say and you know it's true. The doctor certainly won't help you, and I've heard terrible stories about the end result of botched attempts. You'd be very foolish to risk your own safety and health in such an illegal and dangerous way."

"I have to do something." Desperate and stubborn, I thought, and felt pity for her once again.

"Your mother—"

"My mother will immediately tell my father and God, Thea, you can't imagine what that would be like. You simply can't imagine." She gave a legitimate shudder and for the first time I realized that Rachel Holiday feared her father, a very real, bone-deep fear that was more shocking tome than her desire to end her pregnancy. There was no way I could misread the look on her face. The alarm that flashed in her eyes reminded me of the look on Lloyd's face when he awakened in the night in the grip of a wartime nightmare.

"Your father loves you, Rachel." But even as I spoke her head began to shake in vehement denial.

"Please, Thea, spare me. You don't know anything about my father. He's violent and ruthless and proud, all the things Rudy wasn't. That he should live and Rudy should be dead is the greatest wrong in the universe. And if he found out about Rudy and me, if he knew about me now, I believe he'd kill me."

"Rachel!"

"It's true. All he cares about, all he's ever cared about, is appearances, being superior to others and being sure they know it. My God, if he found out about Rudy and me, I believe he'd rather I kill myself than expose him to embarrassment."

"That is quite enough talk about killing yourself," I snapped sternly. "Rudy is dead, yes, but you are alive with a future ahead of you and your father may go to the devil for all I care."

Rachel tried to smile but the upward curve of her lips did not reach the dark, tragic eyes. "That's easy for you to say. You don't live at my house. And I'm not you, anyway. You're always so sure of yourself, so…so competent."

I thought that of all the adjectives the girl might have used to describe me, *competent* was the last one I would have expected her to choose, although she meant it as a compliment. Perhaps.

"You mustn't say a word to anyone, Thea. Promise me." A knock sounded on the door and before I could respond to it, the office door pushed open and Rachel's mother came into the room. Mrs. Holiday was a thin woman whose face hardly showed any of the beauty for which she had once been renowned. Now she was simply an aging woman, who would be described as haggard by anyone seeing her for the first time. For a moment I felt that was the case for me, that I had never really looked at Thelma Holiday before. When entering a room, did her gaze always dart from corner to corner as if she expected to find hobgoblins in the shadows?

She gave me a dismissive look and said, "Here you are, Rachel. The girl upstairs told me you'd be gone only a moment."

You know very well *the girl's* name is Cecelia, I thought, and felt a stirring of camaraderie with Rachel.

"Were you unwell?"

"No, of course, not, Mother." Rachel's gaze flicked quickly to me and then back to Thelma. "Thea and I were just talking about this and that and time got away from us."

"Well, someone was unwell," the woman persisted.

She'd walked by the evidence in the waste can I'd set out in the hallway, evidence which would have been difficult if not impossible to miss, and I found myself saying, "Oh, dear. I thought Kinsey had removed that unpleasant result of my too-heavy breakfast and a bouncy ride back from the train station. I can't imagine why it bothered me this morning when I've made that trip a hundred times completely oblivious to ruts and bumps."

My words sounded so ridiculous that I had a hard time finding the courage to meet the woman's eyes, but when I did, it was clear she took my explanation without curiosity and at face value as something I would be ill-bred enough to do.

"No doubt you have a lot on your mind." Her cursory words dismissing me yet again, she turned to her daughter. "Come along, Rachel, we'll be late. You know your father likes our company when he comes home from the factory for his noon meal." After hearing Rachel's description of her father and her life at home with him I found the words especially pathetic. Did Mrs. Holiday think she had to impress me or was she trying to convince Rachel of their familial happiness?

"I know Father rules the roost, Mother. There's no need to remind me."

Rachel's upset stomach had apparently upset her temper as well and for a moment I thought I detected something anxious in the look Thelma Holiday gave her daughter. Perhaps Rachel's condition was not the secret she imagined it to be. The moment passed, and without even a nod in my direction Rachel and her mother departed.

I stood in the middle of the office for a while, lost in thought, wondering if Thelma Holiday already knew in her heart of hearts that her daughter, her only child, was pregnant. From there my thoughts took a further step. If the mother somehow guessed, might the father have picked up on clues, also? Rachel was sure not and I believed she would be well aware in the close quarters of their day-to-day existence if he suspected anything but, speculating to myself, I tried to imagine her father's reaction to his daughter's condition if he found out. Social embarrassment? Shock? Disgust? Or would the knowledge infuriate Charles Holiday enough to make him confront Rudy? If my father found out he'd be angry enough to kill me, Rachel had said, but I thought it might not have been at Rachel that her father would direct his fury. Violent and ruthless, Rachel had said. A deadly combination if mixed with rage. The thought made me suddenly sit down in the chair Rachel had just vacated. Was this still my peaceful, little town of Blessing, Kansas, the hometown where I was born and raised and where I lived in ignorant happiness for many years? Was it possible that for all its bucolic hominess the place was not the haven I'd always imagined it to be? What other emotions and relationships swirling around me had I ignored or overlooked? And more importantly, what would such emotions and relationships mean to my brother's freedom?

Chapter 6

Thursday, October 9 – Friday, October, 10, 1919

*B*ecause I can read the dates on a calendar as well as the next person, I was well aware that Rudy Stanislaw had been murdered eight days ago and because of that dreadful event, I had first met Gus Davis four days later in the alley next to my store. Yet it seemed to me that in some inexplicable way I had known the man at least half a lifetime. He'd entered my world as effortlessly as a warm knife slides through butter and taken up residence in my daily routine with understated but significant influence. That's what I thought to myself as we sat down to supper in the Hansen House dining room Thursday night. I didn't voice any of my thoughts aloud, of course, but we could have been sharing our evening repast for years instead of days.

Davis spent several minutes assuring me that he'd made good progress on his defense strategy that afternoon, and that he felt hopeful about there not being a single shred of evidence pointing to my brother's guilt.

"I stopped by the undertaker's, and while he agreed that he saw Lloyd leave the garage in a hurry sometime before eight Wednesday morning, he said he couldn't be any more exact about the time. He also said there were a few other people out that morning and they could have been in the garage, too, for all he knew. He didn't see where they came from. From Mr. Hoffman's description of his neighboring establishment, the garage appears to have been a busy place with lots of people coming and going all the time, front door and back." He paused. "At all hours, too, Mr. Hoffman said."

At his final words, I set down my fork and looked at him across the table. "Did you mention the mysterious cargo transfer of last night?" I asked.

"No. That's information we need to keep to ourselves for the time being. Moving merchandise out of your establishment isn't a crime and I don't feel any obligation to mention it to the sheriff."

"Even if it's done after midnight under the cover of darkness?"

"Still not a crime," Gus repeated firmly and reverted to the previous topic. "What Hoffman volunteered was interesting and useful. The number of people around the garage Wednesday morning might offer other suspects, at least in theory. All we need is solid reasonable doubt, Thea."

"But Lloyd's innocent," I said, "and if he's found not guilty simply because there were other people in the general vicinity of the garage that morning, there will always be people that think Lloyd really did murder Rudy, whatever the verdict happens to be. He needs to be fully exonerated, Gus."

"I agree that would be ideal, but as his attorney I'd be happy with a not guilty result."

"Not guilty is not the same as innocent," I pointed out, "and I don't want Lloyd to carry the suspicion that he's a murderer on his shoulders all his life."

"There may always be people who believe that, Thea, whatever happens in the trial."

"Not if we identify the real murderer." I watched Gus Davis's eyes narrow as he considered my words.

"Thea, this isn't some kind of hide-and-seek game. It's not a game at all, in fact, and you would be wise to let the authorities handle the investigation."

"As you may have noticed, the authorities aren't doing any investigating because they believe they have the guilty person locked up in jail." I tried to maintain my usual even tone as I pointed out what should have been obvious to the man. "And even if someone decided to reopen an inquiry into the crime when Lloyd is found not guilty—" I refused to say *if* Lloyd is found not guilty "—weeks will have passed, memories will have

faded, and too much information will be lost. If we don't find the
true killer, Gus, people will always believe that it's Lloyd, no
matter how the trial ends. And that's not acceptable."

"We aren't going to do any such thing." Gus emphasized
the *we* in the statement, but I knew he really meant *you*. My
immediate reaction was to remind him that he was not my
keeper, but I had made the point just that morning and there was
nothing wrong with Gus Davis's memory. No doubt he
remembered our earlier conversation as clearly as I did, and I
truly didn't want to get into an argument with him. I was going
to do whatever I had to do to ensure my brother's freedom and
future, and I didn't need to take up that particular matter with
Davis again. Surely four days in my company had taught a man
with his military experience when he could expect to win an
argument and when he should retreat from the subject all
together.

I could tell he wanted to pursue the topic, the words fairly
trembled on his lips, but after a long moment when he seemed to
be mesmerized by the food on his plate he finally looked at me
and said with a slight smile, "I wonder if you'd pass the butter,
please." For some reason the bland words and his innocent
expression made me laugh out loud.

"Of course," I replied and to reward him for his restraint
added, "I need to tell you about a visitor I had today, Gus. You'll
know if the information is helpful and if you can use it in a way
that will aid Lloyd and not harm the visitor. I hate to think of that
happening, for her sake. It seems Rudy had a girlfriend."

"I've been here four days and this is the first I've heard of
it."

I felt wronged by the gentle reprimand I thought I heard but
responded with equanimity, "I've been here twenty years and it's
the first I heard of it, too," and proceeded to share the details of
my talk with Rachel Holiday. I lowered my voice to conclude,
"And she's going to have a baby, Gus, which is a difficult
situation for any unmarried girl, of course, but she was beside
herself with fear that her father would find out. She said, and I
quote, 'If he found out about Rudy and me, if he knew about me
now, I believe he'd kill me.' What if Mr. Holiday did find out
somehow—I'd bet Rachel's mother suspects—and what if it was
Rudy, not Rachel, that bore the brunt of Mr. Holiday's anger.

He's known to be a hard man, although I've never seen him display any overt temper."

Gus jotted a few notes in his ever present notebook as I talked.

"That's very interesting, Thea. What a deceptive place your Blessing is! To all appearances an ordinary, quiet, and rustic little town but with so much darkness roiling around just below the surface." His words were true and were said without mockery or censure, yet for some reason they stung.

I had lived here my whole life; Blessing was the only home I'd known and I loved it. At least, I loved the Blessing I'd always believed it to be. The Blessing I was uncovering seemed to be a completely new town and nothing like the place where I grew up.

I didn't share my musings, however, and tried not to let on that his words had bruised my feelings. I knew recent events might well have made me overly sensitive to words and actions that I'd otherwise have discounted or overlooked entirely, and I kept my response mild.

"We're human beings here the same as anywhere else, Gus. You never really know what's going on beneath a person's surface, do you?"

He had figured out that his comment about Blessing had affected me in some way and his tone was conciliatory. "You're right, of course. I hope I didn't offend you."

For all my ease with the man, we were in many ways still strangers to each other, learning which topics needed to be approached from an angle and which words had the potential to hurt. I could tell he realized that, too.

"No, I'm not offended. I suppose people are never really what they seem on the outside."

Davis smiled. "Most people, I grant you, erect some kind of facade for protection, but you described your grandmother to me as being transparent as window glass, and I know two more people I'd describe exactly the same." At my questioning glance, he explained, "My mother, for one, and you, for the other."

"Me?" The idea surprised me, and I didn't know whether I felt flattered or disappointed. I wanted to think of myself as a woman who possessed at least a touch of mystery and a hint of inscrutability. Being considered transparent wasn't something I viewed as an especially desirable quality.

Gus nodded, smiling a little, and picked up his fork to finish his now cool meal.

"I meant it as a compliment, Thea." The fact that he recognized my ambiguous reaction supported his observation— so much for the poker face I thought I'd perfected!

After a pause I replied, "Well, thank you, then," and to make my words less grudging added, "My grandmother speaks highly of your mother, Gus, and from a few other things I've heard, you've put me in impressive company."

"Yes, I have," the words matter of fact. "Now if you can spare the time, I'd like to go over your conversation with Miss Holiday again. I think it's very useful information."

"You know," I said, picking my way through the words, "I'd hate to expose Rachel to unkind tongues and social shame if any of it can be avoided. Society is hard on a woman's reputation, Gus. The standards are different for men than they are for women. Men are allowed to sow wild oats with impunity; sometimes they're even admired for their bad behavior, but women can ruin their entire future with one indiscretion. And an unwed mother—" I shook my head, not needing to finish the thought.

"I understand."

"I doubt you understand, not really, but if there's a way to keep Rachel's condition confidential, I wish you would."

"It's bound to be noticed eventually." His careful tone was that of a man discussing a topic of which he had little firsthand knowledge, and it was my turn to smile.

"Yes."

"Then what favor would I be doing her by keeping it quiet?"

"What often happens," I explained, secretly amused at my becoming a lecturer about the delicate matter of pregnancy out of wedlock, "is that the young woman in question takes a prolonged trip, generally to an aunt or cousin that lives out of state. After a sufficient amount of time, she returns home and everyone agrees not to inquire about her absence."

Gus Davis stared at me. "But what about—?"

"You've at least heard about the Crittenton Homes, haven't you?" At his nod, I went on, "One of the things they and other organizations like them do, and do very well I understand, is find loving, happy homes for babies."

"The girl gives her baby away to strangers and her parents allow that?" I heard the disbelief and shock in his voice. The man may have spent the last two years in France, but surely he realized that the society he lived in made it very difficult for an unwed mother to raise a child on her own!

"For some people—not all, but some—placing the baby in someone else's loving home, preferably a home far away, and then trying to reclaim a normal life for their daughter is the least complicated and most reasonable solution. I imagine every situation is as different as the family involved, but for Rachel Holiday with the parents she's drawn, poor girl, I imagine it would be the only acceptable solution. I'm not suggesting they don't love their daughter"—but with the look I'd seen on Rachel's face when she spoke of her father, I couldn't help but wonder how much love there truly was in the Holiday home—"but they're very status conscious. Rachel's father is a personal friend of the governor and her mother sits on several prominent charity boards. Charles Holiday is as far removed from Rudy Stanislaw as the sun is from the moon. In that respect, I can appreciate why Rachel called her father ruthless because that's exactly how he'll react when he finds out about the situation." At Davis's expression, I snapped, ruthless in my own way, "You men made the rules, Gus, and I don't know why you're acting so surprised about them." This time it was my words that stung.

"I am not responsible for those rules, as you call them!" A return snap that almost made me regret my words. Almost. To be fair, Gus was right; he wasn't responsible, not personally responsible anyway, for the common inequities that dictated our lives. Society's duplicitous standards for men and women had been in effect long before he was ever born. And it was the twentieth century now so perhaps in the future, even in my lifetime, men and women would be held to the same standards of conduct. One could hope, anyway.

"Of course, you're not. I'm sorry for the implication." My cursory apology out of the way and the complicated topic set aside for the time being, I began once more to relate the details of my afternoon meeting with Rachel Holiday and her mother.

At the end of my telling, Gus commented, "I believe I need to meet Charles Holiday."

"I'll take you out to the factory tomorrow and introduce you, but he won't welcome the conversation and may decide to have you, have both of us, thrown off factory property."

"I think his reaction to my presence, whatever it is, will be worth the risk." He caught my look and offered, "I won't give anything away, Thea, if that worries you. About his daughter, I mean."

"I know what you mean." I paused for a moment to find the right words for what I wanted to say. "It's harder than I thought to know the right thing to do. With all my heart I want to help Lloyd. He's my brother and I love him, yet I'm very reluctant to bring Rachel into the picture and that makes me feel disloyal to my brother. I guess I haven't mastered the ability to balance right and wrong."

"I don't know anyone who's mastered that particular trait, Thea. Human behavior is so mystifying sometimes and so ambiguous that it's simply not a black and white world. There are a lot of gray areas.

"Even for you? Even working with the rule of law?"

"Even for me." He pushed back his chair, supper and our conversation finished. "And especially working with the rule of law, at least if you're going to put any heart into it." Which was something I thought Gus Davis would do whatever his calling, whether attorney or captain, whether leading a charge of soldiers across Belgian farmland or leading a legal defense in Blessing, Kansas. And that, I decided, was the best thing Lloyd had going for him.

I spent the first part of Friday morning reviewing accounts with Raymond and stopped only because I was scheduled to meet Gus Davis at the end of Main Street for a walk to the Holiday Sugar Company, located about a mile and a half north of Blessing along the train line. The day was warm for October, and I looked forward to the walk more than the meeting.

"Raymond, I want to be sure you know how much I, how much Lloyd and I both appreciate the extra time and effort you've put in this past week. I can't imagine what I'd have done without you. Well, to be honest I can because my original plan was to close the store until the matter with Lloyd was resolved."

Raymond's gray eyebrows shot up at that. "That is never a viable option, Thea. Never. Monroe's has regular hours and people count on the store being open during those hours."

His comment, somewhere past loyalty and just shy of fanaticism, made me look at his sparse, upright figure with different eyes. The man had no family; maybe Monroe's stood in place of family. I'd never really considered Raymond's life outside of work. Did he find going home to an empty apartment as dismal as I found stepping inside the great empty house that sat in stolid darkness directly across the street from the store? Did he welcome a valid excuse for spending extra hours at the store because it kept him among people in a place he found familiar and even welcoming? When I'd grumbled to myself that Raymond was making himself too much at home at Monroe's, perhaps I was closer to the truth than I realized. Since my father's death, I'd viewed what I considered to be Raymond's intrusions into and unsolicited advice about running the store as implied disapproval. But perhaps it wasn't that, at all; perhaps it had never been that.

My mental epiphany generated a soft reply that seemed to surprise both of us. "You're right, of course, Raymond. My only excuse is that I was frightened for Lloyd and sick with worry. I didn't know what to do."

Recognizing my words as an olive branch, Raymond responded, "You've got that Mr. Davis now to make you feel better. He's a man you can count on."

"Yes, and that's why I have to cut this meeting a little short. He wants to be introduced to Charles Holiday, and we're walking out to Mr. Holiday's office at the factory."

I expected some kind of inquiry about why Charles Holiday, if not in actual words at least in facial expression, but Raymond simply nodded and said, "A good idea." I stared at him. Neither his tone nor his eyes showed any curiosity. If anything, the look and the nod he gave me implied a full understanding of the purpose of our visit.

Good heavens, I thought to myself as I jammed on my hat, could it be that Raymond—Raymond, of all people!—knew about Rudy Stanislaw and Rachel Holiday when I was completely oblivious? I could have used worry about Lloyd's health and his erratic behavior as an excuse for my ignorance but would only have been fooling myself. I very much feared that I spent more time and energy on paper accounts and shelves of inventory than on the people that crossed the store's threshold, something my father had never done in all his years of owning Monroe's. The knowledge made me feel ashamed.

The Holiday Sugar factory was the primary factory for the Holiday Sugar Company. I knew there was a second, smaller factory farther north in the state and had recently heard that a third factory was under construction due west at the Colorado border. Mr. Holiday, as I commented to Gus on our walk out of town, must be doing very well indeed.

"Are the Holidays longtime Blessing residents?" Gus asked.

"Mrs. Holiday was born here," I answered. "She was a Pomeroy. I didn't know her father, but Grandmother says that in the old days he owned a number of Blessing establishments and when he died he left everything to his only child and her husband. Charles Holiday sold everything and invested in sugar. My grandmother thought it was a terrible risk, but it looks like the man made a sound decision. The yard's always busy and full of trucks and wagons coming and going. Holiday sugar ships all over the country."

The factory was really a grouping of buildings: a large central grim brick building where the actual sugar beet processing took place, a small train station at the tracks, a pair of warehouses which contained incoming sugar beets and outgoing sugar, and a detached small clapboard building at the rear with the words *Holiday Sugar Company Business Offices* printed in blue block letters on a sign hanging over the front entrance.

As Gus and I walked toward the office entrance, I asked, "Do you imagine this conversation will be just the tiniest bit awkward?" in a tone that told him I already knew the answer and hoped he had given the imminent meeting some serious forethought.

Gus made a non-committal hmmm sound as he pretended to contemplate my question. "Yes, Thea, now that you mention it, I imagine it could be, so if you'd like to wait outside—"

"I am not that easy to get rid of," I replied firmly and stepped into the office interior.

A young man sat behind a desk immediately inside and facing the door. Behind him were two more desks with two more men, those two bent over ledgers and adding machines. The young man at the front desk rose to his feet when he saw me.

"Thea. Hello. What a pleasant surprise to see you!"

"Hello, Frederick. I didn't know you were employed at Holiday's."

"For almost a year now."

"I hope it's working out for you."

"It's working just fine." For some reason I didn't believe him but would have been the first to admit that my feelings were colored by my recent prejudice against Charles Holiday. If his own family found Holiday difficult, how must it be for his employees? Still, that had no bearing on today's visit and after making a quick introduction to Gus Davis I asked if we could speak privately with Mr. Holiday.

Frederick looked down at an open book on his desk and then back at me. "He's not expecting you, is he?"

"No."

"Mr. Holiday doesn't really like to be disturbed when he's working."

"We won't take very long, Frederick, I promise. Won't you please tell him we're here and in need of a few minutes of his time? It's important. Just ask him. Please?" I saw a gleam of emotion in Frederick's eyes that bore an unmistakable resemblance to the flash of fear I'd seen earlier on Rachel Holiday's face. Good heavens, exactly what did Charles Holiday do to make people so afraid of him?

"All right." Frederick knocked discreetly at the door behind him, waited a moment, and knocked again. Finally, we heard a barked response of "Yes?" and Frederick turned the knob gently, pushed the door ajar just far enough to slide himself into the office sideways through the opening, and disappeared into the lion's den. It seemed ludicrous, in a way, this tiptoeing about, this tentative approach to Mr. Holiday, especially compared to the way people barged in and out of my office at Monroe's. I had once threatened to have my desk lugged down to the train station where, I declared in exasperation and only partially kidding, I was sure I'd find an environment more conducive to study and thought.

"Less foot traffic, too, I imagine," Cece had volunteered soberly when I finished my complaining. She betrayed herself with a twitch of a smile and put up a hand to hide it, but it was too late. I caught her gaze and burst out laughing and she did the same. I tried to imagine snapping out a "Yes" through my closed door to someone—anyone—waiting on the other side and gave up on the effort. In all his years at Monroe's, my father had never even closed the office door that I could recall, let alone made a person wait as supplicant on the other side and I thanked the good Lord I was Jeff Hansen's daughter and not Charles Holiday's. Frederick reappeared, leaving the office door open behind him, an indication that Mr. Holiday had decided to stoop from his lofty heights and talk to Gus and me. A disrespectful take on the situation but accurate.

Later, on the walk back to Blessing, I asked Gus why Holiday ever condescended to see us in the first place, and Gus answered wisely, "To find out what exactly we knew." Mr. Holiday hadn't asked a single question all the time we were there, but as soon as Gus replied, I knew he was right.

Charles Holiday did not rise when we entered his office, a small thing, really, but had Grandmother been present at such manners she would have rapped her cane against the floor more sharply than usual and asked the man if he'd been born in a barn. I don't exaggerate. Charles Holiday, richest man in Blessing, Kansas, would have received no more coddling for unacceptable behavior than Benjy Sinclair, the boy that offered two bit shoe shines on the train station platform. Grandma Liza could not abide bad manners.

Neither did Holiday ask us to be seated, even with two vacant chairs opposite his desk. In fact, he said nothing at all, just set down his pen on the desk top and leaned far enough back in his chair that he could look up at us. At his continuing scrutiny, I felt suddenly awkward, immature, and bothersome, no doubt what the man intended, and had to clear my throat before I could speak. Beside me Gus Davis, comfortably at ease, watched Charles Holiday watch us. No throat clearing for the captain, of course, too self-confident, too patient for that.

"Thank you for seeing us, Mr. Holiday," I began, purposefully refusing to offer an apology for our visit's interruption. "This is Captain Augustus Davis, who has taken on my brother's legal defense for the terrible tragedy that happened to Rudy Stanislaw. He wanted to meet you." Holiday did not respond in any way, no nod, no comment. Neither did he look at me as I spoke but kept his gaze fixed on Gus.

Mr. Holiday finally spoke. "I can't imagine why you would want to meet me, Captain Davis."

"You're aware, of course, of the murder charge against Lloyd Hansen," Gus making the point that he had no more time to spend on amenities than Mr. Holiday.

"Blessing is a small town. It would be impossible not to be aware of it."

"Did you know Rudy Stanislaw, sir?" I thought the *sir* a courteous touch but was glad Gus's tone was one of equal to equal without a trace of subservience or awe.

"He once worked on a vehicle I owned, but no, I didn't know him."

"But I understand he and your daughter were friends," the words fully and irrevocably setting the tone for the remainder of the meeting, which I privately thought would not exceed the time it took for Holiday to roar a demand for our immediate exit. Interestingly, he did not roar. If anything, his tone grew quieter.

"What a ridiculous notion, Mr. Davis, that my daughter would have any exchange, friendly or not, with a mechanic and a Stanislaw! You are mistaken."

I watched Holiday as he spoke, trying to identify what it was he reminded me of just then. When those cool words combined with his dark, unblinking stare, I saw him for the first time in the years I'd known him as reptilian. Had his eyes always been so darkly glittering? Had he always been able to go for such long periods without blinking? True, I didn't recall that the two of us had ever held anything approximating a conversation, but I still should have recognized something coldblooded in the man through the years. Or perhaps it was only that he was on the offensive and cultivated the effect for his daughter's protection. Whatever the reason, I had to squelch a shiver.

"But I'm not mistaken, Mr. Holiday. As you said, Blessing is a small town, and there are witnesses to the friendship." Gus's easy tone did not falter at the word *friendship*.

"Then your witnesses are mistaken." Holiday's tone was easy, too, but he sounded nothing at all like Gus.

"Perhaps if I spoke to your daughter she could clear up the confusion."

"There is no confusion to clear up. Rachel had no more of a friendship with young Stanislaw than I did, and she doesn't have time to speak with you. She's leaving to visit relatives in the east and is busy packing. You may take my words as hers." Charles Holiday finally pushed himself away from his desk and rose. "And now I'm afraid I have scheduled a meeting with my foreman in the plant."

"We certainly wouldn't want to delay you any more than we already have," Gus responded. He turned away and then, apparently remembering something, turned back to ask, "By the way, Mr. Holiday, what were you doing Wednesday morning of last week?" The casual brazenness of the question made me smile inwardly. Holiday's only reaction was to lose all color in his face. Restrained fury or a reaction to perceived insult. Perhaps both.

"Whatever you're implying with the question, it's irrelevant, even if it was any of your business. The disgraceful tactic of casting suspicion on innocent people is sad proof of your client's desperate condition. I pity him." The man did not give a care to the effect his statement might have on me, and Gus gave my arm a gentle squeeze, warning me, I thought, not to react to the words.

Gus didn't speak for a moment but kept his gaze on Holiday a bit longer than was comfortable before he murmured, "Thank you for your time," and opened the office door for me to exit ahead of him.

At the outside door, I took a final glance over my shoulder. Frederick was absent from his desk and nowhere to be seen, but the same could not be said of Charles Holiday. The man stood in the doorway of his office, his posture rigid and that unnerving gaze fixed intently on Gus and me until we stepped outside and Gus gently pulled the door closed to block the man from my view.

We were quiet at first, Gus walking with his hands thrust in his pockets and his head down thinking long thoughts, and I quiet because I didn't want to interrupt my companion's concentration.

"Did you know the daughter was planning on a trip?" he asked, finally looking over at me.

"No, and she didn't say anything about it when we talked yesterday."

"Perhaps something changed in the past twenty-four hours, then, and that's interesting." Gus smiled his deceptively pleasant smile. "Very interesting."

"Won't it be a problem if Rachel isn't available during the trial?"

"No. I'd never have put her on the stand because that would only have prejudiced the jury against me as a bully. But I may subpoena Mr. Holiday."

"Which would infuriate him no end."

"If it did and he displayed any public temper, so much the better, especially if Miss Carr will testify that she saw Rachel Holiday and Rudy together down by the river. Will she?"

"For Lloyd's sake, she will. Cece cares a great deal about my brother."

"Ah, I see. I'm glad you told me that before the prosecutor gets after her about making up stories to protect her sweetheart."

"Not sweethearts exactly. Not yet, anyway. More like good friends." I paused. "Will the prosecutor do that, imply Cece would lie for Lloyd's benefit?"

"I would." I'd almost forgotten that prosecution was Gus's bread and butter.

"Maybe Ben Marquart won't."

Gus shook his head at that. "Dream on if you must, Thea, but while I don't know Ben Marquart personally, as much as it's my job to present the best possible defense for Lloyd and have him declared not guilty, it's Marquart's job to bring in a guilty verdict."

"Whose job is it to discover the truth then?" I didn't like the adversarial picture of the legal system he presented and he must have heard the dismay in my voice.

"'Truth will come to light; murder cannot be hid long; a man's son may, but at the length truth will out.'"

"*The Merchant of Venice* is an appropriate source," I replied, trying not to act too surprised by the man's ability to quote Shakespeare at the drop of a hat, "because there's a pound of flesh to collect from someone somewhere, isn't there?" Then in a softer tone I added, "But I believe if truth comes to light, it will be because of you and I thank you for that." My words seemed to startle him as much as his knowledge of Shakespeare had surprised me, and after a quick audible inhale he changed the subject.

"Isn't the church cemetery on this side of town? I don't see a church building."

"The old Lutheran church was torn down years ago and its grander replacement built closer to the central square by our town hall, but, of course, its cemetery stayed where it was, down the next side street. Do you have time to stop?"

"I'd like to, if you don't mind."

The cemetery was surrounded by a wrought iron fence and I pushed through the unlatched gate to follow the dry wheel tracks that wove their way through the graveyard. As usual, I was struck by the simplicity of the place, an expanse of tended, tufted grass and headstones that seemed to extend out into the prairie. We stopped for a moment at the Hansen plot where my parents lay side by side with the stone for an infant son I'd never known at my mother's feet. Grandma Liza's husband, Steven, rested there, too, and her younger son, my Uncle Arnold, whose body was shipped back from the Philippines, a victim of disease not of battle when he was deployed as a young soldier to fight Filipino revolutionaries. My mother's parents, past the age where they could maintain the old Sullivan farmstead and with children scattered across the West, had sold out to land developers and moved away to live with their son in Denver. They and their son were buried there in a cemetery I'd never seen. This little plot in Blessing's Lutheran cemetery was the closest connection I had with my past. It meant a lot to me, and I understood without the need for words why Gus Davis wanted to see the graves of people he'd never known, people that were at best just faded photographs and names from a family album.

We wandered for a while until I called, "Here, Gus! I think this is what you're looking for." He joined me to stare at the two weathered headstones naming Rebecca Caldecott Beloved Wife and Mother and Augustus Caldecott Beloved Husband and Father.

"My older sister was named after our grandmother," Gus said, intent on the markers." He turned to me. "Was there another Thea in your family?"

"No, my father followed the exploits of President Roosevelt and admired the man so much that he named me after him. I've always felt a little relieved he didn't stick me with the name Roosevelt. Father was so enthralled with the man I wouldn't have put it past him."

"That wouldn't have been so bad. You could have been called Rosie for short." The idea made me laugh, despite our sober surroundings.

"Is this the aunt you talked about?" I asked, taking a few steps away from the matching Caldecott markers to look down at a modest stone. Gus came to join me.

"Yes, I believe so." The stone showed only the name Lily Caldecott Fairchild and the years 1854-1880. "My mother never talked about her sister very much. I think my aunt's passing was a deep grief that didn't ease very much with time."

"I'll walk around a little and when you're ready to leave come and find me." Gus had a pensive look on his face, thoughtful and a little puzzled, too, and he only nodded at my words. Thirty minutes or so later he joined me where I sat under a tree at the gate of the cemetery, stretched back on my elbows staring up at the autumn sky. He lowered himself down next to me without a word and I sat upright.

"You can report to your mother that you found the graves. She'll appreciate that."

"Yes," he agreed. Neither of us made any further effort to rise. "I was thinking about roots."

"What about them?"

"Wondering how important they were, I guess, and what they say about a person. Thinking about how people leave their roots behind so they can plant new ones somewhere else and how other people never do that, how they're born and live and die all in the same acre, so to speak."

"That'll be me," I said.

"Is that so bad?" He shifted to face me.

"No, I guess not. I like Blessing and it's a good place to live, I suppose, but the world's bigger than Blessing, and I'd like to see that, too."

"There's nothing to stop you."

I raised a hand and ticked off on two fingers, "Responsible for the store. Responsible for a brother who needs me. Those are two big responsibilities I'll always have."

"I don't believe Lloyd will stay as he is for all his life. I told you I thought he'd improved since I last saw him and I believe he'll get even better. Probably not back to his old self completely, but better."

"I hope so, but if he doesn't get better, I promise not to complain about the situation as long as he's moody outside of a prison cell." Davis rose and extended a hand to me.

"Come along, Thea. I need to get back so I can do my part in helping you keep your promise." I grasped his hand and he pulled me to my feet.

"And I have to get back to Monroe's," I said as I brushed dust and grass from my skirt.

"Because you think the store will fall apart in your absence?" He meant the words as a tease, but I heard an undercurrent of something more serious than teasing in his tone. It seemed to me that he waited intently for my answer.

"No," I answered slowly, drawing out the syllable. "I don't think the store is just about me or relies only on my expertise, but it's mine and as odd as it sounds I find a measure of comfort sitting in my father's chair." If I hadn't had the recent exchange with Raymond I might have replied differently, but now I wanted to rethink a few things, wanted to ponder my own ideas about roots and family.

"I don't think that's odd at all," Gus Davis told me. We started back down the side street, I headed for the store and he the hotel, each of us in comfortable charity with the other.

Chapter 7

Friday, October 10 - Tuesday, October 14, 1919

When I told Gus I would not be able to join him that night for the evening meal, something that had become almost routine without either of us mentioning it aloud, I was sure I saw a hint of disappointment on his face. Truth be told, I felt the same, but neither of us admitted regret any more than we felt compelled to make a formal date to meet for supper. In a way I wouldn't have admitted to anyone and barely admitted to myself, I felt a peculiar kinship with Gus Davis, so much so that after only five days there were times I didn't need words to know what he was thinking. I hoped his disappointment at dining alone was one of those times and not just more wishful thinking on my part.

"Grandma Liza has requested the pleasure of my company," I explained, smiling, "and I've learned over the years that what she calls a request is anything but."

"Having met your grandmother, I can understand." Then, conscious that his words might have sounded less than tactful, Gus tried to clarify them, but in a way that only made matters worse.

Finally, my smile now an outright laugh, I held up a hand. "It's all right, Gus. You don't have to watch your words with me, and all things considered, your response was right on target. My grandmother has always been and will always be a force to be reckoned with, and it's fortunate you recognize the fact."

When I stepped inside Grandma Liza's rooms, she waved a multi-page telegram at me from her chair by the window.

"I've heard from Louisa and Carl today," she stated "It seems they read about the murder of Rudy Stanislaw and the arrest of one Lloyd Hansen on an inside page of The Topeka State journal."

"No doubt the paper saves its front page for home grown violence, vice, and mayhem," I retorted.

"Thea, you assured me you would inform your aunt and uncle about the situation here."

"I planned to, and I started a letter, but I didn't finish it."

"They shouldn't have had to read about their own family's troubles in a newspaper."

I wanted to defend myself further but knew I hadn't a leg to stand on so I sat down in front of her and replied, "You're right. I'm sorry that happened and it's my fault."

Always unimpressed with quick penitence, she did not acknowledge my words and continued, "Now they intend to cut their stay short and be back in Blessing as soon as they can make the arrangements."

"I was waiting until I knew the trial date before I contacted them," I explained, "and then I—well, I forgot. Plain and simple. Just forgot. I've had a lot on my mind and one thing led to another and sending word to Uncle Carl and Aunt Louisa never crossed my mind again. The trial's not for ten days yet and I would've remembered to do it. Eventually. There's no need for them to come back now, anyway, because there's nothing for them to do."

"It might be that Lloyd would appreciate a little moral support from the few members of his family that he has."

"Yes, it might be, Grandmother; you're right again. But I saw Lloyd this morning, like I see him every morning, and he's doing all right." When she opened her mouth to say more, I added, "But Lloyd likes Uncle Carl and I know he'd appreciate his company. When can we expect them?"

"Thursday. I wired them back and told them that if they arrived home by Thursday that would be soon enough. Your uncle now insists we contact his niece Johanna, the one that lives in Chicago. Says she and her husband know a lot of important people there and can find us a good lawyer. Not someone from,"—she peered at one of the pages she held—"an Old Podunk place like Laramie, Wyoming."

"Wyoming isn't Old Podunk, Grandmother, and I hope you told Uncle Carl so in your telegram. It's a perfectly civilized place and Captain Davis is a fine attorney."

"You haven't known the man a week, Thea. Before that he was a nobody."

My contrite mood well and truly over, I retorted, "A nobody to you and me maybe but not to Lloyd and not to the state of Wyoming. Captain Davis is an intelligent, good man, who probably knows more about the laws of Kansas than you and I put together, and he's dedicated to getting Lloyd out of jail. My brother trusts him and so do I. Completely."

At my sharp words she gave me a quick, keen look before she said, "Your uncle has Lloyd's best interests at heart, Thea, and you know that, but I told Carl that for the time being we were more than satisfied with Mr. Davis and he could judge for himself when he got home and met the man face to face."

"That's what you wired Uncle Carl?"

"It is."

"Oh."

My grandmother usually enjoyed throwing me off balance, but this time she said in a surprisingly gentle tone, "You aren't Mr. Davis's only supporter, Thea," my earlier lapse of memory apparently forgiven. "Now while we're waiting for Lizzy to bring up supper, tell me how Lloyd's handling being in jail. I know since he got back from the Front that he's bothered by confined spaces. Did Mr. Davis ask about bail?"

Our former conversation must have covered everything my grandmother desired to say about my forgetfulness because with no further word on that subject she folded up the papers she held and tucked them into the family Bible that lay on a small side table. In the pale late-afternoon light that streamed through the side window where she sat, my grandmother looked her age and then some. She grasped the head of her cane so tightly her knuckles turned white from the effort, and the lines around her mouth were etched deeply into her face. She was often in discomfort lately, although she'd never admit it to me, and I felt ashamed that my bad temper might have had added to her pain.

I thought for a moment about the favorite words she'd quoted through the years: *hard times come and go but family lasts* before I answered, "He did ask," and rose to push

Grandmother's chair away from the drafty window. I went on to relate the disappointing answer we'd received from the judge. With the earlier topic firmly dismissed and the two of us now of one mind, we continued to center our conversation on the coming trial until Lizzy pushed open the door and readied the table for supper.

Gus Davis left the next day on the morning train to Denver where he would connect to his final destination of Laramie. He stopped by the house Friday night to remind me of his departure and caught me in the middle of cleaning the kitchen, my hair held back with an old kerchief and wearing my brother's work pants.

"No one visits unannounced or uninvited after seven o'clock," I told him standing on the back porch with an empty bucket in one hand and a rug beater in the other. "It's in the social rule book."

He didn't look contrite, only slipped off his jacket, tossed it over the porch railing, and pointed to the braided kitchen rug lying rolled on the back porch.

"Sorry. I never made it through that book. Is that ready to go inside?"

"I haven't beaten it yet."

At that he grinned. "Sounds like it's not the rug you'd like to beat."

I met his gaze, a look tinged with humor and with something warmer that I found exceptionally appealing, and had to laugh. "The rug will do for now. I don't go out in public looking like this."

After giving me an objective head-to-toe perusal that could have made me uncomfortable but didn't, Gus observed, "I don't know why not. You look perfectly respectable to me."

"Perfectly respectable," I repeated drily. "My, what girl doesn't long to hear herself described with those words? If you're done turning my head with wild compliments and since you're here—"

"Unannounced and uninvited," he interjected.

"— would you mind helping me throw this thing over the railing so I can give it a few whacks?"

He hefted the heavy rug without my assistance, unfurled it over the iron railing, and stepped back as I smacked the rug long and hard. Then I had him flip it so I could beat the other side equally long and hard. A supremely satisfying exercise.

"Now it's ready to go back in," I directed and went to hold open the door as he maneuvered the bulky rug into the kitchen. Once the rug was replaced on the floor, we lifted the oak table back into the center of the room and situated the four chairs around it.

"Do you always do your house cleaning this late?" Davis asked.

"I was restless," I answered. "I had a nice supper with Grandma Liza, but she looked tired so I didn't stay long, and I stopped at the jail to say goodnight to Lloyd but he was in the middle of a checkers game with one of the constables and didn't need me hanging around. I tried to read when I got home but that didn't work so I just thought it was time to clean the kitchen floor."

That was probably more information than the man expected or wanted, but after I ran down he commented, "Makes perfect sense to me. In fact, I've known my mother to do the same thing on occasion."

I found his easy acceptance of my behavior charming in a way I couldn't explain and to hide the warmth of appreciation I felt said more brusquely than necessary, "Sit down if you're in the mood for coffee and cookies," and turned to light the flame under the coffeepot. He sat.

Later, cookie plate and coffee cups empty, he told me about his departure in the morning. "I'll be back Tuesday afternoon."

"Short trip," I observed.

"Since I didn't know how long I'd be needed here, I left a few matters unfinished in Laramie in case this was all a misunderstanding and I was back with time to spare. That's not the way it turned out unfortunately so I'll go home long enough to make sure everything's handled."

"I'm sorry," I said. "I know this is more than you expected."

"Don't apologize, Thea. This is exactly where I want to be and where I should be. I wouldn't have it any other way."

I wished I could say more, let him know what his coming at the drop of a hat and his willingness to stay as long as he was needed meant to Lloyd and me, but my throat tightened and I couldn't get the words out, could only smile my gratitude.

He pushed back from the table with more force than seemed necessary and stood. "I have an early start and I need to get back, but try not to worry." At my look he added, "I know, I know. That probably seems impossible right now, but I'm serious. If you walk around with a worried expression, people might think there's some truth to the charges against Lloyd. If you can force yourself not to worry, or at least to look like you're not worrying, it will be better for Lloyd and better for you." His voice softened. "I have a good feeling about this, Thea. I think it's going to be all right."

"I hope more than anything that you're right, Gus, and if looking cheerful helps Lloyd, I'll dance down Main Street with a rose between my teeth."

He laughed. "As much as I and no doubt the entire population of Blessing would enjoy the sight, that might be taking it to extremes."

I stood and followed him to the back door. "I suppose taking anything to extremes goes against the grain for a mature, sensible attorney with duties and responsibilities."

"Mature and sensible. My, what man doesn't long to hear himself described with those words?" I stared at him, taken completely by surprise at hearing my earlier words thrown back at me. His expression was innocent but the gleam of humor that lingered in his eyes was evidence that he enjoyed setting me back on my heels.

Because we both reached for the door handle at the same time, I found myself suddenly standing very close to Gus Davis, so close that I could have reached up and rested my arms around his neck, could have pulled him to me and kissed him squarely and firmly on the mouth. The idea was so appealing as to be irresistible and I might have done exactly that except he stepped hastily away and jerked open the door.

"Good night, Thea." His voice sounded as shaky as I felt, and any teasing amusement I'd seen on his face had disappeared, replaced by an emotion I couldn't quite interpret. Something between regret and panic if I had to guess.

"Good night, Gus."

I shut the door after he left and leaned my back against it, aware that for me, at least, something had changed between Gus Davis and me. Oh, lord, I thought, am I falling for the man in the middle of my brother's murder trial? Like I don't have enough on my mind! But I couldn't deny that I wished Gus wasn't going to be gone, even for a few days. And I wouldn't lie to myself in the privacy of my own house and say the feelings churning around inside me were on behalf of my brother or caused by worry about his legal defense. I was going to miss having Gus Davis around because I, Thea Hansen, liked being around him, liked how he made me feel special without words, how an inadvertent touch—our hands meeting on the door knob tonight, for example— made my heart speed up, liked how he was able to surprise me, even liked arguing with him because he treated me as his equal and didn't talk down to me.

"What in the world's the matter with you?" I asked myself aloud. "You need to keep your mind on the task at hand and stop daydreaming like a school girl!" Then, properly chastised, I turned down the kitchen lamp, went upstairs, crawled into bed, and slept the best night's sleep I'd had in several days.

That Sunday was the second regular church service I'd attended since Lloyd's arrest, and it seemed to me that the flock had begun to adjust to the fact that the brother of the woman sitting in the fourth pew from the rear on the pulpit side of the sanctuary was in jail charged with murder. As a lifetime resident of Blessing, Kansas, I'd noticed that it sometimes took a while for really big news to settle in and for people to decide how they were going to react to it. Several congregants murmured greetings, and old Mrs. Tripp even asked about Lloyd, but that was because she was eighty-four and not in full possession of her faculties. Still, I was in no position to quibble about friendly inquiries from anyone, even someone whose question told me that despite the citywide homecoming celebration Blessing had thrown for Rudy and Lloyd months ago, Mrs. Tripp believed my brother remained at the Front fighting the Germans. I told the old dear that yes, I certainly would be happy to have Lloyd home again. Her question, confused as it was, and my subsequent answer had enough truth to them that the exchange seemed almost normal.

Ian and Delta Buchanan caught up with me after the service.

"Thea," said Mrs. Buchanan, "I've had you on my mind so much lately that I can't seem to get much of anything done. Poor Ian's fortunate to find a meal on the table when he gets home at night." Not exactly true, I thought, because the couple had a housekeeper that came in to cook and clean for them, but I understood and appreciated the sentiment Delta Buchanan was trying to share.

"Thank you. It's kind of you to say so."

"It must be terrible for you," the woman continued, speaking with a quick animation not appropriate to the serious topic, "what with the store and Lloyd and that big empty house. I don't know what we can do for you. I said to Ian just this morning, we have to help that dear Thea if we can. She meant so much to our Joey. Didn't I say that, Ian?"

She turned her head to look at her husband, her eyes gleaming in a way that made me slightly ill at ease, the way I always felt when it was apparent Delta Buchanan wasn't enjoying a good day.

"Yes," Ian Buchanan replied, "you said exactly that, my dear."

She turned back to me. "I thought of just the thing during the service. We'll have you over for supper, Thea! Why, I should have thought of it days ago. Just good food and conversation and we'll leave all these dreadful troubles at the door. You'll come, won't you? Say you will, Thea."

"I hate to cause you any bother." From the woman's look and tone, I knew it was inevitable that I would be dining with the Buchanans sooner rather than later, but there were certain obligatory responses I had to make.

"Bother?! As if you could ever be a bother! Tomorrow night. Come tomorrow night. I know you're busy at the store all day. Would seven o'clock be acceptable?" She gave me time for a quick nod of agreement before she swept on. "Oh, won't it be delightful, just delightful to have a young person in the house again? I am beside myself with anticipation! We'll have a lovely evening, won't we, almost like old times?"

I smiled without speaking and shifted my gaze to her husband, who watched his wife with sober care, something sad in his expression and yet I saw admiration there, too, as he studied her face. Delta Buchanan, even on her bad days, was very beautiful, and no one in all the years I'd known the couple would ever have doubted that Ian Buchanan loved his wife with single-minded devotion.

"It will be lovely, my dear," Ian said and to me added, "I hope the short notice won't inconvenience you, Thea."

"Nonsense!" exclaimed Delta gaily, not waiting for me to respond. "Inconvenience, indeed! It will be a lovely break from her routine. Now let the girl enjoy her Sunday afternoon, Ian. You and I have work to do." She placed her hand on her husband's forearm and drew him down the walk away from the church, calling over her shoulder, "Good-bye, Thea. We'll see you tomorrow evening."

"I look forward to it," I replied not quite truthfully. Since their son's death, both Buchanans had changed in ways that sometimes made me uncomfortable around them, but Gus Davis was out of town and I planned to spend this afternoon with my grandmother so why not spend Monday night with Ian and Delta Buchanan? It would pass the time and seemed better than sitting down for a solitary meal at my kitchen table. Even if the floor under the table was cleaner than it had been in a very long time.

The Buchanans' home was exactly what one would expect from a woman whose roots went deep into Georgia clay, a large white clapboard house with front porch pillars, an antebellum mansion transplanted to the plains of Kansas where it sat grand and imposing and even more out of place to little Blessing than the large house in which I lived. Delta Buchanan answered my thud of the knocker on the front door, her husband at her heels.

"How lovely to see you, Thea! I've thought about nothing else all day. Come in now and give Ian your wrap. How was your day?"

I answered her polite question as I handed over my coat and with Mrs. Buchanan's hand on my arm accompanied her down the hallway toward the front room. I stopped abruptly when I entered, however, surprised by the large oil painting of their son hanging prominently over the fireplace directly across from the room's double door entrance. Mrs. Buchanan followed my gaze.

"We had it done after we lost him. The artist did it from a photograph. Isn't it a splendid likeness?"

I walked forward slowly, speechless. It was so good a likeness that one would not have been surprised if the debonair young man looking down on us had stepped out of the black draped frame to join in the conversation. Joe Buchanan, spoiled only child of doting parents, had been absurdly handsome from childhood, with his mother's black hair and dark eyes, his father's manly build, and an infectious smile all his own. In the portrait he rested one foot on a low stool and the artist had captured Joe's essence, the laughing eyes, the smile I remembered, and even—though I doubted his parents would see it—a hint of the casual, devil-may-care disregard Joe had for almost everyone except his two best friends, and even they came in for their share of Joe's clever mockery. I'd always found him quite attractive in a wild way but had never really liked him. Not really. In my heart of hearts I never believed Joe Buchanan could be trusted, not with secrets and certainly not with affections. His was a nature destined to betray. Yet for all that, it was indeed a wonderful likeness, and I felt a queer breathlessness as I looked up at the portrait, something or someone—Joe or Rudy or Lloyd or joy or grief or loss or hope—something or someone gripping my heart in a too-tight grasp that for a moment stilled everything around me. How young he'd been! How bright and gay! And now he, or whatever remained of him, lay somewhere in the mud of France, a boy that could never age, could never be more alive than a painted figure in a portrait. It seemed suddenly so sad that I had to look away quickly to keep the Buchanans from spying the fiddle tears that pooled in my eyes. Joe gone too young and Rudy, too! Only my Lloyd left of that bright and confident trio of Blessing boys. I felt an even stronger commitment to do whatever it took to keep my brother alive and safe.

Mrs. Buchanan, her bright gaze fastened on my face, still waited for a response from me.

"It's wonderful, Mrs. Buchanan! It looks exactly as I remember him."

She smiled, satisfied at my words or at my tone or perhaps at my blink of tears she could not have missed as she stood at my side. "Yes," was all she said.

The three of us gathered in the large, elegant dining room over a delicious meal prepared and served by their housekeeper and discussed everything except what was happening in Blessing. The Treaty of Versailles. Anarchist bombings. The new Grand Canyon National Park. The latest books by Mary Roberts Rinehart and Zane Grey. Mary Pickford in *Daddy-Long-Legs*, the most recent feature at Blessing's movie house. That night Delta Buchanan was witty and entertaining and very clever. More than once her husband murmured her name in laughing reproof at comments she made, but for all their years together, the man appeared as mesmerized by her as if they were newlyweds. For the first time—I don't know why I never realized it before—I saw how Joe had come by his irreverent and sometimes malicious humor. He'd been all his mother's son in that respect. At the end of the meal we adjourned back to the front room and sat with coffee and intricately decorated petit fours under the dark, amused gaze of Joe Buchanan. The crackle of the fire and the glow of newly fitted electric lights made me feel relaxed and comfortable, glad I had accepted the Buchanans' offer of a night free from distress over Rudy's murder and worry about Lloyd. The evening of good food and friends and conversation was exactly what I needed and I was poised to express both my appreciation and my farewell when Mrs. Buchanan set down her cup and leaned toward me.

"Has Ian told you about the surprise we have planned for Blessing?" she asked. Beside her Mr. Buchanan, looking as relaxed and comfortable as I felt, suddenly stiffened in his chair.

"It won't be a surprise if you give it away to Thea," he remarked, but for all the innocence of the words, I detected warning in his tone, warning or perhaps anxiety. Something, at least, that made me straighten in my chair, too.

"No," I replied, drawing out the word. "No, he hasn't said anything about a surprise." I took a quick look at her husband's face and added, "It's late, Mrs. Buchanan. Perhaps we should save the surprise for another time." The mute appeal on Ian Buchanan's face was not directed at me but I felt it, nevertheless, and wanted to spare him because I sensed that whatever his wife was going to share would cause him pain.

Neither of us might have spoken because Delta continued, "We're going to donate a fountain and a statue for our Joe and put it in the square next to the town hall. We've hired a sculptor to present our Joey as the brave soldier he was, not the handsome boy in the picture" —she gestured toward the painting on the wall—"but the valiant American soldier that he was, fighting for country and family, a man of honor and courage, a constant reminder to the citizens of Blessing that they owe our son a debt that can never be repaid."

Owe his parents a debt, I thought, that's what she means. Something in her tone jarred me, something that did not fit the words, and it took me a moment to realize that what I heard was bitterness, bitterness so thick I thought it could have gagged her.

Caught unawares by the sudden, unexpected topic and the heightened emotions in the room, I finally responded, "It sounds like a commendable venture," regretting the adjective as too academic and too commonplace but unable to think of anything else at the moment.

"Commendable," Delta Buchanan repeated. Her dark eyes lost their friendliness and in her voice I heard scorn for so plebeian a word, a word that in her mind did not begin to reflect her intent or the significant impact a statue of her son must certainly have on the small town of Blessing, Kansas.

I wasn't mistaken that I had displeased her because as she took a quick breath to speak, to reproach me for my lack of appropriate admiration, Mr. Buchanan deflected the conversation to himself.

"Thank you, Thea. We think so. But Delta has the project finished already when, in fact, it's hardly begun. We haven't approached the City Council about it yet and the final image isn't approved. There are a lot of steps and stages to this kind of project, and we'd appreciate it if you would keep the knowledge to yourself until everything's in place."

"Yes, of course." I was so riveted by the emotions flaring and fading in Delta Buchanan's face that my words came out flat and distracted. Well, I was distracted, of course, the little scene I'd just sat through was too peculiar to be anything but distracting.

But I was raised on good manners and so I repeated the phrase with firm sincerity a second time adding, "Your secret is quite safe with me. I hope everything goes smoothly for you. I can tell this is something that has quite a hold on your heart." I directed the last words to Mrs. Buchanan as an attempt to placate, and she smiled at me with affection, my latter words acceptable and any earlier insensitivity evidently forgiven and forgotten.

"How kind of you to say so, Thea! You of all people would know about the hold our Joey could have on one's heart." Her comment was familiar ground and with my usual inability to protest the illusion she had about my feelings for her son, I stood without responding directly to her words.

"My goodness, look how late it is! Thank you for a lovely evening." I continued in that vein as Ian Buchanan left the room and reappeared with my coat.

"I'll walk you home, Thea," he offered and would not hear otherwise.

We walked down the residential street, turned the corner onto Blessing's main street, and approached my house. City street lamps shadowed our silent progress down the empty thoroughfare. Only when I stepped onto my front porch did Ian Buchanan finally speak.

"You made my wife quite happy tonight, Thea." I turned at the top of the steps and looked down at the dignified man that watched me from the walk where he stood.

"I was happy myself for a while," I admitted.

He smiled faintly. "About the statue and the fountain—"

"I won't say a word. I promise."

"Thank you. The fact is, despite my best intentions and for a number of reasons the memorial may not happen at all, but her heart's set on it and I hate to disappoint her."

"I can understand why." Our eyes met in understanding before he nodded slightly, touched the brim of his hat as good night, turned, and walked back down the walk toward his home.

Once inside, I went straight up the stairs to my bedroom all the while immersed in memories of the evening and deep in thought. Lloyd had come back from the Front profoundly affected by the violence and the horror he'd faced in the war. It was unlikely that Delta Buchanan had ever seen one violent or horrible thing in her entire life, yet she was as deeply scarred as my brother. How was it possible that physical experience and emotional pain could have so similar an effect on a person? There was so much about life I didn't understand. I felt terribly young yet old as the world at the same time and didn't understand how that could be, either. Exhausted by a complicated world, it was a long time before I was finally able to fall asleep.

In the morning, despite a shortened night's sleep, I was cheerful from the time my feet hit the floor. I whistled my way downstairs to the coffee pot, took the time to eat breakfast, and crossed the street to Monroe's with a light step. The day continued the spurt of warm weather we'd experienced, unusual and welcome for early October.

Raymond, already there and polishing the glass cases when I arrived, remarked, "You're looking quite cheerful, Thea. Is something special occurring today of which I am unaware?"

I paused in the hall on the way to my office at his words. Was there? And then I realized that Gus Davis would be on today's late afternoon train and while the knowledge had never surfaced as a conscious thought, I knew it had colored my mood from the time I opened my eyes. The realization brought me up short. I hadn't missed the man that I could recall, hadn't dreamed or daydreamed about him or thought much about him at all, and yet on some level I must have. How else to explain why my mood had lightened with the imminence of Gus's return? I could try to use coincidence as the reason, but I wasn't going to start lying to myself at this late date.

I wasn't going to tell Raymond the truth, either, so I simply said as I headed for the back, "No, nothing special. It's just a good morning," and went into my office. I suppose the fact that Gus Davis could be absent and still affect my mood should have surprised me, but it didn't. At the time, I thought that nothing between love and death could surprise me anymore, not with everything that had occurred in my life over the last two years. It would not be all that long before I would find out differently, of course, but that particular morning I accepted the fact that I liked Gus Davis a great deal, missed him when he was gone, and left it at that.

Mid-morning I went to the jail to spend time with Lloyd and assured him that Gus Davis would indeed return that day. Evidently I was not the only Hansen that missed the fellow. It was when I was back in my office and opened the file drawer to bring out the ledger books that I saw the anonymous note Davis had returned to me for safe keeping. I had tucked the document into a plain envelope and placed that between the pages of an account book that only I accessed. Safe enough there, although I had no idea why I felt the need to hide it so thoroughly.

Maybe knowing what gets shipped out of Dolf's Garage every Wednesday night would help. A friend

Rereading the words started a train of thought I couldn't derail no matter how I tried. If something moved out of Dolf's Garage on Wednesday night, might that something not be stocked and waiting in Dolf's Garage the Tuesday night before? Whatever I had observed being carted away on Wednesday night had somehow to be carted in prior to Wednesday night, didn't it? And it made sense to me that the cargo would demand the same level of secrecy, whether bringing it in or taking it out of the garage. Maybe, just maybe, tomorrow's Wednesday night cargo would be brought in tonight. Or maybe tomorrow night's load already waited in some dark and hidden corner of the garage, waited for its furtive Wednesday night departure. How it got there to begin with was thought for another day—would I need to spend every night in the alley to find the answer?—but once the idea crossed my mind I knew I would be in the alley behind the garage that night. True, after my last alley venture I had promised Gus Davis that I'd share any information pertinent to the case with him and I certainly planned to do so, but he wasn't around at the moment, and regardless of how he'd interpreted my promise, I never agreed to cease my skulking ways all together.

Chapter 8

Tuesday, October 14, 1919

I waited at the store past closing in case Gus Davis, in the grip of an overpowering and irresistible need to see me immediately upon his return to Blessing, stopped by Monroe's. When Davis's tall figure did not show up in my office doorway I followed Raymond outside, he standing beside me commenting about the increase in shipping costs as I turned the key in the front door lock. In my father's day, we had never bothered to lock up, the same as the rest of Blessing's citizens of the time, but one of my first tasks upon inheriting the Emporium had been to have all the doors fitted with locks. Father and I were of different generations, his hopeful and prosperous at the turn of the century and mine more pragmatic and skeptical. The war's legacy, perhaps, or the influenza's. Whatever the reason, the bright innocence that had characterized my father's time had slowly shifted into something more practical and in its way darker. Keys for the store were a symbol of the change.

Looking down at the key in my hand made me realize that I had no idea which generation could claim Dolf Stanislaw. Did he lock up the garage every night before he climbed the stairs to his apartment? Surely, if he were hiding something in his garage, he would do his best to keep people out. And yet it was Blessing, Kansas, not St. Louis, and for the most part Blessing closed down with sunset. One or two rowdy streets occupied McGill and his constables at night, but they weren't streets on the garage's end of town. And Dolf was right there, besides, living over the garage and close enough to investigate any suspicious noises so why would he bother with the expense of new locks as I had done?

Well, I would start out by watching the alley, just watching, to see if any activity took place. Later, if everything seemed quiet and the opportunity seemed safe enough, I could take a moment and investigate doors and windows. At the time, the plan made sense to me. Honestly, with hindsight I don't know what I was thinking, if I was thinking at all, but sometimes things make sense in trying times that wouldn't hold up to inspection otherwise. My brother sat in a jail cell for a murder that took place in that garage and I was determined to know what went on in there. Something more than Model-T repair, I was certain. Rudy had died in that place and Lloyd could go to prison because of it. For me Dolf's Garage had come to hold the mysteries of Bluebeard's castle, and I was resolved to uncover its secrets.

After supper I waited until the sun was well set and the town fully settled for the night before dressing once more in my prowling costume of dark pants and shirt. Feeling like a veteran burglar by now, I covered my hair with the same dark cap and slipped out my back door. This time I remembered to bring a flashlight tube with me, the newest model with a tungsten filament and batteries that promised extended light. There was something to be said for owning a general store with access to the latest gadgets. When I reached the bottom of the porch steps, I stopped motionless at a rustle of sound from the side of the house. I moved again only when the shadow of a large, long-haired cat made a brief appearance before disappearing once more into the night. Othello, the neighborhood mouser, father of at least half of the kittens born every spring and rodent nemesis, was on the prowl. As was I, I thought, smiling slightly, which would explain why I'd always felt a kinship with the feline nature.

Getting close to the black cold of winter now, the night possessed a thick, almost tangible autumn darkness, stars hidden by a bank of clouds that allowed only a milky moonlight to seep through. A bleak night, dim and not too cold, perfect for my purpose. I wasn't afraid at all. In fact, as I had on my first foray, I rather enjoyed the anonymity of moving among the murky shadows of unlit side streets, past silent houses, and down dark, suddenly unfamiliar alleys. Blessing, Kansas, my slightly dull hometown had a different feel at night—the façade of the bank held a touch of mystery and the barber shop lost its predictability. Blessing became a place filled with strangers and secrets. Too much Mary Roberts Rinehart, I suppose, but only the seriousness of my reason for being there kept me from freely enjoying myself. I was twenty years old and longed for adventure. *Thea Hansen, Investigating Sleuth* had a nice sound to it and held more glamor than *Thea Hansen, Store Owner*.

By the time I turned off Lincoln Avenue into the alley that led to the garage's rear entrance, my eyes had adjusted so well that the night's darkness seemed perfectly natural, and I was able to walk with a comfortable, albeit stealthy, stride. When I reached the undertaker's establishment I stopped and as I had before I first slid down to rest on my heels, alert for any movement or sound no matter how slight, that would warn me I wasn't alone in the alley. After a long stretch of quiet, I shifted to another position that had worked well in the past: seated on the ground with knees pulled up against my chest and arms wrapped around my legs.

The wait seemed to go on forever. What I knew could not have been longer than ten minutes felt like an hour and every successive minute—I began to count in my head *one milk bottle two milk bottle* to measure seconds—stretched out interminably. I should stay huddled here longer, I told myself, should stay small and quiet and observant and definitely not go any closer to the garage for some time yet, if ever. That would be mature, wise, and cautious. With that thought, I figuratively tossed all three attributes to the wind and pushed myself upright, stretched some circulation back into my legs and feet, gave my shoulders a few muffled slaps for warmth, and after taking a deep but necessarily quiet breath, darted across the footpath to stand with my back against the side wall of Dolf's garage. When no one leaped out at me from the darkness I inched my way—literally— in the direction of the rear of the garage with my palms pressed against the wall and my eyes intently watching the corner I approached. When I was finally close enough to peek carefully around the corner at the rear double doors, the doors which last Wednesday had opened for a wagon and a team of horses, I looked both ways down the back alley, looked again just to be sure there was no movement from either direction, looked once more because that's just how I am, and then I slipped around the corner to stand facing the garage's alley doors. I grabbed hold of one heavy wooden door handle and gave it a gentle tug followed by a more forceful pull. The door moved a little, but I could tell it was held firmly closed by a solid inside latch. My heart sank with disappointment. For a woman grounded in good sense I had somehow still expected the doors to swing open at my command. I backed up and gave the whole rear of the garage a good examination, something I'd never done before in all my years in Blessing.

There was an uncurtained, dark upstairs window apparently in Dolf's apartment that looked down on the alley. If Stanislaw had suddenly appeared in that window we would have been staring straight at each other, and the realization made me catch my breath at the horror of imagining such a moment. I hastily backed into the strip of darkness along the plain rear wall of the drug store that sat opposite the garage. Well below the window in Dolf's apartment and just above the garage's double doors was another opening. Not a window exactly, at least by original intent. Probably the place into which, in the old days when the garage was a stable with a loft, one would toss bales of hay from a stacked wagon. I didn't personally recall there ever being such a loft, but from old photographs of Blessing's main street and its early commercial storefronts I thought there could well have been one. Not a full loft, not the kind you'd find in a barn, but a half loft wouldn't have been unusual for a livery stable this size. To enlarge the interior the city fathers of the time probably reworked the old stable to fit their vision of a modern garage and may well have torn out both the loft and the interior stairs necessary to its access. What I felt reasonably certain I was looking at over the garage's rear entry doors was a window-like opening to a now non-existent loft, an opening made up of an old, weathered, wooden frame and two equally old and weathered wooden shutters. I took out the flashlight and shone it upward with a quick on-off gleam. One of the two shutters hung lopsided and loose off its hinge so the pair of them did not quite meet in the middle, and in the brief flash of light it appeared that the latch intended to hold the two shutters together was as rickety as the shutters themselves.

I doubted there was anything behind those shutters but the inside of Dolf's garage, no glass and no screen to impede my entry into the very place I wanted to be. If I could figure out a way to get up there and swing those shutters open, why couldn't I crawl through and drop the distance to the floor below? If I did so carefully and landed lightly enough not to break an ankle and if there was nothing piled below the window that would either cause a commotion or do me a physical injury were I to land on it, I could get in and out with relative ease, at least for someone unused to breaking and entering. Well, those were a lot of *ifs* to consider, but first things being first, I had to figure out how to get up to that window's height. Short of a pair of stilts magically appearing, I needed something solid to stand on. I turned and examined the detritus of the garage scattered around me in the alley. The empty cans tossed out back were no help at all, but those empty crates stacked against the far corner of the garage gave me pause. I eyed them from a distance and then, pressed against the rear of the garage so Dolf couldn't see me if he happened to look down from his upstairs window, I sidled along the wall to get a closer look at the crates.

"Not. One. More. Step." In the still night the sibilant whisper of words sounded like something shouted through a megaphone, and at the shock of it I froze. My heart gave an enormous lurch, stopped entirely – or so it seemed – and then began pounding so ferociously against my rib cage that for a moment I couldn't catch a breath. Not even a small one. For what seemed like forever *Thea Hansen, Investigating Sleuth* became *Thea Hansen, Ice Carving.* I had to fight down an initial inclination to run at top speed down the alley, past the stack of crates, and out into the prairie. Unfortunately, my top speed was nothing to brag about and would not take me far. Not far enough, anyway. Instead, respiration restored, I turned slowly and peered into the darkness at the tall figure standing in the middle of the alley.

"You nearly made my heart stop, you idiot!" I hissed at Gus Davis. As if on cue, the two of us moved to the rear doors of the garage and with our shoulders pressed tightly against the wall turned only our heads to stare at each other. If someone had seen us at that moment, we'd have looked preposterous.

"Which would have served you right," Gus hissed back, no penitence in his tone that I could detect.

"I was just going to—" I began, but he interrupted, "From the way you eyed the window and then the crates I know exactly what you were just going to do. I thought you promised not to indulge in any more reckless behavior."

"No, what I promised was to share with you any information I uncovered that was pertinent to Lloyd's defense. I never promised to refrain from uncovering information."

"Is that what you call sneaking down alleys and contemplating criminal behavior in the dead of night?"

"Neither of which is a crime, Counselor." Pressed against the garage wall as we were, it was too dark for me to see the look in his eyes but that was unnecessary, anyway. His tone expressed his opinion of my venture plainly enough.

"Thea, this is ridiculous and not worthy of you. If you did somehow miraculously manage to climb into the garage without breaking a bone or cracking open your skull, what do you expect you'd find?"

"I don't know." My voice was too loud and I brought the volume back to a whisper. "That's the point, don't you see? Whatever gets carted out of here every Wednesday night must be carted in by Tuesday night, and if we knew what the mysterious cargo was, it might have some bearing on Rudy's murder." Dark as it was, I could tell that despite his better instincts Gus Davis was considering my words, and I pressed the point further. "If we could just get inside, it wouldn't take long to look around. The boxes I saw were big and not easily hidden, and there were at least a half dozen of them."

Gus Davis took a few steps into the alley and peered up at the old, partially shuttered window. For the first time I realized he was dressed in a suit, of all things. The man needed a serious lesson in furtive behavior. He came back, peeled off his suit coat, and handed it to me.

"But a murder was committed here! Why would anyone be foolish enough to continue business as usual with the place under scrutiny?"

"I don't know if they would, but with Lloyd arrested, the place isn't getting much attention at all. Why would it? I can't see what it would hurt just to take a look, a quick, harmless look, and if nothing's out of the ordinary, then we can both go home."

"I don't like this, Thea, not a bit." But like it or not, from his tone I knew I had snared a partner in crime, at least for this one night.

"Then go home."

"And leave you here to break your neck?" He appeared to be rolling up his shirt sleeves as he spoke. "Not on your life." He reached out one hand toward me without comment and when I reciprocated he dropped a pair of cuff links into my palm. "Keep them for me, please."

With me at his heels, Gus headed off for the stack of crates I had contemplated earlier. When we reached the corner, the clouds parted for us with thoughtful accommodation and we were able to examine the wooden boxes without using the flashlight. He found whatever he was looking for—they all looked pretty much the same to me—and picked up two good-sized shipping crates. Together we returned to the garage, I following behind like an eager, well-trained puppy. With a precision I thought he probably brought to any task he undertook, Gus set one wooden box on top of the other.

"I suppose," I muttered with bad grace, "that you plan to be the one that gets to go inside."

"I do." He had both hands on the small stack of wooden boxes and was testing it for stability.

"It was my idea." Aware that I was being irrational and ungrateful, I still couldn't help my cranky words. I felt an odd need to assert that I was just as willing as he to take risks, and I suppose the feeling came from the relief I was experiencing but would never have admitted at having the man there with me.

Gus Davis took both hands from his makeshift ladder and placed them on my shoulders.

"Yes, it was your idea, Thea. Believe me, it's not an idea I'd ever want to take credit for. But I have eight inches on you, more muscle, and considerable experience sneaking into places where I don't belong. The difference is that a few years ago I was working under orders not committing a crime, and being discovered breaking into this garage tonight, as awkward as that might be, will not get me killed." His gaze shifted for a brief moment in the direction of Dolf's apartment window. "At least, I hope not."

I tucked that nugget of information away to inquire about later and said, "But I need to do something."

"You will stand right here and be quiet. If anyone or anything materializes in this alley, you will slip around the corner and make yourself as small as possible against the side wall of the neighboring establishment. You're the brain. I'm the brawn. Such as we are. Agreed?"

He sounded remarkably cheerful for a man about to commit an illegal break in, and I couldn't help a small smile.

"It goes against the grain to admit it, but you're right. So— agreed." He leaned down and kissed me lightly on the lips, a rather passionless and natural gesture that fit the occasion, and stepped back to the crates. At the time, neither of us gave the kiss a second thought, but I guessed I'd spend some time contemplating it later when I was back in my safe and practical world.

"Have you ever been inside the garage?" I whispered to his back.

He half-turned to reply, "Yes. I took a good long look at the whole place front to back, inside and out. It was the scene of the crime, and I needed to have a picture of it in my mind. Stanislaw didn't like it, but McGill made sure I got an unimpeded inspection."

"Well, you'll still need this, "I said, and taking the flashlight out of my pocket I handed it in his direction.

With a quick "thanks," he shoved it into the waistband of his trousers and the next moment he was standing on top of the two crates, his climb so quick and dexterous that I didn't see exactly how he got there. With his chin now even with the bottom edge of the opening, Davis reached a long arm upward, pushed at the unsteady old wooden latch that just barely held the two shutters closed and when the latch finally disengaged he opened one shutter with patient grace until he had pushed it as far as it would go to the side. The old wood gave a complaining creak and at the sound the two of us became suddenly immobile, I watching the upstairs window in case a light—or worse, Dolf's face!—appeared at the glass. After a long moment, Davis moved again, this time using both hands to grab hold of the second shutter. From the start that side had hung slightly on the diagonal, but without its stabilizing partner and the support of the latch it now dangled even more unevenly. Fortunately, it was still fixed to its hinges and the hinges were still fastened to the wall, but even in the dim alley I could see there was a definite risk that the hinges might not hold and the old wooden shutter would come crashing down into the alley. For the time being, however, the shutter hung at a downward angle that offered just enough intervening space for a man to fit.

Gus spent what seemed like an hour testing the edge of the opening, pulling at it again and again for firmness until with an ease I could hardly credit, he pulled himself up and his head disappeared into the opening. His waist rested against the sill for a brief second and then all of him disappeared into the darkness. I stood staring up at the darkened opening, much as a Bethlehem shepherd might watch for another heraldic angel, and when no clattering racket followed Davis's disappearance inside I stepped back and pressed myself once more against the wall of the garage.

Thea Hansen, I thought, how on earth did you get yourself into this? And yet it wasn't fear or any kind of righteous incredulity I felt at the rhetorical question, but a shiver of excitement and the firm belief that I was in the right. Sneaking down side streets and breaking into another person's property but in the right, nevertheless. Something good would come of this night's efforts. I was sure of it. I draped Gus's coat around my shoulders and waited.

I'd be hard pressed to say how much time passed before Davis reappeared at the opening because my attention was fixed intently on my ground level surroundings. In one way it seemed like hours and in another the briefest of moments. All I know is that I heard a faint sound above me, but before I had time to steal a look upward, the man landed on both feet with a solid thud right next to me. He appeared hardly winded, and I realized that while I usually saw Gus Davis dressed in full lawyer regalia, shirt and tie and waistcoat and suit coat, there must be some admirable muscles under all those layers. In more ways than one, this man was not exactly what he appeared to be, and if he were as adept in the courtroom as he was climbing through windows, Lloyd was just days away from coming home.

Without a word, Gus climbed back atop the crates and attempted to get the shutters back to their original position. He fought a losing battle however; the one lopsided shutter was too damaged to creak back to its original place and thus, the connecting latch would not close, either. My partner finally gave up trying and stepped back down to the ground.

"Let's put these back where we found them," he said in a low whisper and reached for one of the crates. I took the other and followed him to the end of the alley. As we passed the garage one last time on our exit from the alley, Gus gave another glance at the stubborn shutter hanging partially open. I knew he wasn't pleased to leave any kind of hint that we'd been prowling where we didn't belong, but it couldn't be helped.

"Dolf will probably notice," I murmured, "but with any luck, he'll think it was just the inevitable effect of time and old wood. You can't do a thing about it, anyway, so forget about it." Gus gave a brief nod of understanding, but I could tell that leaving the old shutter bothered him. I felt some sympathy for his dissatisfaction. No doubt leaving behind any sign of his presence, even one as natural as a broken old wooden shutter, went against the grain for a former military man trained to sneak into places where he didn't belong.

I handed him back his suit coat and then led the way back to my house, the two of us moving in concert through the streets as if we were born for the adventure. Neither of us said a word, but I was always conscious of Davis just behind me, light and lithe on his feet. I could see him stealing behind enemy lines with an easy but competent poise and appreciated the courage it would take, even as I felt an unexpected but very real surge of gratitude for his safe return from the Front. For Lloyd's sake, I told myself, because Gus Davis was a strong supporter of my brother in more ways than one. But grateful on my own behalf, too, for more personal reasons.

"Well?" I demanded as soon as he closed the back door behind us and we were safely ensconced in my kitchen. When I turned back to face him after lighting the lamp, I thought from Gus's face that he looked energized, the past hours apparently more of an adventure than he cared to admit.

"You," I said, trying to sound accusatory and keep from smiling as I spoke, "enjoyed yourself a great deal this evening, didn't you, breaking and entering notwithstanding?"

He gave a brief thought to denying my observation but then shrugged and said with a grin, "No one's perfect, Thea. I admit that I enjoy taking a risk now and then."

I wanted to pursue that interesting comment but reverted to my original query. "I suppose I should find that alarming coming from my brother's attorney, but never mind about that right now. Did you discover anything interesting in the garage?"

"Oh, yes, indeed."

"Well, what?" I prompted with impatience. "It's unkind and unfair for you to tease, Gus. I deserve to know because it's information you wouldn't have if I hadn't led you to it."

"You're absolutely right, my girl. I still can't get over the sight of you headed for those crates. It was clear as day what you planned to do. I couldn't believe an otherwise intelligent woman thought she could scale a wall and drop through a window. However—" he held up a hand to keep me from interrupting "—you're right that I now possess some very helpful information that I wouldn't possess if you hadn't had that outlandish notion."

"Well?" I prompted. I allowed the *outlandish* to pass only because I wanted to know what he'd found in the garage and decided it would be unwise to interrupt his flow of conversation, but I couldn't promise the word wouldn't come up later. Outlandish, indeed.

"I found hooch, crates of it, bottled and ready for distribution."

"Hooch?" I repeated.

"Yes. Illegally distilled alcohol. Spirits. Moonshine. Bathtub gin."

"I know what hooch is," I retorted. "I just can't believe it. Kansas has been dry forever, and after the Wartime Prohibition Act passed this summer, so are all our neighboring states."

"The whole country will be dry in a few weeks."

"You don't agree?" I could tell by his tone that he thought the prohibition of alcohol was unwise and because he seemed like such a straight up kind of man I was surprised. A falling-down-drunk Gus Davis was impossible to picture, even after he admitted to liking risk and being less than perfect. Was alcohol a secret vice?

"I've seen the effects of too much liquor on a man, Thea, and I know that it can confuse a man and make him do things he wouldn't think of doing otherwise, but the urge to drink isn't going to go away just because the government says it's illegal. All that law will do is raise the price of alcohol and push the whole business underground." He shook his head. "Or into the dark corners of otherwise legitimate businesses like Dolf's Garage. I smelled the stuff on Leo Stanislaw the day of the funeral."

"I did, too. And when I stopped to offer my sympathy to Dolf, he fairly reeked of alcohol, but he'd just lost his son and I know men drink from grief." My voice trailed off as I recalled Dolf's ravaged face that day, the terrible look in his eyes, his slurred but furious words.

"Gus," I said slowly, hardly able to put my thoughts into words, "you don't think Rudy was involved in trafficking alcohol, do you? I mean, he was so straightforward about everything and he could be blunt to the point of insult sometimes. He never was good with secrets, not even as a boy. I can't see him as part of a criminal enterprise. I just can't."

"But what about Dolf? Or Leo?" We were seated at the table by then and he leaned forward, interested in my answer.

"That I could picture, especially Leo, but you don't think Rudy was killed by someone in his own family, do you?" The idea was as foreign as Timbuktu to me. "I can't imagine it."

"It wouldn't have had to be Leo or Dolf that pulled the trigger, Thea. There could be a whole network of men involved in the enterprise, depending on how much money's involved and where the liquor came from and where it's going, whether just to the next town over or all the way to Denver and beyond."

"But how was Rudy involved, if he even was, and why would anyone kill him because of it?" I still wrestled with the whole idea of the illegal distribution of moonshine taking place week in and week out like clockwork from the back alley behind Dolf's Garage. It seemed like a headline from a Chicago newspaper, something that happened far away and had nothing to do with Blessing, Kansas. Like you once thought about the Spanish influenza, I told myself, something distant and foreign with no relevance to your sheltered little life. And look at the consequences when that scourge finally found its way to Blessing, the rows of headstones, the inconsolable grief. The world seemed to get smaller every year.

"I don't know that Rudy was involved or that it's important. All I need to do is create reasonable doubt in a jury's mind about whether Lloyd killed Rudy and giving them other reasons for Rudy's death is part of that. The fact that something illegal and possibly dangerous was going on in the back of the garage where Rudy worked offers another motive for the murder. There's no honor among thieves, whatever you might have heard." I should have felt pleased at the hopeful tone in Gus's voice, but I felt more sorrowful than anything else.

"If you try to imply that Rudy was involved in something illegal, he'll take that innuendo with him to the grave, Gus, even if it's not true. Rudy can't defend himself."

For the first time since I'd met Gus Davis, I caught a hint of impatience on his face at my words and perhaps a trace of disappointment, too.

"I am Lloyd Hansen's defense attorney. That's what you wanted when you wired me and that's exactly what you got. Your brother is going to be declared not guilty."

"By blackening another man's reputation?" Davis's expression of exasperation deepened.

"By presenting reasonable doubt."

"It's the same thing in this case," I replied, refusing to let go of my reasoning.

"So I should let Lloyd go to prison in order to spare the reputations of Rachel Holiday and now Rudy Stanislaw? Is that what you're telling me?"

I didn't know what I was telling him. I wanted my brother home again, but it had never crossed my mind that getting what I wanted might hurt others or that there might be unforeseen consequences to finding out the truth.

When I didn't answer his brusque question, his tone softened. "It's complicated, isn't it?"

"Yes," I said. "More complicated than it should be—or would be if we identified the real killer."

"That sounds like you intend to keep poking around in dangerous places and sneaking down alleys and climbing up walls. I wish you wouldn't. I can't keep a constant eye on you, you know."

"No one's asking you to," I countered, and then out of curiosity asked, "How did you know I was in the alley? Are you spying on me?"

He narrowed his eyes in disapproval at that. I might as well have accused him of selling illegal hooch out of the back of Dolf's Garage right along with the Stanislaws.

"No. I am not spying on you," each word clipped and definite. "My train was delayed and I arrived back in Blessing two hours later than scheduled, and I thought you might be— That is, I didn't want you to think I had abandoned Lloyd so I dropped off my bag at the hotel, had a quick supper, and then thought I'd stop by your house long enough to let you know I was back. I came around to the porch and saw that the kitchen windows were dark so I figured you had already gone to bed and started back to the hotel. But when I got to the corner of the house, something made me look back and I saw a shadow move. Something moved, anyway. I thought maybe a cat at first, but it wasn't a cat. No, siree. It was Thea Hansen dressed up like a burglar out for a night of breaking and entering. Imagine my surprise."

"So you followed me?"

"I did."

"All the way across town? I never heard you."

"I learned to be very quiet in the war. Very. Quiet."

"You had some valuable military training, then." I gave the man an appraising look, wondering more than ever what exactly he'd done during the war.

"It would seem so. Valuable if I plan to make a habit of following young women through the back streets of small towns, anyway. Especially if those young women are intent on breaking the law. Very valuable in that case."

His early exasperation with me had faded. It might almost have been admiration that I saw on his face now.

"Breaking the law," I repeated. "If I ever thought I understood the law, I was wrong. What I did tonight felt right. Your plan of defending Lloyd feels wrong somehow." I looked at him, honestly curious. "Does it ever feel backwards to you? The law, I mean."

He stood up from his chair at the kitchen table. "Not very often. It gives me my orders and sets out clear boundaries, and I do my job to the best of my ability and stay within those boundaries. It's not the letter of the law that's complicated."

"It sounds like being in the army," I observed.

"I never thought of it like that, but I guess in a way it is."

"And you liked being in the military?"

"Not very often," gave it a moment's thought and amended, "Well, sometimes."

I shook my head at that and went past him to open the back door. "It's clear as day to me that you liked—no, I'd say relished—military life when you got to be a part of something risky. I imagine that kind of venture suited you to a tee. Nothing that would endanger someone else, mind you, but taking a personal risk of your own, doing something dangerous, well, that was another story, wasn't it? Because I'm not the one that scaled the wall and dropped through a window into a black hole. For all his suits and ties and law books, that person was Augustus Davis. Esquire."

Augustus Davis, Esquire, wanted to argue, wanted to find fault with my words or my reasoning or both. He was a lawyer, after all, and that's what lawyers do. But I was right and we both knew it so all he did was mutter a good night and exit onto the back porch. When I heard his shoe tap against the wooden step, I closed the door after him and flipped the lock, allowing myself a small smile as I did so. There are few conversational experiences as satisfying as having the last word.

Chapter 9

Wednesday, October 15, 1919

Gus's cuff links were a weight in the pocket when I hung up my jacket before going upstairs to bed, and I set the heavy gold links on the kitchen table so I'd remember to take them with me in the morning. I thought they were substantial but plain squares of gold until I saw them again in the morning light and noticed one very small sunflower engraved in a corner of each link. Despite the presence of the flower, however, their look was masculine and solid, much like their owner. I couldn't help but wonder about the significance of the sunflower, the favorite flower of Kansas long before it became official a few years ago. Of course, Gus's mother was a Kansas native, but she left the state of her own free will forty years ago. Did the state still hold such a special place in her heart that she had engraved its most noticeable plant on a gift to her son? A striking gift, I thought, regardless of the giver or the giver's reason.

En route to the store that morning I stopped briefly by the jail to see Lloyd and surprised Gus sitting on a corner of McGill's desk deep in discussion with the sheriff. I thought that when the lawyer saw me an expression that on anyone else I would have described as guilty crossed his face. The look disappeared almost immediately and he stood; Mort did the same. Perhaps Gus Davis was feeling a bit of discomfort about last night's unofficial and illegal foray into Dolf's Garage, standing as he was in the presence of an officer sworn to uphold the law. I didn't have any similar pangs of conscience but did feel cranky on general principles, not enough rest being primary. Awakening at first light out of habit, I could have turned over and gone right back to sleep. Apparently the only obstacle to keep me from a life of breaking and entering into other people's property was the necessity of working night hours because I didn't feel an ounce of shame. Only fatigue.

"Good morning," I said with as much cheer as I could muster. Gus Davis, despite his train trip and all his physical exertions in the alley, looked his usual rested and composed self. Another benefit of military training? Did they teach soldiers how to run themselves ragged and then get up the next day and run themselves ragged all over again? That was training I could have used this morning, although for the most part women seemed to figure out how to work sunup to sundown and then get up the next day and do it all over again without uniforms and formal instruction.

Both men murmured greetings and Mort, used to my morning visits, grabbed the ring of keys and preceded me toward the hall that led to the cells.

Before I followed, Gus said in a low voice, "Can you join me at the hotel for supper tonight around six, Thea? I've got some questions." I nodded wordlessly and hurried to catch up with Mort but was cheered by the prospect of sharing time with Davis that did not involve dressing up like a boy and crouching in an alley. I lost the small measure of good mood I felt when I saw my brother, however. Impatient for Mort to unlock the cell door, I brushed past him to sit down next to Lloyd on the edge of his bunk and reach for his hand.

"Bad night?" although I wouldn't have had to ask. He wore the pale, tense, dark-eyed expression that I had learned early on meant a night of bad dreams. He tried to make light of his feelings, gave a small shrug and a vague, tired smile but didn't try to withdraw his hand from mine.

"A little."

Weighing the wisdom of my next words, I finally said, "Captain Davis told me about the shells and the cave-in."

Lloyd's cheeks turned a bright rose pink. "He shouldn't have told you something like that. He had no right."

"I made him tell me, Lloyd. You know how I can be sometimes." When he didn't respond to my weak attempt at humor, I continued, "And why shouldn't I, your sister, someone who's known and loved you all her life, be allowed to know something like that?" I tried to mimic the same tone he'd used on the final three words.

"Because it's not something you'd understand."

"Maybe not, but we're family, you and I. Hard times come and go but family lasts." He recognized Grandma Liza's words and softened.

"It's not something I want to talk about, Thea. I talked about it enough at the hospital to last me a lifetime, and I still have the dreams, so talking's no good."

"For you maybe, Lloyd, but it helps me." My quiet statement startled him; I could tell it was the first time he'd ever thought about how I might feel.

"I didn't mean to ignore—" he began and I interrupted, "I know that, but when you came home you were a different brother than the one that left, and I was confused. I had to adjust to that new person and I couldn't figure him out. I loved the boy that left and I love the man that came home, but it hasn't been easy for me, either, so I appreciated the captain telling me a little bit about what it was like over there. I know I wasn't in France with you and I know hearing about it isn't the same as being there, but the little bit Gus said still helped me. Don't be mad at him or me."

Lloyd watched me steadily as I talked; the spots of color faded from his cheeks and something about his posture relaxed. When I finally ran down, he smiled the genuine Lloyd smile I didn't get to see nearly enough and squeezed my hand.

"I'm not mad at anybody. Well, maybe the person that killed Rudy, but not at the captain and never at you. It's all right, whatever he told you. He'd know the right thing to say and how to say it. It's all right." The sound of my brother trying to comfort me made me tear up for a moment, and I rose quickly so he wouldn't think he'd upset me.

"Good, because the captain is outside waiting to talk to you and I wouldn't want to be the cause of an argument between you. That would be bad timing since the trial's in five days. Can you stick it out until Monday?"

He stood, too, and grinned. "Are there other options I've overlooked?"

"I suppose I could try to chisel through the bars tonight and break you out."

"As if you'd recognize a chisel when you saw it."

I gave him a gentle punch to the arm and pulled open the cell door, which Mort never bothered to lock when I was there, and looked back at Lloyd a last time before I departed. The sight of him, face haggard and so thin his trousers bagged, grieved me deeply. How many wars would my brother have to fight before he was allowed to be happy? If Gus Davis could keep Lloyd out of prison, I'd never find the words to thank the man. Never.

I replied with a light tone that I was far from feeling. "Don't take that tone with me, brother dear. I might surprise you with what I know."

Lloyd examined my face with objective speculation before he responded, "You might at that, Thea. I'm beginning to see you in a new light."

As I thought about those words on my walk to the store, I almost had to laugh. Seeing me creep through the midnight streets of Blessing dressed in his old pants would definitely be a new light but might be more than my brother bargained for. He was trying his best but still didn't fully understand that he wasn't the only one in the family who'd changed during the years he was away at war.

At the supper table that night, I prompted Gus, "More questions, you said," and waited.

He didn't pause in his attention to the steak on his plate or even look over at me as he answered, "Could I please have one minute to finish the task at hand?" With a final motion of the knife, he set it down and forked the last piece of what is probably the best steak in all of Kansas into his mouth. He closed his eyes a moment at the bliss of it, chewed, swallowed, and only then condescended to meet my gaze. "Aren't you going to eat?"

"Eventually."

He softened. "I'm trying to open up more opportunities for doubt in the minds of the jury. We have other candidates for the murder—"

"Suspects," I corrected. "We're not discussing an election for city councilman."

"All right, we can identify other suspects for the murder, but it's the fact that Hoffman, the undertaker, saw Lloyd tearing out of the garage before the place was open that morning that led McGill to Lloyd in the first place. But besides the fact that there are two ways to get into the garage—" I refrained from pointing out to my companion that the opening above the alley door he'd used last night in a dramatic and illegal way might make it three ways "—we don't know exactly when Rudy was killed because no one knows when he showed up at the garage that morning. The doctor will swear that Rudy was killed sometime after five o'clock, but that's as definite as he's willing to be. Dolf Stanislaw says he never heard Rudy leave, and I believe that because he didn't hear the shot, either, and he should have, sleeping just overhead as he was."

I observed, "It's likely Dolf was sampling illegal goods, don't you think, and that's why he didn't hear anything in the garage?"

"It would certainly explain why the man seems to have slept through his son being murdered just below him." We were both suddenly quiet, struck in the same instant, I think, by the finality and heartache of the awful words just spoken out loud. Then Gus resumed, "If Rudy went down to work early that morning, any number of people could have come and gone without being seen."

"True, and when I left the house around quarter to seven, Lloyd was still asleep in his room. I know I got up a little earlier that morning, around half past five give or take a few minutes, because I had some accounts to look at, and I wanted to leave with the truck to pick up an order at the depot as soon as I opened the store for business. I checked on Lloyd at least once before I left the house, and I'm certain he was sleeping all the time I worked at the kitchen table that morning."

"Which means that between the time when Rudy went down to the garage and you left your house at six forty-five, there's more than enough time for a murder to occur. Rudy could have been killed long before his body was discovered and no one would have been the wiser. And during much of that time, Lloyd has you as a solid alibi."

"Yes." I considered the timing. "You can't get Doctor Petrie to be more specific about the time Rudy died?"

"All he's willing to say under oath is that the murder occurred sometime after five o'clock that morning."

I thought about that morning, what we could know for certain and what we could only speculate about, and finally asked, "Did anyone see Rudy alive that morning? Anyone at all?"

"No. Dolf said he was in bed when he heard Rudy come home the night before. He didn't know what time that was, only that it was after dark. Rudy had been home for supper and then left. He didn't tell his father where he was going and Dolf didn't ask."

"And I can swear that Lloyd was at home by eight o'clock Tuesday night, sound asleep in his bed when I got up the next morning, and still sleeping when I left the house an hour later." I began to understand why Gus wanted to have those morning hours defined clearly in his mind.

"Depending on when Rudy went down to the garage, there could be at least an hour, even more, when someone had the opportunity to slip into the garage and kill Rudy. No one would have been the wiser. The garage didn't open until eight, and I haven't tracked down anyone who would've been there before the place opened for business."

"It's another opportunity to plant some seeds of reasonable doubt, isn't it?"

Gus rested his elbows on the table and leaned toward me. "I know it's not how you want Lloyd to gain his freedom, Thea, but I'd be remiss as your brother's attorney if I didn't use every legitimate means available to get a not guilty verdict for Lloyd."

With the full force of Gus Davis's gaze fixed on my face, I felt for one long moment completely incapable of thinking about anything except the man's clear hazel eyes. Then rational thought returned and I nodded my understanding.

"I know," I said. "In a perfect world Rudy's killer would step forward and admit his guilt and Lloyd would be completely exonerated to everyone's satisfaction."

"In a perfect world," Gus corrected gently, "Rudy wouldn't have been killed to start with."

I shrugged. "It's not perfect, though, is it?"

It took him a moment to agree with me, and I wondered if he was thinking about bombs and shells and broken bodies and men buried alive. The elusive shadow I sometimes saw in his eyes seemed to linger there briefly until he sat back in his chair and willed his memories away.

"No," he said, finally, "it's not," and took a swallow of coffee.

"You seemed awfully friendly with Mort McGill when I saw you this morning," I observed, deciding it was time to change the subject.

"Did I? Well, you seemed equally at ease. Apparently neither of us has an especially sensitive conscience." He gave a small grin at the words, and I couldn't help but smile in return.

"Not many people know this," I admitted, "but my conscience has been known to take a back seat to necessity and rational thought."

"Don't worry. Your secret's safe with me."

"I wasn't worried," I responded in my sweetest tone. "After all, I'm not the only person at the table with a secret, am I?" Something in my words or tone or glance made him choke on his final swallow of coffee.

"Blackmail, Thea? I would have said that was beneath you."

"I've discovered that to get what I want there's not as much beneath me, as you put it, as I once thought."

"So does reaching a moral end justify the means we use to get there? Is that what you believe?" Gus Davis watched me with a care I found somewhat disconcerting; my reply to his question seemed to matter more than was warranted by a simple suppertime conversation. Did he wonder what exactly I'd be willing to do to bring my brother home? Would I lie on the witness stand? Would I falsify evidence? I realized that I wasn't sure about the answers myself any more, and I think Gus was surprised, maybe even troubled, by my hesitant response.

"I think there are still some things that are absolutely right or absolutely wrong, but not nearly as many as I used to think." I didn't know what else to say, still working it out in my own mind as I was, so I pushed my chair away from the table. Meal ended and the evening on the wane, the motion said, the significance of which he did not miss. Good training by his mother and sisters, I thought with approval.

As I lay in bed that night, I recalled that my aunt and uncle would return to Blessing tomorrow on the afternoon train, and from there it was only a tiny leap to thinking about the alley behind the garage and the fact that it was Wednesday night, time for the regular hooch run, as I'd taken to calling it in my private thoughts. Unless transport plans had changed because someone spied the crooked shutter or discovered evidence of Gus's presence and got nervous about keeping the regular schedule. If that were the case, the schedule might have been changed or stopped all together. But wouldn't they be even more anxious to get the liquor out of the garage if they thought someone was on to them? The more I tried to wrestle through the options the less sleepy I became until finally I flung back the bed covers, swung my feet onto the cold floor, and stood. There was no use pretending I wasn't curious about what would or wouldn't happen in the alley this night so I might as well see for myself. By now I had mastered slipping through town in the middle of the night, so why waste a reprehensible but otherwise perfectly good skill? Winter would be here soon enough and even the most enthusiastic of burglars, let alone an amateur like myself, wouldn't be sneaking through hip deep drifts of snow. Best to enjoy the unexpected pleasure of furtive skulking while it was still possible to do so, before the long Kansas winter trapped me inside, a restless and impatient captive of the season.

As I made my way through dark streets, I thought how different this felt from my first expedition of a week ago, how easily I'd adjusted to wearing men's clothes, how quickly I'd learned which houses to avoid because of barking dogs and which alleys to use because they offered the least complicated routes. I knew I'd never have the chance to do anything really exciting in my life, like ride in a dirigible over the ocean or race a Peugeot in the Indianapolis 500 and maybe I didn't have the necessary nerve for that kind of breathtaking excitement, but someday, I thought, when I'm forty, a staid business woman known for her propriety and good sense, I'll remember this night and what it felt like to do something unpredictable and even dangerous. I was more right than I knew at the time. The night would indeed be memorable, just not for the reason I expected.

When I turned into the alley from Lincoln Avenue it at first seemed no different than the night before, just as cold, just as dark, just as quiet, but after taking only a few steps, I became aware of a gradual increase of noise. One moment it was midnight quiet, and then suddenly I heard the unintelligible shout of a man's voice followed by other shouts. Still a woman with some remaining common sense, I stopped abruptly and gave a thought to turning around and heading straight home. Was there an alley fight going on completely separate from the Wednesday night hooch run? I doubted it. More probably, that illegal activity had been discovered by the authorities and the wrongdoers confronted. Because, I suspected, there was only one valid reason why Gus Davis had seemed so comfortable in Mort McGill's office this morning. My partner in crime had shared what he knew about the illegal goods stored in Dolf's Garage with the sheriff with the intention of making the hooch run public knowledge. Davis's doing so made sense to me, but the sensibleness of the action did not keep me from feeling both angry and hurt. He owed me that same information but hadn't bothered to share it. Instead he chewed his steak and drank his coffee, all the while knowing there would be a confrontation in the alley in just a few hours and not saying a word to me about it. Did he feel he couldn't trust me? I was furious with the man and what I considered to be a betrayal of our partnership. The thoughts and emotions sped through my brain with the speed and force of an electrical current, and then I was moving forward again toward the continuing sounds of men's voices. I'd have sooner run down the alley stark naked than turn back like a dog with its tail between its legs. Anger combined with curiosity propelled me forward.

I'd hardly gone any distance at all, however, when I became conscious of the sound of running feet getting louder and coming in my direction. I pushed myself against the nearest wall and waited. A figure raced toward me, the person's identity impossible to make out in the dark alley but a man and one slight in build. I knew someone chased him because I heard a shouted, "You there! Stop!" and heard a second set of running footsteps coming closer, although still far enough down the dark alley that I could not make out the pursuer's figure.

I heard the thuds of the first runner's feet and his panting breaths as he approached the shadowy spot where I stood pressed out of the way, and for some reason—I don't know why but I'm afraid it was probably due to residual anger and unbecoming resentment at being excluded from a venture that was my idea to start with—I simply let the man pass me by. I could have easily stuck out a foot and brought him down long enough for him to be apprehended but I didn't. I made no sound, just turned my head to follow the figure's progress as he raced by me. He paused for the briefest of moments at the end of the alley, apparently deciding which way to go on Lincoln, and it was that tiny pause that gave him away. For just a moment his face was in profile to me and caught by a wash of pale moonlight. The sight made me take a small gasp. Because it was Kinsey standing there, his chest heaving. Kinsey Carr. Cece's brother. My fellow truck lover. Kinsey!

Much closer now, his pursuer, while also panting, still managed to shout out another, "Stop!" The word galvanized Kinsey, who took a quick turn to the right and disappeared onto Lincoln Avenue.

And that's when I made my second unexpected decision of the night: I moved directly into the oncoming path of the constable hot on Kinsey's trail. The big man, Danny Merritt I could see by then, would never catch Kinsey, anyway, too much meat on his bones to match Kinsey's speed, but I thought I could help ensure Kinsey's escape without seeming to do so purposefully. I wasn't foolish about it, however—I intended to keep my own bones unbroken—so I backed up along the wall where I stood and sort of sprang into the alley as if I'd just rounded the corner from Lincoln.

"Help!" I yelled because I couldn't think of anything else to say and shifted to the side as if attempting to turn around and run in the opposite direction, figuring that if Danny wasn't able to come to a complete halt at the sight of me, he would run into my side instead of hitting me straight on.

Admittedly, it wasn't the brightest idea I've ever come up with, but I'm not spontaneous by nature and it was all I could think to do at the time. At the sight of my shadowy figure in the alley, Danny had tried to brake his momentum before colliding into me, but even at half speed he hit my shoulder, exhaling a gusty whoosh of air as he did so, with enough force to knock me flat. I had expected the impact, but it was still a great thud to my system and before I could catch enough breath to identify myself, Danny had grabbed me by the collar and was pulling me to my feet.

"Now," he said in a gruff tone, "just where do you think you're going?"

I'd forgotten that I was dressed in dark clothes, Lloyd's trousers, shirt, and jacket, and that I had my hair pushed up into the cap, so the constable's words took me by surprise as did the shake he gave me as he yanked me upright.

"Danny," I gasped, "it's me, Thea. What's happened?"

If it had been a less critical time I would have found some humor in the look of utter stupefaction that appeared on Danny Merritt's face. The same moonlight that had briefly given Kinsey away now illumined Danny enough for me to see his staring eyes and his mouth opening and closing like a catfish out of water. Poor man. I suppose I should be grateful that my unexpected appearance combined with the pounding foot race he'd just run didn't give him a heart seizure.

Shocked to his core, Danny let go of my collar and I only just managed to keep myself upright at the sudden release.

"Thea?" He injected the two syllables with such horror that for a moment I was nearly offended. It wasn't as if I were some kind of monster, after all. But then I put myself in his place and felt a small pang of guilt for making the constable lose his prey and manhandle me, neither action something he was likely to forget very soon.

"Yes. I'm sorry if I shocked you, Danny, but I know about the garage and what goes on there and about the Wednesday night shipments, too. Didn't Gus Davis tell you any of that?"

My last words were an educated guess proved right when Danny replied, "He didn't mention it to me." Finally past the shock of seeing Thea Hansen dressed like a burglar in a side alley well past midnight, Danny stopped staring at me and glanced down the alley in the direction of Lincoln Avenue. "If it wasn't you I was chasing, then where did he go? Did anybody run by you?"

"There might have been someone," I said, attempting to sound as guileless as possible, "but it was dark and when I came around the corner all I heard was you running up the alley toward me. I didn't know what to do. I sure didn't expect to find all this commotion going on."

Danny removed his hat, ran a hand through his hair, and replaced his hat before he told me, "We were waiting for them, but the two on the wagon scattered in opposite directions down the alley."

Following Danny's example, I took off my hat, too, shook out my hair, and without further discussion began to walk with the constable back toward the garage. After a moment Danny stopped long enough to say to me, "I don't know what Mort will say about you being here, Thea. Maybe you should go home."

Not likely, I thought, still feeling rebellious, but said, "If Mort sends me home, I guess I'll have to go, but I'm here now and I've got my wind back and I'd like to know what happened. I think it might be important for Lloyd."

Danny didn't say anything after that and the two of us started walking again, stopping at the corner of the undertaker's to view the activity outside Dolf's Garage. From the earlier hullabaloo I expected it to be busier, but the alley looked surprisingly calm. I could see in the spill of light from several lamps that Mort McGill was deep in conversation with a short, stocky man that had to be Dolf Stanislaw. *Conversation* might not be the right word, however, because it looked like Mort doing all the talking and Dolf just standing there, body stiff and still, hands stuck into his pockets. I couldn't make out all the words the sheriff was saying since he spoke low and directly to Dolf, but I recognized the insolence in Dolf's answering shrug to whatever it was McGill had asked even before I caught the end of his response.

"—you're talking about. Had no idea someone was using my place to stock liquor." He lifted his head and stared squarely into Mort McGill's face. "In case you forgot, I lost my boy two weeks ago and I ain't been thinking about much else."

I heard those words clearly as Danny and I crossed the footpath between the undertaker's establishment and the garage and approached the horse and wagon waiting there. I stood on tiptoe to peer over the side and saw there were two crates loaded in the back.

They hadn't finished, I thought, and was supported in the assumption by another constable coming out of the garage into the alley and speaking to Mort.

"Half a dozen crates still inside," he announced. Then he looked over, caught sight of Danny, and called, "Looks like you got him, Dan," before he took a second look and added in surprise, "Don't tell me that was a woman at the reins of the wagon!"

"No," the word spoken in a tone somewhere between disgust and embarrassment, "I lost him when I ran into Thea Hansen here." At his words Mort McGill and Dolf Stanislaw both turned to look at me and another man appeared from inside the garage, stopped in the doorway, and stared, too, before taking three enormous strides to end up right in front of Danny and me.

"Thea?!"

If prizes were handed out for the person most astounded and horrified at my presence, Gus Davis would have won the contest hands down. I felt some vindication and not an ounce of guilt that I was able to shock the man to such a degree. He deserved it and more, although I realized I'd have to settle for what I'd just heard. The idea that he'd eaten supper with me innocent as you please, all the while knowing what was planned for the alley in just a few hours still aggravated me more than I could express.

I tried for casual calm. "None other."

"What in God's name are you doing here?"

I eyed him. Close up I couldn't decide if it was mere shock at my appearance that registered on his face or something closer to revulsion. He certainly sounded aggravated, maybe even more aggravated than I felt, which seemed wrong since I was the one who'd been excluded and ignored.

"Same as you, I imagine. It's Wednesday night, after all."

"This is no place for you."

"Well," I pointed out in a reasonable voice, "if you'd told me what was in the works, I would have known to stay away, but apparently I can't be trusted with important information so here I am."

He stared at me, eyes narrowed, before he replied, "It wasn't something I was free to talk about. It was McGill's plan."

I wanted to respond with a vulgar word but figured I'd shocked everyone enough for the night so I simply said, "Ah, I see," and managed a tight smile. Then I turned to Danny Merritt and apologized. "I'm sorry I got in your way tonight, Danny." To the sheriff I explained, "Danny was hot on someone's trail until I tripped him up. I'm awful sorry, Mort."

McGill nodded and then told me to go home. "You'll just keep getting in the way if you stick around, Thea. The captain's right. This is no place for you. We'll talk more tomorrow." The sheriff turned back to Dolf and for the first time I really did feel extraneous and out of place. I patted Danny on the arm one final time by way of both apology and good-bye and started back down the alley. Gus Davis's running footsteps pounded behind me.

"Thea," he said when he caught up with me, "I couldn't tell you." I didn't stop my brisk pace and he walked along with me, speaking all the while. "It was Sheriff's orders. He needed it to be a complete surprise without a whiff of warning." That comment brought me to a standstill.

"And you thought I'd blab it all over Blessing, ring the church bells, and order a special edition of the Banner?"

"Of course, not."

"This is my brother we're talking about, Gus, not some stranger off the train. I can be trusted with information about someone I love, about my family. Family's everything. Family lasts." Then sounding sadder than I wished, I concluded, "I thought we were partners, but I guess I was wrong. Go back to your business. I don't want or need your company."

When he started to reply I held up a hand, the gesture's message clear, and turned away from him to trudge down the alley toward Lincoln Avenue and home. The energy generated by aggravation and excitement and fear had faded. But even then, tired and disappointed, I was already busy with other thoughts in the back of my mind, thoughts about Kinsey Carr and his participation in running hooch. What details did Kinsey have about what went on in the Stanislaw garage? What might he know? Gus Davis had kept secrets from me, I thought with unbecoming childish satisfaction, so turnabout was fair play. Wasn't it?

Chapter 10

Thursday, October 16, 1919

I entered the store the next morning through the warehouse hoping to see Kinsey, but he wasn't there. Maybe hunkered down in the garage with the truck, I thought, but decided to bide my time. Tracking the boy down might not be wise if he were already skittish from the night before.

When I opened the door to the jail for my regular visit with Lloyd before going to the store, I didn't know if any of the participants from last night's adventure would be present, but Mort and Danny and Gus Davis were nowhere in sight. I supposed they'd had a much later night of it than I and were still in bed, which was all right with me. I'd awakened with an assortment of aches and pains, all of which had to do with my alley collision with Dan Merritt except for one small tender spot, a bruise all its own, caused by Gus Davis. I realized he felt obligated to obey the sheriff's instructions, but the knowledge that he'd sat with me only a few hours before the ambush and conversed as if he were completely ignorant of it still stung. Especially since I was responsible for the pivotal information that lay at the core of the raid.

The only person in the office was the constable on duty, Phil Utica, who said, "Lloyd's got company back there, Thea. Dolf Stanislaw. He was sleeping when I checked last but if he wakes up and gets out of line, let me know."

Two weeks ago the idea of Dolf Stanislaw getting "out of line" in my presence would have caused some uneasiness, but I was well past any earlier sensitivities. What could he say that I didn't expect or hadn't already heard?

"Thanks, Phil. I'm not worried." As it turned out, I didn't need to be. The only thing out of line with Dolf that morning was his snoring; he slept through my time with Lloyd.

"Did he say anything when he came in?" I asked my brother, nodding at the cell across from Lloyd's where Dolf lay.

Lloyd shrugged in answer and I waited for more. Finally, "What you'd expect, Thea. He didn't want to wake up and have to look at the face of the man that killed his son first thing every morning. He hadn't done anything wrong and here he was sharing space with a crazy murderer. That kind of thing."

"I'm sorry." I didn't offer more. I'd learned early on that my brother didn't welcome my sympathy, which he considered to be pity, the most offensive of all emotions.

"Well, he was a little drunk and it didn't take long for him to go to sleep. At least having him back here will be a change from the monotony of the past two weeks. Mort said something about Dolf running illegal alcohol out of the garage. Do you know any of the details?"

"I just got up an hour ago," I deflected. "Ask your lawyer about it when you see him. No doubt he'll be a fountain of information."

Something in my tone caused my brother to give me a closer look, turning the tables on me because I was usually the one doing the examining—Sleeping all right? Eating properly? Losing weight? Staying healthy? I discovered that I didn't appreciate Lloyd's scrutiny any more than he appreciated mine. Apparently blue eyes and a straight, inelegant nose weren't the only similarities that had been passed down in our family.

"You and the captain at odds over something?"

"Of course, not. He's perfect and I follow along behind him grateful for any crumb of information he drops in my path."

"Thea—"

"Never mind," I said, ashamed of sharing my bad temper with Lloyd, who'd been staring at the same four walls—four gray and unattractive walls—for two weeks. "I shouldn't have said that. He's your attorney, not mine, and his first loyalty is to you. I'm just being cranky." I gave him a quick and unexpected kiss on the cheek and pulled open the cell door before he could ask anything more. "I hope having him here," I gave another nod toward the snoring Dolf, "won't be too awful." Lloyd stood with his hands in his pockets watching me and smiling a little.

"I'll be fine, Thea." A pause, then, "Don't think unkindly of the captain. You'll never find a better man."

I looked at him through the bars. How quickly I'd grown accustomed to seeing my brother this way, I thought, framed by bars against a gray background! What if that was the only way I ever saw him through all the years to come? The idea, passing and vague, still had the power to make me shiver.

"I know. I just wonder if we could have found a better lawyer," my pique speaking.

"Someone like Ian Buchanan you mean?" Lloyd made a dismissive sound somewhere between a snort and a *tsk*. "The captain believes in me, Thea, believes I'm not guilty. Buchanan would have defended me well enough, I suppose, but in the back of his mind I'd always have been guilty as hell." Perhaps recalling Davis's earlier admonition, Lloyd said, "Sorry," and looked abashed, as if he'd never cursed me with abandon upon awakening from the depths of a bad dream.

"Yes," I agreed. "You're right there. Gus believes as strongly as I do that you didn't hurt Rudy."

"So I made the right choice, then."

I couldn't tell if Lloyd was asking for my approval or asserting his own good judgment. What did it matter, anyway? I thought my brother had put his finger on the strongest part of Gus Davis's legal expertise for this particular case.

"Yes, you did. You definitely did. I promise you I don't doubt the man's competence." On my way out, I stopped long enough to remind Lloyd that Uncle Carl and Aunt Louisa were returning today. "I expect you'll see Uncle Carl before the end of the day." We both liked our uncle and Lloyd brightened at the news. "You may have to repeat your defense of the captain, though," I continued. "Uncle Carl wanted to bring in a lawyer from Chicago, someone his niece, Johanna, recommended. Do you remember her? Johanna Gallagher? Anyway, he said she's got a lot of important contacts and knows a lot of people."

"I can just imagine how a jury of Kansas farmers would take to a big shot lawyer from Chicago! Not a good plan for

Blessing. Once Uncle Carl meets the captain, he'll forget about that idea."

It occurred to me as I left the jail and continued my walk to the store that my brother had made good sense that morning, that he had, in fact, been much more sensible and astute in his observations and advice than I. A happy turnabout, I thought with honest reflection, that probably had as much to do with my lingering hurt feelings as it did with Lloyd's improved mood.

I was surprised not to find Kinsey in the warehouse, where he often started the morning by reviewing current inventory to be sure there was a place for any incoming goods due that day. When he wasn't there, I went in to my office and busied myself with tasks for which I had no enthusiasm until I finally set my pen aside, stood, and headed once more for the warehouse. Still no Kinsey so I went out the side door and walked to the large shed that sheltered the truck at the rear of the alley. The double doors were shut but the small door directly to their side stood ajar, perhaps a sign of Kinsey's presence.

In the dim interior the Olds stood in all its glory—what person would not be captivated by its mechanical beauty?—but I saw no sign of Kinsey until I peered into the back of the truck. The boy slept there curled on his side; he looked impossibly young. I watched him for a while, so much like his sister in sleep that it touched me: long lashes against his cheeks and tousled dark blonde hair. I didn't know what to do, hating the thought of waking him from what must be a sleep of exhaustion but also impatient to talk to him about details of the hooch runs that only he would know. Kinsey stirred and I took advantage of the moment.

"Kinsey. Kinsey, wake up." One eye opened and then the other. He frowned a little, clearly confused by his surroundings, but when I repeated his name a third time he sat bolt upright.

"Thea?"

"Yup." A long pause as I contemplated the boy. "You must have been tired if you needed to take a nap in the truck."

Caution in his tone now. "Yes." He was testing a variety of responses in his head so he drew out the word slowly.

"Late night?" I asked.

"Pretty late." He was getting his bearings, still thinking furiously.

"All that racing around can sure tire a person out, can't it?"

He blinked. "What?"

"Kinsey, I know about last night."

Another blink. "I don't know what—"

My patience evaporated. "I know about the garage and the hooch runs and last night's ambush. I know it all. If I hadn't risked life and limb by stepping in front of Danny Merritt moving at full speed in your direction, you could be sharing a cell with Dolf this morning instead of hiding out in my garage in the back of an Oldsmobile Economy Truck. Wake up and climb out. I want to talk to you." He stared at me as if I'd suddenly begun to glow, but when I repeated my request with even less patience, he stood and hopped to the floor of the garage.

"Did you really do that?"

"I did."

"Well, thank you."

"Don't flatter yourself, Kinsey. I don't have a lot of tolerance for people that thumb their nose at the law. How did you ever get caught up in something like that?"

He looked very young, flushed and uncomfortable and unhappy, reminding me of the time my father had caught Lloyd one Halloween night right after he and Joe Buchanan had toppled the Marks's outhouse. I truly believe Joey never experienced or understood guilt, but my brother had quickly passed the stage of thinking the mischief fun and had received Father's displeasure with the same shamefaced expression I now saw on Kinsey's face.

"I didn't mean anything by it, Thea. It was a way to make a little cash, and Leo said—"

"Leo?!"

"It was him from the start." Kinsey lowered his voice as if Leo Stanislaw might be standing just outside the door and although I knew that wasn't the case, I still looked quickly over my shoulder. The fear in Kinsey's voice was genuine and infectious.

"He said he needed me just the one time, and I thought, what can it hurt? One time and a little extra spending money and who'd ever know? But then there was a second time and a third, and when I finally told him I didn't want to do it any more, he said it was too late. I was in too deep, he said. Knew too much."

Kinsey swallowed, his Adam's apple rising and falling with the gulp. "He said he'd kill me, Thea, or hurt Cece if I tried to back out, said he'd do something awful to her. And I believed him. He's a crazy man. There's something not right about him."

I digested the information, never once doubting its veracity. Kinsey's words had the ring of truth. There definitely was something "not right" about Leo Stanislaw. I had recognized the fact years ago, had felt the menace in his attentions even as an inexperienced, much younger girl, but I'd had my father to step into the gap for me, and Kinsey had no one.

"What did you do for him?" I asked in a gentler tone.

"Not all that much, really. Went in the garage before it opened early Wednesday morning and did a count of what would get picked up that night. Dolf got deliveries all week from a couple of local suppliers. They'd drop off a crate at a time so they never drew any attention. I'd go in Wednesday morning, count what was there, and leave the count with Dolf. On Wednesday night I'd get picked up by the wagon on Lincoln and help load it in the alley. Hardly took any time at all. It wasn't always the same driver and I usually didn't recognize him, but he always knew to drive north a couple miles afterwards, stop, and let me off. I'd walk back home and that was it. I never knew what happened after that, where they went or who the liquor was for."

"But you knew it was liquor," I interrupted.

"Well," I could see Kinsey wanted to deny the fact but he resisted the temptation, "yeah, I did, Thea. I knew it was liquor. And illegal. And I did it, anyway." No defiance in his voice, though, which was hopeful.

"How long has it been going on?"

"Months. Maybe years, I don't know. It started before Rudy got home from the Front because I remember how nasty Leo got when he heard Rudy would be around all the time. He was worried about Rudy finding out and him and his father almost got in a fight about it."

"What did they fight about?"

"Dolf wanted to bring Rudy in on the deal once he got home, and Leo said nothing doing. He wasn't sharing his profit with one more person, he said, and especially not Rudy. Told his father he knew what Rudy was like and how he wouldn't want anything to do with the business. When Dolf disagreed, Leo shoved him up against the wall and said something to him real low. I couldn't hear what it was, but Dolf didn't say another word. He looked scared, Thea, scared of his own son."

I listened to Kinsey's story while a part of my brain was busy processing the facts as I heard them. I knew something important, something really important, was included in all the narration and needed to be separated out from the story. Even when I spoke, some detached part of my mind was sifting through everything I'd heard.

"So Rudy wasn't involved?" I asked.

Kinsey shook his head. "Not that I know of. Leo said no and what Leo said was the rule."

"Kinsey." There must have been something different in my tone because the boy stopped talking and just watched me, waiting. "Go over it again."

"Go over what again?"

I sat down on a nearby box, trying to get all the facts in their proper order and instead of answering his question, said, "You must have been at the garage the morning of the murder. It was a Wednesday. October first was a Wednesday. You must have been there." I looked up from my lap where I'd been staring, deep in desperate thought. "You were, weren't you? You were there that morning."

He didn't answer for what seemed like a long time, as if he knew that his answer had the power to change lives, Lloyd's and mine and his sister's and most of all his very own.

"Yes." One simple syllable.

"And you never said a word to anyone, Kinsey, not a word. Why?"

But I knew why. He'd have had to explain what he was doing there: counting bottles of prohibited alcohol and smuggling them out for illegal sale and all in the employ of Leo Stanislaw. If he said a word, there was the certainty of Leo's retribution and the near certainty that he'd go to jail for his part in the operation. Kinsey didn't answer me and didn't have to.

"Tell me about that morning." Still no response. "Kinsey, sit down," I patted the seat of an old stool next to me, "and tell me about the morning of October first."

At last, his mind made up, he did as I asked after pulling the stool back to extend the distance between us. Was that guilt, I wondered, or did he know that what he was going to tell me would wound me and he didn't want to get caught up in my reaction?

Kinsey licked his lips, looking once more like my eleven-year-old brother standing shame-faced before my father with a furious George Marks lurking in the open doorway. I had to help Kinsey get started.

"Was it business as usual that day to start with?" I asked. When he nodded I asked a second question. "What time did you get to the garage that morning?" I couldn't tell if he realized how important the answer to that question was, but I surely did. I knew I was holding my breath and couldn't help myself.

"Around half past six."

"Tell me what happened." I didn't repeat the words; I just waited. The silence seemed to stretch out for minutes, although I know it was really only seconds, until Kinsey began telling his story.

"I went in like I did every Wednesday morning through the alley door. The door was always open and Dolf was usually waiting for me, except that morning he wasn't there."

"But the alley doors were open when you got there? You're sure?" Kinsey nodded and looked a little put out at the interruption. Once he'd made up his mind to share what he knew, he was impatient to get through the tale without disruption. I tried to look apologetic and was quiet.

"I went in and except for the door being open and Dolf not around everything seemed like usual. I figured maybe Dolf was using the facility or refilling his coffee cup. There'd been a couple of other times he hadn't showed up at all, and I didn't think much about it. I did the count and then I did it again 'cause I knew Leo checked what I wrote sometimes and I wanted it to be right. I was done by seven or so and I waited around a little to see if Dolf was going to show. I worried about being late to the store but I remembered you were taking the Olds to the train depot pretty early that morning, and I figured as long as I was back in time to unload the truck, it wouldn't matter if I was a little late."

I had a quick jolt of memory from that morning: Kinsey looking pale and tired and me worrying that he might be sick, a residual victim of the influenza. And all along he'd been tired out by engaging in illegal activities, conspiring with Leo Stanislaw, of all people! I couldn't have imagined any of it that morning, only two weeks ago though it felt like several lifetimes. I'd been oblivious to so much drama happening all around me, Rudy and Rachel Holiday, Kinsey and Leo, and worst of all, someone capable of murder walking the streets of little Blessing, Kansas. The knowledge of what I hadn't noticed and never suspected made me feel like a stranger in my own hometown, someone friendless and ignorant and incredibly naïve. I was conscious that Kinsey had stopped talking. Even in the dim interior of the garage his face had paled. Not the Spanish Flu, I thought, but the memory of what happened next on the morning of the first of October had sobered him past his years.

"Go on, Kinsey. You'll feel better when you tell the story to the end." He didn't look like he believed me, but he nodded and continued.

"I thought I'd put the count sheet by the register at the front of the garage so I went through to the register and I was going to set the paper down when, when I saw Rudy." I caught my breath at the words. Rudy dead by seven, then. Would that help Lloyd?

"He was lying on the floor behind the stove at the end of the counter. I almost didn't see him because I was in a hurry, but when I went to put the paper down by the register I saw a foot sticking out at the end of the counter and I froze for a moment. At first I thought it was Dolf, drunk maybe or sick. Maybe his heart gave out. I didn't know. I stuck the count sheet in my pocket and went closer and it was Rudy! The front of his shirt was all bloody and his eyes were open, just staring up at nothing. I knew he was dead. I didn't have to go any closer to him, but I bent down and touched the back of my hand to his cheek anyway. He was already cool. Not cold exactly but no living warmth in him, either. You know what I mean?"

"Yes." I did know. Too well.

"There wasn't anything I could do for Rudy, Thea. It was too late for that, and then I got worried that someone would think I had a hand in Rudy getting killed."

"You? Kinsey, nobody would ever think that!"

"Maybe not at first, but if people found out I was involved in illegal hooch runs, they'd think I could be guilty of anything. You know that's true. Look at Lloyd. And then I thought, what if Leo thinks I killed his brother. He'd know I was there that morning." I could follow the panicked boy's thinking as he explained it.

"I went to the back of the garage and I don't know what I planned to do or if I planned to do anything because I heard the bell on the front door jingle. Somebody came in the garage and called Rudy's name. I think it was Lloyd's voice I heard, Thea. I think Lloyd came in then."

As terrible a story as it was, I still wanted to throw both arms around Kinsey and hug him. Rudy was already dead when Lloyd got there, and I had an eyewitness—well, at least an ear witness—to the fact; I couldn't wait to let Gus Davis know. Later I'd remember to my shame that my first involuntary thought hadn't been about Lloyd but about how gratified Gus Davis would be at the news. Not Lloyd but Gus. Something going on there that needed serious evaluation.

"You *think* it was Lloyd?"

"I never saw who it was." Kinsey's voice lowered. "I was scared. I thought that if someone knew about Rudy besides me, I wouldn't have to say anything about being in the garage at all. I went out the back door and down the alley where the track narrows before it connects again with the road leading north. I waited there a while and when no one raised a ruckus, I took a roundabout way back to the store, nobody the wiser."

"And the next week it was business as usual again?! I can't believe that! What did Leo say about Rudy's murder?"

"Not much, but it wasn't a secret that him and Rudy didn't get along. He was mad about it, I think, but mostly he was worried people might get wind of the operation if they were snooping around the garage. He wanted a quick trial and everything back to normal."

"Back to normal," I repeated. I thought that even Leo, warped as he was, couldn't have imagined that life would return to normal anytime soon after a murder.

We sat quietly, each of us lost in thought, until the boy finally said, "I guess you think I ought to tell the sheriff about what I done." The tone of misery in his voice matched the look on his face, but I was proud that he put words to the idea and said them aloud.

"Maybe, but not right now. There's someone else that needs to hear all this first."

"Cece?"

"Yes, Cece, but that's not who I was thinking of. You stay right here and wait for me. I can't tell you not to worry, Kinsey. I'm worried, too, but we'll work it out somehow. I'll be back as quick as I can. Stay right here. Promise?"

"All right," a hesitant concession I would have to trust.

I found Gus Davis still in his room at the Hansen House. He answered my knock and stood stock still, clearly astonished at the sight of me. After a moment he said, "Thea, about last night—"

I shook my head. "Not now. There's something you need to hear. Can you come?"

He didn't bother with questions, just nodded and grabbed his jacket from the back of a chair before pulling the door shut and following me down the hall.

Once outside, he asked only, "Where are we going?" and when I told him the shed where we parked the truck, he never made another peep. When we got as far as the front of Monroe's, I turned to him.

"Cece needs to join us," I said. "I'll get her and meet you at the door of the shed. Wait for us there, okay?"

I caught Raymond downstairs, told him I needed Cece for a while, and asked him to keep an eye on business.

"Flo's in today, too," Raymond told me. Like Gus, he was a man with enough savvy about females to recognize when one wasn't in the mood to answer many questions. "She's been helping out all week and happy to have the work. She'll be all right upstairs by herself. You want me to send Cecelia to your office?"

"No. Send her out to the shed where we keep the Olds. Tell her to come right away." If Raymond was surprised that I'd started holding meetings around the truck, he didn't look it. Maybe, knowing how much I enjoyed the Olds, he'd half expected it all along.

Eventually Gus and Cece, both mystified but smart enough not to pester for information, followed me into the shed where

Kinsey waited obediently, still on the stool where I'd left him. I was relieved to see him because while I wanted to trust him, a part of me wouldn't have been surprised if he'd bolted again. Lloyd in jail for two weeks and never a word from Kinsey! I understood his silence but still felt deceived. Kinsey stood when he saw the three of us, looked at Davis with some surprise but said nothing.

At the sight of her brother, Cece said his name with a sharp inflection to her voice, sent a questioning look in my direction, and halted.

"What's this about?" Something brittle and worried in her voice that I'd never heard before. I supposed my voice carried the same tone when speaking about Lloyd.

Understanding the uneasiness in her voice, I said gently, "Kinsey has something to tell you, Cece, something to tell Mr. Davis, too. It may take a while so find a box or a barrel you can sit on. Kinsey?"

I leaned against the side of the truck and listened to the story again. No embellishments this second time, but I thought he sounded more certain that it was Lloyd who'd entered Dolf's that morning calling Rudy's name. When Kinsey finally wound down, I couldn't decipher the look on his sister's face, maybe disappointment or disbelief, it was hard to tell, but I knew Gus Davis was thinking and thinking hard, his face without expression but something going on behind his eyes.

It was Cecelia that spoke first. "Oh, Kinsey." We all heard the sadness. "What would Mama say?"

Color crept up her brother's face; his eyes looked suddenly teary. The simple question had hit its target, had wounded him. I felt a brief and overwhelming pity for the boy. Kinsey and Cece. Lloyd and I. We were two pairs of the same suit. Each of us had lost one parent years ago and the other in the recent epidemic, and now both brothers were caught up in crime and in danger of jail. The War and the Spanish Flu continued to diminish us all.

Fortunately, Gus Davis took control of the conversation, and I think we all welcomed his prosaic tone.

"Let me be sure I've got this straight, Kinsey. You're certain you were at Dolf's around six thirty the morning of Wednesday, October first. You enter by the alley doors that aren't locked. You're in the back of the garage counting crates and bottles for thirty to forty minutes before you find Rudy's body. During that time you don't hear a thing from the front of the garage, not a shot, not a voice, not a whistle, not a cough, not a thing. Is that right?"

Kinsey nodded.

"And sometime between quarter past and half past seven you hear someone enter the front door and call Rudy's name. The person's voice sounded like it might have been Lloyd Hansen. Did I get it right?"

Kinsey nodded again.

Gus's gaze met mine briefly and he gave a quick, forthright nod. He didn't smile—how could he with both Kinsey and Cecelia watching him with anxious eyes—but I knew he wanted to. This was really good news for Lloyd.

Cecelia turned to her brother. "Kinsey, you let Lloyd sit in jail for more than two weeks! How could you do that? Why didn't you say something?"

"Leo threatened him," I intervened, "and he was right to be afraid of Leo Stanislaw. He can be vicious, Cece. You've heard the talk. He threatened you, too, for that matter, so Kinsey was watching out for you."

Cece's mouth pulled into a straight, stubborn line. "You still should have said or done something."

Kinsey, stung by his sister's scold, retorted, "I did do something. I told Thea." At his words Cece, Gus, and Kinsey turned to look at me in a synchronized way that would have been comical if the situation hadn't been so blasted serious.

"What? You never—" I began and then let my voice dwindle away as I made sense of the comment. "The anonymous note about the Wednesday night pick-up. That was from you, wasn't it?"

"I knew you'd look into it, Thea, and maybe tell the sheriff. If someone started asking questions, I thought Leo might get spooked and move the business, maybe even call it off for a while, and then everything would be all right again. If Leo made himself scarce, I figured it would be safe enough for me to talk to Sheriff McGill, but that didn't happen. You never said a word about the note after I gave it to you so it was business as usual with Leo. He said he had commitments—that's the word he used—and with Lloyd locked up, he said no one would be paying any attention to the garage." After another silence, Kinsey concluded, "The note wasn't enough, I guess, and I'm sorry about Lloyd. I didn't know what to do. If I need to tell what I know at the trial, I'll do it." He swallowed hard. "And if I got to go to prison, then—"

"Prison!" Cece interjected, her initial shock wearing off and finally beginning to understand what it might come to if Kinsey told everything he knew.

"Leo won't like my talking so someone's got to promise to watch out for Cece or I won't admit a thing." Kinsey's mouth mimicked Cecelia's from just a few minutes ago, his lips set stubborn and straight.

Cece whirled toward Gus. "Kinsey won't go to prison, will he? Not if he tells the truth!" She still believed what we'd been told as children, I thought: tell the truth and you won't get into trouble. Admit your mistake and all is forgiven. But it didn't work like that any more, if it ever had. The war and fear and death of these last years had changed all the rules.

Gus had overturned an old tub into a seat. Now, without answering Cece, he leaned forward, elbows on his thighs, hands folded, and looked squarely at Kinsey.

"No one will hurt Cecelia. I give you my word. And you can't be forced to testify in a court of law about anything that might get you yourself into trouble. It's part of the Fifth Amendment. No person shall be compelled in any criminal case to be a witness against himself. That's what the Constitution says."

"But if I don't, Lloyd might not get out of jail."

Gus nodded. "That's right." He paused. "And my obligation as Lloyd's attorney is to get him out of jail."

"It's so complicated." Cece's soft comment echoed my thoughts exactly.

"Yes," agreed Gus, "it is, but just about every worthwhile thing is. It's really up to Kinsey whether he's willing to speak up and say what he knows." Gus held up a hand to keep Kinsey from speaking. "It's something for you to think about and talk over with your sister, Kinsey, and we need to be sure you're kept safe and sound while you do that. Leo Stanislaw is in town. I saw him. He pulled up in front of the jail in a big automobile and after what you told us, I bet he wants to know exactly what his father told McGill. For the time being, it would be smart to keep you two—" Gus waved a hand at the Carr siblings "—out of his way."

"They could stay with me," I volunteered, but Gus frowned at the idea.

"No."

"Why not?"

"It's just not a good idea, Thea."

I wanted to argue further but decided to add it to the list of things I planned to take up with him later. Instead, I asked Cecelia, "Does your mother's cousin still farm north of Scott City?" I'd met the man and his wife more than once and liked them.

When Cece nodded, I suggested, "Then why doesn't Gus take you and Kinsey there to visit for a couple days? You'll have time to think and talk and I can come get you early Monday morning before the trial."

I realized Gus Davis was going to put Kinsey on the stand no matter what the boy decided but that he preferred Kinsey to speak willingly and openly. I felt a stab of anxiety for Kinsey that might also have included a bit of guilt at my contribution to his predicament, yet I also experienced a simultaneous wave of hope as tangible as a breeze. Lloyd freed from those gray walls. Lloyd home. But at the cost of Kinsey's freedom. An ambiguous happiness. Cece was right. Truth seemed so complicated, all of a sudden.

Cece wanted to argue that she and her brother couldn't just appear on their cousin's doorstep uninvited, but Kinsey had grasped the reprieve more quickly than she.

"Dave's always said we were welcome to visit. At Mother's funeral, he told us to come any time and stay as long as we wanted. We should do it, Cece."

"But I'm due at the store."

"Raymond said Flo's there now," I told her, "and she wants the work. We'll be all right for a few days."

Poor Cece. One minute straightening the glove display and the next fleeing to Scott City for an unannounced weekend visit. No wonder she still looked befuddled.

"All right, but just until Monday," Cece's reluctance clear in her voice.

"Daybreak Monday," I assured her. "I promise."

"We need to pack a little something."

"Kinsey can wait here while you do that." I had the plan in my head and outlined it for the others. "You pack a suitcase and walk to the train station and Gus and Kinsey can pick you up there. Kinsey, you stay low in the back until you're out of Blessing." To Gus I said, "You remember the way to Scott City, don't you?"

"Yes, ma'am," with a little ripple of laughter in his voice. I didn't find the situation especially humorous but something I said had brought a quick smile.

"Then it's settled." I gave Cece a quick hug. "It's going to be fine. You'll see. I think you and Kinsey have some things to say to each other and it's better that you both stay out of Leo Stanislaw's way for a while. Kinsey may be exaggerating—" I didn't let Kinsey get in a word of protest "—but Leo's a bully and if he threatened Kinsey, I believe he'd find some pleasure in making good on those threats. Why take the chance? It's just until Monday."

Cece and Kinsey would talk about the situation over the next days and come to realize there was no easy answer, no guarantee of a happy ending, but if his sister was with him, I knew Kinsey would not try to run away from his responsibility to tell the truth. Once Lloyd's home, I told myself, I'll worry about Kinsey, and if it ends up that he needs a good lawyer, I'll know exactly where to find one.

Chapter 11

Thursday, October 16, 1919

$\mathcal{T}$he afternoon plodded along. After seeing Gus and Kinsey off, I walked to the end of the alley and noticed Leo Stanislaw's coupe coming south on Blessing's main street, Leo no doubt making the point that he was doing well and wanting to be sure everyone realized it. I detested the man but his vehicle was another thing entirely, a Paige Six-55 automobile in gleaming black. I'd seen it advertised in a newspaper and knew it had cost as much as my Olds Economy Truck, if not more. It was enclosed, besides. A rarity. I gave a moment's thought to what it would be like to ride through a crisp Kansas autumn evening protected from the elements.

Lost in thought, it took me a moment to realize that Leo had parked along the street, exited the driver's door, and now sauntered in my direction. I looked back at the warehouse door, considering the closest, safest escape because that's how I always felt at the thought of proximity with the man, even a meeting accidental and brief. I was suddenly thirteen again and confronted by something in Leo that I wasn't quite old enough to understand fully but was female enough to recognize as dangerous. My father gone, Lloyd in jail, Gus Davis on the road to Scott City, and no one to stand between Stanislaw and me. I straightened my shoulders and against every instinct took a step, a very small one but still a step, onto the empty walk and toward the approaching man. It was broad daylight, after all, a public setting, and the store's front door only a few feet away. Why should I allow the man to frighten me?

Leo, hatless with hair slicked back and gleaming, came to a stop in front of me, a shade too close, which I knew was his intention. If he expected me to take a step backwards, he was mistaken, however. I held my ground.

"I don't know what your plan is, but it won't work." No alcohol on his breath today. "Maybe you think some bullshit story about my dad running booze will be enough to keep people from remembering that your brother is a crazy coward of a murderer, but it won't make any difference. I won't let it. If the law doesn't take care of him, I will." He grinned suddenly. "I'll take care of you, too, Thea girl, and you might just like it, might say, O Leo, ride me again, ride me as hard as you can." Despite my desire not to react, I inhaled sharply.

"Don't ever speak to me like that again," I said and made myself meet his gaze.

"Or you'll do what exactly? Tell that lawyer about me? Hell, his kind are a dime a dozen. Put 'em in a uniform and they think everybody should bow in front of 'em. You should know by now, Thea, that I ain't the bowing kind."

Behind Leo, the store's door opened and a customer exited, conversing with someone behind her and heading in the opposite direction from where Leo and I stood. The second person stepped out onto the walk and approached us. Raymond. He came to a stop directly behind Leo so that Leo had to turn his head to see who it was.

"We need you inside, Thea," Raymond said without acknowledging Leo's presence. "There's a question about an order that was supposed to be in today." I looked past Leo and smiled at Raymond, although I imagine the smile might have appeared somewhat strained. Leo remained silent.

"Of course." I walked past Leo without any indication that he still stood there and followed Raymond inside. A few customers in the store looked over at me when we entered before turning back to whatever business had brought them there in the first place.

"Are you all right?" I smiled in response to Raymond's quiet question.

"Yes, thank you. Leo Stanislaw isn't a very nice man, but I'm all right." I paused. "I feel pretty certain we didn't expect any orders in today."

It was Raymond's turn to smile. "No? Then I must have gotten the day wrong."

As he walked away, I felt an affection for the older man that I couldn't remember experiencing before. Raymond needed to be added to a mental list that already included Father, Lloyd, and Gus. In the current climate of retribution and distrust I supposed it was more likely than not that an occasion would arise when no one would be available to step between Leo Stanislaw and me. I dreaded the idea and hated even more that I must walk around Blessing, a town that for most of my life had offered nothing but peace and security, dogged by fear and suspicion. Even when Lloyd was found not guilty and was home again—*when*, not *if*—normal life would not and could not resume if we had not discovered who it was that killed Rudy Stanislaw. Living out the rest of my life in that ignorance, never knowing for all the years to come who among the people I walked with and talked with had a heart cold enough to face a young man and pull the trigger to his death seemed an unbearable prospect.

I joined my grandmother, uncle, and aunt at the hotel for supper after I closed the store. I knew from a visit with Lloyd at the end of the day that Uncle Carl had spent time at the jail almost immediately upon his return from Topeka. I wouldn't have expected anything less. Lloyd was only two years old when Uncle Carl's brother died in the far distant country of China, and when Aunt Louisa's brother, our Uncle Arnie, died as a soldier in the Philippines that same year, I believe Uncle Carl made it his mission to act as uncle for both sides of the family. Whatever long-ago motivation and emotion had turned him into an exemplary uncle, it was a comfort to have him home. Lloyd thought the world of Uncle Carl, and I felt the same.

I would be hard-pressed to say the same thing about Aunt Louisa, however. Too much like her mother. She and Grandmother were as alike as the proverbial peas in a pod. The family managed to get along without indulging in bouts of fisticuffs because we knew that besides a definite opinion about any topic under discussion, each woman also possessed a kind heart. The one trait softened the other. I loved them both, besides, and sometimes loving someone makes all the difference in the world.

Aunt Louisa would have started right in on the problem at hand, Lloyd in jail for murder and what was being done about it, but I put up a hand and smiling said, "Since that's the first thing I think about in the morning and the last thing before I fall asleep, rest assured we will certainly talk about it, but first, I want to apologize for not letting you know about Lloyd before you read about him in the paper. It was my fault and I'm sorry." That obligatory task done, I continued on a lighter note. "Now tell me all about Bev and Barb. Are they settled in? Do they live close to each other? Are they happy?"

Besides being opinionated and kind, my aunt was also intelligent. She took a look at my face, saw something there that convinced her that her daughters and not Lloyd might be a better topic of conversation at the moment, and without hesitating shifted into a detailed and sometimes quite humorous description of my twin cousins' new lives in Topeka. Uncle Carl chimed in once in a while but it was Aunt Louisa's show and we all enjoyed it.

Once we finished the meal and Lizzy cleared the table, however, we settled in Grandmother's front room and the silence that settled on our little group indicated that it was my turn to talk.

I told them as much as I knew. Well, that's not exactly true. Of course, I didn't mention that I wandered the moonlit streets of Blessing dressed in Lloyd's clothes. Not a one of them was ready for that information, if they'd even believed me. But I told them what I knew about the crime itself, about Gus Davis, and about the alley activity of the night before. I also told them about Kinsey Carr's role and what he heard and didn't hear the morning of Rudy's death. When I finished, I expected that Grandmother or Aunt Louisa would be the first to speak, but the two women turned toward my uncle wordlessly. I couldn't ever remember such a circumstance before, but then no one in the family had ever been arrested for murder before. I supposed that could explain their unusual reticence.

"That sounds hopeful, Thea, very hopeful, but I talked to Lloyd this afternoon and he didn't say a word about it."

"He doesn't know yet," I explained. "I didn't think it was my place to tell him. Gus will want to talk to him about it and since he isn't back from Scott City yet, I figured he could tell Lloyd tomorrow about what Kinsey said."

"What about Kinsey?" asked Uncle Carl. "Do you believe him? I never thought the boy was a liar, but then I never would have expected him to be mixed up with Leo Stanislaw running illegal alcohol out of Dolf's garage, either."

I pictured the look on Kinsey's pale face earlier in the afternoon, how scared he was and ashamed and anxious not to disappoint his sister. Fourteen, maybe, yet he seemed nothing but a child to me.

"I do believe him," I replied. "I think he got caught up in something and then didn't know how to get out of it."

"It happens," commented my grandmother. I looked at her in surprise; she was not generally a woman tolerant of human weakness. Catching the surprise in my expression, she gave a small, grim smile. "I may not give the impression that I'm as human as the rest of the world, Thea, but I am. It's not all that hard to start down a road and then not know how to turn around." Her remark made me wonder about her past, her life with my grandfather, her lifetime in Blessing, Kansas. Things there that she'd never shared, I thought, more secrets. I felt surrounded by them. Bewildered by them.

"About Davis," my uncle said, changing the subject, perhaps as surprised by his mother-in-law's admission as I was. "Lloyd praises the man so much that I almost thought I missed the Second Coming. I wondered why I hadn't met him yet, but now that you told us he's driving the Carrs to Scott City, I understand why. What's your take on him, Thea?"

My take on Gus Davis. A man of contradictions, I thought. A common enough man at first glance, with nothing remarkable about him, conservative suit and tie and a notebook in his pocket. He could have been a store keeper same as I. But then there was the man that pulled himself up and into Dolf's garage as lithe and graceful as a cat, confident, enjoying the risk of the moment. Lean, brown face and hazel eyes where the shadows of memories sometimes lingered, broad shoulders and long legs. An intelligent lawyer, serious about his vocation, but on occasion something much more than that. I remembered the way his voice had sounded when he'd stepped between Leo Stanislaw and me after Rudy's funeral. No lawyer at that moment but soldier and leader of soldiers, aggressive and accustomed to violence, one who'd step into a fight and perhaps even enjoy it. Gus Davis had deceived me about the previous night and done some damage to my feelings, yet of everyone in my present world, he seemed the person without secrets. What was I to make of him? I was twenty years old, had never been out of the state of Kansas, and thought myself the most uncomplicated person in all of Blessing. How could Gus Davis and I have anything more in common than a mutual desire to see my brother free and home?

Too introspective for discretion, I became aware that the other three people in the room looked at me with expectation and, yes, with curiosity, too. I didn't know what my take on Gus Davis was, not really, but I needed to say something.

"He's a good lawyer." I picked my words with care. "As good a lawyer, I think, as he was a soldier, and Lloyd says there weren't many men better or more highly thought of than Captain Davis. He believed Lloyd to be innocent from the start, which helped Lloyd's state of mind. He has a plan for Lloyd's defense, too, and with what we know from Kinsey Carr thrown in, I think there's a good chance we'll have Lloyd home pretty soon."

"I'm surprised you don't sound more pleased about that, Thea." My grandmother was not a woman to miss much.

"Not guilty isn't the same as innocent. I know Lloyd didn't kill Rudy Stanislaw, but some one did. If we never know who, there will always be people that believe it was Lloyd, whatever the jury says. That's a weight he'd carry around on his shoulders all the rest of his life."

"But he'd be walking around free and clear," Aunt Louisa protested, "whatever people think."

"Not really all that free," Uncle Carl said. He met my gaze and nodded in quiet understanding. "Lloyd already carries a heavy weight of memories from the war. He doesn't need more burdens and he might not be as free and clear as you expect. Being home doesn't mean being free. Thea's right. Not guilty isn't the same as innocent."

We were quiet for a while before I rose, deposited a kiss on three cheeks and said good-night. I knew they wanted to talk further about Lloyd and maybe about me, too, and I wanted to leave them to it.

I had a dark and uneventful stroll home, following the walk along the main street that stretched from one end of Blessing to the other. There was still some foot traffic out and about, but not much. It took some nerve for Grandma Liza to call Laramie, Wyoming, *Old Podunk* considering where she had lived all her life: Blessing, Kansas. One main street with more alleys than side streets. The Holiday Sugar factory that sat north of town was Blessing's largest employer, and that wasn't saying very much. We were an assortment of businesses so small and pedestrian that when the Rexall Drug Store opened five years earlier, the mayor called a holiday and ordered a parade to celebrate. There weren't many people still alive to remember the town's violent Civil War history, but the legacy of those times remained. The citizens of Blessing appreciated a tranquil town and a tranquil life. The façade of Monroe's Emporium showed in the light of the street lamps as I neared home. Beyond it lay the train station, and then nothing but sunflowers and prairie. I knew I should be thinking of Lloyd's homecoming and I was, to a point. But I had lived in Blessing all my life, and as much as I would have liked to see more of the world than what was shown in newsreels at the movie house, as much as I wanted to see it up close and in real life, I couldn't find any reason why I wouldn't live out my life buying and selling tea kettles and long johns at Monroe's Emporium right here in Blessing, Kansas. What else would I do? Where else would I go? I thought Uncle Carl's earlier words were wiser than he realized and didn't apply only to Lloyd: *Being home doesn't mean being free.*

I dressed for bed but still too restless for sleep, made myself a cup of hot tea and sat at the kitchen table. What a difference twenty-four hours could make! Last night at this time there'd been no alley raid, no knowledge of Kinsey's presence at the garage the morning of the murder, no threats from Leo, and no need to spirit the Carrs away for their own protection. No vague feeling of being somehow tricked by Gus Davis, either, no smart of betrayal, however unintentional and necessary. All that balance of hope and harm was still in the future.

I was startled by a knock at the back door and somewhat unnerved. The kitchen wall clock showed it was after ten o'clock and no one came visiting that late, but then I remembered the last time Gus had taken the truck on the road. He'd stopped by late that evening, too. Maybe Laramie, Wyoming, had different rules of etiquette and it was perfectly common there to roust people out of bed for late night chitchat. But I wasn't even close to sleep and I wanted to see him, anyway, so I threw on one of my father's old cardigan sweaters that still hung by the back door and stepped onto the back porch and into a cool clear night.

Gus stood with his hands in his pockets looking out at the view from the top of the back porch steps. At the sound of the kitchen door opening, he turned to face me but did not step any closer.

"Sorry it's so late," he said.

"It's all right. I wasn't asleep or even near it. Too much to think about." When he didn't respond, I said, "I take it you got Cece and Kinsey delivered safely to Scott City."

"Yes, no problem there and I left them in good hands. That cousin of theirs is a big man. I drew a map to get you to his house when you pick them up for the trial Monday morning." He pushed a folded paper toward me, which I took and shoved into a sweater pocket without bothering to open it. No response from me this time. "Thea, I—" He paused and restarted. "About last night. I know you think pretty low of me right now, and I understand why. I can't even say it's not deserved. I'm sorry it happened that way. But I gave my word to McGill and I couldn't go back on it, no matter how much I wanted to."

"I know."

"It's not that I don't trust you. I hope you know that."

"I think I do."

"And I'd never hurt you, not for all the world. There's no woman anywhere I'd rather share things with or be with, but I gave my word and a man has to live by his word. In the end, it's all he has of his own."

We were approaching the black night of an October new moon, but the cloudless sky still held enough waning moonlight for me to see his expression. He was keeping his distance but watching me intently. No apology in his expression but something more, something he wanted me to understand about him, understand and accept. It was clear to me, although I didn't know why I was so certain, that what he'd just told me was important to him and my response was even more important.

I gave passing thought to the idea that it might sometimes be uncomfortable or frustrating living with a principled man but decided, not misunderstanding what I saw on his face as he looked at me, that there would be enough good to offset any passing inconvenience. Then I went up to him, put both arms around his neck, and pulled his face down close enough for me to kiss him, a good, long, and unambiguous kiss. Never do anything halfway, Grandma Liza had told me on more than one occasion, and her advice paid dividends that night.

No doubt Gus was startled. Of all the reactions he might have expected following his stiff little confession, I imagine being thoroughly kissed was at the bottom of the list. But it hardly took him a second to get past his surprise and shift into another emotion, something so powerful that I think we both ended up being surprised by the intensity of feeling we shared. I was twenty years old and had certainly been kissed before, once even by Joe Buchanan, who was as practiced at romancing girls as his father was at the law. That had been enjoyable enough, even when I had to push him away and remind him sternly that I was his best friend's sister and he was going too fast and too far.

But I never once gave a thought to pushing Gus Davis away. Truth be told, I couldn't imagine he could ever go too fast or too far for me but thought it would be a lot of fun to find out if that was possible.

When he finally pulled his mouth away from mine he pushed back far enough to say, "Good lord, Thea. What are you thinking of?"

"I'd make you blush if I answered that truthfully," I murmured and pushed myself closer to him. It was a cold night and among other things, Gus Davis was a warm man.

"Thea!"

The surprise in his voice made me laugh. "We're two decades into the twentieth century, Gus. Maybe it's different in Laramie, but in the rest of the country, it's now accepted that some girls enjoy kissing—and other peripheral activities—as much as boys."

"You being one of those girls?" As usual, the lilt of laughter in his voice had an effect on me that I decided could only be satisfied with further action.

"Yes, indeed," I said and kissed him again to prove the fact.

I don't know how long we stood joined together there on the back porch of the house where his mother grew up and my father died, but not long enough. Eventually, though, Gus's sense of propriety got the better of him. My father's cardigan wasn't all that heavy and I was in my night dress, after all, so I suppose he was wise to draw away.

He got his breathing under control and started to speak, cleared his throat because his voice was so hoarse he might have spent the past minutes cheering on a horse race instead of holding me, and finally stated, "Well, I never expected that." I found his bewildered, slightly confused tone totally gratifying.

"Me, either," I replied, "but everything that's happened these last two weeks has come at me out of the blue."

At my words, he put his hands on my shoulders, pushed me farther away, and stepped past me to hold open the backdoor. When he spoke, his voice was back to normal.

"I know it's been a difficult time for you. You should go inside and try to get some sleep. We'll talk in the morning at breakfast. I have some other information, but now isn't the moment to share it." I just stared at him, suddenly cold and back in the real world of murder and lies, jail cells and court rooms. "Go inside, Thea. Everything will work out," his voice so tender I could have indulged in those fiddle tears he told me about.

Instead of tears, I smiled and moved to the doorway where he stood with the screen door open. "All right. Breakfast, it is."

I stepped past him into the kitchen, turning to face him when he said my name in a low voice. We stood close once again with the threshold between us. Close but not touching.

"Yes?" I said.

"I'd never hurt you." An odd thing to say but I thought he probably imagined me confused and vulnerable, which I wasn't. Not about him, anyway.

"I know."

I felt as I had that evening at the Hansen House when he'd talked about the war, as if he were the one that needed comfort. Gus Davis looked and fought and kissed like a man but there was something boyish about him, too. Something that needed to be protected. Another contradiction. I smiled again so he'd understand that I really did know and wished him goodnight as he closed the screen door.

"Good night, Thea," he said and nothing more, perhaps already regretting his lapse, the way he'd slid from suited attorney to passionate man, crossing some personal line he had set and of which only he was aware. It had been the Gus Davis of dangerous forays and midnight adventures, the soldier and spy and risk taker who'd just kissed me. Even a small town girl with limited experience could recognize there was nothing common or decorous about the way the man kissed.

I heard his feet descend on the wooden porch steps and pushed the inside kitchen door shut. Then I simply stood there in the middle of the floor unmoving, bemused, and as happy as I could ever remember being. My brother in jail and a murderer on the loose, but happy, despite it all. Nothing had really changed about the future I'd contemplated on my walk home. My tombstone might still read *born and raised and lived and died in Blessing, Kansas,* but while the future might not have changed, I thought something inside of me had.

"I believe," I said aloud into the empty kitchen, "that I love Gus Davis," astonished that a condition so significant could happen in a mere ten days. No love at first sight cliché—not Mary Pickford and Douglas Fairbanks meeting at a war bond rally and falling into each other's arms immediately, their peripheral spouses and the war effort suddenly minor annoyances compared to a mutual obsession—yet some kind of deep feeling for the man had settled into my bones when I wasn't looking, a feeling that gave him the power to hurt me even with words he didn't say. So while the present continued to march along with an inexorable predictability, Lloyd's trial just three days away and Leo Stanislaw roaming the streets like a jungle predator, I still felt happy. For the time being, loving Gus Davis made all the difference in the world, and I thought—feared?— that it might always be so.

Chapter 12

Friday, October 17 - Sunday, October 19, 1919

I anticipated some kind of awkwardness when I sat down across from Gus in the Hansen House dining room the next morning, had, in fact, worried a bit about it as I made my morning pilgrimage: jail to store to hotel. But when I dropped into the chair at the table, Mavis swooped over and poured coffee, and by the time she asked if I wanted the usual and I replied that I wanted to step out of my routine and have my eggs scrambled instead of over easy and she laughed and gave me the usual pat on the shoulder as if I were a clever child that needed affirmation, I was able to lift my head, meet my companion's gaze, and wish him a good morning.

He lowered the paper he was reading, smiled, and wished me the same. My, I thought to myself, aren't we two impressive customers? I found myself smiling a little at the cool temperature at the table.

"You said you had some other information," I reminded him without specifics. "Is it a good time to share it now?" I nodded toward his breakfast plate. "Don't wait for me. Your hotcakes will get cold."

"Yes, and thank you," he replied, reaching for the syrup as he spoke. He forked a piece buttermilk pancake into his mouth, swallowed, and went on, "I thought you should know about the subpoenas."

"Subpoenas?" Whatever I'd expected him to share, it certainly had nothing to do with subpoenas.

"They're documents issued by the court to—"

"Gus," I interrupted, growing annoyed at the way the whole morning was progressing and forgetting for the moment that I had pronounced my love for him into an empty kitchen just a few hours earlier, "I know what a subpoena is. I can even spell the word. What about them?"

He took another bite of his breakfast, took a generous sip of coffee, and lifted the napkin from his lap for a decorous pat to the lips. Which I thought, for just a moment, twitched at the corners. Was the man laughing at me?

"I'm sorry. Of course, you know what a subpoena is. I thought you should know that while I was in Scott City yesterday I asked the court to issue subpoenas for a number of people."

I could guess at most of the names but asked "Such as?" so I'd have the facts.

He ticked off the names on his hands. "Kinsey and Cecelia Carr, Charles Holiday, Leo Stanislaw and Dolf Stanislaw. Mort will serve the papers today to the last three and Judge Plumquist said he'd arrange to get them to the Carrs while they were at their cousin's there in Scott City."

Mavis brought my breakfast then and refilled our coffee cups, and even after she left I was quiet for a while thinking about the six people Gus had listed.

"Enough for reasonable doubt, do you think?" I asked finally.

"It never does to be too confident, but I'd say yes, more than enough."

"Time will tell." I decided he was right about feeling too confident and measured my reply. Changing the subject abruptly enough to make Gus blink, I said, "My uncle and aunt got back from Topeka yesterday, and Uncle Carl wants to meet you. Don't be surprised if he comes knocking at your door."

"I'd like to meet him, too. Lloyd thinks pretty highly of his uncle."

"Lloyd and I both love him; he's a good man. Do you have uncles and aunts?" I decided we'd amicably consumed enough hotcakes, eggs, and coffee that it was safe to ask a personal question.

Gus shook his head but then amended his answer. "No living blood uncles or aunts on either side, but I have an Uncle Billy and he's a good man, too."

I recalled the name from my grandmother's conversation with Gus the first time they'd met. "That boy, that slow boy," Grandma Liza had said. Slow maybe, I thought, but loved, nevertheless, and wasn't that the more important detail?

I smiled at Gus and raised my coffee cup for one last sip before pushing away from the table when out of the blue Gus said, "About last night, Thea."

I managed not to splutter my coffee. Instead, trying for a modicum of sophistication, I remained quiet, just looked at him over the rim of my cup and raised both brows in what I hoped was an expression of mild interest.

"Yes?" Inside I gave myself a stern warning not to kick him under the table if he made the poor choice to apologize. Hopefully, he knew enough about women to recognize that no girl would consider an apology at being kissed as a compliment. I certainly didn't want to hear how much Gus Davis regretted taking me in his arms and kissing me like there was no tomorrow, an unfortunate, regrettable mistake and something no mature man in his right mind would ever contemplate.

Happily for my feelings and his shin, he did not say anything even close to *I'm sorry*. In fact, he didn't say anything at all for what seemed like a very long time, so long I envisioned breakfast becoming luncheon becoming supper, the two of us still seated there in our odd little tableau when Mavis dimmed the dining room lights to signify the kitchen was closed. He had brought up the topic, however, so if it took until closing I was determined not to be the one to break the silence.

"What I did last night was what I want to do every time I see you, Thea. I don't know when or how that happened, exactly, but there it is." Not an apology, at all, I thought with satisfaction, and set down my coffee cup. "But—" I'd guessed a *but* was coming and waited to hear more. "I don't think you're quite yourself right now."

"No?"

"Thea," he said, leaning toward me across the table, "in the last two years you watched your father die, took over the running of the Emporium, and worried about Lloyd all the while he was at the Front. After he got home, you've had to live with constant nightmares and a threat of violence from someone who at times must have seemed like a stranger to you instead of a loved brother. Then a childhood friend is murdered and that same brother ends up in jail accused of the crime, running the very real risk of going to prison for the rest of his life. Any woman—any man, for that matter—might find her emotions off balance under those circumstances. I would never take advantage of you, but I think that's what I did last night."

"I wonder if we're talking about the same thing." I don't know how he expected me to respond to his pretty little speech, but I'm certain my reasonable yet perplexed tone took him aback. His eyes narrowed the way I'd come to expect whenever he was in serious thought. "Because my recollection is that you didn't make the first move. As far as I could tell, you'd have been content with a game of checkers."

A slow, small smile from him and the words, "Not checkers, Thea. I always lose."

"It's true," I went on, "that the last two years have changed everything I thought about life, but I am not a shrinking violet, I am not off balance, and you cannot make me do anything I don't fully and absolutely want to do. The one thing I've learned from the last two years is that life is awfully short. Didn't you learn that in the war, Gus? Didn't you?"

Something in the depths of Gus Davis's eyes flickered and then flared with enough warmth to burn up the space between us, light the tablecloth afire, scorch the table, and singe the flatware. For just a moment there was so much heat between us, it might have set the whole dining room ablaze. Then he sat back in his chair and smiled at me. Warmth in the smile, too.

"Yes."

"Then stop worrying about taking advantage of me. I won't let that happen."

"After the trial, when Lloyd's home and I've finished what I'm tasked with right now, we'll talk about this again."

"Finally, something we can agree on," I said, as sensible as he in wanting my brother to have legal representation without distraction, and asked as follow up, "Will it be a long trial, do you think?"

"I'd be surprised, but Ben Marquart's a good prosecutor and I won't underestimate him."

Our conversation was back on safe ground just in time because over Gus's shoulder I saw Uncle Carl enter the hotel dining room and head directly for the corner table where Gus and I sat. I escaped back to the store after introducing the two men, simultaneously glad and disappointed to be back in the safe mercantile world where I passed my time and spent my life. An interesting morning, I thought, and my breakfast companion an interesting man. Well, truth be told, I found Gus Davis more than *interesting* but made myself banish other adjectives for him that came to mind. I had a store to run and Gus wasn't the only one that needed to stay focused on the tasks at hand.

The following day, Saturday, was wonderfully uneventful. Except for my regular stops at the jail before I opened the store and again after closing, I stayed at the Emporium all day, perused catalogs, wrote up orders, reviewed receipts, and walked the floors with Raymond. I thought I was more restless and apprehensive than my brother, who surprised me with his good humor and apparent lack of anxiety.

"Your trial is two days away," I pointed out to him.

"Yes, which means I'm two days closer to being home." In an extraordinary gesture Lloyd gave me a hug. "Don't look so worried, Thea. The captain's got everything under control." My brother comforting me. That hadn't happened in a very long time.

Part of his improved mood could be attributed to the fact that Dolf Stanislaw had been moved to the jail at the county seat. Mort McGill said state authorities had some pointed questions they wanted to ask Dolf and didn't want to have to travel to Blessing to get to him. With the attention the country was putting on Prohibition, Mort added that he wouldn't be surprised if someone from the federal government showed up with a second set of questions. Poor Dolf, I thought. Except for an infrequent personal lapse, I believe I'm as law abiding as the next person, but it seemed out of proportion to place so much emphasis on the transport and consumption of alcohol. Even as a child, I could see that the more a person was told not to do something the more likely he was to consider doing it. I didn't think prohibiting liquor would do anything but make it more attractive. I felt a sudden, sharp pain of longing for my father, who would have enjoyed discussing the matter from both sides and would have made me laugh whichever side he took. But he was gone, of course. As was Rudy. Poor Dolf, I thought again.

I missed Cece's cheerful presence and to my surprise missed Kinsey even more. The boy was a ready figure around the store: warehouse help, box lugger, and all around good lackey. I banished the mental picture of Kinsey in jail. It would not come to that, I hoped, but if it did we'd have to cross the bridge when it was time. Lloyd free and home first, then Kinsey. One innocent. The other not so innocent, just young and more foolish than criminal. Perhaps a judge would see it that way, too.

I joined Grandma Liza for supper, then trudged home and tried to read Willa Cather's *My Antonia*. I had enjoyed her first two books about the pioneers and supposed it was simply that my mind was too full of real life to make room for fiction. My mother, Marie Sullivan, lived with her parents and siblings in a sod house on the outskirts of Blessing until the day she married my father and moved into town. She was a bride at seventeen, a mother at eighteen, and gone from my life before my sixth birthday. I didn't have the chance to ask her about her early years, yet Cather's portrayal of life on the vast plains touched close to my heart. *My Antonia* could just as well have been titled *My Marie*.

I fell asleep in the kitchen rocker with the book open on my lap when the thud of the front door knocker brought me out of what promised to be a comfortable doze. Not Gus at the door was my first thought as I awoke with a start—by now he was accustomed to the back porch and the kitchen—so who, then?

Charles Holiday was nowhere on the list of people I expected to see at my front door but there he stood, a dark figure on a dark October night. He took off his hat when I opened the door and a streak of moonlight made his eyes gleam. For some reason the sight brought an involuntary shiver.

Hoping he had not noticed the small shudder, I said, "Mr. Holiday!" without bothering to hide the surprise in my voice.

"Miss Hansen." We stood looking at each other until he continued in a quiet voice, "May I step inside? I promise not to keep you very long."

"Of course." I opened the heavy front door further and he stepped just across the threshold leaving the door open. To a passerby on the street, the two of us would have appeared as indistinct silhouettes against the light cast by the wall sconce in the hallway.

"I'm sorry to bother you this late. I've just come from the hotel. I tried to speak to your brother's lawyer, but he said he felt conversation between the two of us wasn't appropriate and closed the door on me."

I had the fleeting wish that I'd done the same but said, "He's right, I'm sure. This close to the trial and you a witness." My words caused a grimace to flicker across his face.

"I thought you might have some influence with him, Miss Hansen."

"Influence? I'm sorry, Mr. Holiday, but I'm not following you."

"You know as well as I that the only reason I've been summoned as a witness is to give some kind of despicable credence to the fiction about my daughter and Rudy Stanislaw."

"Are you quite certain it's fiction?"

"Of course, it is."

"Then why are you so concerned about it that you wanted to meet with Mr. Davis? And in his absence, felt compelled to knock on my front door?"

From the look on his face he was not especially pleased with my tone but his voice remained calm. "You know this town as well, maybe better than I. Once Mr. Davis asks his questions, regardless of whether there's any validity to them or not, some people will believe the inference. I'm sure Mr. Davis hopes some of the jury do the same. True or not, kind or not, won't matter." His observation had just enough truth in it to make me briefly uncomfortable. "It isn't right that my daughter's reputation and her life here in Blessing should be stained by innuendo and rumor." His voice shook at the end of his words and I felt a moment of sympathy for the man.

"I understood that Rachel was travelling."

"She and my wife are visiting my wife's aunt in New Hampshire. I don't expect them back for quite a while."

In nine months or so, I thought, but replied with as much enthusiasm as I could muster, "How lovely for them! And if what you fear really occurs, there will be plenty of time for any rude talk to die down, don't you think?"

"Miss Hansen, I am a father, the same as Stephen Hansen was. I care for my daughter as your father cared for you. I'm asking you to find a way to keep Rachel's name and my presence out of the courtroom. I understand that you feel you must fight on your brother's behalf, but do you truly believe that dishonoring an innocent young girl is the way to do that?"

There was so much wrong in what Charles Holiday said that I didn't know where or how to begin to respond. I had never been afraid of my father in all my life, could never have imagined speaking about him with the same words and tone Rachel had used about her father in my presence. And while Rachel Holiday might be young, I didn't think she qualified as an innocent. It wasn't just about intimacy with Rudy Stanislaw, either, but about growing up fearful and oppressed and silenced. That could rob a girl of her innocence, too. Yet when I studied Charles Holiday's face, I couldn't bring myself to say any of that. He was a man difficult to read, and while he might be as worried about his own reputation as he was about his daughter's, I thought I detected something that could have been sincerity in his voice.

"Testimony about Rachel and Rudy might not be necessary, Mr. Holiday."

"Because—"

"Because there's information more pertinent to Lloyd's innocence and a reliable witness to back it up that may make it a very short trial."

"I don't understand." He was the one not following now.

"I can't say any more, Mr. Holiday, but I'll pass your concern on to Mr. Davis." I had the feeling that for some reason my ambiguous comments had worsened Charles Holiday's mood, not improved it, but he was a man used to having the answers, used to authority and his own way. Perhaps the idea that I, a female young enough to be his daughter, held a subtle kind of power over him upset his sense of order.

He nodded. "Thank you."

I watched him as he walked down the front steps, stopping at the bottom to place his hat back on his head straightforward and centered. Nothing jaunty for Charles Holiday. Finally, I closed the door and for no reason I could articulate snapped the lock firmly in place. I'd gone to sleep many nights without doing so, locking doors in Blessing still the exception to the usual practice, but something about the last few minutes had seemed off balance to me.

Perhaps the brief conversation with Mr. Holiday was exactly what it appeared to be: a worried father concerned for his daughter and desperate to protect her. But I thought another motive might have been at work there, too, even if I had no clue what the other motive could be.

Sunday morning the Hansens of Blessing, Kansas, sat in their usual pew, fifth from the front on the pulpit side, and I had the irreverent thought that we could have been mistaken for either a football team or a defensive military line of soldiers. I was at the end of the pew with Aunt Louisa and Uncle Carl to my right and Grandmother in her wheelchair in the side aisle to my left. She did not always manage to attend the worship service, but the October morning was bright and dry, and in good weather, Uncle Carl could push her chair easily from the hotel to the church. Our presence was intended to announce that we were confident of Lloyd's innocence and had not one guilty thing on our collective consciences. It was true, too, as long as I didn't take into consideration my own unlawful complicity in breaking and entering. I thought it best not to spend too much time considering my individual failings. Collectively, we Hansens sent a clear and unspoken message by our unconcerned presence at the worship service, and I only hoped the good Lord understood that we meant no disrespect in the process.

We were ushered out down the center aisle at the end of the service, and I was surprised to see Gus Davis sitting at the back of the church, waiting his turn to exit. Outside, I gave Grandmother a quick kiss on the cheek and told her not to wait for me for Sunday dinner. I wasn't hungry, I said, and had other tasks on my schedule.

Before Uncle Carl pushed off with the chair, Grandma Liza saw Gus shaking hands with the pastor in the church doorway and gave me an enigmatic look, one both curious and knowing, but she contented herself with murmuring, "Of course, you do." As usual, not a woman to miss much.

I waited for Gus at the foot of the walk leading up to the church, nodding and smiling at passing parishioners as I did so. I was a member of this church all my life, grew up with the congregation, rejoiced and grieved with them all, and still there were some that could not bring themselves to meet my gaze. Would a *good morning* have been so very difficult, even if they did think my brother a crazed murderer? But instead of feeling offended, I was only saddened. I had once thought that when Lloyd came home, my life would revert to what it had been, but I realized now that could never be. The war, the influenza, and now this trial had brought with them such profound change that the past was irrevocably and completely gone, to be replaced by a future still ambiguous and a little bit daunting. In its own way, Blessing was gone, too, and that was simply sad.

"A penny for those thoughts," Gus said, stopping beside me and smiling directly into my eyes. At the look on his face I felt my sadness, uncertainty, and apprehension dissolve like sugar in coffee. Here was a man to be trusted. No personal power to shape the future, of course, but someone with the necessary strength to make it bearable, perhaps even happy, not all the time but often enough to make life satisfying.

Much too soon to share these particular thoughts, I told myself, penny or not, and answered aloud, "I'm afraid you wouldn't get your money's worth."

Mrs. Tripp, whose aged grasp on reality continued to diminish although the same could not be said about the dear old woman's inherent kindness, stopped in front of me to ask after Lloyd.

"He's doing as well as can be expected," I answered cautiously, not certain what year she presently inhabited, and was rewarded by her smile.

She lifted one hand from the top of her cane to pat my arm and say, "It will all be over soon enough, I'm told," a true statement whether she meant the war or the trial. I nodded in safe agreement. She turned her eyes on Gus. "Is this your beau, Thea? I don't believe I recognize him."

Since I wasn't sure whether she was aware of the accusations against Lloyd and the imminent trial, I replied, "This is a friend of Lloyd's, Mrs. Tripp. Captain Davis."

Gus smiled, nodded, and touched the old woman's hand in a brief and somehow courtly gesture, saying as he did so, "How do you do, Mrs. Tripp? I'm happy to meet you."

She gave him a light tap on the arm. "Out of uniform, I see. Well, I don't blame you for that, although we girls always have a soft spot for a man in uniform." Her eyes lit with laughter. "Isn't that so, Thea?"

"Absolutely." Truer than she'd ever know, at least in my case.

"I'm going to my son's for dinner today so I haven't much time for chatter. You greet Lloyd for me when you next see him, Captain. That Lloyd's a good boy."

Gus agreed that Lloyd was a good boy and that he'd certainly greet him, and we watched her walk away, eighty-four but a mischievous sixteen inside. I felt unusually fond of her at the moment. After a minute or two and without any further words, Gus and I walked past the churchyard fence, but before we could cross the street in the direction of Blessing's main square, I heard, "Thea!" from behind us. A woman's voice called my name and by the southern lilt I knew who it was even before I stopped and turned.

"Good morning, Mrs. Buchanan." She had invited me more than once to use her first name, but try as I might, I could not get *Delta* to cross my lips.

Delta Buchanan sparkled. How else to describe her? Clear eyed with radiant skin, she might have been a woman half her age. Something was making her very happy. She held on to her husband's arm and the comparison couldn't have been more obvious. Ian Buchanan was as far from radiant as a man could be. I was almost shocked at how old he looked in the late morning sunlight. Gus removed his hat at Delta Buchanan's approach and took a step backwards. I thought that Gus always seemed unusually reticent in the Buchanans' presence and wondered what it was about the couple that made him uncomfortable. Looking at them standing in front of me, an attractive and dignified pair and clearly concerned on my behalf, I couldn't find a single reason to keep them at arms' length.

Mrs. Buchanan must have felt the same about me because after a pleasant greeting to Gus she gave me a warm hug and a kiss on the cheek.

"How lovely you look today, Thea! Doesn't she, Ian? My goodness, I couldn't say what's more blue, your eyes or that bright sky." Her southern inflections were clear and noticeable. "How are you holding up, my dear?"

"I'm just fine," my response one all of us recognized as rote and proper. I couldn't very well say I'm anxious and apprehensive to the point of insomnia. I'm frightened by a nameless, faceless murderer that has taken one life and seems perfectly willing to ruin another by allowing my brother to take the punishment for his crime. *I'm just fine* seemed a much simpler reply at the moment.

We crossed Main Street together and made after-church conversation on the other side: the fine weather for October, the harvest festival planned at the end of the month, how good it was to have Uncle Carl and Aunt Louisa home again, and then out of the blue Delta Buchanan gestured toward the corner where we stood and commented, "This is where the statue and the fountain will go. Isn't it perfect? Right here in the middle of town and right on this corner where everyone, citizens and visitors alike, will see it and several times a day, too."

I knew Gus was about to ask what statue, but before I could catch his eye with a warning shake of my head, Mrs. Buchanan turned to Gus and stated, "I wondered if you ever encountered my son at the Front, Mr. Davis. Joseph Buchanan?"

An infinitesimal pause that I hope only I caught before Gus answered, "Yes, I met him."

"I thought you might have if you served with Lloyd and Rudy. Those three boys were never far apart. My husband and I plan to erect a statue in honor of our brave boy right on this very corner."

"We're still in the petition and plan stage," Ian said, directing his words to Gus, "so it's still not a certainty that we'll get all the approvals we need. My wife, however, is a visionary, an impatient visionary, and not used to the rules and regulations of city hall."

Delta gave her husband's shoulder a light tap. "Nonsense. That's the lawyer in you talking," —she sent Gus a playful look— "which I'm sure is the same language Mr. Davis speaks, but I cannot imagine that there would be any opposition to our erecting a memorial for one of the city's own fallen heroes." At the words her face tightened and the playfulness dropped away so abruptly I was startled. It was as if a cloud had passed overhead, casting a shadow across her face

Ian Buchanan saw the change, too, and reached out for his wife's hand. He spoke quickly. "You're right, my dear. I'm acting like an old fuddy-duddy. We should let Thea and Mr. Davis get on their way. No doubt they have a lot on their minds with the trial tomorrow." All her sparkle was gone now.

"My son died at the Front, Mr. Davis. Did you know that?"

"I'm very sorry for your loss."

"Thank you."

Ian tucked his wife's hand under his arm and turned away from Gus and me. Delta, in a way trapped against her husband, was forced to move with him but she turned to speak over her shoulder.

"Perhaps you could speak a few words at the unveiling, Mr. Davis, since you knew our Joe." Ian said something very softly to his wife that I could not hear and she leaned her head against his arm for a moment, a touching and affectionate gesture, before she straightened and picked up her pace. I heard her murmur something in return and give a low laugh, but I thought she had not reclaimed her bright original happiness.

Neither Gus nor I spoke for a long moment, watching the two Buchanans' departure with such serious attention one might have thought the husband and wife were exotic zoo animals we'd never seen before.

Finally, I asked, "Do you want to tell me about Joe Buchanan?" Gus didn't protest or deny my question's inference.

"I don't know, Thea. I don't know if it's something you need to know or even should know."

"Worried about my female sensibilities?"

The words made him grin. "I know better than that."

"Good." Reflective pause. "I think."

He grinned once more before he suggested, "Let's walk a while. Do you have the time?"

"I'm not the one scheduled to appear in a major trial tomorrow morning. If you have time, so do I."

We walked north along Main Street, past the imposing façade of the Town Hall and the stately front porch of the Hansen House, crossed Lincoln Avenue, commented on the new home of the Fire Department and the old newspaper office that still cranked out a weekly edition of the Blessing Banner. It seemed to me that my companion found a measure of comfort in the commonplace and I could tell it would be no use to try to hurry the conversation along to Joe Buchanan. If that topic came up at all, it would come up in Gus Davis's good time.

Eventually, we found ourselves at the gate of the old Lutheran cemetery where we'd stopped a few days before. He didn't go into the cemetery, just stood with his hands in his pockets looking out over the small fence at the seemingly endless line of headstones and grave markers.

"I can understand why Mrs. Buchanan would want some kind of memorial," Gus said. "I know her son's body never came home and that would be hard."

"Yes. If there was a grave here and a stone, a place where she could come to mourn and remember, I'm sure the idea of a statue would never have crossed her mind." He didn't respond, and I waited, watching him with the same serious expression he gave the cemetery.

Finally, he sighed the sigh of a man twice his age and without looking at me said, "Joe Buchanan was a deserter, Thea. He cut and run and by doing so could have caused others to die. When he was caught, there was a quick military trial and he was executed by a firing squad on a battlefield in France. The men of his own platoon drew straws to decide who'd be in the group that pulled the trigger."

The awful, awful story came at me without warning, and I put one hand over my mouth with the shock and horror of it. Tears welled in my eyes.

"Joe? Joe Buchanan? You're sure?"

"Yes."

I closed my mouth, swallowed hard, and brushed away the tears with my fingertips. When I had regained some semblance of normalcy, I asked, "Were you—? Did you—?"

"No," his reply quick and firm. "I was away on a special mission behind the lines and another officer stood in my place, but I heard about it when I got back. It wasn't long after Lloyd was injured and everything was still pretty chaotic from the constant shelling. No one really liked Joe Buchanan except Rudy and your brother so there wasn't a lot of sympathy for him. He could be—well, difficult to get along with. Superior, even unkind, and he refused a direct order to back up his mates. Maybe the details I heard weren't true, but the word was that he said he wasn't going to put his life on the line for men that didn't know their—" Gus paused. "He said something coarse and insulting, Thea. I won't repeat it. Then he put down his gun—didn't throw it down like a man that's seen and done more than he can bear but put it down very deliberately—turned his back, and walked away. They were getting ready for a charge and his captain at the time ordered him to stop but Buchanan kept going. I think he'd have walked all the way to Paris. They charged the hill without him, but he got stopped up the road so he didn't make it to Paris, after all."

"But to execute him!" I said. "Was that right? Could they do that?"

Gus turned to look at me, face like flint and no trace of warmth in his eyes. For a moment, he looked like a stranger.

"In war, Thea, every man is the same as the next. Nobody's better than anyone else. Family history and reputation and income don't mean a thing. Buchanan never understood that when the shells were crashing around us and the guns were blasting, we were all the same. We were all at risk. In a way, we were brothers, and we depended on the man next to us for our lives. When Joe Buchanan turned his back on his comrades, he left a hole in the line. He left someone unprotected. It can't be allowed. Can you understand that at all?"

I couldn't doubt his fervency or the truth of his words because as much as I wished it weren't so, I could see Joe Buchanan speaking and acting exactly as Gus described.

"I've never been to war," I replied, "so no, I can't understand exactly. How could I? But I can tell you think that what happened to Joe was justified. I haven't known you very long, Gus, but long enough to realize that you know the difference between right and wrong and good and bad, and I trust your judgment." He blinked at my words, surprised. "I understand now why you always act a little stiff around the Buchanans." I paused, our recent conversation with the couple coming to mind. "And now there's that damned statue!" Gus blinked again, this time at my words, for which I refused to apologize. What a complete mess, I thought! A statue erected in the middle of Blessing to honor a man executed for desertion! No hero at all, and who in the world would be the one to give his parents such terrible news? I couldn't imagine Delta Buchanan's reaction if anyone were to so much as hint at such a shameful death. Her darling boy? Her Joey?

"I'm sorry, Thea. I shouldn't have told you." Gus's expression was back to normal, the hard look that had flattened out the planes of his face and cooled his eyes gone.

I tried to smile and placed a hand on his coat sleeve. "Yes, you should have. There are enough secrets already. I don't want there to be any between us. We're partners, remember?"

"Friends," he corrected and brushed the back of his hand across my cheek.

I didn't pull away, just smiled. "That, too."

For all his height and breadth, I had the strong desire to pull the man into my arms and hold him, just hold him, for a long time. For my comfort as well as his. We were a pair; we both carried burdens.

"The kitchen will be closed if you don't get back to the hotel right away, and then I imagine you'll sequester yourself in your room for the rest of the day." I moved the conversation to the commonplace.

"After I talk to Lloyd, that's exactly what I'll do." We started walking back the way we'd come.

"Do you get nervous?" I asked, honestly curious, "about being in court and saying the right thing and knowing the right laws?"

"I used to when I was fresh out of law school, but no, I don't get nervous any more."

"But you're the defense now," I reminded him. "There's a lot more on the line, isn't there, than if you were prosecuting?"

"It's truth on the line whatever side of the court room you sit on. It's all about truth, Thea."

I wondered about that, thought the words too simplistic and idealistic for the modern age and yet wished it were so with all my heart.

When we reached the front of the Hansen House, Gus said, "About Joe Buchanan—" and I gave a quick, decisive shake of my head.

"Let's not talk about it any more, not until the trial's over and Lloyd's home. One crisis at a time, Gus. That's all I have the energy for. Agreed?"

"Agreed," the word decisive, too. "You're getting Cecelia and Kinsey from Scott City in the morning?"

"Yes. I'll leave well before sun up and be back in plenty of time for the ten o'clock start of the trial. I don't want to miss anything."

"You might pass the judge and the prosecutor on the road."

"I might," I agreed, "and if I do, I promise I'll be on my best behavior."

"That's a load off my mind. Take care on the road tomorrow."

"I will."

We shared a smile before he went up the porch steps into the hotel and I continued down Main, planning to stop by the jail to spend time with my brother before I reached the privacy of my big empty house. I needed some time alone with my memories of the handsome face, the banter, and the charm of Joe Buchanan, needed time to grieve for him again, this time grieving the loss of something that might never have truly existed in the first place.

Chapter 13

Monday, October 20, 1919

*I*n the way of Kansas Octobers, Monday morning was frigid. The temperature dropped significantly during the night, frost coated the ground, and I could see my breath as I huffed along to the shed. As much as I loved my Oldsmobile truck, I had no illusions about how cold the trip to Scott City would be, and I had dressed for the occasion in my long wool coat, heavy driving gloves, and a felt cloche pulled down over my ears. If I did happen to pass the judge and the prosecutor coming in the opposite direction on the road, they might recognize the truck but they'd never identify me with only the section of my face from eyes to chin visible.

At the last minute I had remembered to dig the map Gus had given me out of the pocket of my father's old cardigan where I'd shoved it just before kissing Gus Davis within an inch of his life. Even on a cold morning, the memory of that night on the back porch had the ability to warm.

Once on the road, I felt the exhilaration I always felt behind the wheel of the Olds. Driving was good for the spirit, I decided, and if I fell into a funk I should immediately head for the shed and the truck. Mine wasn't a nature prone to funk falling, but it never hurt to have a plan, and all the better if the plan included an automotive component.

The sun rose fully above the horizon when I turned into Dave Montrose's driveway, pulled around the milk house, and positioned the truck nose out and ready for departure. Someone must have been watching for me from the little kitchen window that faced the drive because at my arrival the back door of the farmhouse opened and the whole family trooped out: hefty Dave Montrose, his wife, three mid-sized children, Cecelia, and Kinsey. I climbed out of the truck and approached the group that stood waiting at the foot of the porch steps.

After stilted greetings, Dave Montrose said, "I don't mind telling you that we're all worried about Kinsey, Miss Hansen." I flashed a look at Cece.

"Cousin Dave knows the whole story," Cecelia told me. She looked relaxed and if not quite happy, at least more composed than when I'd last seen her. The time away had done her good.

"I can appreciate that, Mr. Montrose, and I would be lying if I said I knew exactly what the future held, but Kinsey's young and if he helps the authorities, I truly believe any consequences he experiences will be minimal." He thought on the words a moment and finally nodded.

"Fair enough. And the boy's got to do the right thing. We've talked about it. But we want to be kept informed."

"Of course."

"If the sheriff there in Blessing needs someone to vouch for the boy or be responsible for him, I'm ready to do that."

"Good."

We stood in silent tableau until the big farmer lifted the Carrs' bag and hefted it into the back of the truck. A man without much emotion to spare apparently, he said, "In you go, boy," to Kinsey and allowed Cece to give him a peck on the cheek. Kinsey hopped into the back of the truck as his sister said her good-byes to the rest of the family, then climbed in next to where I waited in the driver's seat. I put the truck in gear and with its usual smooth start the Olds headed back down the driveway toward the county road. I thought to myself that I hadn't heard a peep out of Mrs. Montrose and if that was typical, it must have been a quiet couple of days for Cecelia. No wonder she looked so relaxed. I glanced over at my friend.

"Was it all right there at your cousin's, Cece? I don't know them very well." I could have said *at all*.

She nodded and gave a small smile. "Of course, it was. We talked about Mother and I saw some pictures of her when she was a little girl. It was nice," adding inconsequentially, "They're family, Thea."

Her words made me think about how we four Hansens had lined up all in a row in church yesterday, fifth pew from the front on the pulpit side. I thought about Grandma Liza upright in her wheelchair, greeting friends and inquiring about their health as if her only grandson didn't sit in the local jail charged with murder. Had Grandmother been present on the ride back to Blessing— not that she could be bribed to ride in a motorized vehicle since she deplored anything "faddish"—she would have understood Cecelia's words and nodded her approval. She'd said the same thing in different words often enough: *Hard times come and go but family lasts.*

We made it to the trial opening with time to spare because it never took much to convince me to speed up. I took extra care, considering that it might not do Lloyd any favors if I rounded a curve and smacked head on into whatever vehicle carried Judge Plumquist, but as it turned out, the judge and Mr. Marquart had snuck into town the evening before and were sleeping the sleep of the innocent in the Hansen House as I made the round trip to Scott City. There wasn't much to be done about them staying there, it being the only reputable hotel in the vicinity, and no one mentioned anything about a conflict of interest, even if they were trying the hotel owner's nephew. It was 1919 rural Kansas, and the justice system held its own brand of integrity despite the amenability of small town life. Maybe even because of it.

Cecelia, Kinsey, and I stopped at my house when we arrived back in town.

"I want you to stay with me," I said. "I think we should stick together until the trial's over. I don't trust Leo Stanislaw."

"We can't impose like that," Cece protested. "Our regular rooms will be fine."

When their mother died, the siblings had moved out of the rented house where they had lived as a family and for economic reasons taken the upstairs apartment over the bicycle shop. Cece had the bedroom and Kinsey slept on a cot in the other room that doubled as kitchen and parlor. It never seemed right to me that I rattled around in the big stone house at the edge of Blessing while the two Carrs rubbed shoulders in two small rooms over a retail establishment. Having them with me seemed like a sensible decision at the time and whether she agreed with the wisdom of the arrangement or was simply too distracted to argue with me just then, Cece followed me into the house without further discussion.

Kinsey brightened perceptibly when I asked him to return the truck to the shed and met us a few minutes later in front of Monroe's. I changed my clothes into something more decorous to fit the occasion, tried with mixed success to arrange my hair under my best hat, and threw on the good coat I usually reserved for church. I didn't know what to say to Cecelia, Lloyd's freedom perhaps depending on Kinsey's loss of the same, so we didn't speak much, but when we exited the front door of the house, Cece turned at the top of the porch steps to give me a quick and unexpected hug.

"I'm scared, Thea."

"Me, too."

"I care for Lloyd, you know. We're good friends, very good friends, and I love Kinsey. I wish things were different. I don't know what to hope for."

I remembered Gus's recent words and paraphrased them, weak comfort if any, but all I could think to say. "Let's hope that the truth comes out, whatever it is. Then we can figure out what to do next." She didn't smile at the words and I didn't blame her. We both knew that sometimes the truth wasn't all it was cracked up to be.

We met Kinsey in front of the store and the three of us walked north along Main Street, all of us doing our best to act as if going to a murder trial was as normal for us as husking sweet corn in the summer, an annual occurrence prosaic and just a little boring, but inside I believe all three of us were shivering in a way that had nothing to do with the cold morning.

Because Cecelia and Kinsey were summoned witnesses, they weren't allowed into the trial room and had to sit on a bench in the hallway. I felt a little pang of heart when I turned to take a last look at the two before I entered the larger room. They looked so young and alone. Just the two of them against the world. Then I remembered my brother as I'd last seen him in his cell, as thin and pale as he'd been the day he stepped off the train and asked where Father was. He'd come home from the Front in a prison all his own and I couldn't bear the thought of him locked away for the rest of his life in another prison, this one of tangible rock and stone, and especially not as punishment for something he didn't do. One crisis at a time was all I could handle I'd told Gus yesterday, and I wasn't kidding.

Monday ended up being strictly the prosecution's day. Mr. Marquart, older and shorter than I expected, made his case. He questioned several people that had witnessed violent or strange behavior from Lloyd after he returned home from the war, several retelling the incident when Lloyd had turned on Rudy at the sound of an automobile backfire and knocked his best friend flat on his back.

I expected testimony from Dr. Petrie about Rudy's body but that wasn't why Marquart called him to the stand. Instead, reserving the right to talk to the doctor about the victim later, the prosecutor asked the doctor all about what the papers called *shell shock*, what would cause it in a soldier and how a soldier might manifest the condition in his interactions with others. As calm as Dr. Petrie remained and as objective as his answers sounded, I could tell on the faces of the jury that the words *violent* and *unreasonable* and *uncontrolled* damaged Lloyd's case. Under the doctor's clinical terms were secondary, unspoken words: *coward, weak, unnerved, unmanly.* I hated that part of the trial but did my best to keep an impassive expression. It seemed so fundamentally wrong that Joe Buchanan should have a statue in the town square and my brother be accused of cowardice, when Lloyd had done his duty, been buried alive in Belgian mud, and would carry with him all his life the effects of being a good soldier. My grandmother, sitting in her wheelchair in the aisle beside me, surreptitiously reached out a hand and rested it lightly on my forearm, so perhaps my expression was not as impassive as I thought.

Through it all Lloyd listened intently, his eyes focused on Dr. Petrie and his forehead wrinkled in concentration. I thought that since he'd been hospitalized for the very condition the doctor described, none of the details now being related to the courtroom could be a surprise to my brother—although some of them certainly were to me—but perhaps they were, perhaps Lloyd had been so ill at the hospital that nothing he was told there had made an impression. Gus, on the other hand, scribbled notes into his ubiquitous notebook and frequently stood to request clarification and on a few occasions to challenge the doctor's statement all together. Gus looked very lawyerly in his dark suit and high collared white shirt but some of the passion I knew lay below the surface of the man slipped out despite the conservative appearance and modulated voice. I don't think one little fact slipped by him, not one. Gus had clearly done his homework about the condition of shell shock. Despite my frustration and anger regarding the implied accusations of cowardice and weakness directed at my brother, I admired Gus Davis a great deal at that moment and felt a sudden, fervent surge of gratitude that Lloyd had insisted on this man to defend him. No doubt Ian Buchanan was a fine attorney, but he did not have the heart of Gus Davis.

In spite of the doctor's information about shell shock, which he related in an impersonal tone and refused to apply specifically to Lloyd, the worst damage was done by Reuben Hoffman, the undertaker and neighbor to Dolf's garage. He was adamant about the time he saw Lloyd rush out of the garage, looking like a man that had "seen or done something terrible." Gus tried to protest the characterization but Reuben stuck to his statement and would not be intimidated into lessening the impact of his words. If anything, I thought his continued, dogged insistence made his words sound even more reliable to the jury and Gus was wise to dismiss the man from the stand without any more questions.

Dr. Petrie returned to the stand to share information about the wound that killed Rudy. One wound to the chest and through the heart by a common caliber revolver. The bullet entered from the front and exited from the back and Rudy had probably died almost instantaneously.

When Gus rose, he questioned the doctor about the wound itself. "Is there anything you can speculate about either the murder or the murderer from the wound, Dr. Petrie?"

No one present, even the judge, appeared to understand the question at first. We felt about as blank as the doctor looked.

"For example," Gus clarified, "is there any way you could tell whether the shooter was short or tall? Would the shooter have stood quite close to Mr. Stanislaw or did he fire from a distance? Was Mr. Stanislaw seated or standing at the time of the shot? Is there any additional information to be derived from the wound other than what you've already testified, Doctor? Anything at all?"

That was an interesting question, I thought, and one I wouldn't have thought of. I wasn't the only one suddenly interested, either. It seemed that several spectators shifted in their seats and leaned forward.

Doctor Petrie took his time with an answer. "There was no angle to the wound, upward or down," he said with his customary caution.

"Which would indicate what to you, Doctor?"

"That the shooter might have been—*might* have been— about the same height as the victim."

"I see. How tall would you estimate Mr. Stanislaw was in life?"

"Between five six and five seven."

"And were there powder burns on the victim's clothing or skin to indicate that the shooter had pressed the bore of the small pistol against Mr. Stanislaw and then pulled the trigger?" Gus's words made me wince at the mental picture they portrayed, yet I knew the answer was important.

"No. None."

"So it's likely," Gus said, his tone that of a man simply speculating aloud, "that someone, perhaps someone of the same stature as the victim, stood at a distance and shot Mr. Stanislaw one time, killing him."

After a long moment, the judge asked, "Is there a question there somewhere, Mr. Davis?"

Gus smiled in false penitence. "I'm sorry, Your Honor. I'll rephrase. So is it likely, Dr. Petrie, from your examination of the mortal wound that someone no taller than five feet seven inches stood at a distance from Mr. Stanislaw, who was also standing, and shot him one time with a common caliber revolver killing him?" The fact that Gus had for all intents and purposes stated his question twice drove home his point, and I noticed several of the members of the jury turn to look at my brother where he sat. Lloyd, no fool any more than he was a coward, straightened in his chair to his full height of five feet eleven.

Oh, that was lovely, I thought, and saw the day's first hopeful glimmer of reasonable doubt.

The last witness for the prosecution was Mort McGill, who told of not being able to locate Lloyd for several hours after the crime was discovered and of the blood on Lloyd's cuffs when he finally did run my brother to ground.

Gus clarified with the sheriff that they had not found blood anyplace else on Lloyd and that the blood was stained in such a way that it could have gotten there if a person had attempted to move or lift a bleeding, inert body. When McGill allowed that that was one explanation, Gus abandoned that particular topic and asked rather abruptly, "From your experience, Sheriff McGill, what could you tell about the crime itself from the position of the victim's body when you arrived?"

Mort's blank look bore a remarkable resemblance to Dr. Petrie's earlier expression, and Gus once more had to clarify what he was asking.

"I mean, did it appear that Mr. Stanislaw had tumbled backward off a chair, for example, or might he have toppled to the ground from an upright position?"

"You mean was Rudy standing or sitting when he was shot?" Mort asked and an irreverent titter went through the courtroom. Everyone knew what a plain-spoken man Mort McGill was.

"Yes," Gus replied, an undertone of abashed humor in his voice that I doubted was unintentional. *The joke's on the lawyer, and I can take it. I'm an ordinary man just like you and we have a common interest in the truth.* It wasn't the first time that day that I thought Gus Davis might have missed a calling on the stage.

"Well," Mort said, clearly thinking through his response, "from the wound and from what I've seen of dead bodies, my professional opinion is that the boy was standing upright when he was shot. It looked like the force of the bullet knocked him backwards and he fell to the ground landing on his left side. He was a considerable distance from the bench where his morning coffee cup sat, and from the tire and the tools there by the bench it looked like he might have been sitting there working and when someone entered he stood up."

"Could you tell if that someone entered from the front door or from the alley door in the back?"

Mort thought again. "No, I don't think there's any way to tell that."

"But both doors were open and the murderer could have entered from either door, right?" which, of course, is where Gus wanted to get all along.

"Yes, I suppose that's true," the sheriff conceded, and that was the last testimony of the day.

We rose when the judge exited the court room and I stretched, not used to so much inactivity, but I thought of poor Cece and Kinsey cooling their heels on a hallway bench all day except for the break from proceedings allotted for a noon meal and decided not to complain about feeling cramped. When Uncle Carl stepped behind Grandma Liza ready to push her back to the hotel in her chair, he paused.

"He did a good job today," my uncle remarked to me, and I knew he wasn't complimenting Lloyd.

"I think so, too," I agreed. I leaned down to kiss my grandmother on her cheek. "All right?" I asked her.

She looked pale and tired, and I thought I wasn't the only one who had found the day's inactivity difficult.

"Yes. I'm fine, Thea." She looked up at me with a small smile. "He did quite well for someone from an Old Podunk place like Laramie, Wyoming."

I grinned at that but said seriously enough, "It's only just started. Let's wait until we know how it ends." Then to soften what I thought might sound either too critical or too discouraging, I added, "But Lloyd's in the best hands he could be in."

She started to reply, thought better of it, and reached across to give my uncle's wrist a peremptory pat. "Let's go, Carl. I'm ready for a cup of tea. Are you eating with us tonight, Thea?"

"No. I want to stop at the store for a while. And Cece and Kinsey are staying with me, besides."

"Do you plan to cook supper for your guests?" the badly veiled disbelief in my grandmother's tone made my response come out more defensive than I intended.

"I can cook, you know." My three family members eyed me wordlessly until I added, "but Cece mentioned when we went home at noon today that she had something planned for supper."

"Well, that's a relief," Grandma Liza stated firmly. "Cecelia knows her way around a kitchen." *Unlike my granddaughter* might as well have been tacked on to the end of her sentence.

"You try to relax and get some sleep tonight," Uncle Carl advised me. "I'll spend some time with Lloyd after supper, and we'll see you back here in the morning."

In a gentle voice that was totally out of character, Aunt Louisa said, "Everything will be fine, Thea." I thought for one panicky moment that she intended to give me a hug—my aunt is not a hugging kind of woman—but she contented herself with a light pat on my shoulder as she walked past me.

I watched them file out in a proud little procession, Grandmother, Uncle Carl, Aunt Louisa. The Hansens once more in formation. When I would have followed, Gus said my name from behind me and I halted in my tracks and turned around.

He didn't look like he'd just spent the last six hours in court. If anything, he appeared energized by the experience. He loves practicing law, I thought, and felt a brief and ignoble envy. I had the store but I didn't enjoy it with the same depth that Gus Davis loved the law and the courtroom. I hoped he appreciated the rare gift he'd been given.

"I thought it went well today," I told him, "but I'm not the expert. What did you think?"

He nodded. "I wouldn't say *well*, exactly, but I think it could have been a lot worse and will only get better when we put our witnesses on the stand tomorrow."

"How's Lloyd holding up?" I asked.

"Pretty good. He's a good soldier, remember, and he can hold his own."

"He was fortunate to have a good captain." Some color crept up Gus's cheeks at my words and we were both silent.

"Look," he said, "I don't have time right now. I need to go over my notes from today and spend some time with Lloyd, but I want to talk to Kinsey. He's first on the stand tomorrow. Is it all right if I come over later tonight?"

"Of course. Come as late as you want."

Gus gave a nod toward the rear of the room. "Someone's waiting for you."

Cece and Kinsey stood in the doorway, the hallway behind them now vacant. Seeing the two of them side-by-side brought a catch to my voice as I spoke.

"I hope Kinsey won't—" I began and then had to stop to compose my voice.

Gus looked at the Carrs and then back at me, understanding what I wanted to say without the need for more words on my part.

"One crisis at a time, Thea. That's all I have the energy for. Agreed?"

I smiled at the words. "Wise advice."

"From a very smart woman." Another brief silence between us before he said, "I'll see you later, then." He loosened his tie, smiled, and turned away.

I joined Cece and Kinsey and the three of us headed for the store, where it seemed that Raymond had everything in hand and Flo felt right at home taking care of the customers on the second floor. Both Cece and I felt briefly superfluous until we looked at each other and giggled at seeing our own feelings reflected in the other. In private defiance, I didn't go near my office. Instead, I thanked Raymond for his faithful, competent service without feeling an ounce of defensiveness or inadequacy and headed home for the supper Cecelia had in mind. I wouldn't have admitted it to my family, but whatever the meal turned out to be, it was sure to be a vast improvement on anything I could have devised.

Chapter 14

Monday, October 20, 1919

"*G*us said he wanted to talk to you tonight," I informed Kinsey after supper. A lovely warm meal of potato soup that Cece threw together from what I had on hand, with fresh bread and pickles contributed by Dave Montrose's wife, a quiet woman from all appearances but an excellent cook.

Kinsey shot me a quick look. "All right." After a moment, he added, "I didn't see Leo Stanislaw in town today. Didn't he get a summons like Cece and me and Mr. Holiday did? We were all three out there in the hallway at first, only Mr. Holiday said he had a business to run so he got to leave in the afternoon."

"I don't know if Leo got a summons," I answered thoughtfully. "He was supposed to, but maybe Mort couldn't find him to give it to him. Dolf got one, Gus said, and a constable from Scott City is going to bring him to the trial on Wednesday."

"If Leo never got the summons, does it mean he doesn't have to testify?" This from Cece.

"I don't know that either," I admitted. "This is as new to me as it is to you."

Cece stood and started clearing the table, saying as she did so, "Well, I for one would be happy if I never saw Leo Stanislaw again. Good riddance to bad rubbish. He's been trouble all his life and he's never going to change. I feel safer when he's not around."

I made a sound that indicated agreement but thought to myself that it might be safer to know exactly where your foe was and keep him in your sight. No surprises that way. Whenever I'd had the opportunity that day I looked for Leo, too, but didn't spy the man anywhere. Unlike Cece, however, that worried me. The menacing, arrogant boy had grown into a violent, angry, lawless man. Rudy had been blunt to a fault and sometimes rough but never crude or frightening, never threatening like Leo. The brothers were Janus-like, two faces of the same man, and that it was Rudy, the better side and the better nature, who'd been murdered seemed unbalanced, the further tilting of a world that had begun to lose its stability when war raged across Europe and influenza swept away thousands with sudden and shocking regularity.

We sat in the front room for a while after supper, each of us listening for Gus's knock on the door, until I stood and announced that I thought I'd go to the store and pick up the mail Raymond told me he'd left on my desk.

"This late?" asked Cece, a touch of dismay in her tone. "Can't it wait until tomorrow?"

""Probably," I replied, "but whether I'd have time to get to it tomorrow isn't certain and I need a stretch. I'll just grab the mail and be right back. Listen for Gus while I'm gone. He always uses the back door."

"Always?" Cece inflected the word with enough curiosity and surprise to warm my cheeks.

"He's my brother's attorney. We talk sometimes."

"I see."

What she thought she saw made me glare at her in mute denial, a gesture that sometimes worked with children misbehaving in church but which had no noticeable effect on my friend. I chose not to dignify the discussion by pursuing the topic.

"I won't be long," I said. "I promise. I'll just be a minute."

"Take Kinsey with you, then," Cece suggested. She shook her head at her own idea. "Of course, that won't work. Mr. Davis might come while you're gone. Sorry. I'm not thinking straight lately."

"None of us is," I said and to soothe the worry on her face added, "Give me ten minutes to pop across the street. You can send out a search party if I'm gone any longer."

I threw a heavy woolen shawl around my shoulders as I exited the back door and darted across the street to Monroe's. The night was cloudless and cold, the street washed by pale waning moonlight. Another few weeks and the streets would be white with snow. People would forego wagons and motorcars for horses and sleighs and it would be Christmas. Last year's Christmas was difficult, the first without my father and no word from Lloyd despite the Armistice being declared the previous month. This year, I vowed, Lloyd needed to be home and happy for Christmas. He had been away from his family, in one way or another, far too long.

I entered the store through the alley warehouse door and left it ajar so I could maneuver my way through the warehouse without having to light a lamp. One of the last major improvements my father had initiated was to run electricity in the store, but he had balked at the expense to do the same for the warehouse. In hindsight, he probably should have done the whole building because electricity was no more faddish than the automobile and no doubt I would end up paying to illuminate the warehouse within a year or two, probably at an elevated price.

Once I entered the rear of the store, I reached for the switch to light the hallway and headed for my office. Through the open door, the hallway light displayed the promised stack of mail sitting dead center on my desk. Something that has nothing to do with Rudy's murder, I thought with a spurt of anticipation. I stepped behind the desk, not bothering to flick on any lights, and pushed the chair back so I could reach the mail. Against my better judgment I paused for a quick peek through the invoices, circulars, and catalogs, a perfect antidote to the strain and worry of Lloyd's trial, a chance to see what the world outside of Blessing, Kansas, had to offer. At the last minute I opened a top desk drawer and took out the key for one of the cabinets, figuring that I might as well take the order book home with me to match against the invoices. It was a task I could do in my sleep but wouldn't have to; I didn't feel at all tired despite the long day. Cabinet key back in its accustomed place, I was gathering the correspondence in my hands when I heard a noise from the warehouse. Probably a neighborhood cat searching among the boxes for a mouse—and more power to it—but I could not seem to regain my pleasant anticipation of the last few minutes. The idea of a cat made sense, it had happened before, and yet I was conscious of feeling uneasy. Because, I reminded myself with poor timing, you know there's a murderer walking free in Blessing, and with that thought I heard another sound. A subdued squeak from the door at the end of the hallway, the door that led from the warehouse, the warehouse with a side door that I had with the greatest stupidity left open to take advantage of the moonlight.

"Damn!" I whispered to myself, my profanity indicating the sudden lurch of panic I felt in my gut. "What's the matter with me?" I looked around for anything I could use as a weapon, but by then it was too late.

"Well, well, well, if it isn't Thea Hansen. Just the girl I wanted to see." Leo Stanislaw lounged in the doorway with one shoulder casually against the doorframe, hands in his pockets, and a grin on his face that did not hold one particle of humor but something predatory and malevolent instead. I wouldn't have thought it possible, but my panic deepened and spread through more than just my stomach—my heart, my throat, my hands, everything seemed immobile with dread.

"You have no business here. What do you want?" My voice sounded slightly breathless, thirteen years old again and frightened by something in Leo Stanislaw I didn't understand. No father between us this time, though, just an old scarred desk, not nearly enough protection because at twenty, I understood all too well what I feared about Leo Stanislaw.

"I want to know where our friend Kinsey is. I thought you might know."

"Why do you want Kinsey?"

Leo shrugged. "I just want to talk to the boy."

"About what?"

"You always were a curious little thing." Grinning, he let his gaze linger on me in such a way that I had to keep myself from pulling the shawl more tightly across my chest in defense. "Not so little any more, though, are you? All grown up. All filled out, too. Everything right where it should be. You always were a looker, even as a girl. Not a girl any more, of course, no, siree.

Thea Hansen's a full grown woman just waiting for the right man to come along and show her what all her parts are for."

"Why do you want to talk to Kinsey?"

"I don't really want to. Not me, personally. But I've been told by someone who knows that Kinsey Carr needs to be taught a lesson about keeping his mouth shut." As Leo stepped fully into the room, I took a simultaneous and involuntary step backwards, a movement he didn't miss.

"You aren't still scared of me, are you, Thea, like you were all those years ago?" I didn't answer or move. "Your pa come after me like I was the devil out of hell. Said I scared you when all I wanted to do was spend time with Thea Hansen, the prettiest girl in town. No harm there, but your pa wouldn't have it."

"You're spending time with me now." For one moment his implied criticism of my father almost made me more irritated than frightened. Almost. "And I don't know where Kinsey Carr is."

"You're lying to me, Thea, and you always such a good girl, too." He made a mocking *tsk tsk* sound. "I heard he was staying at your house, him and that pretty sister of his, though she ain't as pretty as you, not by a long shot, or filled out as good as you, neither. So tonight I'm watching your house and waiting for the lights to go out and thinking about how I might surprise you after you're in bed. Getting all excited about the idea, too, I don't mind telling you, when what do I see but Thea Hansen herself skipping across the street and down the alley? Kinsey Carr's not going any place, I says to myself, and when else will I have a chance to catch up on old times with Thea? Just the two of us, just her and me all by ourselves. I was right, too, huh? 'Cause here you are, pretty as a picture and all by your lonesome." Leo moved closer as he spoke and the look on his face belied his casual tone.

"I bet your pa wouldn't like it if he knew you were back here all alone with me, would he? Wouldn't like knowing what a sick, crazy bastard his son turned out to be either. That brother of yours killed my kid brother, killed Rudy, and left him laying on the floor like an old oil rag. That wasn't right, Thea. You know that wasn't right."

For all his reasonable tone, there was nothing reasonable in Leo's eyes and nothing friendly, and for the first time I believed the anger and resentment— and could it even be grief I heard in his voice?—was intense enough that I might truly be in danger from him. That vague, intangible uneasiness I'd felt around Leo Stanislaw for so many years took physical shape in front of me. How long had he carried this ferocious anger and why did I only just see it now? The desk was the only barrier between us; he could have stretched his arm across it and grazed my hand with his fingertips. Literally, too close for comfort.

"Lloyd never hurt Rudy. You know it in your heart."

As I spoke I took a couple of small steps to my left because he was no longer directly across from me but had begun to move around the desk to my right toward where I stood. I turned slightly to keep him in my direct line of sight, keeping both hands on the back of the swivel chair and pulling it along with me so when he got behind the desk I would still have the chair between us. Clearly, it would be wise to keep something between Leo Stanislaw and me all the rest of my life because in the last few years he had grown from an ominous youth to a dangerous man. My mind was ticking off escape plans even as I spoke. If I could get him directly behind the desk, I thought I might have a second's advantage to dart out the door and into the hallway. Anything would be better than this feeling of being trapped by a carnivore. I wasn't as strong as he, but I was fast and certain I could navigate the dark interior of the warehouse well enough to escape his reach, but I needed to get to the warehouse before he got to me and that was chancy.

"My heart, Thea? Since when did you ever think I had a heart or any feelings at all? You never gave a damn about me, girl. I was dirt under your feet."

"That's not true."

Leo was on my side of the desk now, one hand dragging along the wooden edge as he moved toward me, the other hand still thrust into a pants pocket. I backed away from him with the same methodical timing of his approach and reached the next corner of the desk, rolling the chair backwards along with me, keeping it between Leo and me.

"Do you know what your pa said to me?"

The man's slow steps and drawling arrogance were hypnotic, snake charmer Leo and Thea the viper swaying to his tune, mesmerized, unable to look away.

"Cat got your tongue, Thea?" Another grin. "Your pa said, 'My Thea's not for the likes of you. When the time comes, she'll do better than a Stanislaw.' That's what he said. Wasn't very nice of your pa, I didn't think." I stepped around the corner of the desk but was stymied what to do with the chair. Drag it on its clunky wheels around the corner's edge with me? If I tried that awkward move, Leo would become even more aware that I was using the chair as a shield between us, my only protection, however pitiful, from his intention to do something more than frighten me and the only ploy I could think of to distract him from that intention. He's dangerous, I thought, but not stupid and suddenly pushed the chair straight at him with all my strength.

The heavy oak chair crashed into him, and I heard his heavy grunt at impact but didn't bother to look in his direction. Instead, I dashed toward the office door and out into the hallway. What little time the gesture garnered got me as far as the door at the end of the hallway, the door that led into the warehouse. But Leo had closed it behind him when he entered and in the time it took me to wrench open the door, Leo's hands were on my shoulders, pulling me back and away from the doorway with enough force to rip the sleeve of my dress. I pivoted, my left hand still scrabbling for the door, and swung back at him with my fisted right hand. The back of my fist bounced off his nose and landed in the middle of his upper lip with enough force to split his lip against his teeth. Blood appeared on his mouth and ran down his chin.

"Bitch!"

Whether because of my blow or the taste of blood, Leo was suddenly enraged beyond rational thought and strong as a bull. He pulled me away from the door, no longer taunting or teasing or whatever he had been just five minutes ago but in his fury intent on punishing me, on hurting me. I was flailing both arms by then in the hope of landing another blow somewhere. The door to the warehouse was partly opened and I needed only enough time to make it through and into that darker, safer interior. But no matter how I struggled, there was no way I could escape the grip of his hands on my shoulders. I tried to bring up a knee thinking even a passing connection might be enough to double him over or incapacitate him, however briefly, but he guessed my intention and pushed me backwards with such brutal force that the back of my head cracked against the edge of the wooden doorframe. I didn't lose consciousness, thank God, but for a moment everything went black and I was unable to move. Leo took advantage of my sudden weakness and pressed against me, one forearm against my throat so that when I made a weak movement of protest, his arm pushed harder and cut off my breathing.

"If you move, I'll kill you. I swear to God, Thea, I'll do it. Your brother killed Rudy. Why shouldn't I take a Hansen in exchange?"

I became very still at his words, the darkness behind my eyes and the dizziness I'd first felt when my head connected with the wooden edge diminishing somewhat, and my apparent obedience lessening the pressure of his arm against my wind pipe so I could catch a shallow breath. Leo was a monstrous sight. Blood, which he made no effort to wipe away, dripped along his lip and caught in the corners of his mouth; eyes gleamed with fury in a face just inches away from mine. I still felt dazed and was not myself. Tiny pinpricks of light sparkled when I closed my eyes and I could feel an odd drumming inside my head. If Leo had let go of me completely, I still wouldn't have had the strength or balance to move, let alone get away from him.

I was conscious that he stared at me, and as he did so I saw something change in his face, something that struck a chord of memory from years ago. Without warning, he leaned forward and kissed me hard. I could taste the blood, sickening and salty and thick on his lips and on his tongue as he pressed closer on me, the restraining arm against my throat removed and that hand now fumbling with the buttons of my blouse.

I tried to shake my head and say, no, don't do this, Leo, but my head hurt and my ears were ringing and then he was kissing me again, pressing me against the wall with his whole body, using both hands to pull up my skirt, saying vile things and moving himself against me in a way that was coarse and demanding and suggestive. I knew what he intended and needed to do something, anything, but couldn't twist away, couldn't even move my face away from his because of the pain in my head that throbbed with every movement.

"Leo, stop. Stop," my words a whispered moan and a shameful pleading for him not to hurt me this way.

And then, just like that, he did stop. He made a loud, choking sound and was jerked backwards, his hands still clutching at my skirts with enough force to pull me with him. Like a childhood game of crack-the-whip, he finally let go of me as he was whirled around to face his assailant—to face Gus, thank God, thank God. With the momentum of my release, light-headed and overwhelmed with vertigo, I must have looked like a dervish as I hit the opposite wall with a thud. I could hear the unmistakable sounds of physical fighting but by then, I couldn't have remained upright no matter what happened around me. My back flat against the wall, I slid down until I was sitting on the floor with my legs stretched out in front of me. I wanted desperately to see what was happening but couldn't make my eyes open. Someone said my name, then said it a second time with greater urgency. Gus's voice. If Gus was here, I told myself, it was safe to relax a moment and stop fighting the comfortable lethargy that crept along my arms and legs and weighted my eyelids. I could tell activity continued around me, but I didn't know—didn't care, either, for that matter—what it was. I needed to rest a moment before I could figure out what was happening, needed to get that dull rapping inside my head to stop. Then I was sure I'd be able to make sense of everything.

I did not get the rest I so longed for because something was crawling on my face, moving over my forehead, down one cheek, across my lips, up the other side, and over my eyes. I tried to brush the bother away, then latched onto the idea that a spider traversed my face. That disgusting thought made me brush once more at my face to dislodge the annoying sensation and try to sit upright.

"Be still, Thea." Gus again, the fierce urgency I thought I'd heard in his voice replaced by calm direction. I opened my eyes. Not a spider, after all, but Gus Davis's gentle hand running along my face.

I realized why he examined my face with such serious intensity and said, "It's not my blood, Gus. It's Leo's. I'm not hurt." I tried to push myself up only to discover that we were both on the floor, Gus now seated with his back against the wall where I remembered landing not that long ago. He cradled me against his chest with one arm and somehow managed to examine my face with the other. When he didn't answer, I repeated the last words. "I'm not hurt, Gus. Honestly. Where's Leo?"

For a moment I felt a quick blaze of panic, remembering what it was like to feel incapable of protecting myself from something dreadful and inevitable, but then Gus answered, "He's gone, Thea. Don't give him a thought. He's the worse for wear and no matter how far he manages to run, it won't be far enough."

"Far enough?"

"To keep me from catching up with him." Something both conversational and implacable in Gus's voice. Had I been a more charitable woman I might almost have felt a smidgeon of pity for Leo Stanislaw. Forever wanted, forever pursued. But I did not feel very charitable at the time.

I heard the sounds of people in the warehouse and Gus explained quickly, "I sent Kinsey for the doctor, Thea. You looked—" He cleared his throat and started again, "There seemed to be a lot of blood and I didn't know whose it was."

I relaxed for another moment, feeling quite at home with his heartbeat in my ear, and without any more words, Gus and I waited the minute it took for Dr. Petrie to find us.

"I hit my head on the door jamb," I explained to the doctor. "Hit it hard. I didn't pass out, but everything stayed dark for a while. I think I'm all right now, though."

Ignoring my information, Dr. Petrie said, "Stretch her flat out on the floor, Davis, but keep her head steady and your arm under her neck."

Clearly, what the patient thought was unimportant so I didn't bother repeating that I was all right and allowed the doctor to probe the back of my head.

Even with his professional, practiced gentleness, when he reached the spot of impact at the back of my skull, I said, "Ow! That hurt."

"I'm not surprised." He turned my head a little to the side, parted my hair, and probed again.

"Ow!" I repeated. "Did I mention that hurt?"

The good doctor crouched back on to his heels and smiled at me. "Yes, Thea, you did. That's quite a goose egg you've got there, but I think you'll live." He looked across me at Gus. "Her eyes are getting back to normal, but keep her awake for a while just to be on the safe side. If the headache doesn't fade in a few hours, let me know."

"I'll tell her grandmother."

"You are not to mention this to Grandmother." I put one hand on Gus's chest, pushed myself away from him, and made it to a position where I could rest backwards on my elbows. "Absolutely not."

"But—" Since both men said the word at about the same time, I didn't know which one to glare at.

"My grandmother isn't well and she doesn't need to be awakened in the middle of the night with something to worry about. I want to go to my own home. Cece's there and she's quite capable of keeping me awake."

From the doorway, Cecelia commented, "I'll do whatever it takes to keep her awake," trying her best to keep her voice light but unable to hide an undercurrent of dismay and worry. I hadn't heard her come in and was surprised to hear her there.

I pushed myself up further to a full sitting position and at the look on my friend's pale face said quickly, "I must look awful, Cece, but I'm really all right. There's no need for you to worry." To Gus I said, "Will you help me stand up, please, so I can go home?"

"No." One blunt syllable of an answer not to be disputed. I stared at him, not quite sure where to go from there with my request. Gus rose, stretched, crouched down once more, and before I realized his intention put both his arms under me and stood upright in one fluid motion. "I'll make sure you get home, Thea, but no, I won't help you stand up. Not just yet."

Doctor Petrie repeated his instructions to Gus and Cece at the end of the walk that led up to my front porch and disappeared in the direction of his office. Once inside, when Gus would have taken the steps to my upstairs bedroom, I gave my head a tentative shake to check for stars and sparks and when none appeared said with as much meekness as I could muster, "I'd like to go to the kitchen, please. I don't want any of Leo's blood on me, Cece, so boil some water and scrub as hard as you have to. I don't want one drop of him on me. Not one touching me anywhere." I heard my voice quiver and realized I was on the verge of tears. "If you don't mind, Cece. If you don't have other plans."

My final words had their intended effect. Gus, who at my initial request had stopped still in the front hallway and tightened his arms around me, took a breath deep enough for me to feel and turned in the direction of the kitchen. Cece laughed, the stricken look on her face gone so quickly I might have imagined it.

"Well, I had plans to drive to Scott City for a night of honky-tonk dancing, but since it's you, Thea, I'll cancel them." It was my turn to laugh at that.

Once he deposited me in a kitchen chair, Gus said, "I sent Kinsey for McGill. If the sheriff wasn't at the jail I told Kinsey not to settle for a constable but to roust McGill out of bed at his house. I'll go watch for him." He looked down at me and gave me a smile so warm I could feel its heat on my skin.

I felt an urge to reach for his hand and not let it go, not let him out of my sight, and maybe my unspoken feelings showed in my face because he reached down to place a palm against my cheek. "I'll be right outside on the front porch."

"I know," but at the moment the front porch could have been in the next county. The kettle started to boil, and Gus vanished from the kitchen at its whistle.

Cece and I talked sporadically and quietly as she worked on cleaning my face. My head hurt and I knew I must not be thinking as clearly as I should and could because something that Leo had said during that awful time in my office nagged at me, something important, but I couldn't get a hold of what it was or why it was important.

Cece, my requested task complete, was busy removing the few pins that remained in my hair and using her fingers to comb through and straighten what had to be a disheveled mess.

"You know," I remarked thoughtfully, "I think Leo said something that was important, if I could just make myself remember what it was."

"I think you should forget what happened. Put it right out of your mind. What if Gus hadn't gotten there when he did?"

"It would have been—" I began but couldn't finish the sentence because there was no word to describe the *would have been.*

Understanding my pause, Cecelia said, "Gus turned into a different man in front of me, Thea. He came in all polite and pleasant like he usually is and after a moment he asked where you were. I said you went across the street to get something from the store and then just like that he was different. His voice got sharp and he wasn't rude or unpleasant or anything like that, but all of a sudden he was a man you wouldn't want to cross."

"I know what you mean. Gus Davis. Man of action and a leader of soldiers."

"Yes, something like that. He snapped his fingers at Kinsey and my brother practically jumped out of his skin. That was a sight I wouldn't mind seeing again." Cece stepped in front of me and eyed my face and hair with a critical eye. "There, you look yourself again."

"Thank you."

She remained standing in front of me and continued with quiet sincerity, "I don't know what the future holds or what will happen to Lloyd or Kinsey or any of us, really. Everything's uncertain and has been for a long time now. War and sudden sickness and the people we care for here one day and gone the next. But from the look and the sound of Gus Davis when he started worrying about you, when he couldn't rest for worry, I believe you have one sure thing in your life, and if I were you, I'd hold on to it."

The hinge on the front door squeaked and I heard a murmur of voices. Mort McGill had arrived.

"I've only known the man for two weeks," I responded. "Do you think that's enough time to recognize a sure thing?"

Cecelia, in her new role as The Oracle of Blessing, shook her head in amused tolerance at my naiveté.

"Oh, Thea." Another headshake. "Sometimes two weeks is longer than a lifetime."

Chapter 15

Monday, October 20 - Tuesday, October 21, 1919

"*T*ell me again, Thea, why Leo Stanislaw was looking for Kinsey." Mort McGill, straddling a chair on the other side of the kitchen table from me, leaned forward and waited for me to respond. I had already related, in as detached a tone as I could manage, everything I could remember about what had happened between Leo Stanislaw and me that night. Because my head began to throb midway through the telling, I felt pretty certain that I wasn't remembering everything properly—except for the look on Leo's face and the taste of his blood and the way it felt to have him pawing at me; those were memories likely to stay as bright as fireworks for quite some time—and I closed my eyes to bring the scene more clearly to mind.

"He said he needed to teach Kinsey a lesson about keeping his mouth shut. That's what I remember." But there was more to it, I thought; I just couldn't capture all the words at the moment. I opened my eyes and tried to smile at the sheriff. "I'm sorry. It seems to me he said more but I can't remember it all right now."

McGill, usually a somber man, smiled back at me as he rose to his feet. "You don't have a thing to be sorry for. You kept your head when another woman might have lost hers. You stayed a step ahead of Stanislaw. And you gave as clear a statement as I've heard in a long while. You did fine, Thea. If your father was here, he'd be proud of you." The kind words brought unbidden tears to my eyes. Mort, seeing what his remark caused, laid a hand on my shoulder as he passed.

"Now I'm the one that's sorry. You get some rest and maybe in the morning you'll remember whatever it is you think you're forgetting."

"Just keep Leo away from Kinsey. He'd hurt him, maybe do worse. I know he would."

"Mr. Davis plans to spend the night here, so you'll all be safe under his watchful eye, and by morning I'd wager we'll have Leo Stanislaw in custody. Him and that fancy motor car of his are hard to miss." He and Gus exited the back door together and stood a long while on the porch, talking. With the heavy inside door only partially closed, the subdued murmur of their voices carried through the screen door into the kitchen. Cold air carried through, as well, and I shivered, though I think it was more than October's night air that made me suddenly shaky.

"Thea." Kinsey had fetched McGill as Gus had ordered and then stayed so quiet I'd almost forgotten he was present.

"I'll go turn down your bed," Cece volunteered. "Kinsey'll keep you company."

When it was just Kinsey and I sitting there, he said, "You didn't tell Leo where I was."

"He knew where you were, Kinsey. I didn't need to tell him. Maybe somebody saw us when we went home from the trial because he said he heard you and Cece were staying at my house."

But who would have seen us this afternoon, known about Kinsey's connection with Leo, and had the time and opportunity to pass the word along? Who would have done that? No one saw Leo in Blessing all day so where had he been and who had known where to find him? There's something I should be able to figure out from all that, I thought, and maybe with a clearer head tomorrow I would.

"Well, thank you for not telling him, anyway, Thea." Kinsey paused. "I wish I'd never got involved with any of this. I wish I'd run in the opposite direction the moment Leo Stanislaw asked me if I wanted to make some easy money. I wish I could go back and do it over."

Those sounded like the words of a penitent soul who's learned his lesson, I thought with relief. Maybe Kinsey wouldn't harbor any more ideas of earning "easy money." As if there were such a thing, as if there wasn't a cost to all our actions, one way or another.

"I know you do."

"But I can't."

"No, you can't."

"If I have to go to jail, I'll just do it. I won't be a baby about it."

"Gus will do his best to keep you out of jail, Kinsey. You've never been in trouble before, you haven't tried to run away, and you're doing the right thing by helping Sheriff McGill. Gus said if you get arrested, the judge will take that into consideration and could choose to go easy on you. That's if you get arrested. There's no use worrying about it now when you're free as a bird."

We sat quietly, the tick of the clock and the murmur of the men's voices on the back porch a comforting cadence.

"I've been thinking, Thea."

"Uh oh."

Kinsey grinned at me and then got serious again. "Do you think I've got what it takes to be a lawyer?"

"Well, I'm not exactly sure what it takes for that," I admitted. Hazel eyes and broad shoulders and a lilt of laughter in your voice when it was least expected probably weren't requirements for being admitted to the bar. "But I think you'd be a good lawyer."

"I want to be like Gus. Just like him in everything." My heart warmed at the words.

"That's a good goal, Kinsey. From what I saw in court today, Gus is an excellent attorney."

"He can fight, too." I blinked, having never considered prizefighting expertise to be necessary for successful litigation. "You should have seen him tonight, Thea. We come in the warehouse and we could hear you and Leo." He paused. "That was pretty awful."

"You're telling me," using a light tone because for a minute Kinsey looked a lot younger than his years. Perhaps he'd never really understood what a man can do to a woman against her will, had never processed it beyond knowing the words. He wasn't likely to forget it now.

"Gus walked light as a cat but fast, too. He was across the warehouse faster and quieter than I ever saw anybody move before and then he jumped at Leo. He put one arm around Leo's neck and a knee into his back and I thought—" I watched Kinsey relive the moment and didn't speak. "I thought he was going to kill him, Thea. Thought he'd snap Leo's neck in two and that would be that or if he'd had a knife he would've slit Leo's throat ear to ear just that fast without it bothering him at all. From the look on Gus's face he sure wanted to do something like that. He looked different. Scary, kind of."

"He was in the war, Kinsey. I guess he learned how to fight then. And he didn't kill Leo in the end, did he?"

"No," a hint of unconcealed disappointment in the word. "No, he didn't. He let Leo go and whirled him around and hit him hard in the face and harder in the gut. Hit him really, really hard." Appreciation colored his tone this time. "Leo didn't know what happened. But then you smacked against the wall and slid to the floor and Gus looked over at you and it seemed he lost interest in Leo and that gave Leo a chance to get away. Gus didn't seem to care, either. He told me to get Doc Petrie and it was like Leo had never been there. Except for you laying on the floor, of course." He paused to relish a final moment of memory. "I never saw anybody move the way Gus did or fight like him either. Not scared about anything. Tough and fast but sort of graceful, too." Kinsey shook his head. "It's hard to explain, but it was something to see. Until you interrupted it."

"I'm sorry I ruined the show," I said meekly. "Next time I'll try to be more discreet when I thud against a wall and collapse onto the floor. I don't always need to be the center of attention, I suppose," and sent him a look to make him laugh.

Cece and Gus returned to the kitchen at nearly the same time, he coming in from the outside and she from upstairs.

"You don't have to stay here," I told Gus. "You had a long day and another one tomorrow. Don't you need to get the defense ready?"

He took a fresh cup of coffee from Cece and sipped from it as he leaned against the sink.

"Marquart needs the morning to close and I'm ready for tomorrow's defense, but I need some more time with this young man before he trots off to bed." He gestured with his cup toward Kinsey.

You're starting off with Kinsey?" Cece's quiet voice gave away her worry.

"Yup." Gus turned his gaze on the young man. "Are you up for it, Kinsey?" Kinsey swallowed noticeably but didn't flinch.

"You bet."

"Then I think it's safe for Thea and your sister to get some rest while you and I talk down here." Gus looked at me. "How do you feel?"

I put a hand to the tender bump at the back of my head. "Incredibly lucky. Thanks to you." I wanted to tell him how safe I'd felt pressed against his heart, but we weren't alone so instead I repeated, "Thanks to you, Gus. Your timing was perfect."

"Well, I'm a good man to have around in emergencies, I guess."

"You're a good man to have around whether there's an emergency or not." If it was just the two of us, I thought, I'd crawl right back into Gus Davis's arms and stay there until sunrise, stay past sunrise if he asked me to.

Cece took a brisk tone. "Gus wants some time with Kinsey, Thea, and you and I should get out of his way. Can you stand up without toppling over?"

"Of course, I can. I feel perfectly fine," and to prove it stood triumphantly upright. "You see?" The sweater Cece had draped over my shoulders earlier slipped off and I saw the torn sleeve of my blouse, remembered with momentary but vivid clarity the feel of Leo's hands on my shoulders, his breath on my face, the taste of his blood in my mouth. This won't do, I told myself, it's over now, but the brief panic of the memory gave me an appreciation for what it must be like for Lloyd. How many times had a sound or smell or sight triggered memories he was desperate to forget? How many times had he told himself, it's over now, but felt his heart speed up and the panic rise in his chest, anyway? My poor brother.

Conscious that the other occupants of the room watched me with concern, I commented, "I think it ripped right along the seam so maybe it's not completely ruined. I always liked this blouse," and followed Cece toward the front hallway. In the kitchen doorway, I paused to say a final good night and add in a confident voice, "I have a very strong feeling that tomorrow will be a good day for the defense," words prescient in their own way but still nowhere near the truth of it.

"Do you want me to sleep in here with you?" Cece asked from the doorway of my bedroom after I entered.

"No, of course, not. I'm not made of glass and I didn't break. I had a fright that left me with a bump on my head and a waning headache, but honestly, Cece, I'm fine."

"Thanks to your Gus Davis." I didn't bother to dispute the pronoun.

"Yes. Do you and Kinsey have everything you need? I'm not a very good hostess, I'm afraid."

"We'll manage. Good night, Thea," she said and pulled the door shut.

I sat on the edge of the bed for a while, my headache slowly ebbing as I thought about a variety of unconnected topics: tomorrow's trial, illegal alcohol and easy money, the mail I'd left scattered on the floor of my office, shell shock, the waning moon behind the closed curtains of my bedroom, Leo's voice as he talked about Rudy, and how secure I'd felt pulled close against Gus's chest. Then with a sigh I rose, got ready for bed, blew out the bedside lamp, and slid beneath the quilts. I expected to lie there wide awake, as sleepless as Lloyd in his cell or Grandma Liza when the pain in her legs kept her up all night, but I fell asleep almost immediately and was not disturbed by so much as one bad dream.

I slept so well, in fact, that in the morning Cece had to roust me awake with a firm knock on the door and after opening the door, an even firmer call.

"Thea, wake up!"

"What? What?" Never at my most intelligible when startled awake, I sat up quickly. "What's wrong?" Cece came farther into the room.

"I don't know if anything's wrong but Gus wants to talk to you."

"What time is it?" Cece was fully dressed and presentable and daylight showed through the crack in the curtains. "Oh, no! I didn't sleep through the trial, did I?" I pushed off the covers and swung my legs over the side, imagining Lloyd looking out at the crowded court room and not seeing his own sister there. What would he think? And what would the jury think? That I was too ashamed of my brother, too sure of his guilt, to show my face?

"It's not quite half past seven, and before you bring up the store, Kinsey already went across the street and explained to Raymond that you wouldn't be in this morning."

"Well, then, what are you banging on my door for?"

"Gus is downstairs and—"

"I know that, Cece. I may have had a knock on the head, but I managed to retain my hearing and most of my mental faculties. Mort told us Gus planned to stay the night."

"It's not that simple." What a good friend I had in Cecelia Carr, I thought, able to tolerate both my interruptions and my bad temper! "Sometime early this morning, I don't know when exactly but well before I was up at six, someone from the sheriff's office came to get Gus. I know that because Gus wasn't anywhere to be found when I went downstairs. He'd made up a bed on the parlor sofa—"

"That overstuffed horsehair monstrosity? It's uncomfortable to sit on, let alone sleep on it. Couldn't we do better than that?"

After an audible sigh—perhaps I gave her more credit than she deserved for being able to ignore interruptions—she said, "If you would just let me finish." I tried to appear chastened, pressed my lips together, and nodded my acquiescence.

"Gus wasn't around anywhere and neither was Kinsey. I didn't know what to think but then Kinsey came back about a half hour ago and said one of the constables came to get Gus sometime before daylight. Kinsey heard him and came downstairs but Gus told him to go back to bed, everything was all right."

"Of course, Kinsey didn't do that," I interjected, having a brother of my own and so understanding the nature of boys.

"No, but by the time he got his pants on, Gus was gone so Kinsey's just been hanging outside the sheriff's office for the last hour."

"Did he see anything? Do you think they caught Leo?"

"He didn't see anything and he doesn't know anything, either. There was some coming and going but Kinsey said he couldn't tell what it was all about, but—" Cece lowered her voice "—Gus just came in and he asked me to get you. Said it was something you should hear first and then you could tell

Kinsey and me. So hurry up and get dressed and come down to the kitchen. I'll go put some breakfast on for Gus while he's waiting, but don't make him wait very long. The suspense is killing Kinsey and me!"

I didn't need to be told twice. I hurried down the hallway to the lavatory, indoor plumbing another proof of my father's progressive nature, all the while lost in wild speculation. I grabbed clothes out of the bureau and pulled my hair back with a ribbon and was pushing open the kitchen door not even fifteen minutes after Cece's direction to hurry up. I felt slightly winded when I got there and at the smell of eggs and ham and fresh coffee also felt hungry. Not just slightly, either, but so ravenously hungry I had to stop myself from marching over to the stove and eating my breakfast straight out of the frying pan.

When I could tear my gaze away from Cecelia at the stove, I found Gus eyeing me with a half smile from his place at the kitchen table as Kinsey, next to Gus, mopped up the last of his egg with a piece of bread.

"Cecelia," said Gus but looking at me as he spoke, "something tells me Thea is hungry. Could you please—?" Like Grandmother, he was not one to miss much, or perhaps I was once again more transparent than I wanted to be.

"Good morning to you, too," I said, trying for dignity and almost immediately giving it up for confession. "I am starving. Can your news wait until I eat something?"

"Sure," a somewhat comforting answer because whatever he had to say couldn't be so very critical if it could be supplanted by eggs over easy.

Finally, everyone fed and the last of the coffee poured, Cece shooed Kinsey out of the kitchen and shot me a quick glance with her brows raised in curiosity as she exited behind her brother. I understood her mute appeal. The suspense was beginning to get to me, too.

"We do have other rooms in the house besides the kitchen," I said.

"My mother says the kitchen is the place for—" He stopped abruptly.

"For what?" I prompted.

"For family, she says. The kitchen is the place for family." The tenderness in his voice when he said the simple words was not for his mother, I thought, and felt a patch of warmth on each cheek. "How's your head?"

"Hard, if you ask my grandmother." I smiled to be sure he knew I was teasing and continued, "My head is fine, Gus. The goose egg is down to half the size it was last night and I don't have a headache at all. I'm right as rain."

"Good." Pause. Then with unexpected intensity, "You scared the hell out of me last night, Thea." The fact that he didn't apologize for his minor profanity told me that in his own way Gus Davis had been as affected by Leo Stanislaw's violence as I. "I knew when I got here last night and you weren't here and Cece said you told her ten minutes but it had been at least twenty that something was wrong."

"Wrong," I repeated. "That's one way of putting it, I suppose. I was so scared, Gus, I didn't know what to do. Leo was so" —I searched for a word and settled for the obvious — "hateful. In a very literal way." I met Gus's gaze directly. "How did I miss that in him? He truly hated me. He wanted to hurt me and humiliate me and I still don't understand why. I mean, part of it was about Lloyd and Rudy but he brought up my father and me as a girl. All that happened years ago." I shook my head at the memory. "He must have been holding on to that hatred for years, nurturing it and letting it grow. I could almost pity him."

Gus reached over and placed a hand on both of mine that I held neatly folded on the table in front of me.

"Don't waste your pity on Leo Stanislaw, Thea," Gus's voice detached and colder than I'd ever heard. "He's not worth it. And he's dead."

I responded aloud with my first thought. "Oh, Gus, you didn't—"

"If I did kill the man, would it make a difference to you?" The unspoken *about me* at the end of his question was understood by both of us, even if he didn't speak the phrase aloud.

I sat there thinking, Gus's hand still warm on mine, and finally answered, "I don't think so," but the idea of Gus killing Leo Stanislaw still troubled me.

"Do you think I didn't kill men in the war? Do you think the rifle and the bayonet were all for show?" If I hadn't heard kindness in his voice, I could almost have felt chastised, a child who hadn't paid attention when the teacher lectured.

"No, of course, not. But Blessing, Kansas, isn't France and Leo Stanislaw isn't a faceless German soldier. There would be more to it, wouldn't there?"

It was Gus's turn for silent thought. He sat back in his chair, removing his hand from mine as he did so, and looked down at the table top for a while. I missed the small warmth of contact with him and contemplated being touched by Gus Davis and being touched by Leo Stanislaw. Why should there be such a world, such a galaxy, of difference? Why would I willingly curl into Gus and run from Leo? Something at the core of the man, surely, or did it come back to my own heart?

Gus finally looked up from his contemplation of solid oak and nodded.

"How did you get so smart, Miss Hansen? Yes, there would be more to my killing Stanislaw than if I'd killed the Kaiser's whole infantry. It troubled me sometimes that I killed men I didn't know. My father warned me about it when I enlisted. He fought in the War Between the States and even fifty years later he remembered what it was like to look down at a man and think you might have liked him if you hadn't killed him, might've shared a love for horses or beer, might've worshiped the same God. He was right, too. I probably think about it more than I should. I did my duty and the war's over and life goes on. But last night—"

No smile in his eyes, no lilt to his voice, but no shame either, when he admitted, "If I'd had a knife with me last night, I'd have slit that man's throat without a second thought. As it was, I came close to snapping his spine and being done with it. I was trained to go behind enemy lines and get past sentries so I have some experience, but last night wasn't like the war where everything was secret and dark and the man on the ground a faceless stranger. To see you there last night and Stanislaw with his hands on you—" I could see him relive the moment. "When I told you that you scared the hell out of me, Thea, that was wrong. *I* scared the hell out of me. Two years at the Front and I never took a moment of pleasure in the fighting, never felt the rage I felt last night. It was always duty that pushed me on, but last night I wanted you safe and him dead. I wanted to kill that man and make him pay for hurting you."

There was still a vestige of surprise in his tone at the notion. I had realized the deep well of passion in the man from our first kiss, but apparently Gus didn't spend much time examining his own feelings. When this is all over, I decided, I'll do something about that.

"But you didn't kill him, did you?" I didn't know how I was so certain, but I was. "So it must have been Mort. Or did one of the constables—?" When he didn't answer right away, I added with a touch of asperity, "Do not make me play *Twenty Questions* this early in the morning, Gus Davis. I don't enjoy parlor games, even in the best of times. What happened to Leo Stanislaw?"

"Very early this morning while you slept and I tried to sleep on that instrument of torture you keep in the front room, Leo Stanislaw broke into the office of the Holiday Sugar Company looking for money and Charles Holiday shot him dead."

At that moment I discovered that *his jaw dropped* wasn't only a poor literary metaphor from a bad novel. The words could also describe an actual occurrence because my mouth fell open and for one of the few times in my life before or since, I was speechless. Simply speechless and for a very long moment.

"Poor Dolf." My words came as a surprise to both Gus and me, but my first thought was that both of Dolf's sons were gone now and what a grief that was for any father! Rudy had been the best of the three, yet Dolf would outlive both his boys and somehow that seemed terrible to me.

Lost in the shock of the words, it didn't register that Gus was no longer seated across from me but rather stood next to me. He took my forearm in a firm but gentle grip, pulled me upright—though I came willingly enough, placed both hands to the side of my face, and kissed me.

"What a darling girl you are!" the words a tender declaration of something yet to be explored.

I smiled at him and pulled him closer for another kiss that triggered a response not as tender as the first but holding an emotion equally as pleasurable, something I would also enjoy exploring in depth one day. Eventually, I pushed him away and returned to my chair.

"Enough distractions. I want to know what happened." I sat down and waited for him to do the same because even then, in the emotion of the moment, I was conscious of a niggling doubt, of something not right in his few words of announcement. "Tell me what it all means, Gus." Once more seated across from him, I was able to watch his face as he thought through his answer.

"I don't know what it *all* means, Thea, not by a long shot," his tone once more that of Gus Davis, attorney at law. I felt a momentary pang of loss for Gus Davis, lover but supposed both had their place in my life and I should get used to it. "It seems that Holiday's statement included a confession of sorts from Stanislaw. Not about his assault on you but about murdering his brother."

"Leo confessed to murdering Rudy?" I didn't bother to hide my surprised skepticism.

"I know, and I agree it seems incredible and too good to be true. I only know the few details McGill shared with me early this morning, but I'll know more in a little while. Judge Plumquist has called a meeting with McGill, with Marquart, and with me in about" —he looked over at the kitchen wall clock — "thirty minutes to discuss the new development. I don't want to get your hopes up, Thea, but if what McGill hinted is true, it would be very good news for Lloyd."

I felt a curious mix of emotions: happiness, of course, if Lloyd were freed and came home, but a level of disbelief and a sense of unease, too. In the absence of an aching head, memories from the night before were beginning to surface. I might wish them away with all my might but feared they weren't going anywhere; and some of the memories were already causing questions about Gus's news that I didn't want or welcome.

"What is it?" He had expected a happier response from me but didn't sound disappointed or hurt. He might have been a little surprised but Gus Davis, attorney at law, was more curious than anything else.

"Nothing," I replied. "At least, nothing now before your meeting. Do you think there'll be a trial today?"

"Plumquist cancelled the trial. For today, I mean."

"But maybe for good."

"That's my hope," he agreed. He stood, shrugged into his suit coat he'd draped on the back of a chair, and began to straighten his tie.

An opportunity too good to miss. I rose and went to stand in front of him, raising both hands to the crooked tie and putting it even more crooked when I pulled his head down to mine.

"Thank you," I said, not sure what it was I thanked him for. Certainly, there was a list from which I could choose.

"My pleasure," he murmured, his lips hovering very close to mine. "Really," and stifled my laughter with his mouth. Gus Davis, lover, was back, I thought with satisfaction, if only for a departing moment, and far be it from me not to take advantage of his presence.

Chapter 16

Tuesday, October 21, 1919

Cece's first question, of course, after I shared Gus's news with Kinsey and her, was what this would mean for her brother. Would he have to testify at all? If he didn't testify, could he still be arrested for his role in the illegal liquor business? Would it still count to his credit that he was willing to tell what he knew even if there wasn't a trial?

I waited for her to run down and gave one blanket answer to cover all her questions: "I don't know."

With my ignorance established as fact, Cece went back into the kitchen to clean up breakfast and contemplate dinner while I wrote a hasty note to Uncle Carl filling in more of what I didn't know and sent it via Kinsey to the hotel at the other end of town. Then, perilously close to twiddling my thumbs, I decided I had to face my office and sooner would be better than later. I repeated last night's route across the street, only this time a bright, warmish morning instead of a cold night, entered through the warehouse door in the alley, and walked into the hallway that led to my office, the hallway where I'd been pinned like a collector's moth to the wall, where Leo's blood was all I could taste and smell, where he had managed to get my skirts well above my knees and I couldn't stop him going further, could hardly move at all without a nauseating clanging going off in my head. I remembered it all clearly but instead of Leo Stanislaw—the man is dead, I told myself, and poses no threat to anyone—

there in front of me was Raymond Cuthbert rising from his knees with a sponge in one hand and a basin of water in the other.

"Oh, Raymond," I said and could hardly speak for the tears lodged in my throat. "You don't have to do that messy job."

When he turned his face in my direction, a face I had once considered old and sour, I saw only an expression of happy welcome, nothing old or sour anywhere. Had he changed or had I? He walked toward me and I told myself that if Raymond, of all people, hugged me, I would certainly burst into childlike sobs, something to embarrass both of us. Fortunately, he did not attempt anything as familiar as a hug.

Instead, Raymond stopped in front of me, examined my face wordlessly, and finally said, "'A quality store is immaculate front and back. What the customer sees and what she doesn't see are equally important.' We both heard your father say those exact words more than once, Thea. I was out early this morning, spoke to Kinsey on the street, and when I got here I happened to notice that the hallway was untidy."

I had to smile at the word. Untidy, indeed.

"Yes," I agreed, "I imagine it was. Well, thank you." Still holding the basin and sponge with both hands, he followed me to my office where the mail was once again stacked in the center of my desk, my dropped shawl neatly folded in one corner, and the chair back in its place, no longer a weapon to be propelled against an enemy but simply a chair behind a desk.

"The account ledgers I had out—" I began, and Raymond nodded toward the file cabinet from which I'd taken the books last evening.

"Well." I couldn't think what else to say and the single word hung between us.

"If there isn't anything else, Thea, I should return to the floor. Flo's by herself."

"Did Kinsey tell you the latest news?" I asked abruptly and by his puzzled expression realized he didn't know. "Leo Stanislaw is dead. He tried to rob someone after he was here with me, and that person apparently shot him dead."

"You don't say." Raymond didn't look shocked or even very interested. "It isn't often one hears of unacceptable behavior so immediately and appropriately rewarded, and I find it gratifying when matters conclude as they should. There's a flyer in your mail from a spice company in New York City that looked interesting and don't forget we're due an order from Sears on tomorrow's afternoon train. If there's nothing else—"

"No," I responded, "there's nothing else. Thank you," and hoped he realized the thank you was for more than scrubbing blood off a wall or reminding me about an order of dry goods.

The morning crept by, every minute an hour, every hour a day until Raymond stepped inside to say, "There's someone to see you out here, Thea."

Gus, at last, I thought with relief, but not just Gus. In front of Gus stood Lloyd, grinning with a sheepish look, as if he felt he needed to apologize for the interruption.

"Oh. Oh." I stared at my brother a moment, stunned into speaking repetitive monosyllables, and then rushed to him and with my arms around him, wept the tears I'd been holding back since the night before when I'd asked Cece to scrub me clean from Leo Stanislaw's blood. Finally able to get out an intelligible word, I put both hands to Lloyd's cheeks and asked, "Are you free, Lloyd, free and clear and can you come home?"

"Yes, to all of the above. Cleared of any and all charges."

Over Lloyd's shoulder, I met Gus's gaze. "Thank you," I said. "How can we ever thank you?"

Gus looked embarrassed. "It's not me you should thank. In a round about way, that honor belongs to Charles Holiday."

I would have asked more but the time didn't seem right. "Can we talk later?" was all I said.

"We can talk whenever you want, Thea. Any time. Any place," some kind of promise connected with those words that I wanted to think about, but later, not now. Now belonged to Lloyd.

"Let's go see Grandma Liza and Uncle Carl," I suggested to my brother. "They'll be as happy as I am to see you, and I'm pretty sure neither one will boo-hoo into your shirt collar."

"Let's wait a while."

"Wait?" I repeated, surprised.

"I want to see Cecelia first. She's at the house, isn't she?"

Cecelia? I thought, surprised again. Lloyd and she were friends—*very* good friends as I now recalled—but Cece before Grandmother, before Uncle Carl and Aunt Louisa? Yet once across the street and at the foot of the front walk, I watched

Cecelia burst out the front door as if chased by wolves, tear down the porch steps, and run straight into my brother's arms and recognized that I needed to amend my original idea. Not only friends but family.

Gus, who'd followed behind, took me by the arm and walked me away from the couple.

"Maybe some privacy would be nice."

"Then maybe they shouldn't be kissing in the front yard," I retorted but spoke the words cheerfully. "I knew they were friends, but—well, I suppose it's something else I was too busy with the store to notice."

"She came to the jail to see Lloyd every day, and it made a big difference to his spirits. Didn't you see the change in him?"

"I'm ashamed to admit that I didn't and even if I had, I would have given myself the credit for any improvement to his spirits. Me. Just a sister. I should've known better." But I didn't mind giving place to Cece, who would be better for Lloyd than I ever could be. "It's humbling, though," I added as an after thought.

"I suppose, but don't let it bother you. There's supposed to be a big difference between a sister and the woman you hope to marry some day. You understand that, don't you?"

Gus took my hand in his as we turned the corner of the house, climbed the back porch steps, and entered the kitchen. Always the kitchen, I thought. The place for family.

I answered his question with, "I do understand that," but refrained from additional commentary despite my interest in the subject. Right at the moment I wanted to ask about Charles Holiday.

"What happened at the sugar factory to make the judge dismiss the charges against Lloyd? I don't understand how what happened out there could have such a big effect on the trial."

Gus waited until we were seated once more at the kitchen table, bowls of last night's soup and slices of day-old bread between us. Not the delectable selections from the kitchen of the Hansen House, but I reassured myself that Gus had survived for two years on soldiers' rations so perhaps he would not mind a meal reheated and slightly used.

"Holiday said he was working late in his office at the factory—"

"It must have been close to midnight! Does that seem probable?"

"He said his wife and daughter were away and he'd lost half a day of work waiting around the court room to see if he'd be called to testify, and that was true enough. Then he went home for his noon dinner and straight out to the factory. He said he got there around two o'clock and time got away from him. I don't think there's anything suspicious in what the man said, Thea, and what would Holiday gain by lying about any of that, anyway?"

I had the glimmer of an idea about something Mr. Holiday might gain, but it was nebulous at best.

"And then—what? Leo Stanislaw shows up at the factory out of nowhere? Why? The man's pretty beaten up, according to you. Why wouldn't he just high tail it out of town, out of the county, in fact? That's what I'd do." I had a sudden picture of Leo's Paige Six-55 in all its black glory parked outside the jail. "Was he driving the Paige?"

"Apparently. As far as I know it's still sitting outside the factory."

"So why stop? There's nothing in the county to catch that thing, probably nothing in the state. Leo could have headed for Canada with a good chance of making the border without any pursuit to talk about." I put both elbows on the table and rested my chin on my palms. "What does Mr. Holiday say happened after Leo got there?"

By this time Gus was watching me carefully, I think surprised at the doubt in my tone.

"Now you sound like the lawyer. Am I on the witness stand?"

"No. Your evidence would be pure hearsay and probably not admissible," and laughed a little at his look of surprise. "I did pay attention yesterday, Gus. Will you finish the story about Leo and Charles Holiday, please? I still don't understand why any of this tale, true or not, should result in Lloyd's release."

"Holiday says Stanislaw burst into his office flashing a gun and demanding money and raving—his word—about how he was the king of crime and not afraid of anybody and if Holiday didn't open the safe he'd take care of him—and here's the important part—like he took care of Rudy when Rudy got in his way."

"He said he *took care* of Rudy? Leo said that?"

"He did. According to McGill, Mr. Holiday was quite clear on that particular subject. Holiday said he feared for his life because if a man would kill his own brother, he, Holiday, didn't stand a chance. So he told Stanislaw he didn't have a safe, that he kept cash in a strong box in the drawer. But he didn't have a strong box in the drawer, he had—"

"A pistol," I finished, deep in thought. "Of course, he would. He's no fool. There certainly were times when he was out there by himself and it would make sense to keep something around for protection. So—" I assembled the incident in my head. "Mr. Holiday is working in his office by himself late at night. A not unusual occurrence, he says, and I'd guess that's true. Leo Stanislaw bursts in." I looked at Gus. "How did he come in? Through the front office, the way we entered the other day? Or is there another door to the office?"

"I don't know that."

"All right. Well, we do tend to leave our doors unlocked if not open in Blessing, even when we know better, and I can personally attest that Leo Stanislaw was practiced at finding open doors." One of those mental flashes again. The squeak of the hall door as I'm bundling the account books and mail into my arms and my heart speeding up at the sound. Then Leo Stanislaw lounging in the doorway, the look of a wolf about him despite, maybe because of, his wide, toothy grin. I looked over at Gus quickly and surprised a look on his face that indicated he might understand why I'd gone so suddenly silent and had stopped breathing for just that moment.

"Anyway," I continued, "Leo demands Holiday open his safe and threatens him if he doesn't comply. Where did Leo get his gun? I can guarantee that he didn't have one on him when he was with me. We were in very close proximity." An understatement if ever there was one. "There wasn't much about his person I wasn't aware of and I'd have noticed a gun."

By the way the skin around his eyes tightened, I knew Gus didn't like that particular implication but only suggested, "In his motor car, maybe?"

"Maybe. So Mr. Holiday says, calm as you please, I don't have a safe on the premises but then volunteers that he has a strong box bursting with cash in his desk drawer. Does he really have a strong box in the drawer?"

"He does, and apparently it's not a secret. He says he thought Leo might have heard about the cash box and because he knew he had that pistol in the drawer, he thought mentioning the box would give him a reason to open the drawer."

"Hmmm. Shades of Dodge City. Mr. Holiday's quite the quick draw, isn't he? Slides open the drawer under the watchful eye of murderous Leo, king of crime, pulls out the pistol and with Leo looking right at him with his own weapon drawn, still manages to shoot him dead. Does that seem reasonable to you, Gus?"

"Judge Plumquist interviewed Holiday and was completely satisfied with what he heard. Ben Marquart did the same. In fact, it was Marquart who made the motion to dismiss all charges against your brother because Leo Stanislaw confessed to the crime." But I could tell from Gus's tone that he was troubled by my attitude. "I thought you'd be over the moon because Lloyd was free. Your brother's home and there's not a shred of suspicion attached to him. No one believes he's guilty because the real murderer confessed. It's exactly what you wanted, Thea."

I smiled at him. "I know what I wanted, but I've been spending a lot of time in the company of someone who thinks there's more to life than getting what you want," and quoted softly, "'It's truth on the line whatever side of the court room you sit on. It's all about truth.'"

"Am I destined to go through life with you reminding me of my past pretensions when I least expect it?"

"Is that a proposal?" I countered, my smile broadening as he suddenly realized what he'd said and how it might be construed. "Never mind," I went on gently. "I won't hold you to it. I expect to be proposed to someday by someone and it had better be a lot more romantic than sitting at an old kitchen table with dirty dishes between us."

He'd recovered his equilibrium, but what he might have said I'll never know because at that moment Lloyd and Cece pushed open the door to the kitchen.

"We're headed for the hotel to see your family, Thea, but I wanted you to know first. It looks like Lloyd and I might get married." Cece's previously radiant face dimmed a little. "I should have said something, I guess, about Lloyd and me but you had so much on your mind and I thought we'd get through the trial first and tell you when Lloyd came home." Good girl, I thought, *when* not *if.* There's a sign of true love.

I stood and gave them both a hug. "I'm very happy for you both." To Lloyd, I said, "I expect Grandmother will want to celebrate tonight so tell her I'll see her for supper and you should take advantage of her good temper when she sees you. Ask to use that new fancy bath room she fixed up at the hotel. You'll get flooded with hot water straight from the tap and she's got those big fluffy towels. I've been dying for the experience myself."

"Is that your underhanded way of saying I need a bath?" my brother asked. We all laughed.

"Sometimes the truth hurts," I retorted. After the two lovebirds departed, I said the words again, looking at Gus this time.

"Sometimes," he agreed. He was standing, too. "Thanks for the meal."

"You'll join us tonight for supper at the Hansen House, won't you?" Gus shook his head.

"No. That's a time for family. I don't belong there." I almost added the word *yet* at the end of the sentence but stayed quiet. Everything in its own time. "And," he concluded, "I have to get my train ticket." The words brought me up short.

"Oh."

"I have a job to get back to and a family of my own that might be wondering if I'll ever be home again."

"Of course. I forgot. Sorry," my response disjointed and sounding insincere, even to my own ears.

"If you come to your own conclusion about Charles Holiday and Leo Stanislaw you'll share it with me, won't you?"

I nodded. "Yes." He looked dissatisfied, the vertical line that indicated a certain level of frustration appearing between his brows. "I need to give serious thought to what Leo said at the store last night, Gus, and while I'd rather put the whole incident out of my mind, I can't. For a lot of reasons."

"But you'll tell me about anything you come up with, won't you?"

"Yes." The vertical line on his face deepened. Then he sighed.

"All right. I have some papers to file with the court this afternoon. I hope you and your family enjoy the celebration tonight."

"We will." Pause. "Gus."

Already headed for the back door, he turned back and waited.

"You won't leave without saying good-bye, will you?"

He must have found the idea more amusing than I did because he had to stifle a quiet laugh before he said, "No, Thea. I wouldn't dream of it. I have to collect my fee, you know."

Since his arrival, I hadn't given one single thought to so prosaic a subject and stammered, "I forgot. I completely forgot. Of course, I'll have it ready and if it's not enough you just need to say so."

"I feel sure we can come to some kind of mutually satisfactory payment." He gave another quiet laugh, more in response to whatever it was he was thinking than to the conversation at hand. "I'll see you tomorrow sometime. Breakfast at the hotel, maybe, for old times' sake?"

"That would be good."

It took me a while to gather my thoughts once Gus was gone—would his departure always leave me with a bereft, unanchored feeling, the man off to the court house in the morning and me wandering room to room unable to get my bearings?—but I eventually managed to clear the table, stack the dirty dishes in the sink, and return to the store.

Several customers stopped me to express their congratulations and good wishes at Lloyd's release, and I made all the proper responses but thought I'd never forget how different they had acted two weeks ago when Lloyd was in jail on murder charges and no dead man's confession was available to change the story.

Ian Buchanan stopped by the office, smiling, clearly happy at the news.

"It is a relief," I admitted, "to have Lloyd home."

"And to know a murderer is off the streets," Ian added.

"That, too."

"How's Lloyd?"

"Surprisingly good. As odd as it sounds, especially with him being in jail for the last two weeks or so, he's the best he's been since he came home. Almost his old self. His eyes don't have that shadow in them and his mind's clear as a bell." He's in love, too, I almost added, but that was something Ian Buchanan didn't need to know just yet.

"That's great news, Thea. Delta wants to have both of you over for supper tomorrow night and asked me to use all my influence to get you to come. If you don't show up, my reputation in her eyes will suffer a severe blow." I laughed at the weak humor because he expected a response. "I know it may not be convenient for you, Thea, but Delta was very worried about Lloyd. He was Joe's best friend, really, so his connection with our son makes him doubly valuable in her eyes. Please humor her and come for supper." I doubted Lloyd's enthusiasm for the evening, and my hesitation must have showed on my face because Ian quickly added, "We think a lot of Lloyd, and it would make Delta happy. Please." How could I refuse after that shameless appeal?

For some reason, after the man left, I found myself remembering Leo Stanislaw's words to me, words spoken on the last night of Leo's life in the very office in which I sat. Perhaps it was Ian Buchanan talking about Joe, about the three "Blessing Boys" off to the Front in gay good spirits and now only Lloyd left. How would I have felt if someone had killed my brother, had snatched him away just when and where he should have been the safest?

I knew the answer. I would have felt like Leo Stanislaw. Furious at his brother's death. Resentful that other people who might have had a hand in the death went on living. And if I possessed Leo's cruel streak, I might have wanted someone to pay for the mortal wound to my family.

That brother of yours killed my kid brother, killed Rudy, and left him laying on the floor like an old oil rag. That wasn't right.

There had been the ring of violent truth in those words. Rage and insult and grief, too. I thought I almost understood him, as much as I would ever understand a man like that. Leo Stanislaw, unaccustomed to honest emotion and how it could hurt, not knowing what to do with his feelings, added the pain he felt at Rudy's death to all the imagined slights he'd ever received from my family and was eager to take everything out on me, Thea Hansen, his own personal human lightning rod, for every vengeful, evil, lustful thought in his head. Leo never killed his brother. I knew it as sure as I knew my own name. Maybe, as Kinsey suggested, the two Stanislaw boys didn't get along, but Rudy was Leo's "kid brother" and Leo wouldn't kill him. But if not Leo and not Lloyd, then who? *Who?*

I pondered the question all afternoon as I went about my regular duties, closing the store by myself for the first time in days. Life settling back to normal after everything normal had been rocked like a boat on a stormy lake. Except, for me, it wasn't normal and couldn't be normal as long as the question of Rudy's death went unresolved to my own private satisfaction. The rest of my family, however, not privy to my doubts, were delighted at the outcome of such "rampant injustice"—my grandmother's words—and we celebrated with a large meal in Grandmother's apartment, followed by glasses of sherry and a toast to Lloyd's and Cecelia's future. Cece had joined us that night, a blushing and happy Cece, and Kinsey was there, too, family by extension.

Later, everyone departed but me, Grandma Liza said, "Don't mince words with me, Thea. I'm too old for it. Carl told me Leo Stanislaw broke into the store last night while you were there and threatened you. No harm done, Carl said in that tone he uses when he's trying to keep something from me, so I know some harm must have been done. Did the man hurt you? Is that why you were so quiet tonight?"

"Was I quiet?" I thought I'd acted my usual self.

"There was something going on behind those blue eyes of yours tonight. Did the man hurt you?" She thumped her cane on the floor for emphasis with the repeated question.

"No," then shook my head and amended, "Not exactly. He wanted to hurt me and tried to rape me."—when Liza Hansen said not to mince words with her she meant it— "He probably would have succeeded, too, because I hit my head on the doorframe and it made me woozy for a while so I didn't have much strength when I needed it. But Gus came looking for me and scared Leo away in the process. Would have killed him, I think. He was pretty fierce about it, except he got distracted by me sitting like a rag doll on the floor, and Leo managed to get away."

Grandmother seemed to age as she listened to the account, even though my tone stayed rational and my demeanor calm.

"He's like his father, then."

"Leo?" I asked, bewildered. Dolf had never been a violent man in all his years in Blessing.

"No. Gus Davis. I wondered about it when I saw him. He looks like his aunt more than either of his parents as I remember them. Lily Fairchild died a long time ago. She's buried in the Lutheran cemetery," I recalled her grave from the day Gus and I went in search of his family's markers, "but he carries himself like his father and there's the look of his father in his eyes. That's the first thing I thought when I saw him. You can put a suit on a monkey but it's still a monkey."

"Grandmother!"

"I don't mean any insult by it, Thea. John Davis had his uses and I suppose in some ways I should have been grateful he was in Blessing when he was. God knows I'm grateful enough now that the apple fell close to the tree." Her color returned as she spoke. "How does your head feel? What did the doctor say?"

"The doctor says I have a very hard head, a fact that will come as no surprise to you, that I was not concussed, and that I will be fine." I reached up and pushed against the spot at the back of my head that had once been the size of an egg and was now simply a tender bruise.

"And Leo Stanislaw is dead," Grandma Liza stated without bothering to hide her satisfaction.

"Yes."

"Killed by Charles Holiday."

"Yes."

"After he assaulted you."

"Yes."

"And after he murdered his own brother." When no *Yes* followed the statement she sent me a keen look. "So that's why you were so quiet tonight. You don't believe Leo killed Rudy."

"I don't know," I responded with a hesitation unusual for me. "He said some things at the store last night that make me think maybe he didn't."

"Then who?" It was like the old woman to go straight to the heart of a matter.

"I don't know that either." Tired of the endless speculation swirling around in my mind, I stood and gave her a quick kiss. "Maybe I'm wrong. Maybe I'm just tired and still suffering the effects of a bump on the head. Maybe I'm just a confused, dithering kind of girl that needs to go home to bed."

"You've never been confused or dithering in your life and I'd say you're not much of a girl any more, besides. You look like a full grown woman to me, with more sense than God gave most men. But I do think you should go home and go to bed. Do you want someone to walk you home?" Because you're still a little frightened, she might have added, because you were exposed to something that would have scared even the brightest and healthiest of women.

"No. Thank you. It's not that late and the street lamps are lit, and it's Blessing, after all. It's home."

"Home's a funny thing."

"How so?" I paused with my hand on the doorknob, curious about such a mysterious statement from my usually straightforward and literal grandmother.

"I think you're close to finding out that Blessing, Kansas, doesn't have much to do with home at all."

I shook my head and pulled open the door at the same time. "Since when did you start speaking in riddles? I could almost be convinced I wasn't the one that got the knock on the head. Good night."

Grandmother returned a good-night without further comment, but I thought I heard her dry chuckle as I closed the door, and it seemed to me from the sound of her laugh that she thought she knew something I didn't. Liza Hansen was a woman that liked to keep the upper hand and from what I'd heard she had always been that way, but whatever she wanted to crow about would have to wait until I worked through the more serious puzzle of Rudy Stanislaw's murder and separated deceit from truth. Not just for my peace of mind, although I wasn't about to lie to myself and say that wasn't important, but also because there should be a true accounting for the young man's death. Rudy deserved that much.

Chapter 17

Wednesday, October 22, 1919

I found myself heading for the jail the next morning by habit, despite the fact that when I left the house my brother slept soundly in his own bed in his own room. Without the added stop, I arrived at the store earlier than usual but, of course, not earlier than Raymond or even earlier than Cecelia that particular morning.

"You're here early," I remarked when I saw her rearranging the shelf of tonics and creams.

"I couldn't sleep," Cece admitted, but to my eye she did not look like a woman deprived of her necessary rest. She still carried a bit of a glow with her, one that had little to do with the state of her health and everything to do with her heart.

"I told you you should have stayed with us last night instead of going back to your apartment."

"Lloyd thinks it's better if we don't sleep under the same roof before we're married." I caught myself before I made an inelegant and telltale snort but made a face at Cece, anyway, so she'd know how I felt about my brother's sudden quest for Victorian respectability.

"I know, Thea, but Lloyd has a newfound respect for public opinion, and it's really rather sweet that he's worried that some residual effect of his being in jail will affect my reputation. As if I give a fig for it, but he's your brother and he can be as hard-headed as any Hansen."

"I can't decide if you just insulted or flattered the family."

She returned my grin. "Oh, flattered, Thea. How could my future sister-in-law think otherwise?" and she flounced off toward the stairs that led to the second floor, her steps bouncing with happiness.

Cece had more than one reason to be happy, too, because at supper the evening before she'd shared the good news that Gus had found her late in the afternoon to tell her that Mort McGill wasn't going to press any charges of any kind against Kinsey.

"Gus said it doesn't mean that the sheriff isn't going to keep his eye on Kinsey for a long time or that Kinsey shouldn't expect to get several lectures about obeying the law, which I'm in full favor of, by the way. Sometimes my brother needs to be told something several times before it sinks in."

She had glared at Kinsey across the table and for a moment he'd looked somewhat abashed in return, although from my side perspective not nearly as remorseful as I might have wished. His mouth twitched at the attention, a sign I had come to know meant that Kinsey wasn't paying much notice to whatever the adults in his vicinity were talking about. The boy will probably give us all a run for our money, I thought, and smiled to myself at the idea of Lloyd carrying the on-going burden of being a good example. It served him right for all the grief he'd given me.

Lloyd seemed to have slept better than I his first night home, but then he thought all questions were answered and all mysteries solved and I knew better. I had, in fact, spent some of the night curled up in the chair in my room, remembering and thinking. I needed to make a visit to someone I'd rather never see again, and my internal debate centered on whether I'd tell Gus before or after I trekked out to the Holiday Sugar factory. I had promised to share any deductions I formed about Rudy's murder that went against the current belief but had purposefully not attached a before or after time to my promise. That I had promised at all was because I realized Gus felt a need to protect me, and as old-fashioned as that was and as much as I didn't need protecting—Leo Stanislaw notwithstanding—like Cecelia, I found the idea rather sweet.

Leaving the store in good hands, I walked the few blocks north along Main Street, past the movie house and the jail and the Town Hall, where Joey Buchanan might one day stand in all his marble glory. How I would ever be able to look at it without remembering Rudy and Lloyd and the true story behind Joe I couldn't imagine. It seemed that one crisis at a time would remain my motto longer than I wished.

Gus was already seated in the dining room of the Hansen House, dressed not in his usual dark and dignified suit but in a pullover sweater, shirt, and plain uncreased trousers. From a distance he looked ten years younger, but when he saw me and stood I thought he had not really changed. Some small vestige of the war still showed in his eyes, and I wondered if I would always see its reflection in their hazel depths.

"You look very collegiate this morning," I observed.

"No meetings. No trial. No plans, really, except the City Council asked to meet with me tomorrow afternoon."

"What's that about? Do you know?"

"I'm afraid it might be about the Buchanan statue for the town square."

"Oh, dear."

"Oh, dear is right. It appears the city fathers want to get my input about honoring Joe Buchanan with a statue since I served with him." He shifted in his chair and leaned forward to speak to me in a lowered voice. "From the little I've heard, he doesn't seem to have been universally liked in his home town."

I pictured Joey Buchanan, a dark Adonis, sleek hair and laughing eyes, clever and cutting and so very attractive. I remembered his offhand arrogance, the jokes that bordered on cruelty, the girls he'd chased and then promptly dropped once he caught them.

"He made a lot of girls cry," I said, "and some of them were daughters of the city fathers."

"But none of them was Thea Hansen." If he wanted assurance, I was happy to give it.

"I knew him too well through all those years growing up with Lloyd. He tried it on with me because I was female and that's how Joey Buchanan was made, but I couldn't take him seriously and he gave up pretty fast. I don't think he minded, either. Conquest was a game for Joe and a girl's broken heart was the prize. That makes him sound awful, doesn't it? But when he was with you, he never seemed awful. Just charming and fun."

"Not charming enough for Thea Hansen, though, so no broken heart there."

"No," I replied, smiling, happy that Gus wanted to be reassured again. "No broken heart there." *Yet*, I added in my mind. No broken heart yet, and wished the Kansas City Southern Railway to the devil.

"Did you buy your train ticket home already?" I managed to ask the question without a tremor in my voice or in my hand, sipping at my first coffee of the day without a spill.

He shook his head. "No, but I have time. The next train scheduled to leave in the general direction of Wyoming isn't until Friday."

"Your family will be glad to see you."

"They don't see me as much as you might think, even when I'm there, but yes, my parents miss me. My mother especially is a warm and positive kind of person, but the two years I was at the Front were hard on her. She seemed older and quieter when I got back."

"Maybe you seemed the same to her. Older and quieter, I mean."

"Maybe." We smiled at each other across the table. "How was Lloyd's first night home?"

"He slept like the proverbial baby. Do you think his dreams will be less intense now?"

"I wouldn't count on it, not right away, at least. But what I read seemed to indicate that the passage of time and a life of normal activities might have a very restorative effect."

"And there's Cece. Even though she's lost a lot in her life, she's like you described your mother, warm and positive. Good medicine for Lloyd, I hope. I've been thinking they ought to have the house after they're married. Frankly, I never liked it and I won't miss it."

"Where will you go?"

"Grandma Liza will find a room for me at the Hansen House. During normal times, I'm hardly ever home, anyway."

"Because you spend most of your time at the store, I suppose."

"I do, and it's not a sacrifice because I enjoy it. Most of the time, anyway. But I still dream about seeing the world outside Blessing and outside Kansas and outside the United States."

"Where would you like to go?"

"Paris, for sure, and London and Vienna and Berlin, all those big, grand cities I've read about in books. I'm not quite sure how to make that happen but someday with Lloyd settled down and the store running smoothly, I might throw caution to the winds and buy a steamer ticket and see the world. It may not seem all that important to you, Gus, because you've seen all those places, but just once I'd like to wake up in a place where no one speaks English."

Mavis brought our breakfasts then, and he didn't say anything in response to my words, just smiled with the same look on his face he might have given one of his nieces or nephews who'd said something cute but childish.

We talked about this and that, and by the time we finished breakfast I knew I wouldn't tell him my plans for the afternoon just yet. Later, maybe. Never, maybe. It remained to be seen. When I stood and grabbed my coat from the extra chair where I'd tossed it, Gus stood, too. Always a gentleman, I thought, except when he wasn't, except when he was slipping catlike into a dark garage or was at Leo Stanislaw's throat wishing he had a knife at hand. Not exactly a gentleman then. The contradictions continued to appeal.

"Is it too much to hope we could do this again? Maybe tonight?" Then he added, "Is there anyplace else that serves a nice meal in Blessing other than the Hansen House?"

"You can get peanuts, pickles, and beer at the billiards parlor."

"That's a hard combination to resist, but—well, you want to go and I need to work so forget I brought it up. Maybe later, though?" A question at the end.

"Lloyd and I are invited to the Buchanans' for supper, I'm afraid. Ian made a shameless request based on his wife's state of mind so I felt trapped into it, and Lloyd agreed to go because he's still basking in residual starry-eyed bliss from his recent engagement. That's not a complaint, you understand, just an observation. If we make it through the evening without something awkward happening, I won't ask one more thing of my brother and will happily pass him along to Cecelia's tender care. It seems odd, but except for greetings on the street or in church Lloyd really hasn't spent any time with the Buchanans to speak of. They didn't offer and he didn't seem to care. They were still grieving and maybe Lloyd felt uncomfortable talking about Joe's death, things being what they were."

"Lloyd probably doesn't know anything except that Joe Buchanan was killed, presumably by the enemy."

"Are you sure?" The thought that I might not have to spend the evening on edge for fear my brother would let slip some fact about the truth of Joe's death was a huge relief.

Gus took the time to think. "Lloyd was shipped out to the hospital by early summer in '18. When I left on special assignment in July of that year, Rudy and Buchanan were both present and accounted for and when I got back a month later, Buchanan was dead. People were still tight-lipped about it, too. Unless Rudy spilled the whole story to Lloyd on their trip home, which I doubt considering Lloyd's condition, it's possible Lloyd doesn't have any idea of the truth."

"I hope that's so. I guess I'll find out tonight."

"Couldn't you just ask Lloyd about it?"

"I suppose, but I don't trust myself to do that without giving something away."

"Well, good luck, then."

"Thanks." We'd been standing all that time, talking to each other across the breakfast table.

"So if not tonight, what about tomorrow night? It's my last night in Blessing." Gus, back to the original question.

"I'd like that," I replied, "and we can try the billiards hall, if you want. I'll face pickles, peanuts, and beer if you will."

"I wouldn't ask it of you, or myself, either." He laughed. "Right here is fine. Tomorrow night, half past six."

That was as good as it was going to get today, I thought as I trudged back to Monroe's, and then just one more day before Gus Davis boarded the train and headed back to Laramie, Wyoming. To say I would miss him was the very definition of understatement.

I stayed busy at Monroe's the remainder of the morning, greeted Lloyd when he finally made an appearance at the store in search of his one true love—it really was sweet to see him all starry-eyed, just as Cece had remarked—and eventually, no longer able to concentrate on accounting columns and back orders, I pushed the ledgers to the side and threw on my coat. Time for another kind of accounting altogether.

The day felt more like November than October, cold, damp, and gray, with the threat of drizzle, maybe even sleet, in the air. The weather matched my mood, which was gray, too. What I had come to believe was the truth had the same depressing effect on me as the slowly dropping temperature. I didn't want to be right but knew I was.

Frederick greeted me exactly as he'd greeted me the last time I stepped into the front office of the Holiday Sugar factory: "Thea. Hello. What a pleasant surprise to see you!"

"Again," I supplied with a smile.

"I was sure happy to hear about Lloyd."

"Thank you."

"It was a close call out here Monday night. You heard about that, didn't you?"

"Yes. How awful! Were you here that late, Frederick, when it all happened?" my question adding stress to the word *you*. No one had hinted that there was a witness to Leo's death. If there was, then I would have to rethink my conclusions, spend another night curled up in my chair not sleeping.

"Oh, no. No."

"How unfortunate that Mr. Holiday was, though!"

"Well, he works late in his office at least once a week, so it wasn't all that unusual for him to be out here."

"As late as midnight?" I asked, keeping a bland tone.

"Later, sometimes, but not usually on a Monday."

"No?"

"Mostly Wednesdays. Not always but mostly. Bad luck that when Mr. Holiday changes his routine, he meets a thug like that Leo Stanislaw. I always knew Leo was a bad one." Finally, realizing that he was doing most of the talking, he quieted. "You must want to see Mr. Holiday, Thea, because it wouldn't be my luck that you came out to see me." He didn't hide the hopeful lilt at the end of his statement and turned a faded pink as he spoke. Apparently, Frederick had developed a crush on me sometime when I wasn't looking and I felt embarrassed that I'd never noticed. Something else to add to my list of *How Did I Miss That?* items.

Frederick was two years my junior so I supposed his feelings would wilt as fast they sprouted, but I felt sorry for his unrequited affection, anyway, and answered with kindness and good humor, "Yes, I would like a few minutes with Mr. Holiday, but it's always good to see you, too, Frederick." Without giving the young man a chance to engage in any further dialogue centered on the pleasure of my company, I added, "I know Mr. Holiday prefers appointments and I know I don't have one, but would you please tell him I'm out here and would appreciate a few minutes of his time? I think he might fit me into his schedule."

Holiday did exactly that, of course, as I knew he would, his curiosity about what I'd heard during my forced proximity with Leo Stanislaw too strong for him to dismiss me without an audience. He even rose when I entered his office, which he had purposefully not done when Gus and I were last there. I took a longer than necessary moment to shut his office door and finally turned back to face him, my mind made up.

"I've been thinking a lot about greater and lesser evils," I began without introduction. He maintained his usual impassive expression, but the little jerk of his head told me I might have surprised him.

"That's to be expected, wouldn't you say, what with your brother in jail for murdering his good friend and then your own recent terrible experience?" he finally responded.

"I've been thinking about the difference between killing someone you don't know in the heat of battle, someone that might be a good man, even a friend under different circumstances, and killing a bad man under a deceptive guise of camaraderie. And if it's truly a bad man, a man capable of hurting others indiscriminately and gleefully, does it even matter how or why he dies or if it was done for purely self-serving purposes, as long as the bad man is removed from society and can't do any more damage? Or—and here's where I get really confused—does the cold-blooded killing of even a very bad man mean there were two very bad men to start with?" I stopped speaking and after a long moment asked, "What do you think about that, Mr. Holiday? What's your opinion?" Neither of us moved, facing off like two prizefighters in a ring.

"I have no idea what you're talking about, Miss Hansen. Perhaps your recent brush with personal violence from a brutish man has unsettled you more than you realize."

I took a step forward, close enough to a chair sitting in front of his desk that I could grasp its back.

"You're right about that. It did unsettle me. That's the heart of the problem, you see, because there's a part of me that is relieved beyond words that Leo Stanislaw will never surprise me alone in my office again."

Everything I said was true and even as I spoke, I wondered what I was doing there. Why did it matter? Why did the truth matter? Was it a reflection of my last two weeks in Gus Davis's company, or did it go back further and more deeply than that?

"But you murdered Leo Stanislaw, Mr. Holiday, and I can't let it go without telling you that I know you did it and I know why."

"I defended myself against a man that murdered his own brother, tried to rob me, and make no mistake, Miss Hansen, would have raped you and enjoyed every minute of it."

"I know from personal experience that the last part is true, but nothing else you said is. Leo didn't murder Rudy and he never told you he did. And Leo wasn't here to rob you. He was here to collect his part of the profits from your liquor business before he got out of the county. Probably out of the state. I think you reached into the drawer pretending you were reaching for the cash box so you could pay Leo and you pulled out your pistol and shot him point blank without a twinge of conscience before he ever knew what happened."

Something about Holiday's immobility, the sudden shuttering of his expression told me I was right, but the validation I might have expected to feel was curiously absent.

"You have a lively imagination," was all he said, still patronizing but edgy, too.

"I've noticed how busy it is at your factory. Lots of coming and going at all hours, so many wagons and trucks it must be hard to keep track of them all, which was perfect for your purposes. I can't imagine how you and Leo Stanislaw ever got on the subject to start with. That's something that does take a lively imagination, livelier than mine, anyway. Maybe it's as simple as a magnet and iron filings, I don't know, but however it happened, Leo used his criminal connections to accumulate liquor at Dolf's garage all week—another place with lots of vehicles coming and going—and on Wednesday night he'd load it up and bring it out here to the factory, where you often were working late. Also on Wednesdays. Kinsey once said that after the pick up from the garage he'd get dropped off before the wagon continued north. North. Always north. Always in the direction of the Holiday Sugar factory. What a smart arrangement! No risk to you, the cargo in at night and out in the morning and no reason a soul would ever notice anything out of the ordinary"

"Even if that were true, Miss Hansen, and, of course, it's not, there wouldn't be a way to prove any of it."

"No," I agreed sadly, "not with Leo dead. He was the only one that knew about your involvement, but Kinsey Carr knew about Leo's role. Leo Stanislaw, a reckless man as far from trustworthy as a man can be, a man who could lose his temper at the drop of a hat. You could never be sure Leo would keep his mouth shut, especially if Kinsey's testimony got Leo arrested. Rudy Stanislaw's death had become very problematic for you, hadn't it? If someone hadn't murdered Rudy, you'd still be shipping illegal liquor all over Kansas. But Kinsey Carr's involvement began to bother you, and that's why Leo said he'd been directed by "someone who knows," by you, Mr. Holiday, to teach Kinsey a lesson about keeping his mouth shut. Was it supposed to be more permanent than that, I wonder?" I shrugged. "Something else I'll never know now that Leo Stanislaw is dead. You knew Kinsey was at my house, too, because you were in the hallway outside the trial room when the Carrs were there." I took a deep breath and let it out slowly.

"So Leo dies conveniently confessing to Rudy's murder and there's no need for a trial and—here's the part I find so crazy or so wrong or so *something!*—in many people's minds you're a hero. A hero, Mr. Holiday. Doesn't that seem ironic to you?"

"What do you expect from me, Miss Hansen?" His reptilian look returned mixed with an unpleasant humor. "Do you expect me to confess to a fiction created by a young woman recently traumatized by a violent act against her person during which she sustained a head injury that has apparently affected her senses?"

That was a good question, I thought, because for all the time I spent thinking and conjecturing and concluding, I hadn't ever pictured how this meeting would end.

"It would be decent if you did, but, of course, you're not any more decent than Leo Stanislaw, so I don't expect anything from you, Mr. Holiday. Not one thing."

Surprisingly, from the sudden glitter in his eyes, my comment about his lack of decency annoyed him.

"You must be hysterical, Miss Hansen. In your confused state of mind, are you accusing me of murdering both Stanislaw brothers?"

"There were two reasons I never believed you had anything to do with Rudy's death," I replied. "First, I couldn't think of a reason. I'm convinced that Rudy died before you ever knew about him and Rachel, certainly before you realized Rachel was carrying Rudy's child."

I thought he might react at the words, but he didn't. Instead, when I didn't continue, he asked with a condescending tone that did not completely mask his curiosity, "And the second reason?"

"Because Rudy stood up when his murderer entered the garage, and he'd never have done that for you. He must have known what kind of a father you were, what kind of a man, and Rudy couldn't tolerate a scoundrel or a hypocrite. He'd never have risen at your presence. He'd have spit on the floor and kept on working. That was the Rudy I knew. Something else I'm sure is true but wouldn't hold up in court."

"So if not Leo and not me, that leaves just your crazy brother, doesn't it?"

For the first time that afternoon, I felt off balance and unsure of what to say, and Charles Holiday didn't miss my expression.

"Before you spread malicious and slanderous gossip about other people, it would be wise if you cleaned up your own house first. Now if that's all you have to say, I have work to do."

He turned his back to me, returned to his desk, made a show of settling himself into his big leather chair, and as an orchestrated afterthought looked over at me as I headed for the door, as eager to be out of there as he was to have me gone.

"Miss Hansen."

I turned at the door. "What?"

"Be assured that you will miss seeing me and my family at your store more than I will miss seeing you. Don't ever come back here. You are not welcome."

What was there to say to that blunt statement, however questionable it was about who would miss the other more? Perhaps if Augustus Davis, attorney at law, had been present, he would have had a snappy lawyer retort for Holiday, but I was all talked out and couldn't think of anything either worthwhile or defiant to say. No one came out on top in the discussion, after all. No one won. It was all just sad and senseless, and I wanted to get back to my familiar store, to the desk at which my father sat until the very day he died, to ledger books and catalogs, to Raymond and Cece and Lloyd, and to Gus. Especially to Gus.

Lloyd and I made our appearance at the Buchanans' home promptly at seven o'clock as directed, and it was a more pleasant evening than I anticipated because of the conversation my brother and I shared before we left our house.

"I never said anything to them about Joe," Lloyd told me as he waited for me by the back door, "and I should have."

"Said what exactly?" I stopped pulling on my gloves so I could watch him as he answered.

"That I was sorry Joe was gone and that I wasn't with him when he died. That he was a good friend and I miss him. That kind of thing." I had been holding my breath without being aware of it and exhaled softly with relief. Nothing marred Lloyd's face but a sincere sadness. I would have known if there was more to his words than their face value.

"You can tell them tonight," I said. "I'm sure they'll appreciate anything you say to them about Joe's service." Except that he was court-martialed for cowardice and executed by the very men with whom he served, but apparently I could stop worrying that Lloyd would give that one significant and terrible fact away. As far as I knew, only Gus and I were aware of that awful information, and when Gus left, I would push the knowledge into a corner of my mind and never think of it again. To do anything else would create a lifelong burden I was not willing to carry.

Delta Buchanan greeted us at the front door, putting her arms around Lloyd and saying quietly, "How wonderful to see you, Lloyd! We never doubted you, not once, did we, Ian?" Her husband stood behind her and stepped forward to extend a hand in Lloyd's direction.

"No, indeed. Welcome, Lloyd." If my brother was embarrassed by the attention, he never let on.

"Thank you, sir." The remainder of the evening followed that pleasant beginning without a misstep. Lloyd reacted with satisfying emotion at his first sight of the large portrait of Joe Buchanan, saying in a choked voice, "It's a good likeness" as he viewed his friend's mischievous dark eyes and charming smile looking down at us from the wall.

"We think so," Delta replied, nothing manic in her tone or glittering in her eyes. Grieving mother still, but her emotion controlled and her tone quiet.

Conversation was easy throughout the meal, and exactly as we had done on my earlier visit, we adjourned to the front room for glasses of cordial to close out the evening. It was then that Lloyd made his brief speech, saying how much he missed his friend and how he wished he'd have been with Joe at the end. Even I, who knew everything Lloyd said was a fiction, still felt touched by his honest tribute. Delta Buchanan dabbed at her eyes with a handkerchief and when Lloyd finished, she went up and kissed my brother lightly on the cheek.

"What a good friend you were to our Joe—I believe the best friend he ever had!" Emotion always enhanced her southern accent. "More of a friend than Rudy was, I'm afraid, but then I thought perhaps the war had affected him in ways we didn't understand and made him unstable."

"I don't understand." Lloyd's bewildered tone reflected my thoughts.

"It seems like nothing now, after all that's happened, but Rudy said some very, very unkind things about Joe when he was here. Didn't he, Ian?"

Her husband said nothing, only kept his gaze fixed on Delta's face as she continued, "I was so taken by surprise at how rude and insufferable he was that I didn't know what to say. He said horrid things. Just horrid." Like Ian, I kept my gaze fixed on her face, too. "Well, Rudy was the quiet one and I always felt he was a little jealous of our Joe, so I suppose I can understand why he was so against the idea of the monument." At Lloyd's inquiring look, Delta explained the project to put a statue of her son on the town square, concluding with, "I have to say that I am completely at a loss to explain what's taking the Council so long to give us the go-ahead. We will absorb the entire cost, after all."

"That explains why they asked to talk to the captain tomorrow afternoon, then," Lloyd responded. "Probably to be sure they've got all the details right."

"The captain?" From the woman's tone, it was clear that Ian Buchanan had never told his wife about Gus's military relationship with their son.

"Captain Davis was our commanding officer. When he wasn't being sent off on mysterious missions behind enemy lines, anyway. He knew Joe pretty well, like he knew all the men under his command. That's the kind of leader he was."

"I had no idea." She turned her full attention to her husband. "I asked him if he knew Joe and he said yes, but he didn't volunteer that he was his commanding officer. I can't imagine why he wouldn't say something about it. Did you know, Ian?"

To my initial surprise, her husband answered, "No. I don't remember that Joe ever mentioned a Captain Davis in any of his letters," emphasizing the last name.

I knew Ian had placed Gus as Joe's officer almost immediately, even though he'd never acknowledged the fact aloud, and I'd been curious about the man's reticence. Wouldn't it have been natural for Ian to seek Gus out for conversation about his son? If he had, I felt sure Gus would have mentioned it. Of course, Gus had been in the middle of a murder trial and perhaps Ian didn't want to know the details about his son's death. Not every father would. I felt a sudden chill. Could Ian have somehow uncovered the truth about Joe, something from Rudy's "horrible" conversation, perhaps, and that was why he hadn't told his wife about Gus being Joe's captain? But seeing the pinched look on the older man's face, I realized that the reason for keeping Delta in the dark was much less complicated, and I felt a spurt of sympathy for him. Considering how erratic Delta had been this past year, how many days she spent behind pulled blinds in a dark house, how she seemed to teeter on the edge of sanity, it was perfectly understandable that he wouldn't have wanted to open wounds just beginning to heal. A wise decision, too, because tonight was the most lucid I'd seen Delta

Buchanan in months and months, reminding me from whom Joe had inherited his devastating charm and sharp wit.

While I slipped into private contemplation, Delta gave her husband's last comment serious thought.

"You're right. He mentioned a captain now and then, but I don't believe he ever gave a last name. Imagine that. Joe's very own captain right here in Blessing for all these weeks and we never knew." Delta's smile took in both Lloyd and me. "Of course, you all had more serious things on your mind."

"We did," I interjected quickly, glad of the conversational opening, "but it's all behind us now, though I admit I feel like I've been running races these past weeks." I looked over at Lloyd and gave the tiniest of nods.

"And jail bunks were never intended for restful sleep," he supplied, reading my mute request, "so as pleasant as this evening has been, I hope you'll excuse my sister and me. I think it's time we headed home."

Neither of the Buchanans tried to argue us out of departing and I wondered if there would be more discussion about Captain Gus Davis after we left. Too bad if you expect to invite him for supper tomorrow night, I thought with uncharitable selfishness, because he's spending his last night in Blessing, Kansas, with me. Which he did, now that I think about it, but not in any way I could have anticipated.

Chapter 18

Wednesday, October 22 - Thursday, October 23, 1919

*O*n our slow walk home, Lloyd and I discussed the evening just past. "They seem to be doing all right," my brother observed, more to himself than to me, "but there was something—"

When he didn't finish the sentence I prompted, "Something?" and Lloyd looked over at me, very serious.

"Off," he said and left it at that. I understood without further explanation and didn't say any more. Perhaps, I thought, Delta Buchanan wasn't as stable as she seemed. Perhaps she would always need to be protected.

Once home, Lloyd headed straight upstairs to bed but I found myself restless and knew I wouldn't sleep. I picked up the novel I'd been trying to read for a month, had no luck with that, sat with a cup of tea I didn't want and couldn't finish, and swept the kitchen floor, keeping my eye on the kitchen clock all the while. I felt uneasy and watchful, which I attributed to the imminent departure of Gus Davis, although somehow that didn't seem quite accurate. The end of the trial, then? Rudy's death unaccounted for, despite Leo's convenient confession before Charles Holiday killed him?

I put on water for tea one more time, climbed the stairs to check on Lloyd, who slept dreamlessly—every night that happened a small armistice of its own—returned to the kitchen and made another cup of tea to pour down the drain. Finally, the ticks of the wall clock created so rhythmic a sound in the still kitchen that I sat at the table, put my head down on my arms, and dozed a while.

I was suddenly jerked awake by a loud, raucous, clanging noise and in the first confused moment of sitting upright felt both mystified and terrified. Then recognizing the fire bell, I hurried to the front porch. A rosy glow of flames illuminated the cloudy black northern sky. The town hall, I thought at first, and then felt a sinking in my stomach. Not the town hall but the Hansen House! I rushed back inside, shouted up the stairs for my brother, and grabbed the closest coat I could find. Lloyd pounded down the steps, his hair tousled and pushing his pajama top into the pants he'd hastily pulled on.

"It's the hotel!" I cried, not far behind him as we both rushed out the front door, but I couldn't keep up with his long legs for long. The street was beginning to fill with other figures, all racing toward the sound of the still pealing bell.

When I finally reached the hotel, a crowd had already gathered and figures stumbled out the front door, looking as confused as I'd felt a few minutes before. From where I stood on the southern side, the building seemed fine, Grandmother's and my uncle's apartments dark and quiet, but the bell hadn't clanged for no reason because flames licked upward on the opposite side of the building, bright flames against a black sky. I picked out Grandmother's wheeled chair at the end of the front walk and pushed my way through to her.

"Are you all right?" I gasped, dropping to my knees beside her. "Where's Uncle Carl and Aunt Louisa? What happened?"

In a calm voice, she answered, "We're all fine, Thea. The fire appears to have broken out opposite the main floor of rooms. I can't imagine how it happened. We're only half full so no guests were put there." Her words stopped abruptly and I caught her thought.

"Except Gus. My God, that's where Gus is!" Grandma Liza reached out for me but I was already on my feet and flying in search of my brother, who would be with his fellow volunteer members of the fire brigade on the other side of the hotel. As I shoved through the milling people, I searched for Gus's tall figure but he wasn't anywhere to be seen. Something was terribly wrong!

Hansen House stood on the eastern corner of Main and Lincoln, and the only fortunate thing, if anything could truly be considered fortunate about that night, was that the Fire Department building with its brand new water pump stood directly across Lincoln Avenue. Water was already gushing through the hose at the blaze, which was clearly contained in just one section of the northern wall, the section where Gus stayed, the window of Gus's room. I found Lloyd with his sleeves rolled up grasping the unwieldy hose with several other fire fighters.

"It's the captain's room," I shouted over all the racket. "It's where Gus is staying, and I haven't been able to find him anywhere."

I saw the kind of soldier Lloyd must have been before the horror of being buried alive had changed him because he didn't say a word to me, just shouted to the man next to him to take his place in line and ran toward the rear entrance of the hotel, commonly used for deliveries. Without thinking I would have followed my brother inside, but he whirled around and gave me a light push backwards.

"No, Thea! You get help! Tell them where the captain's room is and to follow me in. If he's there, I'll need some help to get him out. He's a big man." Then he disappeared into the building. I hesitated too long, suddenly terrified for both the men I loved, and then ran back to grab the first volunteers I could find and beg their assistance.

For what seemed like hours, although it was only a few minutes, I ran between the back entrance and Gus's window, looking for any sign that someone was in there, someone alive. I watched the two men whose aid I had enlisted enter the rear door and almost immediately back out, each reaching to support an arm of a man that lurched outside with them. Lloyd, thank God, who carried slung over his back the burden of another man's body. The men caught Lloyd as he stumbled, reached for the dead weight on his back, and pried my brother's fingers free from his grasp on Gus's arms draped limply around his neck. Because it was Gus's body thumping against my brother, Gus's body sliding to the ground in rag doll clarity.

I made a noise, something between a moan and a shriek and darted forward, one quick look telling me my brother was all right and another, longer look at Gus Davis, who was anything but all right.

The fire hadn't touched him but something—someone—else had. A dark hole showed on his bare skin below his left shoulder from which blood must have originally poured and still continued to seep in a small but steady flow soaking the waistband of his pants. Gus smelled of something that reminded me, strangely enough, of the Olds Economy truck, but after seeing the hole in his chest, I didn't give the smell another thought.

"Get Dr. Petrie!" I cried. "He's been shot!" I couldn't bear to look at Gus's still face. Instead, I took off my coat, folded it in half, and laid it over his chest, then knelt to press both my hands over the location of the seeping wound.

I looked up at the people gathering around me and repeated in a harsh, angry voice that belonged to someone else, "Go get the doctor! Why are you just standing there?"

My uncle crouched beside me and put a calming hand on my arm. "He'll be here in a moment, Thea. Steady, now."

With both my hands pressed against Gus, I watched the slow rise and fall of his chest and caught the sound of his shallow breath, irregular and hesitant. This man of strength and grace, this very good man, could die, I thought. Lloyd, still trying to find the ability to get a good inhale, met my gaze across Gus's form and shook his head at me.

"No," he panted. I might have spoken my fear aloud. "No, Thea. He made it through the war," as if that were proof of Gus's immortality, as if we had not buried Rudy Stanislaw three weeks ago.

I didn't voice a response; I couldn't. Instead, I pressed firmly on Gus Davis's chest and willed him to live at the same time I bargained with God for his life and made promises I couldn't have kept if I'd lived a thousand years. After a few moments, Dr. Petrie pushed me aside, gave Gus's wound a cursory inspection, and ordered him carried to his office. Uncle Carl intervened and offered a room inside the hotel instead.

"It's safe to go back in. Except for the smell, you'd never know anything was wrong. There's a small room at the back of the first floor we can use, close to whatever you need, Harry, and a lot closer than your office in this weather." A light, cold drizzle had been falling for a while and promised to be sleet before very long, and the decision to keep Gus at the Hansen House was an easy one.

It was hard to let Gus go and see him carted off into the night, but he was, both literally and figuratively, out of my hands by then and I had no choice. Lloyd picked up my blood-stained coat from the ground and draped it over my shoulders. I didn't mind. It was Gus's blood.

"Come on, Thea." I turned to my brother and put a hand to his cheek.

"Whatever happens," I told him, "thank you. What you did was very brave."

Lloyd shook his head. "He did the same for men under conditions a lot worse than tonight's. I saw it myself often enough. And I owed the captain, Thea. Still do." He took my hand in his. "He'll be all right. You'll see," and together we headed for the front entrance of the hotel.

Uncle Carl stayed busy, leading Dr. Petrie to a room for Gus and then returning to direct the situation at the hotel and assure the guests all was under control. The fire was out, only the section around Gus's window scorched black, and to help matters—or make matters worse, depending on one's perspective—the wind picked up and the drizzle made good on its promise to change into sleet. The tiny ice pellets carried quite a sting against the skin, despite being nearly invisible, and those customers initially unsure whether they'd be safe back inside the hotel soon decided they'd chance the rest of the night under the roof of the Hansen House, especially after Uncle Carl assured them they wouldn't be charged for their stay. Later, Grandma Liza remarked it was the first time she could remember being grateful for a poor overnight crowd. It was my uncle's offer of free lodging that motivated the comment, I'm afraid, and not that fewer lives were endangered. Sometimes she enjoys the effect she makes and the more outrageous the better.

Mort McGill picked through the remains of Gus's room and questioned the hotel's residents before finally coming downstairs to where I sat next to Gus's bed.

"The doc said he'll probably live," Mort said from the doorway, his gaze on Gus's still form under the blankets, "but he doesn't look so good right now."

"Dr. Petrie told me the same thing," I rejoined, "and I took strong issue with the word *probably*." I couldn't help but follow Mort's gaze. "He lost a lot of blood; that's the worry. The doctor dug out the bullet and said it missed the heart by the width of a hairpin." Just saying the words made me breathless and my last words were so faint only Mort's small smile let me know he'd heard them.

"A miss is as good as a mile, they say."

"This time, anyway," I agreed. "Thank God." We were both quiet.

"Send someone for me when he comes to, will you? I know it'll be a while because Harry told me he pumped something into him so he'd sleep and slow the bleeding."

"You don't want to know what that was," I said. "It's probably illegal."

"Just so it wasn't moonshine," McGill retorted, and we both laughed. The humor was light, but it felt good to be able to laugh. "You staying here by yourself?"

"For the time being. Dr. Petrie said to expect him back in a couple of hours, Lloyd is asleep right upstairs, and Uncle Carl keeps popping in like a jack-in-the-box. Anyway, I can't think of any better place to be."

"Somebody tried to kill Gus Davis, Thea, and in case the bullet didn't do what it was supposed to, he tried to set the captain on fire for good measure."

"What?" I hadn't heard that and felt horror at the thought.

"He shot him and just to be sure the job got done, he poured lamp oil on him. Then he used twisted yarns to set up a fuse of sorts from the hallway under the closed door. Whoever it was went prepared to kill him. His plan must have been to light the end of the fuse and while it burned its way to Davis to make his escape and be well off the scene before anyone was the wiser."

"But I didn't see any burns on Gus."

"No, and it's to the captain's credit that with a hole in his chest, he somehow managed to get out of his shirt and roll under the bed as far away from the fuse and the oil as he could get. Must have hurt like hell."

"Is that why it seemed to take Lloyd so long to find him?"

McGill nodded. "First, your brother had to get into the room and then he had to find Davis, who by that time wasn't any help.

Someone took considerable effort to get rid of the man, Thea. Do you have any idea who or why?"

I'd dwelled on that question ever since Dr. Petrie left and Lloyd went in search of an empty hotel bed to collapse into.

"No. Why Gus?" I put both hands to my head as if stimulating my temples might generate just one reasonable idea but was as disappointed then as I'd been the past hour. "He doesn't live in Blessing, and he was going back to Wyoming on Friday. Even if I could guess at the *who*, I'd be at a loss for the *why*."

Something in my tone caused McGill to look at me more sharply. "You're sure you don't have anything to tell me, Thea? This isn't something to take lightly."

"I know," conscious of Gus lying so quietly beside me, "and believe me, I'm not taking any of this lightly, only—" McGill waited for more but all I could do was shake my head in bewilderment. "Sometimes I think I should be able to see how it all fits together, that it's a big puzzle and I've got all the pieces, only I can't make them fit into a picture. If I could have kept this from happening—" I nodded at Gus "—don't you think I would have?"

Mort heard the touch of tears in my voice and spoke quietly. "I'll be back at sunrise and I'll find Carl before I go and tell him not to leave you alone very long. After Louisa gets your grandmother settled, maybe she could join you down here. In the meanwhile," from under his coat he drew a pistol and placed it ever so gently on the small table next to the bed, "I'll leave this with you. Just in case. Do you know what to do with it?"

"My father taught me when I was thirteen," I replied, remembering that it was his worry over Leo Stanislaw that first prompted the lesson in self-defense.

"That's good, then. You'll be all right, but it's here, just in case. Don't be afraid to use it."

We said goodnight and I heard the creak of the hallway floorboards as he departed. Gus stirred slightly and murmured something I couldn't catch before settling quietly again. Looking at his face, pale in repose and as vulnerable as a young boy's, I felt my throat constrict with unshed tears. I was certainly afraid, but it had nothing to do with the gun on the bedside table and everything to do with the form that lay still as death on the bed.

Time crept along at a slow pace, interrupted once by Cece, who stopped in the doorway and then hurried in to stand beside me.

"I couldn't find you and I was worried! When Kinsey and I heard the fire bell, we got here as fast as we could, but I didn't see either you or Lloyd. I was sorry to hear about Mr. Davis. Will he be all right?"

"Yes," I answered firmly, "he'll be perfectly all right."

"What can I do?"

I smiled at her. "You can go find my brother and hold his hand, if his exaggerated sense of propriety will allow that." Despite the seriousness of the situation, she giggled softly. "Did anyone tell you he saved Gus's life?" She nodded and I said, "Lloyd's been almost himself since he got home, Cece, but you should know that the war is never very far away from him. I worry that if he's reminded of what happened then, he might have some kind of set back. The bad dreams might return, so you should be with Lloyd now. There's nothing you can do here."

"If you're sure," but she had already turned toward the door. Good girl, I thought, not to waste time with questions and to realize who it was that really needed her.

"I'm sure. My brother was dead on his feet and went looking for a room. Ask Uncle Carl where Lloyd is, go find him, and stay with him 'til he wakes up."

"I will, but if you need me for anything, I'll come right away."

After Cece left, I sat with my hands in my lap, once more absorbed by the puzzle I'd told Mort McGill about, all the pieces spread out in front of me but forming no picture. How were Rudy and Gus connected? Surely they were because it strained possibility that in little Blessing, Kansas, two murderers prowled the streets. The two men had the war in common, but so did Lloyd and no one had tried to kill him, and Gus said he hadn't spoken to Rudy since the war ended. Could it be that Rudy's death was somehow connected with the liquor enterprise, after all? But how? Was I wrong about Leo? Had he killed his brother in one of his violent rages? Or was I wrong about Charles Holiday? Had he killed Rudy because of something Rudy discovered about him, and then killed Leo in order to divert the blame? But what threat did Gus hold for any of them? With all his questions had Gus uncovered sinister information that he didn't recognize as such? When I stepped back from my own churning thoughts, I could almost have laughed. A month ago my greatest concern had been whether Cynthia Marks' new china would arrive in a timely fashion and all in one piece. Now here I sat, trying to decide which of several candidates was a murderer.

Uncle Carl stopped in periodically, looking more drawn each time I saw him.

"People!" he exclaimed at the most recent visit. "You'd think I set the fire on purpose just to inconvenience them!" Then, glancing at Gus, he added more softly, "Well, it's little enough bother and I suppose it was unsettling to be rousted out of bed and pushed out of doors in your night clothes. How's the young man?"

"Dr. Petrie thinks he'll probably be all right. He's worried about infection and all the blood Gus lost, but he said Gus is healthy and strong and that's a lot going for him."

"I'm glad."

"Me, too," I agreed and smiled at my uncle.

"He's pretty special to you, I guess."

"Very special. As special as anyone could be," and smiled at Uncle Carl again.

"That's what Liza said, though I was inclined to argue the point." He shook his head. "She has eyes in the back of her head, that grandmother of yours." After a pause, he added, "She's restless and her legs are bothering her, so when Petrie comes back, send him up to her apartment when he's done here."

"Something serious?"

"It's her heart, just like it's always been. Is there anything you need?"

Just one thing, I thought, looking over at Gus. Just that one thing and probably forever.

"Not right now," I said, "Once Dr. Petrie returns, I may ask Lizzy or Cece to keep Gus company while I go home and change, but I'm fine for the time being."

"And no ideas about what happened here tonight?"

"Not a one," I confessed, but it would have been truer to say I had too many ideas, all of them sheer speculation and none of them sensible.

"It'll sort itself out if we're patient."

"I'm sure it will," I replied and thought, if we live to tell about it. The odds for that didn't look all that promising.

After he left, I must have dozed for a few minutes because I was jerked awake by someone saying my name. Gus, I thought at first, but no, he lay as still as ever under the effect of the narcotic the doctor had administered.

"Thea," Ian Buchanan repeated and I turned to see the lawyer standing in the doorway. "I'm sorry if I startled you."

"That's all right. I was resting my eyes."

Ian smiled. "As your father used to say whenever he dozed off after lunch."

"Yes. I'd forgotten that." Ian looked worn out to me and as disheveled as I'd ever seen him, no overcoat despite the weather and no tie, his shirt and jacket wrinkled and messy. "You look tired. Were you helping with the fire?"

"No. I've been trying to assist Carl with a few disgruntled customers."

"He didn't say anything about that, but it's good of you."

I rose to face Ian, placing myself between the bed and where he stood in the doorway, my arms loose at my side, close enough to the night stand that I could feel its edge against the back of my left hand. For no tangible reason, I recalled Lloyd's earlier observation as he and I walked home from the Buchanans' that there was something "off."

"I didn't see you at the fire, Ian, but then I was busy."

"I got there late. The fire bell woke us up and it unsettled Delta for a while. She forgets where she is sometimes."

"I'm sorry. She seemed herself when we were there."

"Herself." He seemed to give the word thought. "My wife hasn't been herself for fifteen months, not since the telegram came." Ian glanced over at the bed. "How's your patient?"

"Better but not out of the woods."

He stepped into the room. "May I sit down for a while? You're right. I am tired."

"Of course. Take my chair. I'll sit here," settling myself on the edge of the bed. He pushed the door shut with a casual gesture and when he looked back at me, the pieces of the puzzle shifted and suddenly, just like that, the whole picture spread itself out in front of me with sad and terrible clarity.

I'm too far from the end table, I thought, and with a nonchalance I was far from feeling tried to move myself closer to the head of the bed. Ian must have noticed but he said nothing. Seated, he looked more haggard than ever, his left hand resting on his thigh and his right arm dangling to his side with his hand out of sight. Was he holding something in that hand?

"It was Rudy's fault, you know. He just wouldn't be quiet about Joe." The words came out of nowhere as both conversation and confession.

"I understand."

For the first time the man looked at me, really looked, examined my face as if he'd never seen me before, and finally said, the relief palpable in his tone, "I believe you do understand, Thea. And you knew Joe. He wasn't a coward." I said nothing at that. "He wasn't a saint, either. Only his mother ever thought that of him, but he wasn't a coward."

"He got tired of the war, though, didn't he?" I said.

"Oh, yes. That's it exactly. He was just tired of it, tired of the mud and the noise and the officers telling him what to do and the close quarters with men he didn't like. He was tired of it all and he wanted to come home."

"I can understand that."

"Of course, until Delta told Rudy her plan for the statue and the fountain I had no idea what really happened. I didn't believe it at first and I told Delta that Rudy was like Lloyd, damaged and delusional, and we should just ignore what he said. She didn't take any convincing because in her eyes Joe was the perfect everything, perfect son and student and soldier, but Rudy's words ate away at me so I had to contact the war office." He sighed. "It was a terrible thing to read, Thea."

"It must have been," I said and shifted an inch closer to the end table at the head of the bed. "I don't imagine Rudy was inclined to be reasonable about Joe's statue."

"No, that was the problem. If I pursued the idea, he said he'd tell the city fathers what happened over there. If I gave up on the idea, he'd be quiet, but Delta—well, her heart was set on it and she never rested from the idea, never stopped talking about it, started looking forward to it, started being happy again."

"I'm so sorry, Ian," I said, and strangely enough, I was.

"You're a good girl, Thea. You always were. A quiet, kind, pretty, good girl. You never took to Joe, did you?"

"I can't lie," I replied. "We weren't well-suited. Joe knew it, too."

Ian smiled. "Always such a kind girl." He moved his right hand into his lap and despite myself, I gave a little gasp at the sight of the gun there. His eyes followed my look and he shrugged.

"I've done some damage with this thing, I can tell you, and it's funny because I'm as far from a violent man as a man could be."

"I understand about Rudy," I said. "I understand that you chose your wife over him, but Gus was here these past weeks and he never said a word about Joe. He wouldn't have said anything, Ian. Not ever. He was going home tomorrow and he would have been out of your way for good. You didn't need to hurt him." He listened to me with an indulgent smile.

"So the rumor's true, then, about there being something between you and Mr. Davis."

"There's nothing yet, but I'd like there to be. Please don't hurt him any more, Ian. He's a good man."

"I never wanted to hurt him to start with, Thea, and if Lloyd hadn't mentioned that meeting with the council about the statue, I never would have. I like what I know of Gus Davis, and he's a damned good lawyer, besides. But I thought if someone asked him a direct question about putting up a statue of Joe Buchanan, Davis would tell the truth. He's that kind of man, isn't he? Truth is important to him."

I moved another inch closer to McGill's pistol.

"Yes, but there's not going to be a meeting now so you don't have to worry about him. You don't have to silence him, too."

"My heart wasn't in it then, Thea, and my heart's not in it now. Frankly, I don't feel much regret about Rudy. He was a blunt, rough young man, and he didn't care that what he said hurt Delta, hurt her deeply, but I am sorry about Captain Davis." He sat quietly, his shoulders slumped, nothing upright and handsome about him now, just a rumpled old man, smiling faintly at the past. "I loved that woman from the moment I met her. You should have seen her, Thea. How she sparkled! Like a princess in a storybook. She was nothing like the women I was used to, and I told her if she'd have me, I'd spend my whole life making her as happy as she made me. I promised her that on our wedding night." For a moment twenty-five years dropped away. Then from his deep sigh, I could tell that he was back in the here-and-now. "In the end, the one true happiness I gave her was our son, and when he was gone—" He shook his head. "Only his memory makes her happy now. It's Joe this and Joe that the first thing in the morning 'til the last thing at night. We live with a ghost in the house. Day in. Day out." He met my gaze squarely, wanting me to understand what his life had been like these past months. Lloyd had put his finger on it right away, I thought. *Something off.* Only I'd applied the words to the wrong Buchanan.

"I loved my son, too, Thea, but I never had any illusions about him." The click of the gun's hammer seemed as loud as cymbals in the small room, and I stood up quickly, still too far from the table and no chance to get to the pistol before Ian Buchanan did something violent and irrevocable.

"So do you plan to kill both of us, then?" Arms akimbo, I glared at him. "Does that make sense to you, Ian? We've buried more than our fair share of people these past few years, and we've already cried enough tears for a lifetime. Isn't life too short already without you making it even shorter? I can't stop you from hurting me, I guess, but I won't let you hurt Gus. He made it through the war and he should be allowed to be safe for a while, safe and happy. I won't have another murdered boy in Blessing, and for sure not my Gus."

Ian Buchanan smiled through words that were meaningless, just useless bravado pretending outrage and fear would be enough to hold off a bullet when we both knew otherwise.

"Oh, Thea, I don't want to hurt you." His voice and his eyes and his words were gentle and sad. "I watched you grow up. Your father was my friend. I promised to make her happy—" it took me a second to catch up with his words "—and I can't do it, so I came to ask if you'd be kind to Delta, but I see I don't have to do that. You were a thoughtful, caring little girl and you've grown up into the same kind of woman." The smile he sent me was sheepish and apologetic, not for hurting Gus or killing Rudy but for damaging the hotel. "Sorry about the fire. I hope Carl won't have to spend a lot in repairs. I thought the fuse would delay the flames and give me enough time to get home before the alarm sounded. I wanted it over and done with and things back to the way they were, but I see now that can't ever happen. I haven't been thinking straight for a while." He inhaled and let his breath out slowly. "You were right when you said I looked tired. I am. I feel like I've been tired forever."

And with those words, Ian Buchanan put the bore of the pistol against his right temple and pulled the trigger.

Chapter 19

Thursday, October 23, 1919, and aftermath

*U*ncle Carl said the sound of Ian Buchanan's pistol reached the front desk with the shock of a bomb going off. The last worried customer had been soothed to her room and he was standing talking to Mort McGill when they heard it. It was worse inside the little room, of course; my ears rang for hours afterwards. What I saw was only a split second of horror, but if I allow it, I can still see Ian Buchanan's last moment in my mind's eye. I don't allow myself that indulgence very often.

When I realized what Ian intended, I cried, "No!" and turned instantly away, turned to Gus and threw myself over him, whether for his protection or mine I couldn't say. I heard footsteps pound down the hallway toward me and heard them stop abruptly in the doorway. Mort McGill said a strong oath and came inside. Uncle Carl entered the room, too, but he walked straight over to me and said my name with urgent anxiety.

"I'm all right," I said, tears clogging my throat and making my voice waver, "but I'm not looking and I'm not leaving Gus. I'll stay right here." I rearranged myself onto the bedside chair, bent and folded my arms on Gus's chest, put my head down on my arms, and stayed that way a long time. I was true to my word and never looked back once, despite all the activity that went on behind me. With Gus's heartbeat as lulling then as when he'd carried me home after the assault by Leo Stanislaw, I would have happily rested against him much longer except the doctor convinced me the pressure on Gus's chest might make his wound worse. Of course, I wouldn't take that chance. As it was, Dr. Petrie had to remove Gus's arm from across my shoulders before I could straighten, although I had no memory of any movement on Gus's part all the while I lay there.

"He shouldn't have been able to move that arm," the doctor reflected, "not with the dope I pumped into him," and I knew from the comment that for all my life to come Gus Davis's first instinct would be to put his arms around me, whether he was conscious or not.

Later, the spattered, stained clothes I'd been wearing taken away to be burned, my hair cleaned and combed, and Gus moved to another room, I sat with the sheriff and told him about Joe Buchanan and Rudy's scorn for hypocrisy, about Delta Buchanan's desperate desire for a monument to her son and her husband's equally desperate desire to keep his wife happy and innocent.

"But Holiday said Leo confessed to killing Rudy," Mort said, all the information clicking into place behind his shrewd, dark eyes.

"I know. No doubt when you inquire further of Mr. Holiday, the man will tell you that he must have misunderstood Leo, that he was in fear for his life, after all, and not paying attention to everything Leo said as clearly as he would have under normal circumstances."

"What else do you know, Thea?"

"I don't *know* anything and I can prove even less, but it wouldn't hurt if you kept an official but discreet eye on what goes in and out of the sugar factory for a while, though I'd guess those glory days are done."

Delta Buchanan was a surprise. I would have been happy never to see or speak to her again, although not for any fault of hers. Grief took a hold on her and never let go, grief and the past and love obsessed and it was a terrible combination. A deadly combination. Still, I didn't want to be reminded about her husband and how I'd last seen him, but when Aunt Louisa volunteered to give Delta the bad news, I said no. Ian had trusted me to be kind, I said, and I have an obligation.

My grandmother said a vulgar word at my pronouncement, adding, "Good lord, Thea, you don't owe a thing to that murderous man," but I knew I did, even if I couldn't explain why.

At first, my plan was to lie about Ian's death, but on the walk to their house it dawned on me that Delta might ask to see her husband's body and that must not be allowed. I had been informed by Dr. Petrie, with purposefully ambiguous words and unmistakable meaning, that the effect of a gunshot to the side of a man's head at very close range was not something for a widow, for anyone for that matter, to see.

So I was prepared to tell Delta Buchanan the truth, or at least part of it. We sat in the front room under the laughing gaze of perpetually handsome, perpetually young Joe Buchanan, and I began by saying that Ian was dead.

She didn't bat an eye at the news, only asked, "Did he take his own life?" I thought I was prepared for anything but the abrupt question made me gasp, anyway.

"Yes," I said, recovering quickly. "Yes, he did, Mrs. Buchanan. I am so sorry for your loss." Her face softened and I expected tears, but none came. None ever came that I saw, from that moment through the funeral and to the day she moved out of Blessing.

"I always knew he mourned our Joe more than I did. He hadn't been himself since the day we got the telegram." That omnipresent, eternal telegram, I thought, its words holding the power of life and death in ways no one could ever have imagined. "I always knew his heart was broken. A wife knows." I couldn't help but wonder if she only ever saw her own grief reflected back to her in Ian's behavior.

Except for her overt and unrelenting animosity toward Blessing's City Council, she remained the southern belle that must have charmed her husband all those years ago, dignified in her grief and always courteous. Imperial in a way, the citizens of Blessing, Kansas, mere commoners compared to the royal Buchanans. Perhaps the façade was how she protected herself. Delta Buchanan sold her house with all its furnishings but one and without a backward glance returned to her Georgia birthplace with only the portrait of the crown prince in tow.

Most important of all, my Gus lived. The first time he opened his eyes and said my name, I began to cry like a baby and couldn't stop. Alarmed at first but still weak, he tried to sit up and reach for me until I choked out, "Don't you dare move. Don't you dare." He lay back down obediently, still watching me. I continued to sob in fits and starts that made me sound like an engine with something clogging its fuel line. Finally, out of both energy and tears, I slid to the floor next to the bed, close enough for Gus to rest his hand on my head.

"I'm not going to die, Thea."

"And don't you forget it!" I retorted.

He must have heard something in the words to make him laugh because I heard a chuckle followed by a stifled groan.

"You be still, Gus Davis," I ordered and he quieted, the only movement his fingers weaving softly through my hair. We remained in that awkward, lovely posture for quite a while.

I met Gus's parents without warning because my grandmother neglected to tell me about the wire she sent the morning after the fire, but when two people appeared in Gus's room Saturday afternoon I didn't need an introduction. He looked like both of them and in another way like neither of them. His own man, but I could still tell Gus came from that particular family tree. Their son was alert and even sitting up in bed when they showed up, for which I was grateful. I saw the look on his mother's face lighten at the sight.

I stood quickly, smoothed my skirt, and after a brief introduction—"You must be Mr. and Mrs. Davis. I'm Thea Hansen."—moved to the side and then toward the door. Mrs. Davis, her eyes taking in Gus's condition, put one hand on my arm to halt me but didn't speak.

It was her husband, in a quiet, courtly manner completely contradicting Grandma Liza's characterization of him as a violent man, that completed the courtesies.

"How do you do, Miss Hansen? Thank you for your care of our son." The man charmed me from that moment, a blue gaze not hazel, silver hair not auburn, bearded not clean shaven, and yet Gus in his eyes and in his smile.

Assured of her son's well-being, Lou Davis turned to give me her full attention. Gus had understated her qualities. He'd described his mother as warm and positive but she was more than that, a woman lit by an inner reservoir of joy.

"Please stay, Thea." She paused a moment. "I knew your father when he was a boy. I'm sorry to hear he's gone. And I can see something of your grandmother in you. Liza might have mentioned that we were friends for many years." There's a story behind that past tense, I thought. Then Lou Davis gave me the full effect of her smile and leaned toward me to say so softly only I could hear, "I believe my son loves you, Thea. Thank you," more than gratitude for nursing skills contained in the words.

Her eyes glistened momentarily and without thinking I asked, "Fiddle tears?"

Surprise made her laugh out loud, and with the spontaneous kindness I would discover was as much a part of her as gray eyes, she kissed me lightly on the cheek before wordlessly turning away to sit on the edge of the bed and reach for Gus's hand.

There was never a doubt on anyone's part, mine included, that I'd marry Gus Davis, but when Gus was fully recovered and capable of scaling the alley wall of Dolf's vacant garage if circumstances again warranted an illegal intrusion and he still hadn't proposed, I began to wonder if I needed to take some action of my own to move the situation along.

In November, Gus returned to Laramie and resumed his work as a prosecutor, took the train to Blessing as often as he was able, and wrote daily letters when we were apart. But he didn't propose, either on paper or in person, and once Christmas passed without a declaration, I decided I'd have to act on plans of my own.

Shame on me for doubting the man. On the first Saturday of the new year, with my brother banished to Cecelia's for the evening, Gus and I sat together in my kitchen, the evening meal over but the table still cluttered.

Gus, who by this time was not hesitant or uncertain in any of his actions toward me, seemed uncharacteristically awkward that night. Finally, he pushed the supper dishes to the side and asked without prologue, "Thea Hansen, will you marry me?"

Instead of a yes or no, I replied, "Several months ago in this very room, I warned you that sitting at an old kitchen table with dirty dishes between us was not the romantic setting I hoped for when I received a proposal of marriage. Do you happen to recall that moment?" I said it with a smile because we both knew what my answer would be.

"Yes."

"And are you telling me this is the best you can do?"

At my words he took two decisive actions, a soldier with a planned offensive and the will and nerve to carry it out.

"No," he said.

First, he placed a small black box on the table and flipped it open to reveal the most glorious, gleaming ring I'd ever seen. The kitchen lights caught in the stone and made it flicker like fire.

Then he rose and came around to where I sat, pulled me to my feet and into his arms.

"I love you, Thea Hansen, and I am not about to face the future without you," after which he proceeded to kiss me breathless. Literally. Breathless.

Finally able to speak and thinking he shouldn't get used to having the upper hand all the time, I managed to say with credible composure, "So is that the best you can do?"

His mouth lingered for a moment on mine before he pulled away to murmur, "Oh, no, Thea," that seductive lilt of laughter in his voice and the promise of the future in his eyes. "The best is still to come. I guarantee it." I gave a passing thought to continuing the conversation, but Gus distracted me from the idea almost immediately. To this day, he maintains the ability to distract me in similar fashion.

The one time I told him as much, surprised—pleased and satisfied, too, but I didn't need to say so at the time—at his continuing ability to breach my defenses so easily, he grinned and corrected me.

"Not *maintained* the ability, Thea. Perfected."

By then it was obvious to both of us that for me to argue the point would be both futile and hypocritical. So I didn't even try.

Epilogue

We married on Valentine's Day, 1920, four weeks to the day following Lloyd's and Cecelia's wedding. My brother was one year older than I and used his seniority as the reason he should get first nuptials. I put up a half-hearted opposition, but it made sense for me to wait a few weeks longer because we had to make room for all the Davises: Gus's parents, two sisters and a brother, their respective spouses, and a confusing number of nieces and nephews that it took me weeks to keep straight. Grandma Liza, to her credit, made good on her promise to Gus that if he managed to bring Lloyd home, the entire Davis family could stay at the Hansen House without charge for the rest of their natural lives. There were more people in the family than she planned for but none of them stayed for the rest of their lives, so everything evened out in the end.

I didn't stay in Blessing for the rest of my natural life, either, which came as more of a surprise to Gus than to me. Walking down Main Street one cold January day, he said, as if it were already a given, "With Ian Buchanan gone, I think Blessing can support another lawyer, don't you?"

I stopped. "Are you talking about you?"

"Yes. I thought—well, the store is here, and I know what it means to you to sit in the same chair your father sat in."

What a gem you've got here, Thea Hansen, I thought to myself, a man that takes to heart the whole cleaving to one's wife section in the book of Genesis. I slipped a gloved hand under his arm and started him walking again.

"Oh, dear, that means I forgot to tell you, doesn't it? It's harder than I thought to keep everything straight with two weddings in the family just four weeks apart."

"Tell me what?" Smart man to have that edge of wariness in his voice. I intended to keep him just a little off balance, one way or another, for the rest of our lives.

"I sold the store."

His turn to stop this time. "What?!"

"I sold the store to Raymond Cuthbert for one dollar with the condition that he teach Lloyd the business. I put it all in writing, of course, and we both signed because my grandmother taught me never to do business on a hand shake."

"But, Thea, Blessing is your home." I turned away from him and made a slow rotation, looked north and south, took in the newspaper office at one end of town and Monroe's on the other, and then came back to the look on Gus's face.

"Now that's a funny thing," I said. I'd reached my conclusion some time ago but was still a little surprised at the outcome myself. "It's true I love the store and at one time I loved Blessing, too. I wanted to see the world and I still do, but I always planned to come home to Blessing at the end of my travels and live out my life right here. But over the last months, I realized that Blessing wasn't what I thought it was, and some people I'd known all my life ended up being strangers."

The world wasn't going to slow down, I told myself. If anything, it would move ever faster. Everything around me was going to keep changing. I didn't mind the idea. In fact, I viewed the future with anticipation. There would be so much that was new and exciting! But I needed one constant in my life, something I could count on to be there even if—especially if—my world spun out of control. Augustus Davis was my balance, my center, my heart and I expected it would always be so. The one constant I could count on in an unpredictable world and an unsettled future was the man standing in front of me.

"I made Blessing into what I wanted it to be, Gus, and never saw that it was just an ordinary place full of ordinary people. It doesn't feel like home now, and I don't need or want to live here. I want to be where you are, and you want to be in Wyoming."

"I can't let you do that."

At that, I put both gloved hands on the lapels of his overcoat and kissed him hard, let him go, took a breath, and kissed him again. It was so cold that our lips might have frozen together, a fate that carried some attraction at the time and still does.

"You had better get over the notion that you *let* me do things, Mr. Davis, smarty-pants lawyer. I have a mind of my own and I intend to keep using it. In fact, I'm already considering opening a branch of Monroe's in Laramie. Why not?"

I thought if we stood there looking at each other any longer we'd freeze into statues, so we started walking again, headed nowhere in particular, just the two of us walking side-by-side straight into the future.

A lot of the loose ends from that terrible October of 1919 never got tied off. Charles Holiday lived in Blessing for another ten years until he lost everything in the crash of '29. Then he and his wife disappeared and no one ever heard from him again. Rumor had their daughter, Rachel, marrying a rich man in New York City, but I don't know if that's true. She may be rich as Croesus for all I know, but I always think of her as *poor Rachel*. Dolf Stanislaw faded from memory and Kinsey owns the garage now. Not a lawyer, after all, but a mechanic—with a sense of humor. The name of the garage is in bold capital letters across the front of the building: CARR'S.

We go back frequently to visit Lloyd and Cece and their children and grandchildren. Grandma Liza is gone and Uncle Carl and Aunt Louisa, too. Gus's parents have passed on, as well. I learned to love Lou Davis as if she were my real mother, and I miss her. I miss them all.

We fought another war and had to return to Blessing to bury Lloyd and Cece's oldest boy, Steven, my grandfather's namesake. He died on the Solomon Islands in November of 1943. I had to look the place up on a map and could hardly see for the tears. That the boy we had welcomed into the world as a hope for the future of Blessing, the family store, and the family name, the dearly loved, always smiling boy with his father's fondness for poetry should have died so far away from home in a place I'd never heard of was an immeasurable, irreplaceable loss. But then war is always an immeasurable loss for somebody somewhere, even if you're the victor.

My nephew on Gus's side, Will, the only one of the Davis clan of fighting age when the Japanese bombed Pearl Harbor, came home safe and sound, a Navy man because, as he said, Wyoming was land-locked and he wanted to see the ocean. I never saw Gus's sister Katherine or her husband anything but cheerful all the time their son was overseas. It was only when Will stepped off the train in 1945 that Katherine began to cry with the same abandon I'd felt the time Gus opened his eyes after Ian Buchanan tried to kill him. Whole in life and limb and safe and home at last. I knew exactly how Katherine felt.

Today, the term *Cold War* is bandied about by people who ought to know better, as if war can be cold whenever men die, whether in the Philippines or France or the Solomon Islands or Korea, as if tears don't burn and hearts don't melt.

Dwight Eisenhower was recently reelected for his second term and we have television and a vaccine for polio and women athletes beating men at their own games. Time keeps marching on and we all keep getting older.

My sister-in-law Becca was widowed last year and Uncle Billy, that "slow boy" my grandmother recalled, who grew into a gentle man and aged more gracefully than any of us, died this past summer, eighty-nine and playing his fiddle at family gatherings almost to the end.

Yes, we all keep getting older. At family reunions, I'm part of the elder generation, the youngest of the Davis children and their spouses, although on some days fifty-seven doesn't feel all that young. Gus is closer to seventy than sixty and his older brother, John Thomas, won't see seventy-five again. When did that happen? I always knew life was short but just an instant ago it seems I was pregnant with our first child, our Liza, and suddenly I have four grown children, and our grandchildren work in the store for their summer jobs. We've replaced the Olds truck many times over, our current vehicle a 1954 Ford F-100 truck, a thing of beauty, for sure, but wasn't it just a moment ago that I was bouncing along Kansas roads in that Oldsmobile Economy truck? It surely seems so.

Sometimes when I see Gus playing baseball with the grandkids or deep in conversation with Jeffrey, our youngest, the boy that came as a surprise after we thought we had our family in place and the only child to follow his father's profession, I feel something take hold of my heart and grip it hard. One day I will not wake up with Gus Davis lying beside me, will not be able to offer him the comfort of my arms after a bad dream, will lose the sound of laughter in his voice all together. My father died in my arms, after all; I am a realist. One day Gus will rest, we will all rest, in the family cemetery. I've lived through three wars and cannot soften or deny that truth, but even as a gray-haired grandmother, the thought of life without Gus is more than I can contemplate. Despite what the younger generation thinks—and we all thought it at the time—love is not bound by years or desire lost with age.

But then Jeffrey looks over at me and for an instant I see Gus in the turn of our son's head. I've heard my father's laughter bubble up from his grandson, our Caldecott, and caught my own reflection looking back from Rie's high school graduation picture. My younger daughter is a beauty where I never was, but for a moment I'm there in her smile.

A trace of Grandma Liza is in my children, too, and Lou Davis and her husband John, and I think even Gus's Aunt Lily, although I never met the woman who died long before I was born. I remember a five-year-old Rie running in from play and how Lou stared at her, eyes suddenly bright with fiddle tears. When I asked if she was all right, Lou gave me her lovely smile.

"I'm fine, Thea. I caught a glimpse of the past in Rie, is all. For just a second she reminded me of someone I loved a long time ago, but it's gone now."

I never forgot the moment and the curious combination of surprise and sadness and delight I heard in Lou's voice. She always said Gus favored her sister, Lily, and of our four children, it's Rie that is the image of Gus.

Well, unlike my brother, sober business man and pillar of the community, I seem to have grown more fanciful with age, delighted when the past generation pops up in the present and constantly surprised by the relentless rush of time.

Speaking of surprise, my husband remains a man of boundless surprise in his own way, equal parts law and order, risks and passion, and each trait likely to make an appearance when I least expect it.

Gus Davis, a man of contradictions that still appeal.

On our wedding day thirty-six years ago, Gus promised to show me the world, and, in fact, we traveled the globe for a while as newlyweds, Gus recruited as special emissary of the United States to report on conditions in Europe after the Armistice. When we eventually came home, we settled in Cheyenne and lived there for a few years until we made our last move to Laramie, a good place to grow old together. I had my chance to see the great cities of Europe, and it was a dream come true.

Gus Davis, a man of his word.

I'll show you the world. His whispered words for my ears only that morning, the two of us standing in front of the church, strangers five months before and now man and wife. We chose each other for better and for worse that day, and through the years experienced just enough worse to make us treasure the better.

I'll show you the world. A promise of things to come, of sights to see and love to share, home and family, children and grandchildren, laughter and tears, sickness and worry and arguments, too. I will not lie about the hard times, though by now I admit that the reasons for the arguments completely escape me.

I'll show you the world. A man of his word and then some, that Gus Davis, because after all these years, I realize he did more than just show me the world.

He gave it to me.

If you enjoyed this book, look for the other novels in *The Laramie Series,* all available in both soft cover and digital formats. You can also order signed copies from the author's website: www.karenhasley.com

The Complete Laramie Series

1. *Lily's Sister*
2. *Waiting for Hope*
3. *Where Home Is*
4. *Circled Heart*
5. *Gold Mountain*
6. *Smiling at Heaven*

"…one wonders if the people [met] in passing will turn up in Hasley's next captivating book."

(Akron Beacon Journal, 1/10/10)

Wonder no more.

Other books by Karen J. Hasley
- *The Dangerous Thaw of Etta Capstone*

- 'The Penwarrens'
  3 light-hearted Victorian romances ~
*Claire, After All * Listening to Abby * Jubilee Rose*

Made in the USA
Charleston, SC
14 December 2014